**RICH, ELECTRIC, CRACKLING
WRITING SETS IT APART."**
—*Washington Post*

They had the same marks. Cheeks, breasts,
lips. The Jewish prostitute, the nun from
St. Louis, U.S.A., and the young Arab
hustler. A slish/slash signature carved in their
flesh. Consistently marred flesh. Were they
serial murders? Ritual killings? Pattern
crimes?

For police Detective David Bar-Lev, the case
is unfathomable. But as pieces emerge and
connections are made, a list of suspects leads
him to the depths of vice and the heights
of power . . . and closer and closer to a
terrible truth that is agony to face . . .
impossible to escape. . . .

PATTERN CRIMES

"INGENIOUS AND ENTERTAINING!"
—*Cleveland Plain Dealer*

PATTERN CRIMES

A NOVEL BY WILLIAM BAYER

A SIGNET BOOK

NEW AMERICAN LIBRARY

PUBLISHER'S NOTE

This book is a work of fiction. Names, characters, places, and incidents either are the product of the author's imagination or are used fictitiously, and any resemblance to actual persons, living or dead, events, or locales is entirely coincidental.

NAL BOOKS ARE AVAILABLE AT QUANTITY DISCOUNTS WHEN USED TO PROMOTE PRODUCTS OR SERVICES. FOR INFORMATION PLEASE WRITE TO PREMIUM MARKETING DIVISION, NEW AMERICAN LIBRARY, 1633 BROADWAY, NEW YORK, NEW YORK 10019.

SIGNET TRADEMARK REG. U.S. PAT. OFF. AND FOREIGN COUNTRIES
REGISTERED TRADEMARK—MARCA REGISTRADA
HECHO EN CHICAGO, U.S.A.

SIGNET, SIGNET CLASSIC, MENTOR, ONYX, PLUME, MERIDIAN and NAL BOOKS are published by NAL PENGUIN INC., 1633 Broadway, New York, New York 10019

First Signet Printing, April, 1988

1 2 3 4 5 6 7 8 9

PRINTED IN THE UNITED STATES OF AMERICA

FOR PAULA

ACKNOWLEDGMENTS

Many people helped me with this book, but none of them is responsible for its concepts, its fictionalized "facts," or the political views held by its various characters.

Thanks, first, to the director and staff of Mishkenot Sha'ananin in Jerusalem for warm and wonderful hospitality. Mishkenot is, indeed, "a peaceful dwelling," and a true paradise for a writer.

Thanks also for help, encouragement, and/or assistance to: Arlene Donovan, Riva Freifeld, Peter Gethers, Joseph Katz, Avraham Kotzer, Dubi Leshem, Joan Nathan, Mildred Newman, Kenneth Pressman, Geoffrey Weill, and the "Wednesday Night Gang."

And finally very special thanks to three Israeli detectives whose names, for obvious reasons, cannot be given here. They were most generous with their time, but the responsibility for any errors which may appear in these pages belongs solely to me.

W.B.

I have set watchmen upon thy walls,
O Jerusalem, which shall never hold
their peace day or night.

—*Isaiah*

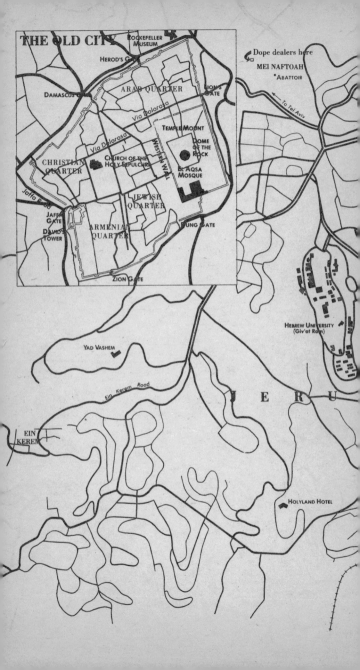

THE OLD CITY

ROCKEFELLER Museum

HEROD'S GATE

ARAB QUARTER

DAMASCUS GATE

ZION'S GATE

Via Dolorosa

TEMPLE MOUNT

Via Dolorosa

DOME OF THE ROCK

CHRISTIAN QUARTER

CHURCH OF THE HOLY SEPULCHER

WESTERN WALL

EL AQSA MOSQUE

Jaffa Rd

JEWISH QUARTER

JAFFA GATE

DAVID'S TOWER

ARMENIAN QUARTER

DUNG GATE

ZION GATE

Dope dealers here

MEI NAFTOAH
"ABATTOIR

To Tel Aviv

HEBREW UNIVERSITY
(Giv'at Ram)

YAD VASHEM

Ein Kerem Road

J   E   R   U

EIN KEREM

HOLYLAND HOTEL

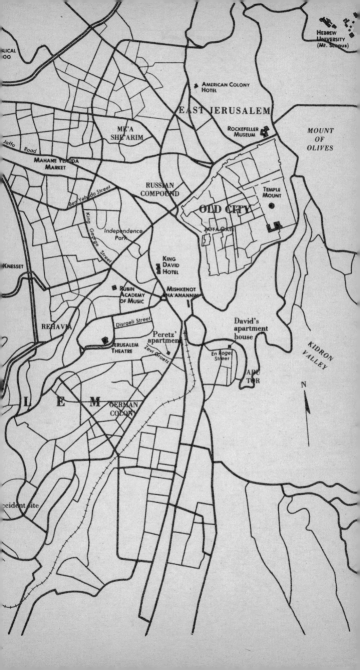

A POSTCARD FROM VIENNA

BIG SUR, CALIFORNIA

He woke up suddenly and then he remembered: Today was his birthday. Today he was sixty years old.

He was sweating. The sheets were damp. His nightmare had been terrible.

"Anna!"

No answer. He opened his eyes. Light was streaming in through the shutters. He squinted. Another blinding California day. They were all blinding here.

The dogs! Where were the dogs?

"Irina!"

When he heard her footsteps he lay back against his pillows and composed his face.

"Happy birthday." She gave him her look when she said it, the one she'd been giving him for years. It reminded him of her expression of amusement and contempt from the days, so long ago, when they still made love.

The dogs bounded in after her, Boris and Peter, great black shaggy leaping things, eyes moist, excited, gums wet, salivating. He petted them, massaged their ears. The maid followed with his breakfast tray.

"Felicidad, Señor Targov." She was Mexican, young, pretty, dark. A good figure too—he often spied on her when she swam laps up and down the pool. While she arranged the tray, he watched Irina throw open the shutters.

"Take the dogs out with you, Bianca," she instructed the maid. Targov gave them each a final roughing of the ears.

"Why exile the dogs?"

"To talk privately."

"And you're afraid they'll overhear? Really, Irina, I think maybe you should go back to that psychiatrist."

She ignored him. "There's a load of mail. Letters, telegrams. The phone's already ringing."

"I'll look at it all later. Rokovsky can handle the calls."

"That journalist, Boyce—he's coming for lunch."

"Fine. Serve something good. Not that salt-free stuff. Good Russian food today."

She didn't reply, and when he glanced up from his breakfast tray he saw that she was studying him.

"You're going to say something awful. I can feel it. So go ahead, Irina, say it now and leave."

He glanced at her again just as she smiled. Then it seemed to him that her entire face turned into a net of fine wrinkles and lines. The effect reminded him of a slow-motion film he'd once seen of a bullet fired at a pane of safety glass. The glass smooth and perfect, then suddenly crosshatched. When she smiled her face became a web.

"Anna wants to go." She announced the fact triumphantly.

"I'll talk to her."

"She's made up her mind."

"After all we've done for her."

"She acknowledges everything. Very grateful too. But now she's ready to move on. She doesn't like it here. A 'hothouse' atmosphere, she says."

"Hothouse!" He laughed. "Well, she may be right. . . ."

"Of course she is. And much too young to be cooped up with us. Very comfortable here with the pool, the servants, but she's suffocating. She must get out, perform, and be with people her age."

"Find a nice young man. Isn't that what you mean?"

"Oh shut up! Here! I've been holding this." She flung a postcard at him. "It burns my hand!"

The card came at him fast, then stopped in midair, then fluttered down slowly until it settled on his quilt. He reached for it, but not before he glanced at her again. This time her expression was more than triumphal. It was gloating, crowing. *God, how she must hate me,* he thought.

He examined the card. A few words in Russian, a signature hastily scrawled. Then, when he understood what it was, he gasped and put it down.

"So he's out."

"At last!"

"Vienna?"

"A transit camp." She still wore her conquering look. He photographed her with his eyes, wanting to fix this image of her forever, knowing that someday he would look back upon this moment as one of the most crucial of his life.

"This didn't come today. Too big a coincidence. You've been holding it back."

"Only saving it for the proper time."

"My birthday! Irina, you're a snake."

"And what are you, Sasha?" she hissed. "Tell me— *what are you?*"

"I'm an old man," he said finally.

She laughed. "Sixty. That's nothing! You're strong as an ox."

"The nightmares. . . ."

"You've always had them. Ever since. . . ."

"My sheets are soaked."

She came beside the bed, touched the sheets. "Just night sweats. Nothing to worry about."

She sat down on the bed and arranged his napkin so

he wouldn't spill coffee on his quilt. It was an amazing quilt. He'd designed it himself, a multicolored patchwork filled, like a Russian futurist painting of the 1920s, with curves and arabesques. People admired it. A collector wanted to buy it. There had even been an inquiry from a commercial bedding firm asking if he would consider licensing the design.

"Tell me about your dream."

"What?"

"Your nightmare, Sasha. I want to hear."

"Oh." He tried to remember. "I was to be assassinated. But I saw it all through the assassin's eyes."

"Tell me." Her voice was comforting now. She took a corner of his napkin and carefully wiped his brow.

"He had a rifle with a telescopic sight. He was up on the hill, in the woods above the road, and I was there too since I was him. He was waiting for me, lying prone in the leaves. There'd just been a rain and I could smell the earth. Then I saw myself through his sight. Do you understand? I saw myself enclosed in a circle, everything foreshortened, as if through a telescopic lens. I was on the terrace playing with the dogs. He set his cross-hairs on me. I could feel his excitement. And then, when he fired, I could feel the rifle jump. Next thing, I saw myself leaning over Boris, pressing my ear against his chest. Peter was crying. My beautiful Boris was dead! I became enraged. I saw myself furious, through his sight again, turning to him, shaking my fist."

"And?"

"I woke up. Ten, fifteen minutes ago."

"Oh, Sasha," she wiped his brow again, "not so bad. Not really. A little nightmare, that's all. Just a little birthday morning dream. But," she added, "interesting."

"What?"

"The way you see yourself, my dear. As a target.

Furious and impotent." She laughed. "Isn't that a joke?"

"You pretend to be sympathetic until you get the goods. Then you turn nasty again."

She shrugged, got up from the bed, went to the window, looked down at the Pacific, the surf crashing against the rocks. "You really think you're a government in exile? *You!* You have a Trotsky complex, Sasha. You dream of your assassination as if you're important enough for them to send out a special man to shoot you down. Such dramatizations! Such an ego you have! Meantime, the truth is you're bored and bottled up. You've barricaded us here in this super-luxurious concentration camp, and now you long for excitement, anything even a KGB assassin to come and take a shot at you. So, okay, you want to be killed, why don't you go someplace where that will happen." She turned to him, her mouth twisted. "And now you know just where to go, too, don't you? *Don't you, Mister Toe-Kisser?*" She flung the postcard at him again. "I'll see you at lunch." She turned her back and swept out of the room.

Boyce, the journalist, had intelligent eyes. He was in his late twenties with a good, young, well-shaped, eager face. The last interviewer, an awful British woman, had written Targov up as a nasty scold. But he was shrewd, was never burned twice. Boyce had written three intelligent letters, he'd sounded solid, and Rokovsky had checked him out. Many reporters had asked; only one could be chosen. In the end, he'd decided Boyce was worth the risk.

So, what must he think of us, our curious ménage? Targov wondered. The burly lion, sixty years old today, his white hair flowing like a mane. The bitter wife with the spider-web face. The beautiful young cellist, dressed in jeans. And Rokovsky, the secretary, gaunt, balding, serious, suspicious. Quite a little group we must make, eating like peasants in the kitchen of our fancy fenced-in ranch beside the sea.

"Hope you don't mind eating in the kitchen, Mr. Boyce. We Russians always speak more candidly in our kitchens."

"I've had the pleasure of being received in many Russian kitchens, Mr. Targov. Little Moscow kitchens mostly. Never one like this."

"A kitchen is a kitchen," Irina said. And then in Russian: "Do you think he'd like it better if it stank of cabbage?" Anna and Rokovsky laughed.

"I do speak Russian."

"Please excuse my wife. She's often rude. And now some questions. How is it you Americans put it? 'Shoot!' "

"As émigrés—"

"Exiles. You see, Mr. Boyce, we were thrown out. Or, to be precise, we were allowed to travel and then, just as we were about to go back, they denounced us and stripped us of our citizenships."

"They insist you made a deal to get out."

Targov laughed. "The KGB peddling trash. Their lies are so transparent, clumsy but dangerous. *Very dangerous*—don't you agree?"

"They're circulating—"

"I know. They've been showing it around for years. They'll try anything to discredit me, or anyone who dares to criticize. Have you heard their line on Solzhenitsyn? That he betrayed Vitkevich! They offer proof, a transcript. It's so laughable! From 1944!"

"Are you in touch with Solzhenitsyn?"

"Not anymore, but there was a time. . . . His trouble, you see, is he has no charm. They invite him to Harvard, he decides to give them hell—believe me, I'm all for that! But then he botches it, puts on his stone face, thrashes his arms like a cossack, and harangues them in Russian until they snore. I hope some-day they invite me. I'll have a few things to tell them about their great and bountiful West. And maybe they'll listen because I won't make Solzhenitsyn's mistakes. For one thing, I'll address them in English. For another, I'll plunge in the needle where it hurts."

"What are your main criticisms of the West?" Boyce held his pencil poised.

"Moral cowardice. An obsession with money and success. A total misunderstanding of art. The most successful people here, and I include the artists, remind me of the hacks who rule our artists' unions back home."

"Yet you've been very successful here, Mr. Targov. And no one calls you a hack."

"Perhaps I am. That's for others to say. Or perhaps I'm simply bitter. You see, Mr. Boyce, when you're sitting in your freezing hovel in Moscow, unable to work, unable to gain commissions because your style doesn't suit the bureaucrats and their stupid party line, you think: 'In the West they care! They know how we suffer! They're our friends! They're petitioning! For them we must survive!' Then, if you're lucky enough to escape, you discover no one gave a hoot. Not only were people here totally unaware of you, when they do finally meet you they find you tiresome. You're so serious. You complain. You bite the hand that feeds you. Their worst accusation is that you're ideological. Can anything be more boring than that?"

"Do you respect American artists?"

"I respect Noguchi. But as a sculptor I cannot speak ill of sculptors. Painters are a different story." He winked at Boyce. "Who are your painters?"

"Stella. Rauschenburg. Fischl."

"Stella's a decorator. Clever, interesting sometimes, but I don't take him seriously."

"Robert Rauschenburg?"

"A distinguished artist, yet I wonder if he really cares. As for Fischl—" he laughed. "A puppy. Cute."

It was hours before Boyce left. When he did, Targov was exhausted. Such a show he'd put on, so many ripostes. Being alternately cagey, brilliant, supercilious, and profound had used up all his energy. He went to his room, wrapped himself in his quilt, tried to sleep but without success. Later he searched for Anna but she and Rokovsky had gone out for a walk. He wandered through the house, then crossed the grounds to his studio. He hadn't been in it in a week. *Today of all days,* he thought, *I must enter and try to work.*

He unlocked the steel door, entered the vast room. The first thing he saw was Anna's cello. She had spent the morning practicing, had left her instrument on the platform along with her stool and music stand.

Barrels of clay were arranged to one side. Scaffolding stood ready to be assembled. Tools were laid out like a surgeon's before an operation. Maquettes of earlier work sat on stainless steel shelves.

He moved to the big window, the great wall of glass that looked out over the sea. Trees had been cut to open up the view. The weather was closing in. Fog was moving down the coast, would soon conceal the rocks and spume below.

Sergei out. He drops a casual postcard from Vienna. On his way to Israel. . . . Oh God!

He looked at the large photograph of his Chicago crucifix bearing his writhing, defiant Christ. "I love the crucifixion in art," he had told Boyce, "the great ones are so *controlled.*" He had also repeated for the nintieth time his maxim: "I ask the clay what it wants to be and when it tells me I begin to sculpt." A moment of weakness—he had said it too many times, and now he hated it; he knew it was meaningless and fake.

He picked up the phone, dialed the house, was pleased to find Rokovsky back. "Send her to me in the studio," he told him. Then he stood before the window and watched the fog close in.

She knocked before she entered, a polite young person, though he was horrified at the sweat shirt she wore, black with the name of some ridiculous rock group scrawled in silver across the chest.

"Sasha. . . ." She came to him. He took her in his arms.

"Irina tells me you're leaving."

She nodded. "Tomorrow. I'm going to New York."

"Tired of me?"

"Oh, Sasha."

"The lion is sixty now. Too old. I understand."

"Please."

"I've tried to help you."

"You have, you have."

"The introductions. The concert in Washington with Rostropovich. The top émigré circle—I got you in."

"Yes. . . ."

"But now you want to go."

"I can't stay forever. Besides, Irina hates me."

"She hates everyone."

She broke away from him, shook her head. "You know I must go. They've found me an accompanist. I must play before audiences. Music is my life."

He nodded and turned away. *Yes, just as sculpture once was mine. . . .*

After they made love he went to the refrigerator, brought out a bottle of Stolichnaya, poured them each a glass. "I've been wondering about you, Anna, whether you're really a Komsomol girl."

"What?" She was shocked. "How can you say a thing like that?"

"Could be," he teased her. "You've found out all my secrets, from me in bed and from Rokovsky too. Yes, I think you are a spy. They set up your 'defection' to confuse me. You were trained to be a *femme fatale,* then sent here to attach yourself, hold me, drain my vitality, render me impotent. Yes?"

"Oh, Sasha." She laughed. "Not impotent at all." She rose from the daybed and began to dress.

He emptied his glass, turned serious. "There's one secret I haven't told you yet."

"What's that?"

"I did something once."

"What did you do?"

"Named a name, betrayed a friend. You see, it's true, that old lie. I fibbed to Boyce."

"What are you talking about?" She was hooking her bra.

"My best friend . . . supposedly. Some friend! He was fucking my wife behind my back. I betrayed him, he was sent to the camps, and now after fifteen years he's out, out of the country too. He's a Jew—they're letting him go to Israel. I can't sleep. Have nightmares. Can't work anymore. Haven't felt the clay in my hands in months. I try to forget, want so much to forget. But every morning Irina reminds me. Her vengeance, of course. It keeps her alive."

She came to him, put her arms around him.

"I was an informer, Anna."

"But he betrayed you first."

"No excuse." He pressed his cheek against her hair and wept.

Later he asked her to play for him. "The 'Arpeggione.' A last request."

"Without a piano—impossible."

"It doesn't matter. Your birthday gift to me. Play it alone, just the adagio. Please."

She paused, considering, then went to the platform, picked up her cello and began to tune it.

"That ridiculous sweat shirt—it has to come off."

"Really!"

"Off!" he demanded.

She pulled it over her head.

"And the bra too. You look silly in it. The jeans are fine, but I want you bare above your waist."

She shrugged, unhooked her bra, threw it at him. He caught it, grinned, gazed back. He loved her leanness, the way her ribs showed taut beneath her pale skin, and above them her breasts, so firm and sassy, the nipples hard and arrogant.

He poured himself another vodka, then switched on the spotlights creating a kind of stage. When everything was finally ready, the cello tuned, the lighting perfect, he sat back upon the couch. "Now you may begin."

She played the Schubert marvelously, and despite the sentimentality of the piece, he was moved by its dark feeling, so moved that, as she launched into the long melodic line, he lost himself in fantasy. He saw himself, a leonine old man, making love to this proud and beautiful cellist. And then, as she played on, bowed the last long dark passage, he shut his eyes and recalled the bitter cold of a windy winter afternoon fifteen years before, and then his rage as he had entered the living room of his Moscow flat and found Sergei Sokolov screwing Irina on the couch.

MARRED
FLESH

JERUSALEM.
ONE YEAR LATER . . .

It snowed that winter in Jerusalem. Deep drifts piled up against the walls. Roofs were blanketed and icicles hung from battlements. Men walked stooped before the gently falling flakes.

When the snow stopped, the city dazzled, a maze of white cubes sparkling in the sun. One night in January, David Bar-Lev sat before the large window of his apartment in the residential district of Abu Tor and gazed in wonder as the snow-covered capital glowed a strange blue-silver beneath the moon.

For a long while he stared, across the Hinnom Valley, through encrusted olive trees and cypresses toward Mount Zion, the Mount of Olives, the Dome of the Rock brooding upon the Temple Mount. Beyond the chilled glass, Jerusalem was silent; the only sound he heard was Anna breathing lightly in her sleep.

He looked toward her. Her cello stood in the corner like a sentinel. Her comb and face cream and pearl necklace lay entangled on the little table beside the bed. The planes of her face glowed like the moonlit roofs. Her thick black hair was glossy as a cat's.

He reached for the gray silk dress in which she'd performed that evening, from which a quarter hour before he'd watched her step so carefully. It lay just where she'd left it, across the back of the couch. It was still damp from her concert, and he remembered the droplets he'd wiped from her forehead in the dressing room and again in the car before they'd driven home.

He held the silk to his lips as he tried to match his breathing to the slow even rising of her chest. He loved her and he wondered then whether he could only love a mystery—women who were puzzles, crimes that were difficult to solve, designs he sensed but could not read, this city in which he'd been born and raised but whose pattern he had never grasped.

The first killings came with the spring.

The snow melted quickly; the runoff was huge. By late March the Judean hills were coated with desert grass, almond blossoms, and budding poppies. Before dawn, the smoke from fires in Bedouin camps drifted in to perfume the city. The sky above Jerusalem was a deep dark blue and the winds brought air so cold and pure it seemed to cut one's lungs.

When the telephone rang, David was sipping coffee. Anna wore a white terry cloth robe and her hair was still wet from her shower. Her eyes followed him as he carried the phone to the window and peered out into the dawn. He was looking for something a thousand meters across the valley. He nodded when he found it—a tiny whirling light.

"I can see your flasher, Rafi."

"So you could have been a witness. Want to come over here? It's cold."

"Are you calling because I live across the way?"

"David, David—what a question!" David pulled the receiver from his ear; the patch-in with the patrol car was bad. ". . . have to leave, have a meeting. Want you to take a look before things get disarranged. No need to take charge. There's a sergeant here already. So—is there a pattern? Maybe. We'll talk about it later in the morning. But it's really cold. You have gloves? If you don't, maybe Anna does. But don't bring her, David. I don't think she'd like it. See you later. . . ." Rafi's voice drifted off and then the connection was cut.

The body, discovered before sunrise by an Arab boy riding his horse along the walls, lay amidst stones and other debris between the Dung and Zion gates. The limbs protruded at terrible angles no living creature could simulate. Crumpled, David thought. She was killed somewhere else, then brought here and dumped. Thrown out of a car like trash.

Liederman was in command. David knew him slightly, a small graying middle-aged man with thick glasses and a wizened Polish face. An old-style Ashkenazi policeman recruited in the 1950s, before the force was flooded with immigrants and cops were classified with garbagemen.

"Rafi says wait for you." Liederman's voice was hoarse, his fingers stained from smoking. He wore a beaten-up leather commando jacket. "Says I should tell you everything."

"So go ahead. Tell me."

Liederman shrugged as he danced from foot to foot to fight off the morning chill. "She's young, maybe eighteen, twenty. Throat cut. Beaten and mutilated. Found naked under that old army blanket there. No ID. No idea who she is."

An empty tourist bus rounded the corner, stopped, and blocked the road. The driver peered at them and then at the body.

"Hey! Get him out of here," Liederman yelled at one of his men. "Keep traffic moving. I told you that."

"Jewish?" David asked.

"How the hell should I know?"

"Use your instinct."

"I don't have any instinct. I'm just an old cop. This year, thank God, I retire."

"Ask him." David gestured at the Arab boy who was sitting on the ground; his horse was grazing the sparse plants that grew along the base of the wall. Liederman grinned and fumbled with his Polaroid. David walked closer to the body, shivered, and stared down.

The girl's face was puffed. Her skin was already turning blue. Her cheeks were marked, two shallow vertical slashes across each, cut quickly, David thought, like a pair of bars drawn across a check. There were similar pairs of marks, harsh, ugly, brutal, cut into her lips and breasts and a neat slit across her throat. Very little blood. No expression on her face, no frozen look of agony or fear. She was very young. Her eyes were closed and there was a residue of kohl around them. Attractive, perhaps even pretty. He could hardly bear to look at her. He turned away.

Liederman called to him. He was standing with the Arab boy. "He thinks she's Jewish," he said.

David walked over. "You've seen her?" he asked the boy in Arabic.

The boy nodded. "She stands by the Damascus Gate."

"A prostitute?"

The boy nodded again. He was wearing two brown sweaters, the outer one old and torn.

"A Jewish prostitute?"

"I think so."

"Did you ever go with her?"

The boy shook his head.

"You ride down here every morning?"

He explained that he exercised the horse, which belonged to his uncle who lived beyond Ramat Rahel on the road to Bethlehem.

"So why ride this way?"

"I ride her to Shiloah. Besides I find it beautiful."

David looked around. "Yes, you're right. It is beautiful here. Especially just at dawn."

The boy stared deeply at David, then patted the neck of his horse. He had the very gentle sort of Arab-Christian face that always filled David with guilt. No angry PLO kid from Hebron University but a sweet thin Jerusalem boy with large sad injured eyes.

There were more cars now. Cops were blowing their whistles trying to keep the traffic moving up the hill. People gazed out of car windows, their faces curious and disturbed. An ambulance arrived. Several pedestrians stopped by the side of the road to watch. David looked over at Abu Tor, found his building, wondered if Anna was standing before the large window rubbing her hands together, or sitting on her stool in the middle of the room already at work practicing her scales.

Liederman followed David to his car. "How did you know he'd know if she was Jewish?"

"I'm a detective."

"Yeah, I see that. But how did you know?"

"Just a guess."

"A good one. I've heard about you. I've heard you're very good." Liederman threw down his cigarette, then leaned in through the window so he could speak in confidence. "Rafi wouldn't have called you here if he wasn't going to give this to your section. If it turns out she was definitely Jewish, this could turn out to be a pretty interesting case."

David waited. The sun was up, already caressing the walls. In a few minutes it would strike full force and set Jerusalem aflame.

". . . I never worked a good case, never worked anything that wasn't shit. I can't wait to retire. I've got other things to do. I have an archive. Books, old newspapers, documents. It's stashed in a room in the German Colony. An old lady's house. I do odd jobs for her, stay there when she's gone and keep an eye on everything. And for that she lets me have the room."

"What sort of archive?"

"Early 1940s. Poland. My father's collection. And I've added to it on my own. Thing is, I wonder if you'd come out one day and look it over. You've a good eye. You see things. I've heard that and now I know it's true."

"What could I see in all your papers?"

"Well, you might see something if you looked." Liederman stopped. "You don't like that kind of study, do you—examining the past?" He backed away. "I'm sorry. You're young. You were born here. People born here don't like that kind of thing. I understand."

"I'm thirty-six years old," David said. "Examining the past is my passion. If you think I can help, then of course I'll look at your stuff. Sarah in Rafi's office has my schedule. Pick a day when both of us are free."

At ten that morning he was sitting in the office of Rafi Shahar, Chief of Criminal Investigation, staring at stripes on the terra cotta floor projected by the sun through Rafi's blinds. Through the open window he could hear the buses grinding their way up Jaffa Road, and in the courtyard patrol cars revving up. He could also hear phones ringing unanswered in other offices, and echoes from the hall beyond the door, people striding, talking, cursing the coffee machine, and the quick high-heeled steps of the Moroccan girl who worked in Superintendent Latsky's office, who wore tight sweaters and used henna on her hair and fought with her fingernails and for this had been dubbed "The Claw."

Rafi sat back, his eyes watery and sad. The sun made a halo around his balding head. He held the headset of his phone between his cheek and shoulder and drummed his fingers on his desk. Every so often he nodded at Sarah Dorfman, who sat at her little table across the room listening on the extension and taking notes.

Finally, when Rafi put down the phone, the stripes on the floor compressed. David looked up; the back of Rafi's chair was crushing the blinds against the sill.

"So?"

"Nasty marks. Unusual."

"That's all you have to say?"

"Well—"

"What?"

David glanced back at Sarah Dorfman, then down at the floor. "Maybe whoever killed her marked her to say 'She's mine, belongs to me.' "

He looked up at Rafi, saw his eyes enlarge behind his glasses. Since the day David had met him, he'd been aware of the sadness in his eyes. Rafi was only five years older, but his remaining hair was graying above his ears and he had developed the pale complexion and growing paunch of a ranking officer who now, to his great regret, was forced to work behind a desk.

"Marks of ownership. Interesting, David. You've always had an interesting kind of mind."

Rafi stared at him a moment, then leaned forward. From the clutter on his desk he picked out a pipe. Pipes and orchids: Rafi liked Turkish tobacco and bred air orchids in his greenhouse after work. Though David considered him a friend, he was aware of the methods by which Rafi distanced himself: hiding at work behind clouds of aromatic smoke, performing his solitary hobby behind a wall of glass.

Rafi lit his pipe, then selected a file folder. He pushed it across the desk. There were photographs inside. As David examined them, he felt his stomach tighten. When Rafi spoke again, it was in a hoarse whisper that filled the little room.

"Same marks. Cheeks, breasts, lips. Found ten days

ago in a wadi on the side road that leads up to Mevasseret. A nun from St. Louis, U.S.A. Staying at the Holyland Hotel. Doorman saw her get into a car, thinks it had Tel Aviv plates. No one else saw her after that."

Rafi pushed across another folder containing another set of photos. The same marks, except this time they were on the face and body of a boy.

". . . Halil Ghemaiem. Arab street kid. Drug user. Male hustler. Sometime transvestite prostitute. Worked the beach in Tel Aviv. Picked up about one A.M. last Tuesday by a well-dressed gentleman. Driven away in a foreign car. Found dumped up here five days ago behind the Augusta Victoria Hospital at a construction site."

David heard a snap. Rafi's chair was crushing the blinds again. "You see what we have here, David? Marred flesh, consistently marred flesh. We have a pattern crime and," Rafi paused, "perhaps our first Israeli serial murder case."

Rafi accompanied him to the hall, stood with him as he fed coins into the coffee machine, getting half of them back, trying different ones from his pocket. The machine finally delivered scalding coffee with a hiss; it overflowed David's plastic cup.

". . . kind of thing that happens in America. So maybe if we're lucky it'll turn out the killer's an American." Rafi started banging on the machine; he hadn't gotten his coins back and hadn't gotten any coffee either. "But suppose he's Israeli? Wouldn't surprise me much, the way things are going these days. A suburban housewife in Haifa feeds rat poison to her husband. A nice South African-born gentleman, technician at the Weizman Institute, injects his aging mother with kerosene. Beautiful kibbutz kids refuse to join the army. My younger brother, a tank commander, wants to move to New York and drive a taxi."

Rafi stood back and gave the machine a tremendous kick. Coffee started gushing out. He often spoke to David like this, bitter, ironic, contemptuous of what he called "the new mores," which he blamed upon the present government.

"A government elected by pickle sellers, so what should we expect? Much as I hated the old light-unto-the-nations crap, it was a lot better than this meanness we exhibit now." He sipped some coffee. "Still, David, now that we've got ourselves a crazy American-style society, isn't it time we got an American-style murder case? Long overdue, but," he shook his head, "very very difficult to solve. Random victims, no prior connection—don't need to tell you how tough that's going to be. A great big mess." He gazed at David. "I'm handing it to you. Refuse if you like—I'll understand."

"It's a pattern crime, Rafi. How can I refuse?"

"You can't." Rafi slapped him gently on the back. "Get the dossiers from Sarah. And give my best to Anna." He shook his head. "I like her, David—very much. What will she think of us when she hears about all of this?"

As he walked back to the Pattern Crimes offices, he turned over Rafi's phrase: "Consistently marred flesh." Of all the possible pattern crimes, he thought, consistently marred flesh was probably the worst.

The PC Unit, of which he was commanding officer, was located on the second floor of Jerusalem District Police Headquarters in a complex of buildings known collectively as the Russian Compound, a hundred meters up from Bar Kokba Square.

The building was old, its ceilings twenty feet high, and its cavernous tiled corridors, lit by fluorescent lamps suspended from iron chains, echoed and re-echoed with the footsteps of cops, clerks, detectives, prisoners, informers, witnesses, and an occasional lost citizen looking for a place to lodge a complaint. The beaten-up pay telephones and recalcitrant soup, coffee, and candy machines in these corridors were notorious, the interlocking squadrooms a maze. Few outsiders could find their way around this rabbit warren carved out of what once had been the huge intimidating offices of police officials in the period of the British Mandate.

David Bar-Lev did not think anyone would be intimidated by his office, barely wide enough to contain his desk. Dossiers were crammed into bookcases. A bulletin board was crowded with overlapping notes. There were two heavily chipped black metal chairs, two telephones, and a carefully cropped photograph of his daughter, Hagith, with just the left hand of his ex-wife, Judith, showing beside her arm.

Although the walls here had been soundproofed and a false ceiling installed for privacy, David always left his door open to the room where the rest of the PC Unit worked. Here the partition walls were barely taller than a man so that raised voices and ringing phones from the squadrooms of adjoining units swirled together and merged. No single word was ever intelligible out of all this restless sound, but David felt there was an underlying harmony. "Crime and Torment," he called it, as if it were a piece of music, a piece he sometimes struggled to decode and at other times loathed so much he would make up any excuse no matter how absurd to escape it, fleeing the building, taking to the streets, even driving out into the Judean hills . . . and sometimes even then it would still ring in his ears.

"Shoshana!"

She appeared almost instantly in his doorway, a short young woman with eager black eyes, tight black curls, and olive skin.

"Where's Dov?"

"Working the Rehavia burglary case. A lady came in. Said she saw some of her silverware in East Jerusalem. He went out to check."

"Micha . . . ?"

"With Uri having coffee. My turn next unless things start picking up."

"So you're bored, Shoshana?"

"Not really bored. It's just that here I never get a chance to fight."

She'd been in a narcotics unit when David met her, an unhappy office mascot. She wasn't getting along with her boss and was angry at being assigned to cover the phones while the boys got to work the streets. She had the plump fresh cheeks and guileless smile of a high school girl, but there was cunning behind the facade. David liked her, and when he saw her perform at a police karate competition, all flashing black eyes and short black curls, he was so impressed by her self-assurance he arranged her transfer to Pattern Crimes.

"We don't fight. We investigate. If you like to fight so much, go back into the army." She grinned. "While you're considering it, go downstairs and see if you can find us a halfway decent car."

"Where are we going?"

"We're going to check out a place where an American nun was dumped."

He heard her footsteps as she ran out through the squadroom; he was fascinated by her sudden entrances and exits. One moment she was there and the next was gone, yet he could never remember actually seeing her come or go.

He told her to drive, thought that might use up some of her restless energy. The car, a delapidated white Subaru, had ripped seats and dented fenders. On their way up Jaffa Road, he told her what he wanted her to do.

"Get good photos. Then go with Uri to the Damascus Gate. He stands aside while you talk to the women, as nonthreatening and sympathetic as you can be. Find out who she is. Name, address, everything. Did anyone see her get picked up last night? Does she operate for a pimp? It may turn out the kid was wrong. Maybe she wasn't a prostitute. But talk to them anyway. See if they heard about any guys who like to cut. Tell them about the marks, but not about the breasts—we're going to keep that to ourselves. . . ."

There was a traffic jam in front of the Mahane Yehuda market, trucks and cars stalled, blasting one another with horns. A woman lugging a market basket wove her way across the street. A group of schoolchildren, five- and six-year-olds, waited with perfect discipline at the curb.

"What the hell is this?" Shoshana wiped her forehead; it was eleven o'clock and getting hot. David thought of Anna practicing, her bow cutting across the strings, filling the apartment with dark rich sounds. Every so often she too would wipe her brow.

"I'll put on the siren."

David shook his head. Something was happening in the market. People were pouring in but few were coming out. "Meet me up there on the right," he said. Then he stepped out of the car.

As he made his way down the dark arcade that was the market axis, he heard the shrill whistles of police. He pushed past stands piled with eggplants, onions, Jaffa oranges, past vendors and buyers, through the debris of fruit skins and discarded vegetable greens, then took a shortcut through one of the little cross alleys until he came up against an immobile human mass.

"What is it?" he asked a stooped old lady in black who was grasping her purchases to her chest.

She looked at him, lips tight. "Katzer." And then all around David heard the name. Some whispered it, others hissed it, a few yelled it out like a cheer: "Katzer!" "Katzer!"

Suddenly David caught a glimpse of him, escorted by police, bobbing along behind a phalanx of his supporters, sullen young males in knitted skullcaps bullying their way through the crowd. There was something thuglike, dull and stupid, about this vanguard, but the rabbi's small hard eyes gleamed with calculation.

David watched, fascinated, as Katzer embraced a seller of olives, a seller of fish, an old man with a cane who sewed buttons and hems. David was surprised at how short he was; although he knew his face well from TV, this was the first time he had seen him in the flesh. Now he was struck by his animal magnetism and rabid quality too: moist eyes, sweaty beard, mouth that twisted as he spoke. Nothing otherworldly about him, nothing pious or Talmudic. This was a politician who thrived on touching faces, patting shoulders, grasping extended hands. His supporters needed him, wanted to feel his power, and Katzer eagerly obliged. But then David noticed something else. The rabbi's eyes squirreled up at the sound of a passing airplane, and then again at the pop of a beer can being opened up. A glimmer of fear: He was political meat and knew the passions he unleashed could also put a bullet in his chest.

The cops blew their whistles, the thugs marched past, and Katzer was swallowed by the mob. Making his way back past the butcher's stalls to find Shoshana and the car, David felt his shirt sticking to his back.

It was a drainage ditch, dusty, overgrown with brambles, separated by bushes from the narrow access road that led up to Mevasseret. Police stakes tipped with orange fluorescent paint marked the place where the body had been found. David circled the site, careful not to walk upon it, then leaned against the car. There was a constant roar of traffic from the highway, a harsh whirling sound of speeding cars and trucks. Just the sort of spot, he thought, you might pull up to if you were starting down to Tel Aviv and then decided to stop and take a piss.

"She was seen getting into a Tel Aviv car," Shoshana said. "Looks like whoever killed her pulled off at the exit, threw her out, then continued on his way."

The sun was beating down full force. David looked up at the white villas glittering on the barren heights. The people who lived up there were wealthy, the kind who owned two cars. They'd drive past where he was standing several times a day. Someone would notice the body pretty quick.

"If he really wanted to ditch her, he would have taken her into Judea. He didn't care if she was found."

"Why care? He was done with her."

"So just pull in the way we did, drag her out, toss an old blanket on top of her, don't even bother to cover her legs, then zip on down to the sunny coast?"

"What's wrong with that?"

"Nothing, if he wasn't trying to hide his workmanship. Maybe the best solution, if he wanted it displayed."

"Think that's what he wanted?"

David shrugged. "He couldn't have chosen a better spot. Except for his spot this morning. That was better." He took a last look at the orange stakes, then turned away.

Back at the Russian Compound, he smiled when he saw them, Micha and Uri in sloppy army jackets, Dov Meltzer in striped track pants sporting an oversized

submariner's watch. All three wore the beaten-up run-
ner's shoes that were the trademark of Jerusalem plain-
clothes cops. They were sprawled out in swivel chairs
while prim, smiling, orthodox Rebecca Marcus, clerk
of Pattern Crimes, sat upright typing reports on her
vintage Royal, her legs and arms nicely covered, her
head wrapped neatly in a scarf.

"Murder case?"

"Triple," Shoshana said.

"Report says the nun was tortured, but no sign of
intercourse."

"Madonna, girl-whore, boy-whore," said Dov.
"Sounds like psycho-time."

"It's psycho-time all right."

He looked at them. They were excited. Detectives
in other units sometimes called them "David's Dogs."
Now they had a new and very disturbing case, perhaps
the best they'd gotten in a year.

"Shoshana and Uri work the girl this morning. Micha,
you get the Arab boy, and Dov, you take the nun.
They say the boy was a drug user, so find out if he
dealt. This Sister Susan Mills—was she really a madonna? How does a woman like that end up in a
ditch?"

"What about the marks, David?"

"I'm very interested in those marks."

"Report on the sister says the cutting was done after
she was dead."

"Ten to one it's the same with the other two."

"An afterthought?"

"Some kind of ritual?"

"Sarah says you thought it could be some kind of
brand," Dov said.

David nodded. "A brand says: 'She's mine.' But
this could be more. A signature. Signature says: 'I did
this work. My work.' Could be either one."

He ran Pattern Crimes like a small unit in the army—

first names, anyone could say what he thought, minimal distinction between commanding officer and men. He felt closest to Dov, whom he considered the smartest, but Uri Schuster was formidable, a tracker, a bloodhound on the streets. Uri, David thought, could have been a criminal, which was why he was so valuable, and why, despite complaints that he was rough, sometimes even brutal, David was determined never to let him go. Micha Benyamani was the unit chess player, sad-faced, gaunt, a thorough paperwork-and-telephone detective. Shoshana Nahon—self-styled fighter, she made up for her inexperience with zest.

He told Rebecca Marcus to telex to the Israeli police liason in New York. "The U.S. Justice Department has some kind of serial killer clearinghouse. Send them a straight query: Have they ever seen these kinds of marks?"

Rebecca smiled sweetly. "Whenever anything horrible happens, Rafi always thinks it's an American."

"An American Jew."

"Yes." She giggled. "But never an Israeli. Oh no! Never!"

He called in Dov. "What happened this morning?"

"Found a pair of candlesticks. An Arab trinket dealer on Salah el Din."

"Good stuff?"

"Nothing special. That blue-dye-job who was robbed last fall says they aren't worth much."

"How did he get them?"

"Had a story. Flea market in Hebron. But, David, there was other stuff there. Judaica. And that doesn't fit."

"Good Judaica?"

"I don't think so. It's a pretty dumpy place. I saw some Torah crowns. That bothered me. You don't fence stuff like that in East Jerusalem."

"You're thinking . . . ?"

"Our scrolls case. It's been months. I practically forgot about it until I saw those crowns. I didn't say anything. Wanted to tell you first. The Rehavia burglaries and the stolen scrolls. We never put the two together."

David thought about it. He didn't think they belonged together. "Silver is silver," he said. "The people burglarizing fancy houses in Rehavia need a place to unload silver that isn't worth shipping out. Meantime, the people stealing Torahs for resale in America have to get rid of the crowns because the crowns identify the origins of the scrolls. We're talking about items of fairly limited value. East Jerusalem's good for that. What time does this dealer close?"

"Eight o'clock."

"Okay, let's go over there around a quarter of and have ourselves a little talk."

At four that afternoon, Shoshana and Uri brought him the girl's name: Ora Goshen, nineteen years old, born of Moroccan-Jewish parents in the settlement town of Bet Shemesh. The boy on the horse had been right—she had indeed been working as a prostitute by the taxi stand at the Damascus Gate. The drivers knew her and a number of her colleagues stepped forward too. She was described as "attractive" and "friendly with a seductive timid manner," a girl who could turn four to six tricks a night and often started work in the early afternoon. She rented half a room in an apartment in Katamon but never took her clients there. Sometimes, when she needed a place, she'd pay an hourly rent to one of the other girls, or have her client hire a taxi, have it driven to a remote spot, then perform while the driver took coffee at a café.

"She'd go with Arab men, Jewish men—she didn't care," Shoshana said, "but most of her clients were foreigners or Arabs. She didn't charge much and she liked it quick. Her landlady says she thought she was a hotel maid. She also says that Ora spoke of having been molested by her brothers and of running away from home, first to Beersheba before she came up here. Everyone agrees she's been in Jerusalem three or four months at most. No knowledge of any boyfriends, and no mention of anyone resembling a pimp. One of the girls says she and Ora have been employed several times by a well-dressed gentleman from the Foreign Office. They were paid ten times what they usually got for which they were required to attend black men, African diplomats, staying at the King David Hotel. They both used the money to buy themselves winter coats. Another time, she says, Ora was rejected by a client because he said she looked too dark. In regard to Arabs, it's apparently fairly important that a Jewish girl make clear that's what she is. Seems part of the thrill for the Arab client is to be serviced by a member of the oppressor race. As for Tel Aviv, no one knows if she's ever been there. And as for cutters, no one's ever heard of such a thing."

Shoshana was beaming—she knew her presentation had been good, and the best part was still to come. David glanced at Uri who nodded back—he had extracted the greater part of the information and now was enjoying listening to Shoshana weave it together into a tale.

"Okay, last night, around eight o'clock, the traffic's thinning out. It's getting chilly. A tan car comes by and starts to cruise the parking lot. Fairly recent model, maybe a Renault. Maybe it had Tel Aviv plates—no one's sure. There was a man, fairly young, fairly decently dressed, European-type—no one saw him well because it was pretty dark. He gestured to Ora, she walked over to the window, they talked for half a minute, she waved to her friends and got inside. He pulled out and must have made a U-turn up the road because a minute or so later one of the girls saw them headed back toward new Jerusalem. That's it. She didn't come back, and by nine they finish up and everyone heads for home. Three points: this guy and Ora didn't act like they knew each other; no one recalls seeing the guy before; there was nothing special about the encounter—it was a typical automobile pick-up, kind that happens fifteen or twenty times a night."

"So . . . ?"

"What?"

"How many witnesses?"

"Just two girls, her friends."

"Will they submit to interrogation by a hypnotist?"

"Didn't ask them."

"Go back tonight, Shoshana, and ask. Meantime, call the police up in Bet Shemesh and get hold of a social worker. The family has to be told and someone'll have to come up here, give us a positive ID, and waive objections to an autopsy. Make sure the social worker understands that even if the family objects we can have one done. It'll just take longer and then everyone down there will know Ora was molested and that's why she became a whore."

"Okay. Now what do I do if the girls refuse to be hypnotized?"

"Point to Uri, tell them how he'd love to run them in for vice and then how badly it stinks in the Russian Compound jail. Then tell them how much we'd appreciate their cooperation since basically the guy who did this is a potential threat to them and we wouldn't want to see them sliced up too."

He called Anna to tell her about his case and that he had to go to East Jerusalem with Dov. "We'll probably grab some dinner at the Ummayyah. You like Dov. Why don't you meet us there?"

But she had bought groceries and was at that moment in the midst of making Borscht Moskovskii, which she'd been thinking about the entire day. "If I don't eat it now I'll go crazy. Don't stuff yourself, David. There'll be a big bowl for you when you get home."

They always spoke English; she had started studying Hebrew but wasn't ready yet to practice seriously. The expression she liked best was *boker tov,* "good morning," which she whispered sensuously into his ear every morning to wake him up.

"How did it go today?"

"I practiced all morning, then went to Yosef's. We worked together for four hours." She and her accompanist, Yosef Barak, were preparing the Beethoven cycle for their May European tour. "Then I shopped at the Supersol. There was a terrible scene at the checkout. A woman started screaming. 'Prices, robbers. . . .' Then she started to sob. I kept wanting to tell her how lucky she was, how the store sold practically everything and you never have to wait in line. But I knew I couldn't help her. She was—what's the word? Inconsolable?"

Yes, he thought, the perfect word to describe people suddenly breaking down, incredulous at the daily erosion of their savings. But he was touched by Anna's desire to console the woman, explain to her how lucky she was not to live in the sort of society which she, Anna, had escaped. The society she was happy to have left but the country she still desperately missed— thus her compelling need to taste Moscow-style borscht.

At the end of the day, Micha and Dov reappeared. Micha had driven down to Tel Aviv to interview the one witness to the pickup of Halil Ghemaiem on the beach. As he spoke, he slumped deeper into his chair, sneaker-clad feet stretched to David's desk, arms hanging loose so that they touched the floor.

"Ali Saad, heroin addict, worst eye witness I ever met. The jerks who dug him up didn't bother to try him on the IdentiKit, so I brought out mine and put him to work. Drove me crazy. We'd get a composite going, then he'd say no, it wasn't right. So we'd start again and then he'd choose a different set of eyes, ears, even formations of hair. Finally I said to him: 'What is this shit? What are you covering up?' Blank stare. Then I understood: He couldn't remember. Been too long and his brain's been fried by drugs. The only things he'll swear to are that the guy who approached Halil was dark, clean-shaven, spoke Hebrew, and was decently dressed. I got excited about the Hebrew—seemed to clinch it that he was Israeli. But then I realized this kid barely knew Hebrew himself. All he heard was something like: 'You come with me? Fuck? I got nice car.' "

"Did Halil deal?"

"Strictly small-time. Just enough to pay for his own."

"Rumors of any cutters?"

"You kidding? These kids pack knives, David. It's their clients who get cut."

Dov had done better with his investigation of Susan Mills; listening to him David could feel how much Dov liked the murdered nun.

". . . here's an American school teacher on pilgrimage to the Holy Land, backpacking, using her Bible as her guide. She's been everywhere, Nazareth, the Galilee, Jericho, Bethlehem, you name it, and she's not on some goody-goody tour, and she doesn't dress in a habit like those nuns you see around Notre Dame de France. She wears normal stuff, T-shirts and jeans, shorts, too, when it's hot. She stays at hospices, carries an expensive Nikon and takes a million shots. Meets people wherever she goes. Priests, professors, archaeologists. In the mornings she jogs. She rented snorkling equipment in Eilat. A very modern lady. So what do Rafi's *schmuck* jerk-offs conclude, the great homicide investigators assigned to track her stay in Israel? That she must have been forcibly abducted from the Holyland 'because,' and here I'm quoting from their report, 'holy Christian women such as this *never*'—their emphasis—'*never* go out except in pairs.' Un-fucking-believable. Where does Rafi get these slobs? Point is, David, the big deal about Susan Mills getting into a car turns out to be no big deal at all. This morning you asked how a nun winds up in a ditch. Well, however this particular nun wound up in one I don't think it had much to do with her affiliation to the church."

The three of them walked downstairs together. Cops and staff thronged the corridors. The Claw, from the superintendent's office, was gossiping with Sarah Dorfman. A jail guard, carrying a tray of cheese sandwiches, nearly slipped on the tile floor.

The bomb disposal truck was parked near the compound gate. Micha Benyamani spotted it, turned away, quickly shook their hands, then hurried off to catch his bus. Son of a watch maker, he had been a bomb disposal specialist who quit the unit when his hands began to shake. David first met him on the police firing range, where he noticed that Micha's shooting was extremely accurate; he'd squint at the very moment that he pulled the trigger, and, for that moment at least, all his trembling would stop.

David and Dov walked on to the police parking lot. It was dark and getting cold. They got into David's car. David pulled out onto Heleni Ha-Malka, where he honked at a trio of Ethiopian monks—black faces, black robes, black skull-tight hats. Traffic was heavy. The floodlit Old City walls looked stark. David slowed the car as he approached the Damascus Gate, paused at the entrance to the taxi lot. A girl, standing in the shadows of the wall, studied them a while, then walked toward them with a slow hip-swinging stride.

"Jewish?"

Dov waited until she was twenty feet away. "Yeah, think so," he finally said.

"Looking for a date?" She was young, still in her teens. Something about her, a cherubic quality, made David think of Rebecca Marcus without a scarf.

"We're cops."

"So what? Cops don't date?" She laughed. "Screw cops." Her walk back was angry, sluttish, tough.

"Bitch," Dov muttered. "Nasty bitch."

David glanced at him. "Ever see Katzer, Dov? In the flesh, I mean."

"Yeah, once, at a funeral down in Netanya. He and his goons were working the crowd. A woman had been killed by a terrorist bomb. He likes situations like that where everyone's nerves are raw."

"I saw him this morning. Short guy, shorter than I thought. You know how he rants on about 'Jewish whores'?"

"He's got a big bug up his ass."

"So, when I saw him, it occurred to me—maybe this is just the kind of guy we're looking for. Ora Goshen, a prostitute—Katzer's said a Jewess who fornicates with Arabs ought to be stoned to death. Taking off from there, reversing the reasoning, someone could say the same of an Arab boy who offers his ass to Jewish men."

"Okay, Ora and the boy make sense. But why Susan? Why kill a Christian nun?"

"Who knows? We're talking about a fruitcake. The kind of person who's very angry. Angry very deep inside."

He turned onto Salah el Din, honked his way through the nightly blockage of cars double-parked while their owners exchanged eroding shekels for black-market dollars inside Arab shops. He found a parking space around the corner from the National Palace Hotel, carefully locked the car and armed the alarm. Then he and Dov walked back toward the main business street of East Jerusalem.

It smelled and sounded different here than in the Jaffa-Ben Yehu-da-King George triangle downtown, more like the Middle East, the scent of cardamom, the faint aroma of hashish, the pulsing rhythm of Egyptian love songs played on radios blasting out of stores. A busload of Americans tourists trudged into a belly-dancer joint. A souvenir shop owner, sucking on his waterpipe, caught David's eye and smirked.

"Wow, they make us quick over here. Course, we make them pretty quick too on our side of town."

"Actually, Dov, I think it's you they make. Only an Israeli detective would wear striped track pants and that enormous watch."

They were fond of one another. David thought of Dov as a younger brother, endearing on account of his absurd wardrobe, thick neck, unkempt head of black curls, and the poetry he wrote—sweet and savage verse that combined the mellowness of a Jerusalem child-hood with the emerging bitterness of a young Israeli cop.

The bric-a-brac shop was up two flights, above a store that sold electronic equipment, radios, cassette recorders, electric guitars. There was an acrid smell of cat urine on the first floor landing and an office door marked "Magic Supplies."

The junk dealer, a Mr. Aziz Mansour, was middle-aged, overweight, and worried. Behind the steel bars that divided his shop from its small entrance off the stairs were dusty piles of treasure: plates, utensils, ladles, bowls, serving platters, candlesticks made of silver, bronze, and brass.

Dov, dropping all signs of informality, respectfully introduced David as "Captain Bar-Lev."

Mansour bowed to show he acknowledged Israeli authority. "As I told the sergeant this morning, I purchased the candlesticks from an itinerant peddler in the flea market in Hebron several weeks ago. Of course I had no idea they were stolen. And now I must suffer a loss for that, since I shall doubtless never again see the swindler who sold them to me, and whom I now curse for what he did."

Like many Jerusalemites of his age, Mansour spoke a formal British-inflected English. But there was something undignified about him, a cringing quality David didn't like.

"I'm afraid it's not so simple."

"Why not simple? I give you the objects. I do not wish to profit from stolen things."

"We have to seal up your store. Tomorrow we'll send a truck. Everything must be brought to our offices and examined against lists of stolen goods."

"But surely not! I have never heard of this procedure."

"It's one we reserve for special situations."

"Why? What is special here?"

David looked around. "Something here is special, I'm sure. But if you object, Mr. Mansour, you must consult your lawyer. Israel is a free country. We respect the rights of everyone. By all means fight our confiscation. Meantime, your store will be sealed."

"Confiscation! You said nothing about confiscation! Just to examine the objects, you said."

Dov was now on the far side of the room, directing his gaze at the small collection of Torah scroll crowns he had spotted that morning amid the dusty piles.

"Perhaps we could find a way to shortcut the procedure."

"I can do something for you? Yes? Tell me—what is

PATTERN CRIMES · 51

it that you want please." Mansour was angry, but David could feel him calculating, wondering what this stern police captain really wanted, whether he was hinting at a bribe, and, if so, how large.

"Frankly, for me the candlesticks are trivial. If you bought them in Hebron, then you can't be held responsible for the fact they were stolen from a house on Ramban street. We believe the robbery was committed by Jews. We have no use for such people. I'm personally much more disturbed by a Jewish thief than by an Arab fence."

Dov, now standing behind Mansour, queried David with his eyes. But David didn't think he'd gone too far.

"Sir, excuse me, I am *not* a fence. I promise you I bought the candlesticks in Hebron. Possibly one of the Jewish settlers there—"

"If you're going to tell lies, at least tell one that's plausible. Israeli settlers may steal Arab land but not this kind of junk." He peered around the shop with great disgust. "I'm going downstairs for a coffee. Meltzer, stay with the prisoner, advise him of his rights. When I return we'll make a preliminary search."

He walked out without looking back. Dov would wait at least a minute, until his footsteps were no longer audible on the stairs. Then he would sit across from Mansour, gaze at him with his most pitying expression, and start to explain how tough things were going to get.

Yes, Dov would lay it all out, the nature of the captain's "preliminary search," how he would methodically tear the shop apart, break all the breakable objects, crush all the fragile ones, and then how various other items Mr. Mansour probably didn't even know he had would appear miraculously on the inventory list and would be identical to objects stolen from fine Israeli homes. Mansour could certainly call his lawyer but he should be advised that the captain might then turn the matter into a security affair, in which case, of course, certain rights would be suspended and the interrogation could become extremely harsh. No, of course this wasn't political, but poor Aziz had acted stupidly from the start, when it was obvious that the only thing the captain wanted was to develop a new informer in East Jerusalem. Yes, that's all. Didn't Aziz understand? Israeli policemen don't take bribes. They value information—against crooks, burglars, Jewish burglars at that, against the very people who were using poor old Aziz's shop as a place to fence the junk they couldn't sell abroad or down in Tel Aviv. . . .

David ordered a coffee at the National Palace café, picked up a copy of *Al-Fajr,* the Jerusalem-based Palestinian newspaper, discovered various interesting things he hadn't learned from his readings in the Israeli press, and, when he thought that Dov had Mansour sufficiently softened up, paid for his coffee, left the newspaper on the table, strode back up to Salah el Din, and then noisily ascended the stairs.

Dov gave him the nod as soon as he walked in, the big nod that said Aziz was begging now to talk. David walked straight over to the pile of Torah crowns, scooped them up, brought them over to the desk, slammed them down, then addressed Mansour in short stabbing phrases while staring hard into his imploring eyes:

"I want a name, a full description, everything you know, and I want it straight and fast. From whom, Mr. Mansour, did you obtain these silver ritual objects now piled on your desk?"

Dov's first words when they were back on the street were about how amazing it was the way the good-guy/bad-guy routine never failed. They talked about it on their way to the Ummayyah.

"Fear of an enemy, need for a friend—it's so basic it has to work."

"But corny, David. Everyone knows we use it."

"Doesn't matter. The need's too deep. Even an experienced cop'll fall for it if you do it right."

"So is this what we do—run scams, play tricks?"

"Yeah, of course, it's one of the things."

At the Ummayyah, David ordered a salad. The place was filled with journalists, archaeologists, Palestinian politicians, a large, noisy Arab restaurant where everyone was welcome, even a couple of tired Israeli cops. Dov ate ravenously—scooping up hummous, pulling meat off skewers, gobbling it up, devouring an extra portion of baklava for dessert. Something about the encounter with Mansour had hungered him—perhaps, David thought, his pleasure in it, a pleasure Dov now wanted to deny. Watching him eat, David recalled the day that they were bonded, that morning three years before when they'd burst together into a youth hostel on Nablus Street, guns drawn, hearts pumping, ready to capture, perhaps even to kill.

They'd been tracking narcotics dealers, four youths whom they knew were armed. The entire PC Unit had staked out the hostel for a week, boring but demanding work. Finally David had had enough. "They're in there; let's get them. Now." Dov had grinned. He was new to Pattern Crimes. He was wearing a Mickey Mouse T-shirt and a pair of beaten-up Adidas sneakers—just the garb for a frontal assault.

The place was run-down, a two-story building with odd-shaped windows and balconies on the second floor. The usual money-changer downstairs, a motor scooter parked in front, a glass shop next door from which a huge mirror was just then being loaded onto a truck. Ten o'clock in the morning, quiet, a perfect time to make a charge. David and Dov glanced at one another, David nodded, then together they hit the door.

A rush through a dingy yellow hall past a decrepit reception desk. A charge up a set of sagging stairs. Yells in Arabic. Curses. A young man in underpants suddenly dashed in front of them across the hall. A crash. He had jumped off one of the balconies. They heard the scooter revving up below. After a chaotic chase and a quick exchange of fire, David and Dov cornered two of the dealers on the roof while Uri captured a third slipping out the back. Micha had fired at the one fleeing on the scooter and had missed, but his shots had cracked the mirror. As a result, when David and Dov came back out onto the street they were confronted by strange distorted images of themselves: heads not straight on necks, limbs askew, reflections which startled them, then made them laugh, and before which they instinctively embraced.

"Aren't you hungry?" Dov was looking at him.

"Anna's saving me some Russian soup."

Dov grinned. "That's a good woman, David. You're different since you met her. Everyone says you are."

"Yes, I'm different. Mellower. Easier to get along with. Less of a shit. Right? So are you finished?"

Dov nodded, grinned.

"Good. Let's go. I'll drive you home."

They didn't talk much as he swung around the Old City Walls, up by the place where Ora Goshen's body had been found. David paused at the spot, looked over at his own building across Hinnom, saw the lights in his apartment. Anna was waiting there, probably listening to music or reading a book or an American magazine.

"What are you thinking?"

"There was an old cop here this morning, Moshe Liederman. Said he thought this could turn out to be an interesting case."

"Don't you think it is? I do. You always love a pattern."

David nodded. "Yeah, but a pattern like this? Too much brutality, Dov. A man who hates women so much he'll even kill a boy who dresses up like one. Look at how he dumps them—out of his car, like trash, trash he covers up with an old army blanket because the carcasses are naked and he wants to protect the poor things from the cold. Except he doesn't cover them up all that well because he wants them found in the morning. Wants people to see what he's done. Feel his fury. See his work. Learn to fear him. Know his power. *Know.*"

The four-lane highway to Gillo was empty. When David hit it, he accelerated.

"What do we do about the Torah case?"

"Check out this guy Gutman. I think Mansour was too frightened to lie."

"No scrolls stolen in a while."

"Doesn't matter. It's a long-term racket. We have the new case, sure, but we still have our inventory to clear. Scrolls has been around too long. I'm getting sick of staring at the file."

They decided how they'd do it, put Shoshana on Gutman, the man Mansour had identified as the source of the Torah crowns, have her watch him on and off. Then, if Gutman looked like he might be right, send in a guy from the intelligence branch wearing a mike who could play the role of an American, say from Arizona, looking to buy a Torah for his new-built synagogue. Another scam, and it might work, and in any event they'd have developed a new informer. Except when they drove into Gillo, the modern bedroom satellite town, David knew the scroll case was nothing compared to the torn and marked-up bodies of Ora Goshen, Halil Ghemaiem, and Susan Mills.

David dropped Dov in front of his building, one of fifty huge apartment slabs, cold sheer residential bastions for the New Israeli Man. On his way back into town David was mad. A man like Dov, a police sergeant and a professional, couldn't save up enough in the New Israel to buy himself a car.

Back in the city his temper cooled. The streets were deserted; although only ten o'clock, Jerusalem was asleep. As he swept around Bloomfield Park, he was filled with a disquieting love for the place. But Jerusalem evaded him; for all his efforts to know her she continued to hold herself aloof.

On En Rogel Street he searched for a parking space, found one near the entrance to the Jerusalem of Gold Folklore Club. When he shut the car door a dog barked out, then other dogs in adjoining gardens, the barking spreading house by house through Abu Tor, then down to Shiloah and up the slope of the Mount of Offense. With a simple noise he had started a wave that now rolled across the hills.

In front of number sixteen a bar of yellow light cut across the stoop. He punched out the code that opened the apartment house door, entered, and closed it carefully behind. As he mounted the stairs and passed the various apartments, he could hear bits and pieces of the late evening news. Another big car-bomb explosion in Beirut. Katyusha rockets fired at Qiryat Shemona. An ultra-orthodox demonstration in Petah Tikva. Collapsing bank shares. The King of Jordan in Washington restating Arab claims and asking the United States for new long-term credits to purchase arms.

On the third floor he caught a hint of Anna's borscht and the sound of Janos Starker playing Bach. She was waiting up for him, just feet away, and now he paused to savor what lay in store. She would greet him, kiss him, feed him, talk to him, make him smile, lead him to their bed. There they would make love, the night city spread out before them, sparkling, still, and cold, and afterward they would lie entwined.

He slipped his key into the lock, turned it, opened the door. The aroma of the borscht and the music of Bach flowed out into the hall.

"Anna, I'm home. . . ."

And then she was there before him, her smile so brilliant, her eyes so clear, her love for him so evident, that for a moment he felt he had to turn away lest he be blinded by so much radiance.

DOUBLECUTS

He strode out the back gate of the Russian Compound, past the Ticho house on Ha-Rav Kook, up narrow Ethiopia Street, then into Me'a Shearim. A mere five minutes by foot from the Pattern Crimes offices in Jerusalem Police District HQ, but for David Bar-Lev a walk into the enemy camp, the only neighborhood in Jerusalem he truly disliked.

And yet he *had* to come here.

It had been a year since his father had sold his apartment on Disraeli Street, closed down his practice, given away most of his furniture and moved to a shabby single room on an alleyway off Hevrat Shas. To devote himself to the study of Jewish mysticism, he said, to discover God within. Not that he ever actually pronounced the name of The Creator—among Kabbalists God was written G-d.

The light was fading fast, street lamps were already lit as David made his way among the clusters of yeshivas toward his father's little room. Black-suited Hasidim strode briskly by, jewelers, scholars, forgers for all he knew. An old bearded Jew with a bent back struggled up the street with a pair of canes. Cloaked youths with curled earlocks glared at him with suspicious eyes. Men in flat fur fringed hats. Men dressed in the costumes of eighteenth-century Poles. Didn't these people realize they were living in the Middle East?

Israel, of course, was their country too, but David couldn't help himself—these ultra-orthodox filled him with disgust. Was it because he knew how hypocritical they could be, how cleverly they could cheat and steal? The way they cowed their women? Their exemptions from military service? Their professed hatred of the Zionist State which protected them, financed them, and in whose politics they participated with a disproportionate obstructionist power?

Yes, all that angered him, as it did all secular Israelis, but David's dislike had deeper roots: a love of the Hellenic, the humanistic, the heroic Zionist ideal; a distaste for medieval, self-righteous, self-limiting ways of life, Jews who, even as they claimed a monopoly on truth and virtue, stoned other Jews and called them "Hitlers."

And yet here he was trudging his way into the very lair of their intolerance. If a year before someone had told him that Avraham Bar-Lev would come here to live, David would have held his sides and roared.

It was dark now. Black-garbed religious people flitted like phantoms down the narrow streets. Squashed fruit on the narrow sidewalk. A smell of cooking oil and boiled cabbage. The aroma of old cracked sewers. The sounds of people chanting, praying. A large graffito on a wall, the work of a fanatic: "Zionism and Judaism Are Diametrically Opposed."

His father's building was part of a complex of old structures, connected by courtyards, divided and subdivided again. Walls so thin you could hear the neighbors, unpainted thin old concrete walls sweating moisture and maybe grief. To live here was to live in the old Pale of Settlement. To renounce. To turn backward. To truly become a Wretched Jew.

Avraham took him in his arms—these embraces, too, were new; in the old days Dr. Bar-Lev was far more formal. But at least then David knew where he stood with him. Now he was never sure. The flowing white fringe was the same, the trimmed white beard, the thick glinting glasses, the powerful grip he remembered from his boyhood. But now he had no notion of what was going on inside his father's head.

Two old armchairs and a worn old couch, remnants of the psychoanalyst's consulting room. On a side table, framed photographs of David's mother and younger brother, both now dead, and one of himself taken years before when he was married to Judith and Hagith was a tiny child. A shelf crammed with books but containing no works by Freud, Reik, Rank, Ferenczi. Instead the Zohar, Moses Cordovero, Isaac Luria, and the Kaballah studies of Gershom Scholem.

"Well?"

"What?"

"The meaning of this visit please."

"Must it have a meaning, father?"

"Usually you drop by. Tonight you phoned."

"To be certain you'd be here."

"And where should I go?"

"Well, father, I'm sure you go out sometimes. At least I hope you do."

Avraham did not respond. He was like that lately, listening but refusing to acknowledge, gazing at David with curiosity, waiting. The old analyst's trick—waiting the patient out.

"It just occurred to me how odd it is you even have a telephone." Still no response. "That suggests a little less renunciation than you'd have us all believe."

"And who is this 'us' you speak of, David?"

"Those of us who know you."

"I don't recall ever using the word *renounce*." This was true—he had simply stated that he was going to give up his profession and devote the rest of his life to study. There was even doubt among his friends that he had actually turned religious. Many thought his study of Kabbalah was a scholarly pursuit that had nothing to do with belief.

"Well?"

"Why am I here? I need help."

Avraham smiled. "A brave reply."

"I have a case. Multiple homicides. The most difficult I've ever had." Avraham nodded, encouraging him. He was good at that, getting a person to talk.

As David began then to describe the killings, he was surprised at his own clarity. Surprised because, whenever he pondered them, which now was always, he found a pattern that tied him up in knots.

The first three victims had suggested a vague but graspable symmetry—sex crimes committed by a classic serial murderer. An apparently well-adjusted American nun; a transvestite Arab street hustler; a prostitute who, in fact, had been a sad lost child of oriental Israel.

But that very morning a fourth victim had turned up, and now the symmetry was broken: Yaakov Schneiderman, bachelor, fifty years old, fine military record, loyal reservist, owned his own truck, specialized in local hauling around Jerusalem. His body found by the side of the road near the UN House on the Hill of Evil Counsel. Same killing method, same marks, same blanket, same signs of abuse after death, but now suddenly nothing fit.

Two men, two women; one Arab, one Christian, and two Jews; two sexual people, two not-sexual; three young, one middle-aged. A pattern yes, but a pattern of technique, not one that suggested a man coherently disturbed. What was in this killer's mind? Did these strange marks he left convey a message? Did he simply slay at random out of bloodlust, compulsion, some irresistible need to kill and mark?

Oh yes, father, in case you're about to ask, we have employed the latest in investigative techniques. De-

tailed autopsies. Checks for tooth marks. Fingerprints.
Debris beneath the victims' nails. Fibers. Tire tracks.
Possible eye-witness sightings at the dumping sites.
Investigations into the victims' pasts. Research into
the meaning of the marks. . . .

Avraham's eyes did not leave his—clearly he grasped
everything. In the end he nodded and summed it up.
"You have a psychological case. You bring it to me
because I am a psychologist."

"I need criteria, father. A profile of this man. What
does he think? What's he like? So we are convening
experts. I'd like you to be on the panel."

"Who have you got?"

David mentioned some of the names, the criminolo-
gists Shimon Sanders and Professor Haftel from the
University of Haifa, various experts too on political
extremism, sociology, and psychological stress. "I believe you could help. You've helped me understand
criminal behavior before. The criminal's 'calling card.'
The compulsion to confess."

Avraham was silent. Finally when he spoke it was
not in response to David's request.

"Tell me, please, why do you do all this?"

David winced; he had heard it all before. How
could the son of a Disraeli Street psychoanalyst and a
French-Hebrew literary translator choose a career with
the lowliest arm of government, the police?

". . . a life of risk, terrible hours, ridicule, lousy
pay. Do you pride yourself on that, David, on being a
dustman, a man who picks off the vermin from our
fine Israeli streets?"

"No, I don't pride myself on it."

Avraham's glasses glinted as he shook his head.
"Crimes, crimes. You may solve a few, but do you
ever cure the underlying ills?"

"That isn't why I do it."

"Why then? I want to understand."

"The same reason you sit here and study. Because I like it. It's my work."

Avraham turned away. His gaze was now on the family photographs. On the one of beautiful serious Gideon, David knew. Gideon—sensitive warrior-poet, fighter-pilot, family prince.

"Anyway, I don't think that what we do is all that different," David said. "Detectives and psychoanalysts—we work to uncover the truth and render the demons harmless."

"Harmless? That's your delusion. Anyway, I'm no longer a psychoanalyst."

All at once David was irritated, tired of their duel. It had turned sour, and he felt it was his father's fault. "Look," he said, "will you be on my panel or not?"

Avraham turned back to him, suddenly looking tired and old. His voice became a meager whisper: "I need help too."

Help! Dr. Bar-Lev would ask his policeman son for help! Unprecedented, but still there was something thrilling about this grand reversal of their roles.

"My old papers. Suddenly some are missing." Avraham shook his head, perplexed. "The files of my practice, some going back many years. I had them stored at Blumenthal's, in the garage behind his house. And then just a few days ago he phoned to tell me someone had broken in. I went over to see and yes the lock was broken off the door, my papers scattered everywhere as if someone had gone through them very fast. I have the impression some are missing. I'm sure of it, in fact. But I don't understand why. They'd be of no interest to anyone. I should have burned them. I thought of it but didn't." Avraham shrugged. "Now I wish I had. . . ."

A curious story, David thought, for he had listened to it as a detective. And perhaps it was not really the story that was so curious as the way his father had told it—in the classic manner of a victim reluctant to file a complaint.

"Did Dr. Blumenthal report the break-in?"

"Of course."

"And the police came?"

Avraham nodded impatiently. "The point is there was nothing valuable to steal."

"You insist your files were of no interest?"

"None at all."

"Yet some were taken, so then they *were* of interest." Avraham did not react. "My feeling, father, is that very few people would take that kind of stuff. Only two thoughts come to mind: a former patient looking to clean up his past, or a prospective blackmailer searching for information he can sell. If you want me to help you'll have to be specific. Make an inventory, determine exactly what is missing, and then I'll look into it. How's that?"

Avraham's eyes turned cagey. "I have a feeling you're very good at what you do."

"Thank you. I try to be."

"So, anything else?" Avraham stood up to end the audience. "Yes, I'll come and try to analyze your killer. Tell me where and when. Perhaps it will even do me good. To get back to that kind of work for a couple of hours—yes, I will do it. Of course. . . ."

Rafi Shahar turned Pattern Crimes into an SIT, a Special Investigating Team. All other cases were to be temporarily shelved. Focus now was on the solution of the killings. Five new detectives were added, including Moshe Liederman, who had approached David privately and begged to be allowed to join.

It was interesting, David thought, the way each of them had his favorite victim. Uri liked Yaakov Schneiderman, perhaps because they were both large physical men. Dov was extremely fond of Susan Mills, and Micha identified in some strange way with Halil Ghemaiem. But no one cared for Ora Goshen except Liederman and himself.

David had asked for a large bulletin board. Uri brought in cork panels and nailed them to the unit room wall. Photos of the victims were pinned up, and a large map showing the locations of the dumping sites. Detectives came in, stared at these displays, then went out again. Rebecca Marcus, head always covered, disposition always sweet, manned the continually ringing phones, while David, with Dov as deputy, supervised from his office in the back. Everyone worked "skeleton hours," grueling duty, twelve on twelve off. And no one came up with anything. Yet all sensed the homicides would go on.

Certain facts were established:

The most important was the plate number of the car, recalled under hypnosis by Ora's friends. A light tan Renault stolen from a lot in Independence Park. The owner had a solid alibi. Much excitement when finally the car was found, parked in Gonen on a residential street. The forensic specialists swarmed over it, but in the end declared it immaculate. Every print wiped clean. A professional job. Which suggested to David a little less passion and a far cooler approach than the vicious mutilations had implied.

Nothing new on Halil. His friend, Ali Saad, continued to make havoc with Micha's IdentiKit. Meantime, Susan Mills's Israeli friends all agreed she'd been a modern but not a reckless nun.

Dov uncovered more: that she'd been deeply disturbed by the hatred that gripped the Holy Land, a woman who had longed for peace and had believed in universal brotherhood. Thus a sucker, he theorized, for Palestinean tales of woe. Perhaps she'd befriended one and he had killed her—Dov wanted to follow this notion up. David set him loose to interview everyone she'd met, but Dov's search for an "Arab friend" yielded no result.

Schneiderman, of all the victims, presented the greatest difficulties. Break Schneiderman, they told each other, and you begin to solve the case. This was not a man who would be easily overpowered. Burly, strong, accustomed to heavy physical work, brash in his dealings, kind but curt, described by his brother and several friends as "an honest, no bullshit guy." No evidence of homosexuality. No weakness to attract a predator. No signs in his modest Talpiyot flat of forced entry or a struggle. A homely man; one might even describe him as ugly. Which left two questions: How could the killer, if unknown to him, have lured him into a position where he could cut his throat, and what about Schneiderman could have attracted the killer anyway?

As for the old army blankets thrown over the mutilated bodies, investigation revealed these were standard issue, available by the ten thousand in flea markets throughout Israel.

Ten P.M. Hananya Street, one of the sweet-smelling streets of the German Colony near the big public swimming pool off Emeq Refaim. A cool Thursday evening the first week of April. The season of icy nights was done. Passover was coming and, soon after that, Easter. Jerusalem was filling with tourists and pilgrims, and flowing with rumors about a "slasher" who had stymied the police.

David, Dov, and Shoshana Nahon were waiting in an unmarked police Subaru in front of Jacob Gutman's home.

"It would not be wonderful if we got spotted here." Dov had been opposed to the foray. It would not do for the commander of an important SIT to be observed staking out a man suspected of brokering stolen Torah scrolls.

But Shoshana had been adamant. She'd been watching Gutman for a week. Now the case belonged to her, her first real case, and she was certain Gutman was behind the thefts. She didn't want to share the arrest with an undercover officer, and if David wouldn't let her have this chance then she might as well go back into the army—at least there a young person could prove what she could do.

So now they were waiting, Shoshana coiled with tension, chain-smoking in the back seat while Dov munched potato chips in front. He and David passed the time tossing around ideas about Schneiderman and how he could be made to fit the pattern of their case.

"Suppose Yaakov had knowledge," Dov said. "He'd seen something, suspected who the killer was. He tried to blackmail him and the killer said okay. Then, when they met to make the deal, the killer sandbagged him and did him up like another victim in the series."

"You're nuts!" Shoshana was puffing furiously. "Gutman's in there. He's a pushover. Why the hell are we sitting around?"

"Don't get impatient, sweetie. It's not too smart to go into apartments until you're sure how many people are inside." Suddenly Dov turned around and grabbed her cigarette out of her mouth.

"David!"

"Okay. Enough. Let's get this over with." Tired of their bickering he was relieved to get out of the car.

Silence on the street. No one around. A single window lit in the first floor apartment. Jacob Gutman lived there, and it was there, Shoshana was convinced, that he kept his store of stolen goods.

She'd done a thorough job, talked to his neighbors,

identified him as a private dealer in rare Judaica. An old man, German born, Gutman had immigrated to Palestine in the thirties. He'd joined the Jewish Brigade, later served in the Palmach. Distinguished himself in the '48 war, lost his wife in 1960 and his only daughter in an automobile accident in 1972.

Shoshana had photographed him surreptitiously, showed her pictures to Aziz Mansour, gotten a positive ID that this was the man who'd sold him the Torah crowns. She'd tracked him through the city, found no evidence he had an outside stash. Assumption: The stolen scrolls were stored in his apartment. Based on proof which she had submitted that several of the crowns had come off of stolen scrolls, a judge had issued her a warrant for a search.

In the entrance hall of the subdivided house David read the tenant roster: Rosenfeld, M.; Rosenfeld, E.; Cohen, L.; Levi, L.; Gutman, J. A purely German building. He looked at Shoshana and nodded toward Gutman's buzzer. "Your bust," he told her. "Your case. You ring."

She nodded, rang, then rang again. No answer, but half a minute later an elderly man in a frayed gray bathrobe came to the glass door and peered out.

Shoshana held her ID against the glass. "Police." Gutman cupped his ear. He was bald on top with tufts of unkempt hair protruding from the sides of his head. *"Police."* The second time she shouted. The old man's eyes darted as he took in the three of them, then he brought his finger to his lips, opened the door, and stepped into the hall.

"What? What?"

Shoshana showed her warrant. David watched Gutman carefully. He was pale, poorly shaven, and he looked scared. But there was also in his manner a subtle hint of relief. David had seen this before: the reaction of a man who, having engaged in illegal activity for years, is finally relieved to be rid of his fear of being caught.

"So, in Israel now the police come in the middle of the night?" Gutman's eyes gleamed with righteous anger. "To humiliate an elderly person before his neighbors? Are these the approved tactics of officials in our Jewish State?" Suddenly he presented his wrists. "You have manacles of course? And instruments of torment? No! But you must extract my confession. You will use pain as a lever. Yes? Am I right? Oh, the pain! *Oh! Oh!*"

He muttered something about "storm troopers" as he led them back into his apartment. But when they ignored him and Shoshana began her search, he seemed to realize the game was up. "I'm a Jew like the three of you. I fought in the War of Independence. Why pick on me? Why don't you go after bad guys? Child-murdering Arab terrorists?"

He didn't even bother to turn when Shoshana announced her find. "Scrolls. A closet full of them. Other stuff too. Menorahs, pointers, candlesticks."

"So," Dov asked, "are you the broker or the thief?"

"The menorahs are all legal. I have proof!"

"Sure. They'd be recognized. But scrolls all look alike. Did you organize the robberies or do you just fence the loot? Come on, talk!" Gutman stared at the floor. "You'll talk, old man. In time."

Shoshana glowed. Her first bust and she'd hit gold. This case would make the papers: Stolen Torahs were much better than diamonds and furs.

But then a strange thing happened. For the first time since they'd come into the apartment Jacob Gutman turned to David and stared into his face. "I know who you are," he said. "You're David, aren't you?" He smiled, then slowly began to nod. "Sure, you're David. That's who you are. You're David. David Bar-Lev. . . ."

"He kept staring at me, all the way back to the Compound. I asked him several times how he knew me but he wouldn't say. He just kept smiling and nodding as if I were someone he'd run into unexpectedly, someone meaningful in his past whom he hadn't seen in years."

"No idea who he is?" David, naked, was lying on his back. Anna, wearing just a T-shirt, sat astride him, knees gripping his flanks, sensuously massaging around his neck.

"Just this old crook, that's all I know. Claims to be religious, but then he brokers stolen Torahs."

"Maybe you arrested him once."

"I'd remember." He groaned with pleasure. She had powerful Russian hands and an instinctive ability to locate knots of tension and smooth them away.

"Maybe you knew him in another context. Now he's older, looks different, and you can't remember because he doesn't fit."

"This is a man I'd remember. I'd remember his eyes."

"So how does he know you?"

He blinked. "Can't figure it out."

He twisted beneath her pressure. She bent down to kiss his chest. "Well," she said, "maybe he knew you as a child."

Yes, that could fit with his smile. Gutman had smiled at him the way one smiles at someone one hasn't seen since he was small.

"He could have known my parents." David shook his head. "What a strange thing. I'm glad I didn't know before."

He reached up, slipped his hands beneath her shirt,

ran his fingers along her sides. She was a lean girl; he could feel her ribs, ripples beneath her flesh. When he grazed her breasts she trembled slightly, rose, then sat down again directly on his sex.

After they made love, they lay together beneath the covers, clothes scattered where they'd tossed them. Jerusalem hung like a backdrop framed by the window, illuminated towers, domes, and walls dark amber against a deep black velvet sky.

". . . Gideon was always the handsome one. Golden youth, golden man. He had beautiful features. Not like mine. Beside him I looked rough."

Anna, running her fingers lightly over his face, protested with her lips.

"No, it's true. People always said I had a good Israeli face, whatever that's supposed to mean. But Gideon had my mother's eyes and her beautiful fine carved lips. Artist friends of my parents were always asking to draw him. People who visited from overseas would take our picture together and then a separate one of him. As he grew older I began to notice that people stared at him, men and women both. He had that special kind of face people can't tear their eyes away from. But there was something wrong with him—I think I always knew there was. It was as if he was somehow *too* perfect—perfect student, perfect son. And something bad was going on in the family. I still don't know what it was. Some kind of complicity between my parents—whispered conferences behind closed doors, my mother emerging with tears in her eyes, my father with his unhappy worried face. And then those quicksilver alliances between the three of them. . . ."

He paused, trying to recapture an old feeling of separateness, of being part of his family and apart from it too. She was watching him, her eyes large, her compassion written on her face.

"I think that's why you became a detective," she said. "To figure out your family's mystery."

She was right and he loved her for understanding him so well. Also for the quickness of her mind, the direct way she spoke, and, too, for her sensuality, the uninhibited joy she took in making love.

He described for her again Gideon's death, that strange last self-destructive flight, how, on a training mission, fully loaded with bombs, he had suddenly broken formation, flown out over the water, then turned his Phantom to the sky and begun a steep ascent.

"Heading higher, higher, until finally he went too high, blacked out, and lost control. The plane flipped over, then dove straight down into the sea. The news seemed to break my father. Afterward he was never the same. As if somehow it was *his* fault, *his* failure, as if he was responsible for Gideon's self-destructive streak. Gideon always had it, of course. He was forever fracturing a wrist in soccer practice or breaking a leg on a camping trip. It's a wonder they didn't catch on to him in the Air Force—they're supposed to watch the pilots so carefully. Anyway, a month after that my mother was diagnosed as having cancer. Three months later she was dead. Father stopped taking new patients, phased the old ones out. So now he sits in his little room gazing at Gideon's photograph. And then I drop by, a mere detective, mere captain in the police, and I can see the disappointment in his face."

Anna's dark brown eyes were staring straight into his. She held her palm against his forehead. "Why go on like this, David? Why torment yourself?"

He shrugged. "Sometimes it helps to talk. Now I wonder how Gutman fits in. I'll ask father, of course. But he may not tell me. He's like that lately. He hears the question but half the time he doesn't bother to reply. . . ."

The conference room of Jerusalem District Police HQ, between Superintendent Latsky's suite and Rafi Shahar's CID. It was late in the day, shadows were long; fading sunlight reflected off the top of the conference table adding luster to the old worn wood.

Rafi sat in the head chair, pipe and tobacco set out in front of him, his sad watery eyes scanning the others as they spoke. David sat to his right. Sarah Dorfman perched behind vigorously taking notes.

Dr. Sanders and Professor Haftel had done most of the talking, but the five other specialists had contributed too. Including, David was pleased to note, Dr. Avraham Bar-Lev, who had spoken not with his usual lethargic delivery but with his former clarity and force.

And yet what did it all come to? David wondered as Rafi tried to reconcile and then summarize their views. So much that was obvious, so little that was new: that the killer was almost certainly an Israeli male between twenty and fifty years old; that he had almost certainly served in a military unit where signs of psychological disturbance may have brought him to the attention of a staff psychologist. Possible criminal record, suggested by his expertise in stealing cars, though that was far from clear. The killer knew Jerusalem well, so he either lived here or had done so in the past. A strong possibility that he also knew Tel Aviv.

Such were the objective parameters that could be fed into various computerized data banks, the basic one that held the Israeli national identity list as well as those of the police and the IDF.* But as Rafi had pointed out very quietly at the beginning of the conference, he expected such a search would produce between one and two hundred thousand names.

Which left the psychological criteria, not entered

*IDF: Abbreviation for Israel Defense Force.

into any computer system and thus not useful as a means to screen the citizenry.

"We are dealing here with an entire country of suspects," Dr. Sanders announced. "There're at least a million and a half adult Israeli males. We can give you a feeling of what this man may be like, but we cannot tell you where to find him, or even where to begin to look."

A loner, they all agreed, perhaps even a brooder, but socially adept too, able to inspire confidence, get people to go off with him, lure them to a lonely place. With Ora Goshen and Halil Ghemaiem he had been a man in search of sex, but with Susan Mills and Yaakov Schneiderman he had assumed a more subtle identity which these victims had believed.

Once he killed he owned his victims' bodies, believing he had full permission to "sign" their flesh. Autopsies revealed Susan Mills had been tortured before she'd been killed, but that the others had only been mutilated after death. This change in method struck Dr. Bar-Lev as an important, perhaps even vital clue:

"She was his first victim, so he may have learned from his experience with her that he couldn't bear to hear human screams. Then he decided that in the future he would work only on bodies that were dead. You see, really he's a butcher. The live person doesn't interest him at all. He's less a sadist than a man detached from life. He could be a worker in a slaughterhouse or a mortuary, or an actual butcher in a meat market, or a hunter who likes to skin and cut up game."

Rafi nodded at David—the old man was sharp; he had indicated certain professions and thus places to begin a search. But then the others started in. It was the double marks that interested them, those quick cuts, slash-slash across the cheeks, the lips, the breasts. Stigmata, perhaps, marks of derision or disgrace. A possible religious dimension there, or some form of ritual punishment. Perhaps the killer thought of himself as a sacred executioner who marked his victims so that those who found them would know they had offended God.

That was one line of interpretation; there were others; one could speculate endlessly. One thing, however, was agreed upon by everyone: The message was in the marks.

The shadows grew longer in the conference room. No one bothered to turn on the lights. The table gleamed. The participants became energized. Their faces were etched, half lost in gloom, half illuminated with brilliant light.

"He wants us to *know* him. He doesn't want his victims confused with those of anybody else."

"He wants the bodies found, his work recognized, his purpose feared."

"Attention. Fame. Notoriety."

"He's a megalomaniac. A kind of terrorist."

"He may not be aware of this self-aspect. Or even of the contempt he shows by the way he dumps them— amid rubble, in a drainage ditch, at a construction site."

"But compulsive, too. The blankets suggest this. Perhaps he has purchased a certain number. Perhaps if we knew how many we would know how many times he intends to kill."

"He may stop suddenly, or go on indefinitely. We have no way of knowing without knowing what his purpose is."

"He strips them to reduce them. Naked they are like dead animals."

"The lack of semen suggests he's impotent. These are sex crimes, certainly, but extremely devious ones by which, most likely, he conceals their sexual content from himself. . . ."

Later David would not recall the exact moment when the idea struck. "Inject the dye and wait for it to circulate," he said. "Then, when it reaches him, hopefully it will stain."

They were all staring at him. He had stood up, had his palms planted on the table.

"The best detective in Israel," Rafi was saying. "So go on, David, tell us what you mean."

He glanced at his father, saw a querying look. "An analogy with the tracer-dye method of the bone-scan radiologists," he said. "Look, it will be extremely difficult to go out and find this man, but listening to you talk I think there may be a way to make him come to us."

"Explain please." It was Dr. Bar-Lev. David nodded to him and went on.

"You all say he wants recognition, that he's sending us some kind of message. So why not attract him by doing in public just what we're doing here? Hold an open forum, give him the opportunity to hear us speculate about what kind of man he really is."

"Would he come?"

"If we make ourselves accessible enough, how, really, could he resist? And even if he doesn't, he can write in for a transcript. We'll publicize that too, print up the text and mail it out on request. Meantime, we'll covertly videotape our audience. If you provoke him enough he may react. At the very least we'll end up with a manageable list of suspects. Anything's better than two hundred thousand names."

They decided to hold it in the auditorium of the Rubin Academy of Music—centrally located, no security gate, yet a perfectly credible place. The "forum" would be held under the auspices of a fictitious *ad hoc* group they decided to call "The Society for a Better Israel"—a name consistent with those of other wound-healing groups that had sprung up to protest the break-down of civility in Israeli public life.

Stories about the conference were planted in newspapers. A poster was printed and placed in strategic locations around Jerusalem and Tel Aviv. The *Jerusalem Post* ran a tantalizing article quoting some of the ideas of Professor Haftel. Shimon Sanders, Israel's foremost criminologist, was interviewed on the radio, along with David Bar-Lev, who played a typical no-nonsense cop.

One particular interchange was carefully contrived:

SANDERS: *To catch this man you must understand his mind. There is brilliance there, evil perhaps, but brilliance nonetheless.*

BAR-LEV: *The guy's a savage, that's all I know. An animal. I'm tired of hearing how damn smart he is.*

Outside the Rubin Academy, tables were set up. People entering could sign petitions and anyone wanting a free printed transcript had merely to leave his name. Pattern Crimes personnel mingled with the audience, exchanging whispered views with strangers who appeared especially engaged. The videotaping of the speakers was carried out by a single cameraman stationed at the back. Nothing threatening about him—he was shooting over the tops of people's heads. But three unattended cameras were concealed beneath the speakers' table, remotely controlled from a van parked around the corner on Balfour Street. From here, cramped in with three technicians, David and Rafi watched the symposium on a bank of monitors.

"This set-up cost me one hell of a bundle of favors." Rafi had borrowed the special equipment and personnel through a friend in the Mossad.* "I always feel humiliated by these informal arrangements, David. Wheeling and dealing for decent stuff. The intelligence guys get the goodies while we get surplus radios and crappy cars. The politicians say they want professional police, but they won't vote the money to back us up."

Rafi's oft-repeated gripe. He claimed he hated *protektzia,* the system of influence in high places, the old-buddy-in-my-reserve-unit way of doing business. But even more than that, he seemed to hate the present era, the way the government careened from crisis to crisis—corruption scandals, cabinet meetings that ended in insults, physical shoving on the floor of the Knesset, lawlessness, tribalism, violence, pervasive cheating, rage, and greed.

Dr. Bar-Lev was speaking now. Listening to him David was amazed. His father had rudely interrupted Shimon Sanders, and now was putting on an astonishing performance, provoking and arousing the entire audience:

"This killer thinks he's maybe The Messiah but we know he's the most despicable kind of Jew. The self-loathing kind, the Jew trying to kill in others that which he hates within himself. Pervert. Sadist. Secret homosexual, terrified of women, furious with men. A coward but he can't admit it. On the symbolic level, when he cuts his victims, he affirms to us his impotence. . . ."

Rafi nudged David. "Your dad's terrific."

Blow up frames from the videotapes, turn them into photographs, mount them in rows on the PC Unit bulletin board. One hundred seventy Israeli males at-

*Mossad: Israeli Foreign Intelligence Service.

tended the symposium. All of them were suspect. The first job was to give them names.

Some of the more agitated people were followed home. Meantime, David showed the tapes to cops in other units. Whom did they recognize? Whom did they know? More names. Run them through the computers, check out military records, identify professions, discover which men were qualified to drive. Marital status. Police and medical records. Identify, collect data, analyze, and set priorities. Likelies, possibles, unlikelies, impossibles. Refine the lists, then start to winnow, eliminating from the top.

Three days into this new phase of the investigation, David received an unexpected call. A man named Ephraim Cohen, a friend, from youth movement days, of Gideon Bar-Lev.

"I remember you, of course," David said, though he wasn't positive he did.

"Saw you on TV in connection with the nastiness. Have something interesting you'd maybe like to hear."

"Please. I'll listen to anything."

"Well, this isn't something I can talk about on the phone."

Why's he being so careful? "Want to meet? I'll come to you." No response. "What's the problem?"

"David, I'm with another service. This would just be something I'd pass on in a strictly informal sort of way."

They arranged to meet at seven that evening at The Garden, a dairy restaurant near the YMCA on King David Street. David arrived first, found a quiet table on the terrace, ordered tea, and settled down to wait. He was forced to endure a lecture then, given by an American tourist, holding forth to his wife and be-dazzled tablemates. The man was loud, his voice carried across the terrace, and he was very sure of himself, an instant expert. Listening to him explain the parameters of the current political situation, David was amazed at how every single "fact" he recounted was wildly distorted or else completely false.

After ten minutes a well-dressed, well-groomed man appeared. David, guessing his age at thirty-one or two, recognized the fine edge of arrogance he associated with officers in the Mossad.

After a few seconds this stranger caught David's eye, smiled, strode over, extended his hand. "Hello. Nice to see you. I'm Ephraim Cohen."

"Yes," David said, "I *do* remember you." And he did. Ephraim had been one of those beautiful boys Gideon always used to choose as friends: Nordic, blond, with carved cheeks, and sensitive eyes and lips.

"It's been a long time. I wrote your parents when Gideon died. How's your father?"

"Retired. He's become a Kabbalist."

"Oh?" Cohen raised an eyebrow as if to say, "That sounds a little batty, but who am I to judge?" David studied him, decided he didn't like him: Cohen was too good-looking and much too cautious. David glanced at his watch. "Well, here we are. You were going to pass something on."

"You understand this is strictly unofficial."

"Yes, yes." *Why do they always have to say that a hundred times?*

"Well. . . ." Cohen hesitated. Watching him work himself up to speak, David was happy he had not chosen the intelligence service instead of the police. "Seems one of our technicians, guy who worked your little job a few nights back, his name's not important— seems he recognized someone in that audience. Someone he served with once." Cohen cleared his throat. "Someone, he says, who used to like to cut."

"Liked to cut?"

"Yeah, that's what he says. He didn't mention anything to you about it at the time, because, after all, he works for us. But some of us talked it over this morning and we thought we ought to pass the information on. Maybe nothing to it. Maybe you know it already. But this case is very disturbing to everyone, and we thought the least we could do is try and help."

How very good of you, you slimy bastards. "So, who did he see who 'used to like to cut'?"

"Guy named Peretz."

"That's a pretty common name."

"This Peretz was a professional military officer, a major. Major Chaim Peretz. That ought to give you a start."

David nodded. "Would your guy be willing to come in and point him out on the tapes?"

"Afraid not. Policy is to stay out of police affairs."

"What about unofficially, as a private citizen performing a civic duty?"

"Well, we rather feel he's done that already. Don't you, David? After all, here I am passing on the name."

Rafi may have loathed the old buddy system, but it was a lot quicker than working one's way through the IDF bureaucracy. That evening David started making calls. By ten the following morning he found what he was looking for: a friend, Yehuda Merom, now a colonel, whom he'd served with in Sinai during the '67 war.

"Oh, sure, David, I know Chaim Peretz. Even had a feeling one day I'd get a call like this."

"Why's that?"

"We'd better meet. Unofficially, of course."

"Of course."

"A drink after work?"

"This is pretty urgent."

"Okay. Let's have coffee. You know the Pie House? Meet you there in fifteen minutes."

On his way out the door David told Dov to drop what he was doing and find Peretz. "Used to be a major. I want to know what he looks like and where he lives. Try doing it the easy way: Start with the phone book. If that doesn't work, then use the computer."

It was a perfect Jerusalem spring day—deep blue sky, the smell of blooming shrubs and trees. Even the traffic on Jaffa Road was bearable. The old buses spewed out fumes but not enough to spoil the pure dry April air.

Yehuda embraced him, then they clapped each other's shoulders and punched lightly at each other's girths.

"David, we're middle-aged."

"Listen, we're still alive."

"So you're a big-shot detective now. Saw you on TV."

David shrugged. "Seen any of the guys?"

"A few. Shai. Yig'al. I saw Zvi Shapira at the airport about a month ago. Making a fortune in computerized imaging. He was on his way to Japan."

They spoke briefly of old comrades, and then of how they'd cheered that first morning when they'd seen the planes return. David remembered: the terrible heat, the blisters on his face, the dust and the wind, then the roar of the fighters just above their heads and how they'd jumped up and down upon the burning sand: all the Arab air forces destroyed on the ground. The great conquest had begun. Heroic days.

"It's not the same now, is it? Remember how we all adored Arik? Then Lebanon. I was there. It stunk. Bastard! We didn't know it then. '67! That's when everything started going wrong."

"Tell me about Peretz."

"In connection with the murders, right?"

David nodded. "His name came up."

"I'm not surprised." Yehuda looked uneasy. David didn't say anything, just waited for him to talk.

". . . a perfect commander for reprisal assaults, which I suppose is why he got the job. It was a covert unit. Strictly volunteer. But there was a level of brutality even the toughest types couldn't take. So then Peretz came up with this idea, a way to staff it out. Fill it out with criminals, guys in trouble, violent guys. They had these guys in stockades, and they didn't know what to do with them. 'Let me have them,' he said. 'It's a filthy job so give me filthy guys.' "

"So what exactly was this filthy job?"

"Counterterror. They do bad things to us, we go do even worse to them."

"Crossing frontiers?"

"Nothing new about that. We've been doing it for years." Yehuda looked away. "Of course this was different. Real nasty stuff. The justification was that it was aimed at the hard-core terrorists, the ones who sneak in, kill kids, and shoot up schools."

"What are you saying?"

"I'm not saying anything, David. The unit was small, covert, and when it was disbanded all the records were destroyed. You won't find anyone now who'll admit it ever existed. No one wants to own up to having signed off on the damn thing because of the way it got out of hand."

"I heard something about Peretz, that he 'liked to cut.' "

Yehuda nodded.

"They *cut* people?"

"That wasn't the purpose. The purpose was to strike back hard."

"So what's all this about cutting?"

"Stories. Tales. You couldn't prove any of them. It was all hearsay kind of stuff."

"What kind of hearsay?"

Yehuda looked away again. "The way it started out, the unit was supposed to leave some kind of mark. That way people would know we had a reprisal squad and that the squad always got its man. So let's say they did a termination, they'd leave these cuts on the guy, their signature. But then, later, with this violent criminal element involved, it got out of control." He tightened his lips, squirmed in his seat, then looked David directly in the eye. "There were, at least we heard, some mutilations, things like that. You know, ears, eviscerations—though I find *that* hard to believe. Women and children too, somebody said. Tell you the truth, David, I don't really want to talk about this. It makes me want to puke."

"So what happened?"

"The unit got disbanded."

"What about Peretz?"

"The army quietly let him go."

"Just like that?"

"Actually, they found a desk job for him. But he didn't like it, so when he complained they suggested he resign."

"No investigation? No inquiry?"

"The stories couldn't be verified. The witnesses were criminals. As for Peretz, he was an outstanding officer who took on a dirty job and did it well. Relentless, maybe merciless, but at first no one was too concerned. They wanted results and he gave them results. Later, when they got to know him better, there developed this feeling that he might be getting off on it, which is when they began to have second thoughts. I think that's what really bothered them. Not that Peretz did these things. We're at war. Counterterror's not supposed to be a boy scout jamboree. But if the commander was actually enjoying his work, as opposed, you understand, to treating it as a dirty job. . . . I mean, if it'd been you or me, David, we'd have tried to get out of it, or have griped until they pulled us out, or, failing that, done it half-ass. But Peretz didn't do it that way. He *liked* it and after a while everyone could see he did. So in the end that was the real reason they closed him down."

Yehuda sat back. Then he gave David a bitter little smile. "I could get into a lot of trouble if it ever came out I told you this."

"Forget about that. It won't. But I've got a couple of questions. You say the unit records were destroyed. Does this mean I can't get a list of the men?"

"No list. The unit didn't exist. It didn't even have an official name. Whenever anyone mentioned it he'd just say 'Peretz and the boys.' Peretz recruited for himself, so he might remember. Didn't occur to me till now, but he might have some kind of informal list of his own."

"Second question: What exactly was the 'signature'?"

"I don't know exactly but I have a vague recollection of hearing it discussed one time. I think the original idea was to convey the notion of double trouble, two-for-one. You know, like in Hosea: 'They have sewn the wind, and they shall reap the whirlwind.' I remember something about sets of cuts—double cuts, something like that."

They found Peretz very quickly on the videotapes, and when they did they all wondered why they hadn't spotted him before.

"He's so *still*, David." Shoshana shuddered.

"Guy doesn't move, doesn't react."

They rewound the master audience tape and ran it again. The striking thing about Peretz was his total lack of affect. In a sea of highly disturbed people he was a noticeable island of calm.

"As if nothing anyone said touched him at all. How did we miss him?" Micha asked.

"We were looking for the wrong thing," David said.

"But still we *got* him! We *got* him!" They were excited: David's long-shot scheme of the false symposium had worked.

"Not so fast," he warned them. "He's a suspect. Now we watch him. No pressure. He mustn't know we're there. Full-press covert surveillance around-the-clock, which means constantly changing shifts. Not three guys wearing Ray-bans parked in a white car across the street."

He put Dov in charge of organizing the surveillance, gave Micha the job of digging into Peretz's past. But Micha was put out when David assigned him Moshe Liederman.

"He's a burn-out. He isn't any good. All he talks about is his retirement."

"Try and use him anyway," David said. "He told me in thirty years he's never worked a case that wasn't shit. I'd like it if, when he retires, he could tell people he worked one hell of a case one time."

That night, the Seder night of Passover, he called Avraham. "Do you know a Jacob Gutman?" No reply. "I know you do, Father. Please tell me who he is."

A long pause, then finally a response: "Jacob Gutman is a man who has been wronged."

Driving home the second evening of the holiday, passing Herod's Gate, David glanced up at the Rockefeller Museum and smiled. He remembered the day he had spotted Anna here, the day that had changed his life.

It was the previous November, just three weeks after he'd broken off his affair with the journalist Stephanie Porter. He'd bought himself a ticket to a recital at the Lutheran Church of the Redeemer. An exciting new Soviet-émigré cellist was being featured along with her Israeli accompanist. There'd been an article about them in the *Jerusalem Post*, an interview with Anna Benitskaya and also her photograph. Perhaps it was the inviting look in her eyes or the expression on her face. Something intrigued him. When he discovered he had a free evening he decided to go and hear her play.

The recital moved him. He loved chamber music, and when she played the third Beethoven sonata he found himself entranced. He couldn't take his eyes off her. She was a beautiful young woman but it was more than beauty that he saw. Vulnerability, something open and yet mysterious, a haunting quality too, an impression of depth that belied her youth. She had worn a gray silk dress, a pearl necklace, and tiny pearl earrings which glowed like soft little lights beside her head. She played with passion and her forehead gleamed. When the concert was over he left the church wondering wistfully where she was staying and whether it would be possible to meet her and if he did what she would be like.

Then, the next day, there was one of those coincidences that seemed to occur so often in Jerusalem. He had been driving midmorning past the Rockefeller Museum on an errand concerning some now-forgotten case when he saw her walking alone up the entrance drive.

My chance, he'd thought. *I mustn't let it pass.* He quickly circled the museum, found a parking place, hurried back to the gate, bought himself a ticket, and entered too.

It didn't take him long to find her. There were few tourists that time of year, and the Rockefeller, an archaeological museum, was not one of the more popular sights. There were perhaps a dozen visitors mov-

ing quietly through the galleries, but when he found
Anna she wasn't studying the collections. She was
walking slowly beneath the vaulted arcades that lined
the central sun-filled court.

He watched her. It would have been too obvious to
follow her directly, and in any case he was a detective
and knew how to follow without being seen. So as she
moved slowly under the arcades he moved more quickly
through the adjoining interlocking galleries, catching
glimpses of her every so often through interior windows open to the cloister.

After a while she crossed to the center and sat down
on an old stone bench. It was nearly noon. The sun
was shining directly on her, showering her with brilliant November light. She shut her eyes, turned her
head for warmth, and as she did, revealed her face.
Her forehead gleamed as it had during her concert and
then he caught a glimpse of skin glistening at her
throat. Something so intimate about that gloss of perspiration: He was filled by an image of her writhing
and moaning in sexual abandon that filled him with
desire.

Perhaps he spent a quarter hour watching her. He
remembered being fascinated and also feeling like a
spy. When she left the museum, he followed her down
the drive, across Suleiman, along the Old City walls,
and then, turning the corner, along a little footpath
that ran between an ancient Moslem cemetery and the
massive Turkish wall.

Some Arab boys were playing soccer in the dust.
There was a scent of pine resin in the crystal air, the
leaves on the olive trees flashed silver, and the golden
dome of the Dome of the Rock glowed brilliant beneath the sun. She stopped several times. At first he
thought she was looking at Gethsemane. But then, as
he drew closer, he saw that she was gazing upon the

chalk-white graves that coated the slopes of the Mount of Olives.

Suddenly she glanced at her watch, then broke into a run. His heart stopped when, plunging forward, she almost tripped upon a step. He watched as she ran into the Jericho road, flagged down a taxi, then was gone, speeding back toward the center of Jerusalem. And then he knew he had to meet her, that if he did not he could not live.

Sarah Dorfman arranged it. Poor wonderful Sarah, Rafi's loyal middle-aged secretary, abandoned by her husband for one of those aggressive young German girls, the kind who come to Israel "to confront my parents' guilt" but in fact, or so it always seemed to David, came for a quick tan and to make love to a lot of swarthy Jews. Still, Sarah never complained, and now her life was devoted to the CID. Her only outside interest was music. She knew everyone in the Jerusalem music world and delivered on her promise that David would meet his cellist within the week.

All that had happened less than six months before and now Anna lived with him in Abu Tor. What if he had not driven by the Rockefeller that day? Would they have met? Or would he have forgotten her face and the extraordinary way she'd played? David did not know but he believed in the magic of Jerusalem, that it was a city of intersecting lives.

A rumble of thunder as he pulled into En Rogel Street, a flash of lightning as he parked. Just as he stepped out of his car the rainstorm began. He dashed to the doorway of number sixteen where he frantically stabbed out the code on the touch-tone combination lock.

He was soaked before he got inside. In the lobby he took off his jacket, held it away from him, and wrung it out. A spring rainstorm at last; the country needed rain. Water was a problem even more serious than the confrontation states.

Anna was wearing a faded yellow shirt. There was a crease between her eyes.

"What's the matter?"

"Rafi just called. You're to call him back right away. He sounded tense." She shook her head, disturbed.

He kissed her between her eyes, then strode to the phone. Dialing the Russian Compound, waiting for them to patch Rafi in, he threw her several more kisses as she stood by the kitchen door.

"David?"

"It's me."

"There's a terrific rain coming down."

"I know. I just got in."

"You're going to have to come out again."

"Another one?" He knew the answer and even before Rafi responded he could feel the dull ache again, the ache he had felt in his stomach ever since he'd been assigned the case.

"It's near you, anyway. A Dumpster on the south corner of Bloomfield Park."

He gulped. "Two minutes ago I passed within fifty feet."

"If I'd seen you I'd have flagged you down."

Anna had his poncho out, was smoothing it by snapping it in the air. He glanced out the window and at that moment a bolt of lightning cracked the sky. Anna held the poncho, he ducked under it, then straightened up so that his head was in the center hole. She pulled the hood up for him.

"When you come back we'll make love," she whispered. "And then I'll make us eggs."

Rafi wore a bright orange slicker, like a fisherman,

David thought. Micha wore a trench coat, Moshe Liederman sucked on a cigarette beneath a poncho, while Dov Meltzer stood in soaked sneakers holding a pin-up magazine above his head.

"I heard it on the radio," Dov said. His T-shirt was soaked; through the wet fabric David could see dark curls of hair covering his upper chest.

"Peretz?"

"He's home. We spotted him around five going into his building. I've got four guys watching him now. Thought I ought to meet you here."

The Dumpster loomed before them like an over-sized coffin, huge and black, difficult to see, except when the lightning struck and then it was etched out. Five patrol cars and an ambulance were parked around it at converging angles. The forensic team was waiting for the illumination. A sergeant was setting up porta-ble quartz lights, clipping the lamps to the door frames of a van.

David went up to Rafi. "Female?" he asked.

Rafi nodded, pipe clenched between his teeth. "Found by a couple of teenagers looking to scrounge up some discarded wood. Very young this time, like the third one by the wall. But I have a bad feeling she's not a prostitute. Five is too many, David. We never had a case with five."

"You said it before. Our first serial killer."

"But the scale's wrong. Know what I mean?" Rafi reached under his slicker, brought out a lighter, tried unsuccessfully to light his pipe. "Everyone's always talking about scale. We go to war, lose a thousand guys, and we say that's like the fifty, sixty thousand the Americans lost in Vietnam. So figure it out. Five is like two hundred fifty. Yeah, I know it doesn't work that way, but that's the way it seems." Another light-ning bolt. Rafi winced at the thunderclap. Now the rain was slashing down in sheets. "Shit, don't know what they think they're going to find in there. With rain like this there'll just be soup."

"Same blanket?"

Rafi nodded.

Suddenly David was furious. "Pricks!"

Rafi squinted at him. "Anyone I know?"

"Mossad bastards. Their guy spotted Peretz but they had to wait a couple days before they clued me in. Now this. We've only been on Peretz since five o'clock today. He could have done this last night. We'd have seen him approach her. We could have stopped him. You understand, Rafi? If Peretz did this, then the blood's also on their fucking heads."

A SHAPE
IN THE CLAY

BIG SUR.
SIX MONTHS BEFORE . . .

"Oh, Targov. . . ."

She was like that—after she climaxed she always moaned his name: "Targov, Targov . . . oh . . . oh. . . ." Then, always, she fell asleep.

She was a big girl, this one, taller than Anna, California-grown with a quick smile, a dimpled Irish face, and a Milky Way of freckles across her chest. Strong hard breasts and a ribbon of reddish hair between her legs. She jogged. She took dance class. She lifted weights. Her hair was long and auburn. Her hands were powerful. She was a potter.

He left her on her mattress amid rumpled salmon sheets. There was no bed in the loft, just the huge mattress and her clothing, costumes really, stored in straw baskets scattered on the floor. Smaller baskets, containing underwear and stockings, hung from the ceiling amid her hanging plants. A ladder led down to her studio. He descended it, his cock swinging. A little tired, a little droopy, he thought, but still it swings and rings. . . .

He went to the refrigerator, poured himself a vodka, sat down naked on her sofa upholstered in musty olive cordoroy. Then he inhaled the aroma of her freshly made pots sitting on their wheels, still wet and wrapped in towels.

They had a date every Tuesday. He drove up to

Palo Alto in the morning, taught his Master Class, met Maureen for a quick pizza near the campus, walked with her to her studio, screwed her brains out until five o'clock, then drove back down to Big Sur, arriving home just in time for dinner.

Irina knew. "Dish him out more soup, Rokovsky. Poor thing's exhausted. Look at the circles beneath his eyes." Then she'd smile her cunning smile and then she'd glower. Later, when she retired for the evening, she'd make sure they heard her throw the latches on her door.

"Targov? Where are you? Come back up here, naughty man!"

Maureen wanted him again; he obeyed her summons, ascended, and then paused on the ladder so she could see him only from head to waist. Her fiery green eyes focused on his navel. He took another step. She stared and moaned. Yes, he thought, the lusting lion is back to mount the rutting sow.

After his birthday he ordered Rokovsky to collect the mail early so Irina would not be able to intercept. It was torment waiting to hear from Sergei again, but perhaps torment was what he had in mind. How could he write just once from Vienna and then not a second time? But, of course, that was his method; he would torture his betrayer slowly by degrees. Men in camps fantasized such things, used fantasies of vengeance to keep themselves alive.

Anna had written from New York. She was so grateful for all the contacts he'd helped her make, and too for all the loving memories. Her agent had introduced her to an Israeli pianist, they'd played together, there was instant rapport, and then they'd given a hastily prepared recital at the prestigious YMHA.

One critic praised her "expressive clarity"; another

described her tone as "dark and sensuous" and her phrasing as "limpid and full of nuance." There were some reservations: a wish for a little better balance and a little less "Russian imperative." But the reviews were excellent and now the agent was booking them into small halls all over Europe.

There was something else in her note that saddened him, the delicate suggestion that as lovers they were finished. He accepted that, had known, even as she was leaving, that she was probably departing forever from his life. At least now he had Maureen, not so silken as Anna, nowhere near so refined, but much more exotic, an American primitive and insatiable. God only knew how much longer he would be able to keep her satisfied. . . .

A week before, there'd been a tremor. Outside the sea was wild. A winter storm was battering the peninsula. The coast had been gouged and now mud slides blocked the road.

This morning he knew, even as he unlocked his studio, that his hands were ready to work. He grasped up some clay, took it to his bench, closed his eyes, began to work it between his palms. Yes, he felt something—there *was* something there. He tried to discover what it was.

A subtle curve across the top. A ridge down the center with shallow recesses on either side. Like a back perhaps, bent in supplication, the spine exposed, the head bowed to the ground.

No! Impossible! Targov's figures never bowed. They suffered but didn't plead. But still he found something moving in the curve. Forced to bend, the head twisted to one side perhaps, but the face, the features, the posture would repudiate. Yes, that was it, the suffering body would resist.

He worked through the morning, playing with the

clay, and then, in the afternoon, the work turned serious. Outside he could hear the wind. Through the big window he caught glimpses of trees thrashing in the storm. He started on a larger model, one as wide as his own chest, roughing out a wire skeleton, piling the clay on quickly, chopping out an image, then using a wide knife to carve and cut and smooth.

By nightfall he had something. He took it to the platform, placed it on a dolly, turned it beneath the spotlights, studied it some more. Something powerful about it, which surprised and almost frightened him. To be naked like that, bent over, struggling against a merciless power—he didn't know why but he identified that posture with something important in his life.

He slept in the studio. In the morning the storm was over. The sea was rough, not wild, and the trees swayed in a gentle breeze. He looked at his model, circled it once, and then, suddenly, he saw it clear. Hurrying to the main house to eat and bathe, he didn't give the sea a glance. He must instruct Rokovsky—he would move into the studio and from now on take all his meals there. Now, at last, he had what he'd been seeking, a work into which he could fling himself. A vision to be wrested. A shape to be released. He would sculpt a martyr.

MAJOR
PERETZ

Her name was Yael Safir, she was nineteen years old, and she was everything Rafi had feared: pretty, smart, well-liked, a soldier girl working in the computer room at the IDF Command Center in Tel Aviv. She was, moreover, the daughter of a national hero, Captain Asher Safir, killed and posthumously decorated for bravery on the Golan in '73. She'd been last seen hitchhiking her way home to Kibbutz Hulda for the Passover holidays.

The outrage in the country was immense. Yael Safir was a member of the Israeli elite. She left behind a mother, two sisters, two brothers, a pilot boyfriend, and a large circle of grieving and angry friends.

As the story hit the press a great outcry was heard. The old lady who lived upstairs stopped Anna in the hall. "What kind of an Israel do we have," she asked, "that a soldier girl can be picked up like that, then mutilated, and killed?"

Rafi walked into David's office holding a letter. "This just came into the superintendent's office. Latsky's pissing blood."

David read the letter aloud: " 'What's wrong with you people? While a madmen kills our children, you're writing out tickets on Bezalel Street.' "

"Anonymous, of course. One of half a dozen or so

that came in today. There were more yesterday and there'll be more tomorrow."

"What are you telling me Rafi?"

"That the pressure's on."

"You don't think I feel that?"

"Of course you do." Rafi sat down. "Watch TV last night?"

"Katzer?" Rafi nodded. "I feel ashamed a man like that is even listened to. Anna was astonished; she couldn't take her eyes off the screen."

"Sure. Katzer's magnetic, and this is just the kind of situation he knows how to exploit. The worst of it is that he only repeats what ordinary people say: 'It's got to be an Arab. No Jew would do such a thing!' " Rafi shook his head. "An Arab transvestite prostitute and a Moroccan Jewish whore—no one gave much of a shit. An American nun—that was trouble, but we were coping with it. Schneiderman was bad, but this Yael Safir is something else. To quote Latsky: 'Now we got ourselves a capital-M Murder Case.' "

"If it does turn out to be an Arab, Rafi, you know what a field day the reprisal groups will have. Can't you just see them barging into some pathetic Arab village bristling with self-righteous anger and freshly sharpened kitchen knives?"

Rafi gazed at him. "Yeah, and I can hear them too. 'You cut our girls, we cut yours.' " He shook his head and left.

Shoshana retraced Yael's movements. She had left the Command Center at 4 P.M., then waited with other soldiers at the hitching shelter just beyond the gate. She and a girl friend had gotten a lift to Ben-Gurion Airport where a couple hundred more soldiers were also waiting for rides. The scene was chaotic with drivers stopping every few seconds, picking the young people up, then speeding off into the hills. Yael's friend left first—she was heading for Jerusalem. The cars were coming fast, she said, and she doubted Yael waited ten minutes more. Later a male soldier thought he saw Yael get into a dark blue American-type van with Jerusalem plates. Kibbutz Hulda was about a twenty-minute ride from Ben-Gurion. Yael never arrived and was reported missing. She was found twenty-two hours later in the Dumpster in Bloomfield Park.

"Passover eve," Shoshana explained. "Kids desperate to get home and the drivers desperate too. Everyone wants to get to his Seder. Yael's friend's family was a little religious, so Yael pushed her to take the first ride. 'My people don't care all that much,' she said. They kissed and then her friend took off. Yael just waited her turn."

"Can't anyone remember the driver?" David asked.

"Van had those kind of windows you can't see in. Even under hypnosis my witness can't recall the digits on the plates."

"Didn't anyone else get a fix on the car?"

"David, you've forgotten what it's like. When you go on leave all you think about is getting home. You're so wrapped up in that you don't pay attention to anything else. The man who picked her up probably knew that too. He chose the perfect time when those hitching stops are wild."

And now Shoshana has a favorite victim too, David thought.

The tan Renault that had carried Ora Goshen was stolen, so there was reason to believe the blue van with the one-way windows had been stolen too. David put out an all-Israel alert. No reports came in. Then he had Rebecca Marcus forward a request to the police computer unit. He wanted a printout on every dark-colored van in the country, broken down first by city, then by make. If necessary, he would have every owner checked.

Peretz: Dov had him thoroughly covered now. Five teams were on him, watching him day and night, and Dov didn't think Peretz was aware of them—he'd made no visible alterations in his routine.

"He's a strange guy, David. Doesn't go out much. Stays home most of the day. Doesn't seem to have a job. But then he takes a long walk around five, six in the afternoon. No particular direction or destination, but there's a manner he has that bothers me. Couldn't put my finger on it at first. Then I realized what it was. The way he moves—like a certain kind of dog. A hunter. A tracker. He moves around Jerusalem like a guy maneuvering in the woods."

Although there was risk, since he was publically identified with the case, David knew he had to see this for himself.

The apartment was on Zevi Graetz, heavily perfumed this time of year by flowering jasmine. A street of fine houses and lush gardens and a sweet smell that reminded him of his boyhood. Walking here to meet Dov he remembered spring evenings playing with Gideon on Disraeli Street, kicking around a soccer ball, then bicycling through the thick aromatic air that settled with the dusk.

Dov was waiting in an old Volkswagen squareback, parked a few doors down and across the street from Peretz's home.

"He's got the whole top floor. Looks like it was added on. There's a terrace. Uri can see it from the other side. Sometimes Peretz goes out there and stands by the railing. View's probably terrific. Place must have cost a bundle."

David knew Peretz had money. Micha Benyamani and Moshe Liederman had pulled together a fairly decent file. He'd inherited from an aunt who lived in the States. The money came through just about the time he left the army and since then, as far as anyone knew, he hadn't bothered to find a job.

Some crackling over the field radio. Then Uri's voice: "Lights going out." David looked up at the apartment, saw the windows suddenly go dark.

"Going from room to room turning them off," said Dov. "Coming down now for the evening stroll."

David focused on the building door. This would be his first look at a living breathing Peretz. He had read through the dossier and studied the tapes, but so far had no clear impression of the man.

"Okay, now watch the way he sniffs the air."

And, indeed, when Peretz appeared, he paused, looked both ways, gave the air a sniff, then took off for Wingate Square with an aggressive swagger.

"Seems to like the posh parts of town." Dov started up the car. "Jerusalem Theater area, that sort of thing. Three out of four times he goes this way. Still, he always looks both directions before he starts."

Dov turned the car around, zigzagged through a couple of streets, came out by the Mayer Institute of Islamic Art. "Okay, he should pass by in a minute or so. He can work himself up to quite a pace."

Uri's voice on the radio: "He's on Chopin Street." Then: "Hey! Wait! There's a taxi-load of torchers heading your way."

Just then an old Mercedes taxi came reeling around the corner with half a dozen bearded youths packed into the back. David caught a glimpse of fanatical eyes peering out of windows. He recognized a gang of ultra-orthodox who drove the city at night. Offended by the seminudity of models in advertisements affixed to the sides of bus shelters, they were no longer content to paint the posters out; now they burned the shelters down.

"What I'd give to arrest a couple of those creeps," Dov said. The taxi passed. "There! See him? There he is."

David slid down in his seat as he watched Peretz pass in profile. He was striding swiftly now, head thrust forward, hands locked tightly behind his back.

"From here he usually heads for Zarefat. We had some trouble the first two nights, but now that we know him it's getting easier. There're always two of us out there on foot. Every couple of minutes we change off." Dov started the car again. "I'm going to do a pass."

David sank down again but kept his eyes on the rear-view mirror. "Now!" For an instant he caught Peretz's face and was surprised to find it troubled and grim. On the tapes he'd seemed so calm and self-assured. *So,* he thought, *Major Peretz wears a mask.*

As they took up various other positions to observe other segments of the walk, David asked himself how much he really knew about his quarry. Only son of secular South African-born parents. A loner with no close male friends. A lifetime bachelor apparently without any woman in his life—which seemed to fit with the lack of sexual assault upon the victims. Still not much to go on. Ali Saad had not been able to identify him, and neither had the two prostitute friends of Ora Goshen. But his appearance at the symposium and his former use of the double slash signature made him a plausible suspect, so far the only one they had.

"Oh oh, he's turning into the park." Dov grabbed his microphone. "Careful, Uri. It's a maze."

They were parked across from the Supersol, where Anna did most of her shopping. Peretz had just strode by them, and then, opposite the American Consulate, had turned suddenly into the labyrinthine lower portion of Independence Park.

"You know, David, it's Queersville in there this time of night."

Dov was right, this was the place and time for homosexual trysts. There were other such places, in the Old City and in East Jerusalem, but the southern base of Independence Park was notorious, and in the summer months there were always incidents, gay foreigners mugged by addicts, assignations made in expectation of pleasure but ending in beatings or fights.

"Three's not enough."

"I know." Dov ordered two more men in, then got out of the car himself.

"I'm coming too."

"He knows you."

"Can't worry about that now." They jogged along the street together, Dov trying to attach his field radio to his belt. "We'll split up and try to flank him. Shouldn't be too tough if he's just passing through. But if he's hunting. . . ." They turned onto a footpath, then into a stand of trees.

That cloying odor again, of flowering jasmine, hanging in the still night air, thicker this time, almost like a syrup. It was a humid evening, and now, away from the street lamps, cut off from the city, wandering alone amid these silent woods, David asked himself why that particular aroma conjured up such sharp memories of his past. *Gideon,* he thought—something to do with him, and he realized at once that the association was stronger now than it had been earlier when he'd made his way down Zevi Graetz.

He took the right fork, skirted the edges of the Mamillah Pool where a dozen young men in tight-fitting clothing lingered against the thick trunks of eucalyptus trees.

No sign of Peretz. David was about to cross to his left when he remembered that the Renault into which

Ora Goshen had stepped that night by the Damascus Gate had been stolen from the public parking lot just four hundred feet up the slope. *Suppose he's not here for prey? Suppose he's after another car?* He began to run toward the lot. As he charged through some bushes he nearly tripped over two men lying together on a patch of grass.

"David!" It was Dov, standing on one foot in the middle of the parking lot picking thorns out of his socks. "He's up by the Arp statue on King George. Shoshana'll be around in a minute to pick us up." He pushed in the antenna of his radio and grinned. "Almost forgot about that car."

"Garbage detail." Shoshana dumped the bag onto the desk. "Or should I say the gleanings, since I kindly removed all the soggy old teabags, raunchy old yogurt cups, and yukky orange rinds downstairs?"

Eleven A.M. The Pattern Crimes Unit room was nearly empty. Micha was on the telephone, and Rebecca Marcus, cherubic as always, straight-backed and neatly scarfed, was typing up surveillance reports. Liederman was out doing legwork for Micha, and the rest of the expanded unit was either home asleep or on Zevi Graetz waiting for Peretz who, according to Dov, had been acting increasingly nervous and thus might finally be getting ready to make his move.

David spread out the gleanings. Shoshana's delivery of extracts from Peretz's garbage sack had become a mid-morning ritual. Micha came over and together they went through the stuff, pulling out papers, uncrumpling then discussing them, while Shoshana watched, hands on her hips, in order, as she put it, "to learn detective work."

"Still scissoring," Micha said, examining various discarded newspapers from which items on the case had been cut. David scowled. He'd once read in an American criminology textbook that psychotic murderers often assembled scrapbooks on their crimes. It had rung true to him then, but now it didn't: To clip out articles on the murders was consistent with showing up at the symposium, and thus proved nothing but an interest in the case.

"Angry. Look how he ripped this one in half." Micha passed David a fund-raising letter from the West Bank settlers' party, Gush Emunim.

"Politically he's sympathetic. 'A Greater Israel for Greater Security.' But we know he hates the mystical religious crap. Never mind the prophets' graves."

"Wonder if he's considering a political career. Look at this stuff. On every mailing list of everything right of center."

"He's an ex-officer."

"Now here's something, David."

Micha was examining a sheet of paper apparently torn from a pocket-size flipover spiral notebook. He handed it to David. The name "Bar-Lev" had been scrawled across the top.

"You or your father?"

"If he's our killer he'd have reason to hate us both."

Micha scratched his cheek. "Funny, he puts this in his garbage. I wonder if maybe he knows. . . ."

"What?"

"No, that's impossible." Micha shook his head. "He couldn't."

Just then Rebecca called to him. "Man named Raskov downstairs. Some kind of contractor from Haifa."

Raskov! Shit! "Find out what he wants."

Rebecca listened, then covered her receiver. "He's asking to see you, David. Says it won't take long."

He didn't normally receive unofficial visitors in his office—the unit area was for police only, its exhibits and bulletin boards off limits to the press. But Raskov was special, he was in some awful way "almost family," and David was extremely curious. He had never met Judith's new husband, now stepfather to Hagith.

The moment Rebecca brought him in, David's first thought was: He looks just the way I knew he would. But then, after a minute in his company, David decided his imagined Raskov had been a lot better than the real thing.

"Hi. Call me Joe. Excuse the English but my Hebrew stinks."

A short husky individual with lightly greased wavy salt and pepper hair, Raskov had the body of an aging athlete, thick and strong through the chest. He wore the old 1950s Zionist uniform, shirt open, flowing gray chest hairs showing in the triangle, shirt collar worn outside jacket collar and lapels. Yes, the old Labor Party look even down to the tufts of hair David thought he saw sprouting from Raskov's nose and ears. Perhaps he was imagining these tufts. Perhaps he merely wanted to be disgusted by them. One thing, though, he did not imagine and which didn't fit at all with the Zionist image: the blue and white wool knit yarmulke perched on the back of Raskov's head.

"English is okay."

"Yeah, Judy told me you speak it pretty good. Look, I'm sorry to barge in on you, but I'm in town just for the day. Bunch of damn permits to get signed. So I thought—what the hell, I'll just drop in." Raskov peered around the office. It was clear he wasn't impressed. Then his eyes fell on the photo of Hagith. He motioned toward it. "On account of her."

Already David loathed him, couldn't believe Judith, his slim and elegant mathematician ex-spouse, had actually married this buffoon. But Raskov was rich, in the contracting business he was virtually a tycoon, and in any event the only thing that mattered was the effect living with this cretin might have upon his daughter.

"Don't expect you to fall all over me, Dave. But we're both grown-up guys and I think we ought to talk. Guess you know the story. Judy was doing bookkeeping for my company, she had your daughter to take care of, and she wasn't getting much out of life. So, okay, you two got divorced. I'm divorced myself. That's why I moved over here. New start, build a new life, help build a new country too."

Yeah, I've seen your ticky-tacky housing blocks. So get on with it, Raskov, get to the point.

". . . fell in love. And Haggi, too." *Haggi!* "She and I, we got along from the start. Now it isn't easy being ten, eleven years old and your daddy's up in Jerusalem and a new guy comes along and marries your ma. So, okay, we all gotta adjust. I got a twenty-five-year-old son back in the States. An okay kid but he couldn't hack it here. So, okay, we adjust a little bit. . . ."

If only the clown could get his daughter's name right then maybe, David thought, there might be something hopeful in his slobbering good will. Judy, Haggi, Dave— these American-style nicknames grated on his ears. Still he said nothing, just gazed intently at Raskov, waiting for him, as he understood they put it in the construction business, to get to his bottom line.

"Education—no problem. I can give her the best. Bryn Mawr, Vassar, Brandeis if she wants. And I figure being around me these next few years won't hurt her English either."

"Anything wrong with Hebrew University?"

"Course not. Damn fine place. But you can't beat American training. Look, Dave, no one's trying to cut you out. But let's face it, I can give her advantages. That's why I'm here. Wanted you to see I'm not that bad a guy. Which is why I'm asking you, for your own daughter's sake—"

"What *are* you asking me?"

Raskov paused. For the first time since he entered the office he seemed to be at a loss for words. "I thought Judy spoke to you."

"About what?"

"Adoption."

"You want to adopt Hagith?"

"Yeah. Look, I thought Judy said—"

"What did she say?"

"Said she spoke to you and you said forget it, you'd never go along."

"She didn't have to speak to me. She knew that's what I'd say."

"Okay. I hear you. But think about it, will you? Don't just rule it out."

David stood up. "Yeah, I'll think about it, Joe. Meantime, I'm running a murder investigation here."

After Raskov left, David sat alone in his office depressed because he wasn't a rich and mighty man. But after ten minutes he'd had enough. Okay, he thought, Judith married an asshole, so that's no reason for me to feel bad. And, having decided that, he told Rebecca Marcus he was going out, then stalked down to the corner of Jaffa and King George where he quickly devoured two falafels in a row.

Micha and Liederman were on the phones trying to locate the owners of dark-colored vans. David worked with them a while, then conferred by radio with Uri, in charge of the daytime surveillance, who assured him all was quiet and Peretz was home. Then, near the end of the afternoon, he went back into his office, dialed the Raskov Construction Company in Haifa, and asked to speak to chief accountant Judith Weitz.

"It's me."

"Who?" She sounded busy. He could hear the clatter of an automatic printer in the background, most likely keeping track of Raskov's billions.

"David."

"Oh, *you*." Her voice was flat. "I saw you on TV."

"Bad time to call?"

"No. Joe's away. Things are always quieter when he's away."

"He came to see me this morning."

"Really?" She sounded amused.

"Know what he wanted?"

"I can guess."

"Well—"

"It wasn't my idea. Once Joe gets an idea, there's no stopping him. He just bulls his way right on through."

"Guess that's why he's been so successful here."

"So what are you so sore about?"

"Do I sound sore?"

"Yes. You do."

"The guy's got dirty fingernails, Judith. He calls my daughter 'Haggi.' He calls me 'Dave.' "

"I think that's cute."

"I don't."

"I don't much care if you do or not. To tell you the truth, David, I don't care at all."

"What is he? Some kind of clown?"

"What?"

"Way he dresses. Half Ben-Gurion with that settler's yarmulke perched on top."

"He's entitled to his political beliefs. Frankly, if we were all as soft on territory as you, I wonder if we'd still have a country here."

So where was Joe Raskov when I was slogging through the Sinai? "Sounds like you've changed your mind about some things."

"You bet I have. I'm keeping kosher now."

"What a splendid luxury. Arab servants help you out?"

"Look, if you're calling to express sour grapes about your lot. . . ."

"I'm calling about my daughter! Adoption's out of the question. That he would even think! Must be out of his mind! So okay, he's a jerk. But I'm not standing by while he tries to turn her into some kind of intolerant small-minded mean-spirited self-righteous right-wing Arab-hating spoiled little bitch. . . ."

A silence. When Judith finally spoke he could hear the new hardness in her voice. "How long since you've seen her?"

"I called last week."

"You think calling's enough?"

"We're on skeleton hours here. I'm on a major case."

"That damn police lingo. Thought I'd heard the last of it. I'll tell you something, David. I never said this to you before, but since you seem to think it's okay to call me up and discuss the condition of my husband's fingernails, I gather all the old social taboos are down and I can let loose with what I really feel."

"Go ahead." She sounded enormously angry. He imagined the set of her mouth, remembered how tightly she could draw it, so tight it almost became a line.

"As far as I'm concerned, having Joe Raskov in her life is the best thing that could happen to Hagith right now. Want to know why? Because you, David Bar-Lev, are the worst, the absolutely worst father in all Israel. *The worst!*" She hung up.

Two nights later David transported Anna, her cello, and her accompanist, Yosef Barak, down through the hills to Ben-Gurion Airport on the plain. David had always liked Yosef, a tall, serious balding man in his middle forties who hunched over the piano keyboard when he played. Yosef was a superb musician but lacked the ego and ambition to become a star. He wanted, however, to serve a star and was pleased to play that role for Anna. She, in turn, thought of him as a kind and diligent older brother whose impeccable musicianship and precise technique were perfect foils to her temperament.

David waited with them in the transit lounge for the announcement of their flight, listening to their tense excited talk, envying them their adventure, wishing he could leave with them, go to Europe, forget his case. Over the next thirty days they would play in twenty cities, in Switzerland, Austria, Germany, Belgium, and France. Then they would return to Jerusalem to prepare for summer appearances at the European festivals, then Jerusalem again to work up another program for a winter series in the United States.

The flight had been announced and passengers were boarding, when David heard his name called over the public-address. A last embrace with Anna, a farewell shake of Yosef's hand, a final cry of "Good luck! Great trip!" He watched them board, then rushed to the nearest telephone. Seconds later he was connected to Dov.

"Peretz. He's moving. He just got into a *sharut* for Tel Aviv. Almost filled now. Ought to be leaving any second. We'll follow him, of course. We got five cars. Since you're down that way, we can pick you up. Park by the side of the road just before the airport cutoff. When I see you I'll stop, Micha will take your car, and you can get in with me."

This is it. I know it. I *feel* it. All the time I'm getting spooked by this guy, I know sooner or later he's got to make his move."

Dov was pumped up. His Mickey Mouse T-shirt (a sure sign to David that he was prepared for war) showed wet beneath his arms. His eyes never wavered from the long maroon Mercedes taxi just ahead.

"Eight nights on a guy, you get sensitive. Those weird long walks of his, the tension building up. Last couple days I felt it, he was walking different, taking longer strides, twitching sometimes when he stopped. So tonight he does the usual, except when he hits Jaffa Gate he boards a number thirteen bus. At the bus station, when I saw him head for those *sharuts*, I called you because I knew it was tonight."

"How are we covering him?"

"Two carloads, six guys, waiting at the other end. Two of us, plus three more cars including Micha and Shoshana, makes fifteen. No matter what he does, walks, runs, takes a bus, grabs a cab, we're on him. Figure first thing he'll do is try and steal a car."

"If he does we'll let him take it," David said. "If he goes for a victim we'll follow him as far as we can. Instruct the others: Don't go in unless I give the command. Only exception, if they're certain a life's at stake. But when we go in, we really move. I mean fast, Dov. Very fast."

While Dov passed all this on, and the confirmations came back from the different teams, David loosened his collar and wondered if he was really close to ending this awful case. Then, as they entered the outskirts of Tel Aviv, he became conscious of the heat.

The city, normally so dry, was steeped in a heavy noxious fog. And as always, when he entered Tel Aviv, he found himself feeling oppressed. First great modern Hebrew city, city of Bialik, the Habima Theater, the brilliant street life and literary cafés of his father's time, it now seemed shabby, bedraggled, in need of a good coat of whitewash, smelling of automobile fumes and greasy falafel stands and seething with the anger of downtrodden oriental Jews.

"Okay, they're pulling in." Dov steered through a

street of low-cost shoe stores that led to the bus station, extremely busy this time of night. "He just got out. He's paying. Uri's on him. See him? There!"

David caught a quick glimpse of Peretz pushing his way through the crowd, an El-Al flight bag slung over one shoulder, Uri right behind him flanked by two other detectives on his team.

Peretz paused just in front of the station, sniffing the air, looking this way and that. Dov muttered "Here we go again," but David sensed greater energy than before. When Peretz finally took off, they followed him down the maze of narrow streets, ten of them on foot, the other five in cars. He led them rapidly to a small cheap hotel on Allenby Road, The Zion.

"You don't think this is *weird?*" asked Dov. They were parked across the street. Micha, who had a better view of the lobby, reported that Peretz was checking in. "Guy with a beautiful apartment in Jerusalem checks into a fleabag hole like this. Kind of place you do a drug deal or maybe take a whore."

"Soon as he's up in his room, I want Micha to identify himself at the desk. He's to find out if Peretz is using his real name and if they've ever seen him here before."

Micha reported Peretz had checked in as Meir Shikun, that he had stayed in the Zion several times, and that not only did he have good ID, but a business card on which he was listed as a salesman for a Petah Tikva plastics firm.

"Okay," David said. "Get adjoining rooms. Either side of his and across the hall. Put three guys up there, and someone with the operator in case he uses the phone."

But even as these arrangements were being made, Peretz reappeared without his bag and set off again on foot.

"Let me bust his room," Dov begged. "See what's in that bag."

"No justification. He hasn't done anything yet."

"At least let me put in a mike."

"Forget it, Dov. That could botch the case."

They followed him to a stop on Allenby, where he boarded a bus that took him up Pinsker to Dizengoff Square. Shoshana and Uri got on the bus with him. The rest of them followed in cars.

"Knows Tel Aviv better than I do." Dov was keyed up but David tried to relax, staring out at the peeling flat-topped buildings, laundry strung from balconies, roofs forested with TV aerials and solar water-heater tanks. The night sky, he observed, wasn't pure black as in Jerusalem, but faintly tinged with yellow.

Once off the bus Peretz did a complete circle clockwise around the square, pausing at each intersection, waiting patiently for each light to change. Then, when he was finished, he abruptly changed direction and did another circle counter-clockwise the same methodical leisurely way, the way of an animal who fears nothing because he has no predators.

"He's nuts," Dov said, and David had to agree: They'd never seen Peretz act like this. It was more now than tension; there was something compulsive and yet extremely purposeful about the way he moved.

On Dizengoff, David got out of the car. The masses of milling people provided him with protection, and he was happy for a chance to stretch his legs. Cars streaked by. Neon flashed. For all the shabbiness of Tel Aviv he recognized the city was alive. The latest Israeli pop tunes poured out of record shops. Uniformed army kids on leave, rifles slung over shoulders, strode the wide sidewalks in search of girls. Young couples stood in line at cinemas. Street money changers and dope dealers plied their trades. The cafés were filled—people sat in them gesturing, arguing. He caught tail-ends of conversations: the mess in Lebanon, a deal on diamonds, a place to get a good TV set cheap. No visible religious people. Clothing was lurid. Flesh showed hot and moist. There was an atmosphere of informality, sex, flirtation. The modern hell-bent Israel.

Peretz entered a modest restaurant, took a table facing the street, ordered a blintz, ate it slowly, then sat watching the parade.

"Look how sharp he is. Like a big cat about to strike." He and Dov watched from a café across the street. Three detectives were in Peretz's restaurant. The others were scattered about on either side of Dizengoff.

"Yeah, he's changed since he did those loops around the square. Street life turns him on. So, what's he up to? What's his move?"

"He's getting ready now to look for what he wants. And then go after it," David said.

It was more than an hour before Peretz moved again, just after midnight when the crowds began to thin. He called for his check, paid it, then took off fast. The circle formed around him, scurrying to keep up. He led them a little further down Dizengoff, then turned abruptly left on Arlosoroff.

"Shit!" said Dov. "He's headed for the beach."

It was the famous bathing beach of Tel Aviv where Halil Ghemaiem had been picked up. Crowded with innocent bathers, mothers and children, by day, this long wide stretch of sand became a sordid flesh-market at night. Prostitutes of both sexes congregated, but despite complaints the Tel Aviv police were unable to contain them. Patrols went out, engaged in sweeps, but as soon as they left the whores returned.

Here, on the sand, away from the lights, figures moved like phantoms, dark gray silhouettes against the yellow-tinged night sky. The tide was out, the beach was wide, and something phosphorescent created sparkles in the tiny waves that lapped the shore. A solemn sort of dance, David thought, as he watched the transactions taking place. Figures approached one another, huddled, discussed in quick subdued tones the services required and a range of price. If no arrangement could be made, they separated again. If a bargain was struck, they moved together off the sand.

He felt useless. Peretz was out there searching for a victim and all he could do was stand by and watch. Something frightening too, he thought, about being so close to madness as it filled and drove a man.

Dov kept his back to the water, didn't want his radio seen or heard. "Contact," he whispered, "hundred fifty meters south. Foggy. Difficult to see. Shoshana thinks it's a boy. Okay—Uri says they're walking south together now, edging closer to the road. Says they're headed for the Sheraton taxi stand."

They exchanged looks, then ran back to their car.

No difficulty tracking the taxi; it drove straight to the Zion on nearly empty streets. The boy got out first, waited while Peretz paid. David got a good look at him: young, Arab, slight, with fine smooth features and dark skin. So, another male, but not a transvestite. This one wore a white tennis shirt, scuffed sneakers, and tight-fitting faded jeans.

"Seems Mr. Meir Shikun likes the boys." Dov had just returned from the lobby to their room next door to Peretz's. Micha was standing, his ear pressed against the wall. David lay exhausted on the bed.

"How often?"

"Maybe four, five times. Clerk didn't want to talk, but when Uri told him this was homicide he blabbed. Says Peretz always makes the same moves—checks in, goes out, then comes back very late with a 'friend.' "

David turned to Micha. "Hear anything?"

Micha shook his head. "They were talking and laughing, but not anymore."

"What do you think?" David asked Dov.

"What're we supposed to do? Wait till he kills the kid?"

David sat up. "Okay, let's bust him."

Dov and Micha smiled then the three of them stepped into the hall. Uri and Shoshana were waiting. Dov gave them the thumbs up. Everybody grinned.

Uri approached Peretz's door, then walked backward slowly on the tips of his toes counting off the paces in pantomime. He took a deep breath, psyched himself up like a man about to lift an enormous weight. Then, his features set, he ran forward and flung himself against the door.

The lock snapped easily, the door gave way, and all five of them rushed inside. Peretz and the boy, both nude, were embracing on the bed. They turned, there was a moment of silence, the detectives gawking at the lovers, the lovers gaping back. Then pandemonium. The boy panicked. He screamed, jumped up, charged forward, trying to slip between Shoshana and Dov. Uri caught him, grasped him in his arms, then lifted him up, wriggling, off the floor. While he struggled, Peretz sprawled upon the bed, threw his hairy legs apart, and thrust his genitals forward as if they were an offering.

"So garbagemen—which one of you is going to suck me off?"

"Fuck yourself, you fuckin' pervert." Shoshana glared at him and spat.

Seven-thirty A.M. They were back in Jerusalem down in the cellar of the Russian Compound, in a small windowless sound-proofed interrogation room. A single light bulb, protected by a grille, burned brightly overhead. Two straight-backed wooden chairs, one small worn wooden table with microphone, a cement floor slightly slanted toward a drain. A narrow slit of inch-thick safety glass exposed the proceedings to Rafi and the video-camera operator seated in the observation cubicle next door. The dank damp stench from a leaking sewer pipe mingled with the smell of human sweat.

"Tell me about it," David said.

"The 'tell-your-story' method? Don't be an asshole, Bar-Lev. I used to interrogate guys all the time."

"So why did you go to the symposium?"

"Hey! Was that a setup?" Peretz gave David a mock two-fingered salute.

"Why did you go?"

"Fascinated."

"By what?"

"The marks."

"What about them?"

"Already answered that."

"You said you heard they were like the marks you used to leave. I want to know who said they were."

"And I told you I heard it around. You can't keep something like that quiet, not here. Cops tell other cops. Medical examiners tell the wives. Nurses drop in on autopsies. Pretty soon everybody knows."

"Who told you?"

"An old army friend, and that's all I'm saying. I don't squawk on guys who help me out."

"What makes you think this guy helped you?"

"He was one of the few who didn't turn on me when things got tough. He knew about our unit signature, and he heard about how these bodies were getting marked. Called me, said he thought I ought to know. Well, I tell you, I was pissed. Someone out there forging my signature—I wanted to know who the fuck he was."

Forging his signature: on that subject, it seemed to David, Peretz was deranged. As if the five killings were some sort of forgery case; as if the issue of "forgery" was what it was about.

"How many nights were you watching me?" Something crafty now in Peretz's eyes.

"I ask the questions."

"But not the right ones. Eight nights. Surveillance started the second night of Passover. It was carried out by approximately a dozen men, led during the day by that huge Germanic type who smashed his way into my room, and at night by the fuzzy-headed kid wearing the funny T-shirts. So tell me: Am I right?"

David turned toward the observation slit to show Rafi how he felt. Their high-powered surveillance had been a farce. Peretz had picked up on them within the hour.

"Don't feel bad, Bar-Lev. You're looking at maybe the top reconnaissance man in Israel. I got the highest marks ever recorded at Ranger School. Your guys were good but I'm the best. I like urban tracking games. I could have played them with you guys for weeks. That part was fine. The part that wasn't was that you thought I'd killed without a reason!"

There it was again, the self-righteous rage coupled with mockery and arrogance. A truly unbearable man, David thought, the kind you send out on reprisal raids.

". . . so I led you a good chase, staying home all day, going out at dusk, testing to see whether I could throw you off. Even sent you a little note in the garbage. Get it?" Peretz laughed. "Yeah, I think you did. Okay, a joke. Nothing personal, Bar-Lev." He leaned back balancing his chair on its two back legs. "Anyway, it was from my discovery I couldn't throw you off that I figured out how many of you were there." He moaned. "How I wanted to go into the Park, find someone, bring him home. Went in once but your guys were all over me. That's when I decided maybe my strategy wasn't right."

"What strategy?"

Peretz leaned forward again. "Method I'd worked out to clear my name. Make it easy for your people to follow me, reasoning that sooner or later the mother-fucker would strike again, and then, since you had me under close surveillance, I'd be cleared and you'd go on to someone else. But after that foray into the park I realized I was a prisoner. So I thought: 'I'll go down to Tel Aviv and find myself a boy. Then, if they stop me, I'll finally have it out with them, and that'll be the end of that.' " He laughed.

David stepped outside to talk to Rafi. He found him, wearing an expression of supreme disgust, puffing smoothly on his pipe.

"So?"

"Makes a pretty fair case for himself."

"Could be a bluff."

"You'll check it out."

"Story on the marks won't hold unless he identifies his 'old army friend.' "

"He won't, David. Man like that won't tell. Not his style." Rafi shook his head.

"So what does that prove? That he can stonewall?"

"Getting on your nerves?"

"Damn right he is!"

"You had too much invested in him."

"Maybe so. And maybe the reason I had so much invested in him was because I didn't have any other place to invest."

"That's why I want you out of here. Go home, relax, take the rest of the day off. You're tired and you're overinvolved. I'm going to throw in a regular interrogation team."

"Come on, Rafi, it's my case."

"They're experts."

"He's an expert, too, don't forget." Then he thought: *Screw it!* "Fine. You're right. Put them in. I *am* tired. I *will* go home. See you later. Good-bye."

He woke late in the afternoon. The apartment seemed lonely without Anna. He missed her cello in the corner and her music stand which she'd folded up and stored away. Her make-up jars were gone from the dresser, the closet was half-empty, and he missed her earrings and her pearl necklace which she liked to leave on the little table beside the bed.

He went out to walk. It was nearly sunset. The air was scented with the fragrance of the wildflowers that had sprouted all over the city's hills. It took him twenty minutes to follow the road that circled the Hinnom Valley, ascent to Mount Zion, pass the bell tower of the Church of the Dormition, then enter the Old City through the Zion Gate.

Once inside the Jewish Quarter, away from traffic, he moved quickly through the maze of angled alleyways, courtyards, hidden gardens, plazas, rebuilt synagogues, and carefully preserved archaeological sites all pristinely uniform now that the ruined quarter had been rebuilt. There were boutiques up here, tiny groceries, religious shops, galleries, restaurants and cafés, but he was interested in none of these, was intent instead upon finding his favorite overlook.

After a few false starts that led to dead ends, he found it finally by following a slinky Jerusalem cat. It was a narrow terrace beside an elegant apartment building, nothing more than a tiny balcony containing a single bench. At its edge there was a low wall, its hollow center planted with wisteria. From here there was a steep drop exposing the view: below the great pedestrian plaza; above the brooding, silent Dome of the Rock; and in between the magnificent sight he'd come to see—the Western Wall.

At this hour the light was intense, endowing the Wall with a special quality as if its enormous stones were somehow illuminated from within. This was the luminescence that he loved—Jerusalem's stones were famous for reflecting light, but only the city's natives knew how at certain times of day they changed color, turned red-gold, then almost seemed to burn.

The huge plaza was dotted with people—perhaps a thousand in a space that on Holy Days could contain a hundred thousand or more. David watched them: black-suited Hasidim whirling, dancing; solitary old religious men, wearing tefilin, rocking rhythmically as they prayed. Tourists in shorts and T-shirts gawking. A group from Poland choking, weeping. A wedding party rushing about for the traditional photograph before the sky turned dark. Panhandlers, soldiers, mystics, crazies, Jews who longed for reconciliation and others who favored expansion of the Zionist State.

Nightfall was at hand; in minutes the sun would disappear. And then, from the minarets in the valley of Shiloah, David heard the muezzin call the Arab faithful to prayer. The voices echoed, overlapped across the valley, haunting cries that God was Great. The murmuring of people below on the plaza, the cries from the valley, the bells tolling in the churches on the hills—this, he recognized, was the Jerusalem of the guidebooks, the city where members of three great faiths lived together in perfect peace.

But it was not his Jerusalem. His was a very different city: tense and angry as a wound-up spring, inhabited by criminals, whores, dope dealers, sex-killers, filled as much with evil as with good. And the three great religions—he knew about them too, how, beneath the facade of harmony, fanatical factions plotted to spill each other's blood, seize every shrine and stone, and then claim the city exclusively for themselves.

But still he loved the place.

Micha said it *had* to be Peretz, that his alibis *had* to be faked. "Too pat," Micha said. "It all suddenly ends the night we start watching him? Come on! Then he cruises the exact spot where Halil Ghemaiem was picked up. What a joke!"

"Go ahead. Punch a hole in it," Dov said. "Just one tiny little hole."

They'd been over it a dozen times. Peretz was on vacation in Egypt when Susan Mills and Ora Goshen had been killed. An airtight alibi. A group tour. A dozen witnesses. All Israeli and Egyptian borders closely watched. No way he could have slipped out of Cairo, then back again in time for the Nile cruise. He didn't have alibis for Ghemaiem and Schneiderman, but the first night of Passover, when Yael Safir was picked up, he'd attended a seder at the home of friends.

But Micha was a chess player, his mind reeled with plots and schemes, and so he devised a theory of a conspiracy, a second killer who murdered the women while Peretz killed the men.

"So who's this second killer?" Moshe Liederman asked.

"It's possible. It could work."

"Yeah, it could," David agreed, "if you could name both conspirators, show they knew each other, and then prove that they conspired."

"Say two freaks get together, they agree to use an identical method and arrange airtight alibis for the murders they don't commit."

Shoshana said that sounded like a movie she'd seen, *Strangers on a Train.*

"How do they get together? Answer an ad in the *Jerusalem Post?*"

"Great try, Micha."

"It was just an idea."

"So now what do we do?"

"Forget about Peretz. Start tracking down guys from his unit," David said.

"You didn't 'fail,' " Rafi said. Hard mid-morning light striped his office floor and walls. "The symposium idea was good. You developed a suspect. No break-ins, no wiretaps. From a technical point-of-view, your investigation was a model."

"He's crazy, Rafi. You know that. He *could* have done it. He's crazy enough."

"Maybe, but he didn't. So now—"

"Yeah. The investigation-must-go-on."

Rafi nodded. "Go back to it. Less pressure now since the killings stopped, and Horev-Isaacson hit the news."

Aaron Horev and Ruth Isaacson: adulterous lovers found murdered in their love nest. This new murder case, assigned by Rafi to his regular homicide team, had fascinated the public. People couldn't get enough of it; it rang true to them, was imaginable, a crime of passion, not crazy like the serial case.

David asked for a last meeting with Peretz, a final go at him before they sent him home. Rafi agreed. "But be gentle, David."

"Of course. What do you think? I'm going to hang him by his heels like a Turk?"

Rafi laughed. "Watching the two of you I got the feeling you didn't like each other very much."

"So we don't. So is that any reason we can't do a little business? He knows who was in his unit. I need a list. That way I don't have to track down every fuck-up who's ever been in a military prison."

The final go-around took place in a corner booth at Fink's, a small, cozy, dark, and very middle-European restaurant-bar, a hang-out for politicians and up-scale foreign journalists.

Waiting for their table, David and Peretz bantered lightly about who was going to be the guest of whom. They struck a bargain, Peretz would pay for the drinks and David would buy the dinner.

After they sat down and ordered goulash, Peretz planted his elbows aggressively on the table.

"You hate my guts."

"Hate may be too strong a word."

"Cut the crap. I don't even care."

"So why do you bring it up?"

"Ah, the analyst's son." A mocking smile.

"Should I be impressed you checked me out?"

"Didn't have to. I knew your brother. Quite the handsome fellow was Gideon Bar-Lev. He and I used to play tennis. Well—are you surprised?"

"Since you ask, I wouldn't have thought you'd have been quite each other's type."

"Oh, we were each other's type all right. He just had a lot of trouble admitting it."

David said nothing.

"What's the matter?"

"What are you driving at, Peretz?"

"How much do you know?"

"I don't know anything."

"*Really?*"

"Are you telling me you went for him and, poor you!, he didn't give in?"

"Who says he didn't?"

"Who cares?"

"You care all right. You hate the thought."

"Oh, I get it. Now that he's dead you can smirk around about how he was a queer." David shook his head. "You're fucking impossible to talk to, you know."

Peretz seemed to make an effort to calm himself. When he spoke again the hostile edge was gone. "Maybe you're right. Talking's not my thing. Fighting is. But now I can't do that anymore." He took a long swig of beer. "You know why they got rid of me?"

"Way I heard it, they thought you played a little rough."

Peretz shook his head. "Wasn't that. It was my . . . proclivity. They couldn't handle it. Not in their manly army." He laughed.

"So, you see yourself as quite the tragic figure."

"More like a first-rate officer who served his country well and then got screwed." Peretz shook his head again. "Know something, you're not like Gideon. You don't even look like him. He was delicate and you're kind of burly. The difference, I guess, between a pilot and a cop."

"Why are you so contemptuous, Peretz?"

"I'm not—at least not of everyone. But I am, I admit, contemptuous of you. You should be in the army not the police, out in the field where the real murderers are running loose." He made a sweeping motion. "Oh, I know what you think, that I'm some kind of psychopath, that we're all the same, terrorists and counterterrorists, bunch of nuts running around blowing each other up. I know your type. Don't believe in reprisals. Think it's self-defeating. Think the way to end the cycle is to sit down, talk it out, nobody gets too little or too much. That's the kind of bullshit you hear in the soft elite circles where nobody puts anything on the line. 'We all have to live together here on this Holy Land, nod good morning to each other, be polite, ask after each other's wives, make the desert bloom, blah-blah, blah-blah.' Meanwhile, of course, we hate each other's guts. But never mind that, just share the blessings and respect each other's precious faiths. The old bullshit. See, we're enemies, Bar-Lev. I'm contemptuous of you, and now that you know my views I'm sure you feel the same." He started to eat. "Incidentally, a very attractive lady at the bar keeps looking over this way."

David turned. It was Stephanie Porter, seated on a stool between two standing American newsmen. She mouthed "Hi." He did the same. She smiled, then turned back to her friends.

"Who is she?"

"A free-lance journalist."

"Been giving you that look, the kind that says 'I'd like to get inside his pants.' "

"You're vulgar."

"Yeah, sorry about that."

"Look, I still have a case to solve. I could really use your help."

"I knew we weren't here on account of our shared political beliefs. So what do you want?"

"List of the guys who were in your unit."

"Don't have a list."

"You could write one up."

"Tell me why I should."

"Because of the marks."

"A lot of people knew about those marks."

"Sure, but your old unit's the place to start. You say you're pissed off because someone forged your signature. Now here's your chance to get even, help catch the forger and bring him in."

"Don't sweet-talk me."

"Please consider what I said."

"I have considered it."

"And?"

"I can't see any reason I should help."

"Why not?"

"You think it's all a joke, don't you? 'My signature' —you think that's cute. But, see, to me it *isn't* cute. I invented it, just like I chose the guns we carried and the boots we wore and everything else. I decided everything. I handpicked every man. I was feared from Beirut to Damascus. I loved that work, loved the sport of it. That unit was my life."

"Look, Peretz, I never said—"

"Let me finish, Bar-Lev. The way I look at it, the person who killed those people tried to set me up. He carved my name onto them to try and pin his crimes on me. So now I'm going after him. If he was one of my old boys, I'm going to find him, too. When I do, I'm going to punish him. And when I'm done doing that, I'm going to break his head."

HIDDEN SYMMETRY

Five victims in four and a half weeks, then, suddenly, the killings stopped.

Rafi was right: the serial case, so incomprehensible to the Israeli mind, had been replaced in the public imagination by the double murders of Aaron Horev and Ruth Isaacson.

For David, Horev-Isaacson came as a welcome relief; the enormous pressure that had been on Pattern Crimes was now transferred to the Jerusalem homicide squad. While the Israeli press and public feasted on the extramarital scandal, the PC Unit went quietly about its business, assembling lists of violent men who'd been in military prisons.

He called in Shoshana. As always, she appeared in his doorway in an instant.

"What's new on Gutman?"

"Refuses to say a word. He's got himself a first-class lawyer, Abramsohn. They're going to make a motion for bail."

"He's still in the lock-up then?"

"Prosecutor told the judge he's got lots of money and there's reason to believe he might try and flee."

"Plus, I suppose, the 'heinous nature of the crime.' "

Shoshana nodded. "They put him in a cell by himself. Worried he might get hurt. Meantime, most of

129

the scrolls have been identified. I've been talking with
Netzer, who's going to try the case. As the arresting
officer I'll have to testify. He says even with Abramsohn, Gutman doesn't have a prayer. The evidence is
strong, he won't get any sympathy, and about the only
things he's got going are that he's old and doesn't have
a record."

David phoned his father. "What does it mean: 'A man
who has been wronged'?"
   "You arrested him."
   "Did I wrong him?" Silence. "He calls us Nazis."
   "Well?"
   "You think that's what we are?"
   "Let me ask you something, David: Do you think
Gutman's nothing but a shrewd old crook?"
   "Tell me about him."
   "Talk to him."
   "He won't talk."
   "No, of course not. Stupid of me. Of course he
won't." A pause and then a change of tone, as if
Avraham wanted genuinely to help. "Think of it this
way: there's a colored translucent screen between you
and Gutman. Don't mistake the colored light that
passes through for the hard white light that burns
behind."

Anna called from Strasbourg. The recital series was
going well. So far the reviews were good, and now
there was a chance the tour would be extended to
Amsterdam.
   "I'm always thinking of you, David. I love you very
much."
   "I love you too."
   "How is Jerusalem?"
   "Beautiful. There're flowers everywhere."
   "Your father?"

"We're getting on better now." He paused. "I miss you, Anna. Coffee together in the morning, you in your white robe, the light streaming in. And at night when I come home. And watching you practice. And in bed, holding you, kissing you, tasting you, whispering. Listening to you breathing in the night. . . ."

"I've been thinking about Micha's theory."

"It's nonsense."

"Yeah. But there's a germ of something, especially when I put it together with something my father said to me the other night."

He had taken Dov to lunch at the Mei Naftoah, an arcaded Iraqi-Jewish restaurant on the edge of Jerusalem. Below the sunlight glittered upon the ruined roofs of an abandoned Arab village. Beyond the gully lay the stony Judean hills.

"Forget a conspiracy between two killers, but keep the notion of two classes of victims, 'easy' and 'hard.' Easy victims are whores and hustlers and soldier-girls hitching rides. Easy to pick up. Young and sexual. You stop, exchange a couple words with them, they get into your car, and you've got them. Right?"

Dov nodded.

"Okay, up till now we've been thinking of this as a serial murder case. That's what it looks like. That's the pattern. And it fits with the easy victims—no problem there. But it doesn't fit with Schneiderman and Mills. They're hard. They're not the kind you can get into your car. They're not sexual either. It's as if . . . there are two different things going on at once."

"The marks are always the same, David. The blankets, the method. Everything."

"Forget all that. I'm talking victims. Ever hear the expression 'hidden symmetry'?"

Dov shook his head.

"Particle physicists use it, biologists too, to describe

a situation where two totally different results derive
from one unseeable source. For example, the crab that
has two claws, one big one small. That kind of crab
looks unbalanced, but there's symmetry—it's just not
visible. Both claws derive from a single gene. You
have to understand genes and the purposes behind
them before you can recognize the symmetry in what
at first you think is just a weird lopsided crab. So,
okay, we have two classes of victims. The symmetry's
concealed because we don't know the killer's purpose.
So suppose we forget serial murders. Let's ask ourselves what other purpose he might have had. Start by
throwing the easy victims out. Then what have we
got? Schneiderman and Mills. So why were the others
killed exactly the same way? Maybe to make it look
more complicated than it is, give it a shape, a pattern
that disguises what was really going on."

"Three innocent people killed just to throw us off?"

"It's a possibility. All I know is that when I throw
out 'serial killer' I get a whole new angle on the thing.
Look, suppose we've got a pattern that conceals another pattern? Suppose we've been so blinded by what
we've been shown that we haven't looked at what
we've really got?"

"What do you want to do?"

"First, keep searching for Peretz's men, because,
whatever his motive, the killer used their unit signature. But I want you to split off and concentrate on
Schneiderman and Mills. Track back and get as much
detail as you can. Don't worry too much about looking
for connections. Just bring in the data. Then together
we'll see if we can't find something that links them up."

Micha was frustrated. The lists of imprisoned men
were long. Peretz's unit had no name or designation.
The task was to find men who'd been suddenly and
unexpectedly released.

"Since Peretz is out looking for his forger, wouldn't it save a lot of time if we just let him do the work?"

"You mean follow him?" David laughed. "I don't know, Micha. Seems to me we tried that once before."

Stephanie Porter: After she waved to him that night at Fink's, he had a feeling she would get in touch. The night she did he was sitting home, lights off, staring out at the city, feeling lonely and powerless and somewhat scornful about himself.

He'd just spoken with Hagith. The conversation had not gone well. His daughter was polite but distant, dutifully answering all his questions but sounding as if she wished she were doing something else. He wondered if he was losing her, whether she was being infected by Joe Raskov's vulgarity and Judith's sour view of life. A notion tormented him: that the little girl he loved might grow up to become a woman he wouldn't like.

Just then the telephone rang. He picked it up. "Hello?"

"How are you, David?"

That calm, low-pitched, seductive voice—he recognized it at once. "Well," he said, "this is a surprise."

"Oh, I don't think you're all *that* surprised. Your friend, the cellist—is she there?"

"Away on tour."

A throaty giggle. "I hear she's very talented." Then: "Guess it's been a while."

"More than six months."

"And now you're a bachelor. How lucky to call you at just this time."

"What's on your mind, Stephanie?"

"As if you didn't know." She laughed, her knowing laugh. It annoyed him. He was certain she had known that Anna was away.

"Did it occur to you that . . . ?"

"Come on, David. What do you think *she's* doing tonight? She's probably balling her accompanist."

"He's gay."

"Sounds interesting." She giggled again, then her tone turned serious. "Listen, why don't you come over? I'm all alone. I won't force myself on you. We can talk, have a drink, in the bar if you'd feel more comfortable. Or do anything else our little hearts desire. Am I being brazen? I think I'd be a fool if I weren't. No obligation. I promise, David. Really. So, okay? Will you come?"

Even as he started up his car he knew he would probably regret the visit. But he went anyway, over to the American Colony Hotel where she lived in permanent luxury. Driving there he asked himself: Why am I doing this? The only explanation he could come up with, an explanation that maddened him, was that he was curious.

He parked in the dark lot concealed by palms just behind the portico, sat in his car reconsidering the venture. Then, disliking himself for not returning home, he entered the hotel.

"You know, David, I really liked you a lot." They had had a drink in the bar, now were seated on the couch in her room. She stared at him, swung her head so that her precision-cut hair flicked across her face, then fell back to the exact place it had filled before.

"Maybe not all that much."

She smiled. "Well, no, we weren't in love if that's what you mean."

He knew he had not loved Stephanie but he had certainly lusted for her. At her suggestion he'd called her "Lynx" in bed. An appropriate name, he thought, on account of the way she moved. She wore a lecherous feline smile when she unclasped his belt and when they made love she shrieked like a cat and scratched and simmered and fussed and curled sensually around his limbs.

She took his wrists in her hands.

"I think it was your wrists. I was very conscious of them from the start. The hair and the thickness of them. I noticed them the first time we met at what's-his-name's, that boring journalist."

"Menachem."

"Yes. And then the hair that shows in the opening of your shirt." She eyed it. "I had a kind of erotic vision of you. I undressed you in my mind and imagined how the hair at your wrists and at your throat would connect—the pattern on your body, up your arms, across your chest." She sat back, looked him up and down. "I thought about that a lot, actually, got all hot thinking about it. It got so I couldn't put it out of my mind and then I had to see you stripped. So I set up that meeting at the King David swimming pool and when I saw you there, saw your body was just the way I'd imagined it, well. . . ." She giggled.

"Do you remember what we did that afternoon? God, I'll never forget it. For days I'd wanted to do that particular thing. As I remember the occasion I did it under the sheets." Again she tossed her head to flick her tawny hair across her face.

He remembered, and at the memory felt his cock grow hard.

". . . ever wonder why? You, the detective, I bet you did. I wanted to hide from you because I knew if you saw my face you'd know how much I liked it. I imagine my face is very lewd when I'm doing a thing like that. Hey! What's the matter? Don't go away. I'm not going to leap on you, poor man!"

He was up on his feet now and halfway across the room, feeling like a fool. He knew she knew she had him aroused and was getting ready to pounce. He knew too that he had not come to see her just out of curiosity, but because something about the way she'd stood at the bar at Fink's and her voice on the telephone had turned him on.

"Tell me," he asked, "did you care for me, or did you just sleep with me for information?"

"Of course I cared for you. Jesus, David—do you think I'm some kind of slut?"

"You were in half a dozen beds far as I could figure out."

"That's what I do, how I find out what's going on."

"Then you *are* an agent."

"I'm a journalist."

"You're an American agent, Stephanie. And a cop like me with access to all sorts of dossiers—I suppose I could have been a useful contact if I hadn't caught on to you so soon."

She laughed. "You underestimate your attractiveness, David. I have plenty of sources. I didn't need you."

"Anyone in the police?"

She shrugged. "Maybe. Maybe not. But I can tell you I've got at least one cabinet minister in my pocket. And, this may surprise you, he knows exactly what I do. Better that way—he only tells me stuff he wants me to find out. That's the game, you see. They leak stuff to me and I pass the stuff along. And from all those deliberate little leaks, certain inferences can be drawn. I don't personally draw the inferences. Other people do. I just bring in the raw stuff and let the inferences fall where they may. And you know something else? I like it. I like getting into the sack with powerful men and getting them to tell me things. But you, David, you were something else. I was crazy about you. Your body, yes, and something more. I think it was your inaccessibility. Because you weren't really there. You held something back. Day and night, no matter what we were doing, you were always a cop.

You're one now. It's quite maddening. A maddening trait you have."

She got up then and began to stalk around the room, and as she did he was conscious of her breasts and that she wasn't wearing a bra. *Her breasts!*

". . . you'll never be able to really love a woman. Not even this new one you have, the cellist, what's-her-name, Miss Pluperfect, Miss Great Performing Artist, whatever she thinks she is. You love your work too much. Shit, David, have you any idea how maddening, *maddening* it was to hang out with you when you were on a case?"

She stopped at her dresser, poured herself a small glass of Scotch, took his glass and refilled it, then sat down.

"You *do* love her, don't you?"

He nodded.

"Good for you. I really hope you do. But it's interesting that you picked the two of us, neither of us Israelis or even Jews. I'm not saying I blame you. There're some hot little numbers walking around, but your basic Israeli female is an earth-mother. Boring, too, compared to the mythical commando girls, the ones on the covers of the gaudy paperbacks. Breasts straining against khaki shirts, sunburned skin, fabulous legs showing out of the military shorts. Ever get it on with one of those?"

"Maybe."

"And?"

"What?"

"What was she like?"

He studied her. "You want me to tell you you're a great lay, don't you, Stephanie?"

She laughed. "I admit I wouldn't mind hearing you say it, since I happen to know you think I am. Thing is, David, I have this feeling that no matter how much you may love your cellist, you probably got bigger hard-ons for me. I don't expect you to acknowledge that. No point. But I wonder why you never fell for me. Would you mind explaining that, now that we're quits?"

"How could I love a woman who wasn't honest?"

"I wasn't *dis*honest. I just didn't tell you everything. Question is: Is *she* honest with you? *Is she?* Do you really understand her? Totally? Completely? Do you really think you know everything?"

He didn't answer. He knew he didn't understand Anna, that as much as he loved her she still remained a puzzle. Perhaps because she too held herself apart. But in Anna's case this didn't madden him; it intrigued him all the more.

"I'm asking for a reason. It would be great to make love with you tonight, if you decide you'd like to stay, but even if we do I wouldn't expect us to go back to being lovers the way we were. And I'm not out to hurt you, or to interfere with your sweet domestic bliss over there in scenic Abu Tor. But I have to tell you that I know a thing or two about your cellist. I wonder if you'd like to hear."

What could he say? Of course he'd like to hear. But there was no way he was going to ask.

"She has a past, you know."

"Everyone has a past."

"Hers is more complex than most. Just the fact she's Russian makes it more complex."

"What are you trying to tell me, Stephanie? Are you speaking to me now as my friend?"

"I want to be your friend. And I admit that if from time to time I could go to bed with you, I'd enjoy that too. But even if you never touch me again in my entire life, I still think I should tell you what I know."

"So what's holding you back?"

"What's holding me back is that you won't come straight out and ask."

"You'd feel better if I asked?" She nodded. *Damn her!* "So, okay, I'm asking: What do you know?"

She lit a cigarette, inhaled deeply, then slowly blew out the smoke. Then for the third time she shook her head to fling her hair across her face. "It's like this, David. Your Anna Benitskaya—yes, of course I know her name—has been involved with a prominent Russian émigré, a man the KGB want to discredit. She was his mistress. I'm not saying she is now. I can't be sure. But she was very much involved with him, and there's a school of thought that goes that she was sent out to the West to go after him, get close to him, and maybe not just him either, maybe some other important controversial émigrés as well. Her defector story, you see, has got some holes. Makes good copy, that tale about leaving her state-owned Montagnana cello under the sheets in her hotel bed, slipping out to the U.S. Consulate, begging for asylum, all of that. But did it really go down that way? Or was she ordered to do it? To gain credentials—you see what I mean? To gain a super credibility so no one would suspect her later on."

"If you're saying she was a false defector, that's a load of shit."

"I knew you'd be angry. And I expect you to be skeptical considering this is coming from a woman who admits she gets horny just looking at your wrists. Look, I'm just passing on what certain people think, based on information obtained in Moscow and confirmed by at least one other source I know about. It was interesting that the people who accompanied her were never punished. The man she was sleeping with at the time, that conductor, Titanov, he's been allowed to travel to the West since her so-called defection and that doesn't add up because he was responsible for her—unless of course he was in on the deal too. Now hear me out, David. She's a world-class musician, no doubt of that. A star cellist, not a spy. But there could have been a trade-off. Something like: 'You defect, build yourself a career in the West, make lots of money, and become a star, and in return for our letting you do all that you'll get close to certain people we're interested in, find out what they're up to, and report back on them to us.' "

"What you're saying is that she's just like you. I don't believe that. But suppose you're right. Then what the hell is she doing with me? I'm of no use to a spy."

"Oh, I don't know, a smart young Israeli police officer, a man who might have a big career ahead of him. A man, moreover, who's in a certain position right now, involved in a case that could have implications that go beyond . . . well, I'm only speculating."

He looked at her sharply. "What do you know about my case?"

"I saw you on TV. I know you're up to your ass in something big."

"How big?"

"I don't know, David. All I've heard is rumors."

"What rumors?"

"I gather there're some people around who're getting . . . well . . . upset." Suddenly she seemed nervous, as if she'd said more than she'd intended to. She shrugged. "I see I've offended you. All I can say is that your Anna may have reported back on a man named Aleksandr Targov and that it wouldn't surprise me now if she were also reporting back on you."

He set down his glass, stood up, then walked over to the door. She watched him. She didn't look too happy. He turned to her, ready to leave. "I don't know what to think of you, Stephanie. Whether you're a lying little schemer or just a run-of-the-mill American bitch. Whatever your game is, I'm not interested in playing. I'm sorry I was stupid enough to come."

She nodded. "Okay, David, if that's the way you want it. But please trust me on this: I'm worried for you. I think you're in over your head and that if you keep on the way you're going you might end up getting hurt. I wouldn't want that. I'd be very upset if something bad happened to you." Their eyes met. She blew him a kiss. Then, as he was shutting the door, he heard her light another cigarette.

Later, when he thought back over their conversation, he realized she'd offered only one detail: Titanov, the conductor, whom she said had been seen recently in the West.

Anna had spoken of this man several times, described how much she'd loathed him and her pleasure in knowing that when she'd fled he had taken most of the blame. Her defection story was rock-solid. She'd left her cello in her bed because she wasn't a thief and so that when Titanov looked in on her he'd think she was asleep. But there was a fifty percent chance he'd come in anyway—that had been her greatest risk. He thought nothing of awakening her. "My discovery, my property," he called her. "I own you body and soul." She'd defected, she'd told David, as much to get away from him as to live freely in the West.

Now Stephanie said Titanov had been seen, and that was a fact that could be checked. He took it to Sarah Dorfman, who inquired of her music world friends, one of whom even telephoned a knowledgeable impresario in New York. Word came back. Titanov had not toured outside the Soviet Union since the day Anna Benitskaya had asked for asylum in Milan. He was still in disgrace, still blamed for her defection. Sarah's sources, David knew, were absolutely reliable, so Stephanie's single "fact" was proven false. For David that was enough to discredit everything else she'd said.

An American nun on tour of the Holy Land and a working class Israeli trucker. Could they somehow be linked? Could their lives have crossed?

Susan Mills had kept a travel diary. Dov, Uri, and Micha had each been through it several times. Names, dates, places—it was the basic source for their attempts to trace her friends. She commented on the weather, the impact of first seeing certain important religious shrines, everyday encounters with Israelis, her excitement at walking where Jesus Christ had lived and trod. No mention of a truck driver named Yaakov, or of any truck at all. David reread the diary, and then looked at her photographs, including ones developed from the roll found in her camera after she'd been killed.

These photographs amounted to a diary in themselves. Susan seemed to have shot two or three thirty-six-frame rolls a day. Her camerawork was excellent. She changed lenses, shot interiors and exteriors, all perfectly focused, perfectly exposed, perfectly framed for the scrapbooks she would make.

Together, David and Dov examined every shot. They were looking for Schneiderman, or possibly his truck. Nothing. But everything else was there, every shrine described in the diary, every person mentioned, even the facades of the hotels where she had stayed. If she mentioned getting into a conversation with an old bookstore owner, there would be a photograph of him standing before his shop. Susan was a documentarian. She was on a once-in-a-lifetime trip. She had carefully constructed a record of it. But they could find no Schneiderman, no matter how hard they looked.

"We have to go deeper, Dov. She tells us a lot, but she couldn't put down all of it."

"Deeper how?"

"Several times she says: 'Wrote Margaret today.'"

We ought to have a look at those letters. Check her address book. Search for a 'Margaret.' Probably her closest friend."

While Dov went through Susan's personal address book, David turned back to the papers taken from Yaakov Schneiderman's flat. Again, he, Dov, and the others had been through the material several times. Bills. Receipts. Business correspondence. Tax forms. Check stubs. An appointment book. Cryptic, hurriedly written notes and orders for pick-ups and deliveries all over Jerusalem.

The amount of material was massive, but it struck David as a pathetic remnant of a life. A man like Schneiderman would not confide in a diary. His fantasies, illusions, beliefs, and dreams had died with him, and all that was left were papers having to do with money.

"Okay, there's a Margaret Dupuy, Convent of Mary, St. Louis."

"Susan's convent." Dov nodded. "Try and get her on the phone."

The connection was clear and Sister Margaret Dupuy's voice was warm.

"Yes, the police, I understand. I'm so happy you haven't forgotten her. We won't ever forget her, of course. But you didn't know her and love her the way we did."

"Did you keep her letters?"

"Oh yes, every one."

"Could we read them—if they're not too personal?"

"They are lovely sensitive letters and I'll be happy to share them with you. I could read them to you now, but it would take too long. How would it be if I made copies? I'll mail them to you tomorrow."

"We'd be grateful," David said.

The search for men who served with Peretz was proving slow and difficult. One wall was posted now with the lists of men who'd done time in military prisons. Micha's, Uri's, Shoshana's, and Liederman's desks were covered with computer printouts from IDF central files.

These four detectives had gone home at six. David and Dov now sat alone in the PC Unit office. Dov was discouraged. "I don't know, David. We've been through this stuff a dozen times."

"That's the thing about hidden symmetry, Dov. It's very difficult to see. You have to try out different pieces in different combinations. So now we go through it all again."

They had divided their material, placed it on separate tables: Schneiderman's miscellany; Susan's diary and photographs. David had decided they would confine themselves to the period of Susan's stay in Jerusalem. They would forget the early part of her trip, concentrate instead on the final eight days of her life.

He and Dov tacked up a fresh plastic overlay over the large street map of Jerusalem on the cork-covered wall. Then they stuck pins in every place that Susan Mills had gone. The main clusters were around the great Christian shrines. She wasn't an extravagant woman, had used public transportation to get around. And since the Holyland Hotel was in Ramat Sharett, there were limitations on the bus routes she would have had to use.

She walked a lot too—that was evident from her descriptions and her photographs. So they began to chart, as best they could, her probable itineraries on each of her eight final days. They did this by connecting up the pins with different colored threads. Yellow for the first day, blue for the second, orange for the third, and so on until they had a mass of crisscrossing daily routes.

Next they charted Schneiderman's movements, the various deliveries and pickups he had made over the same eight days. Household furnishings transported from Qiryat Moshe to Talpiyyot; a refrigerator from a store on Nathan Strauss to an apartment in Emeq Refaim. . . . Again yellow for the first day, blue for the second, orange for the third, etc. And they didn't forget that he had started out each morning from his home and returned with his truck there every night.

Wherever two threads of the same color crossed, they went back to the documentation to see if the crossing fell within a couple of hours. There were many instances of crossings. The work of checking on each was laborious. Most often, it turned out, the crossings were not true intersections but had occurred at completely different times of day.

David made a decision. If they could pinpoint a crossing which they could estimate had fallen within three hours or less, then there was a possibility that Susan and Schneiderman had met. After four evenings of work they came up with six such possibilities. They circled each one in crayon, then sat back and studied the map.

"What bothers me, David, is that it's all so chancy. Susan must have done things she didn't document, and as for Schneiderman, in a city like this there're just too many different routes. Suppose he glances at his gas gauge, sees he needs to fill up. Does he go out of his way to a favorite gas station, or does he just continue until he spots one on the road?"

"We can only use what we've got. Now we know a meeting's *not* impossible. Before we thought it was. So we keep on searching. That's all, really, we can do."

When the letters arrived from Margaret Dupuy there were things in them they hadn't found in Susan's diary or photographs. Feelings mostly, sensitive reactions to the shrines, and occasional notes on Israel as an embattled, imbittered nation-state.

"I do so admire the Jewish people," she wrote, "but here sometimes they *do* test my love. I've never seen so many chain smokers or such pushing and shoving in crowds and shops. Nobody likes to stand in line here. It's 'me, me, me' and never mind the rest. But they can be saintly too. An old lady goes out of her way to show me a street. A busy teacher spends hours explaining an archaeological site. And then I'll encounter rudeness again. It's because they have so many terrible problems, I think. . . ."

One reference from the letters leapt out at David: "Had a very unpleasant encounter today with an extremely nasty cop. Usually they're so polite but this one was awful. 'You must do this, must do that.' Just like a German. And perhaps he was a German Jew. . . ."

An encounter with a nasty cop in Jerusalem. She wrote that it had occurred that very day. The letter was dated March 12. David went to the map to trace her route.

The white thread: It didn't lead to a direct crossing with Schneiderman but there were two times when they'd come fairly close. Back to the documentation. The second instance seemed possible. Susan had eaten lunch at a suburban dairy restaurant near her hotel and around midday Schneiderman had been driving empty toward Romema, having completed a hauling job in Gonen Bet.

"Wait," Dov said, "I think that's when he had his accident."

While Dov rummaged through Schneiderman's papers David thought about Susan's reference to a nasty cop. When Dov found what he was looking for he read it aloud, a computerized notice from Schneiderman's insurance company concerning a collision he had had on March 12.

The notice stated that according to the motor vehicle registry office the reported plate number of the other vehicle did not exist. Would Mr. Schneiderman please consult his notes and as soon as possible submit an amended form.

Across the bottom Schneiderman had scrawled the plate number, and underlined it twice. He had also scrawled a name, Igal Hurwitz, and then another number, A29103.

The insurance company was in Tel Aviv. Dov and Micha drove down early in the morning, were waiting at the door when the office opened at eight. They brought back a copy of Schneiderman's original report, which included a crude diagram of the accident. They also brought back the extraordinary information that the other vehicle, the one whose plate number could not be traced, had been described as a late-model dark blue Chevrolet van, and that Igal Hurwitz, a policeman, serial number A29103, was listed not only as the cop who had taken charge at the scene but as a witness to the accident itself.

The only trouble was that when Dov checked with police personnel he was told there was no Igal Hurwitz. There was no such serial number either. A29103 did not exist.

An iron-gray windy afternoon. David, along with Dov, Shoshana Nahon, Uri Schuster, Micha Benyamani, and Moshe Liederman, drove in two white police Subarus to the alleged collision scene. Following Schneiderman's diagram, they positioned their cars and then tried to reconstruct the accident.

Schneiderman, according to the statement filed with his report, had been driving at reasonable speed along Yehuda Ha-Nasi in his empty truck, when, quite suddenly, at the intersection with Berenice Street, the Chevrolet van had pulled into his path. Nearly all the damage had been done to the van; Schneiderman's truck was barely scratched. No other information had been provided on the form, since, Schneiderman wrote, patrolman Hurwitz had taken detailed notes.

A fairly bleak intersection—not much going on during the day. A suburban area, private houses mostly, a few small apartment buildings scattered about. The usual service stores: a small grocery, a laundry and dry-cleaning establishment, a shoemaker, a newsstand that also sold candy and film. Yet within the past three weeks this modest neighborhood had become notorious. Around the corner, at 49 Alexandrion, was the borrowed apartment where the bodies of the murdered lovers, Ruth Isaacson and Aaron Horev, had been found.

While the others marked the street and photographed the scene, David and Dov strode three blocks against the wind to the little dairy restaurant just off Ya'aqov Pat, where Susan Mills had eaten lunch.

David stood outside while Dov went in to interview the waiters. When Dov came out he shook his head. He had shown Susan's picture, but it had been two months and no one could recall her face.

"Still," David said, "it's looking good. At around the same time on the same day we can place them within a hundred meters. She comes in here for lunch. Afterward she decides to take a walk. She arrives up there at the corner just in time to see the accident, and that's when she has the encounter with the 'nasty cop.' But it's better than that—the nasty cop turns out not to exist. Neither does the Chevy van, and we know our wildcard, Yael Safir, was picked up in a dark blue American van we've never been able to trace. Phony nasty cops. Unlisted vehicles. Witnesses killed off and then easy victims picked up and killed and thrown in as a disguise. Doesn't feel much like a serial murder case now, does it? More like a conspiracy and coverup."

They started to walk back to the accident scene. Then David changed his mind. "Let's take a look at Forty-nine Alexandrion."

Dov nodded. "Sure."

When they reached the building, they stared up at the windows of the famous love nest on the second floor. David shook his head. "Horev and Isaacson. Okay, it could just be a coincidence about the neighborhood. But the timing bothers me. They used to get together around noon, spend their lunch hours making love. That's too close, Dov. Too big a coincidence. Suppose they also saw the accident?"

"But they were shot, David. Point-blank range, two each in each of their heads."

"Sure. Take them out clean. A professional hit—that would add another layer of concealment. No point trying to blend them into a phony psycho murder series. They were adulterous lovers so make it look like it was done by a killer hired by an angry spouse."

Back at the intersection the wind was blowing harder and the clouds were darker, about to burst. David called Micha, Uri, Shoshana, and Liederman together into the middle of the street. A flock of black birds tore across the sky.

"Canvass the neighborhood," he told them. "Every house, every apartment, every shop. Find me a witness. They couldn't kill everyone. There must be someone who saw this accident who's still alive."

THE
WITNESS

In every district there's a busybody. Find her, play up
to her, get her talking about her neighbors. Discover
who stays home during the day, who goes to work,
and did she hear anything about an accident? Knock
on doors between noon and two when the accident
took place. Talk to the newsstore owner, the shoemaker, the garbage collectors, the Arab maids. Make
lists. Figure out which apartments overlook the intersection. Talk to the residents and if they're not at
home come back in the evening when they are. Show
familiarity. The woman who lives on the corner—is it
true her son's retarded? What about traffic patterns,
and who owns those cars parked out on the street, and
who's reliable, and who's not, and who takes a midday
snooze?

At last David had set a task at which Moshe
Liederman excelled. He was good at chitchat, spoke
excellent Polish, was patient with the old ladies, generous with cigarettes. In four days he and the other four
detectives heard a lot about Aaron Horev and Ruth
Isaacson. But no matter how many people they asked
about an accident, they couldn't find anyone who knew
anything.

David said this was impossible, that when a truck
hits a van and there's a confrontation between a nun
and a cop, someone *has* to see something or at least

hear some noise. But the intersection was nearly deserted that time of day. This was a bedroom community; no orthodox people; most of the wives held jobs. There were kids of course, but they were either infants or at school. Still, maybe, on that particular day, for one reason or another, someone had stayed at home.

Go back. Ask again. It's hard, but people will help if they see how much you care. The intersection could be viewed from thirty windows. Check each one again. There has to be a witness. *Has to be.*

Amit Nissim, six years old, short, pixieish, with bangs of light brown hair and playful dark brown eyes, was home from school that day with a cold. Her aunt was in the hospital recovering from gastrointestinal surgery, her mother had to visit her, so she asked old Mrs. Shapira next door if she would look after Amit while she was gone. Mrs. Shapira said sure, and could Mr. Nissim help her by changing some lightbulbs when he got home. Yes, certainly. A bargain was struck. And when Mrs. Shapira lay down for her noontime nap, she left Amit on her sofa with a doll.

Later Amit heard noise, people talking loudly on the street. She went to the window, saw a woman quarreling with a man. Was there a truck? She wasn't sure. She remembered a woman clutching a camera and a man in uniform trying to snatch it away.

Mr. and Mrs. Nissim did not like the way their daughter was being questioned. Amit was blinking, a sure sign to them that she was under stress. She wasn't used to so much attention, six police officers hanging on her words. She was intimidated. Couldn't they tell? Anyway, she hadn't seen any accident so would they all please leave now before the child became even more upset.

David sent the others out, then tried to calm the Nissims down. Mrs. Nissim hid her pregnancy beneath a cotton smock; Mr. Nissim lounged in a faded tennis shirt and polyester shorts. David peered around their living room. Behind the maroon sofa with the bright orange cushions, he observed a new Japanese stereo and a pile of tape cassettes. A short shelf contained the usual books: Hebrew editions of *Exodus* and *Story of My Life* by Moshe Dayan; copies of Michener's *The Source* and Kurzman's biography of Ben-Gurion in English. An oil painting of an old Jew praying at the Western Wall was prominently displayed, the paint laid on very thick, the scene garishly sentimentalized. David could see that the Nissims were good people— decent, law-abiding Jerusalemites. He knew that if properly approached they would cooperate.

"Your daughter has seen something very important," he told them. "But you were right to stop us. We didn't interview her properly. The proper way, without exerting pressure, is to turn the interview into a game. Amit is a vital witness. Would you consider allowing us to talk with her a second time? There'll be no intimidation. We'll videotape the interview, and when it's over that'll be the end of it. We won't bother her again."

After a brief whispered consultation, the Nissims solemnly agreed.

Since there could only be two interrogators, David asked himself who in the unit would be best. Shoshana? Too impatient. Liederman? Too old. He finally settled on huge weight-lifting Uri Schuster who, though tough, even brutal on the streets, was a lovable teddy bear with kids.

They set the whole thing up in Mrs. Shapira's apartment, just the way it had been that day: at noon with no one else around and a dark Chevrolet van and Schneiderman's truck positioned on the street just as they were in the insurance diagram.

David and Uri brought along two cartons of toys: a van, a truck, little buildings to create a model of the intersection, and various male and female dolls including dolls dressed in different military uniforms and one dressed as a Jerusalem cop. On one of the females they pasted a tiny photo of Susan Mills, and on one of the males, a photo of Schneiderman. They also made up dolls for Ora Goshen, Halil Ghemaiem, Yael Safir, and the murdered lovers, Ruth Isaacson and Aaron Horev, and they had a dozen more faceless figures with them too.

When everything was ready, Uri escorted Amit to the window, showed her the cars out on the street, and then asked her to use the toys to make a model of what she'd seen.

"That's right, Amit—the truck here at the corner, yes, and the van has just driven into it so they're together just like this. . . . Now look at all these girl dolls. Do you see one that's like the woman with the camera? This one? Good. Put her just where she was when you saw her having the argument. And which of these boy dolls looks most like the uniformed man? The policeman. You're sure? And that they were standing together on the sidewalk here, like this, facing the truck? Uh huh. . . ."

Yaakov Schneiderman was driving the truck—now Amit remembered. She also remembered him standing beside it after the collision, hand on his hips, shaking his head, inspecting the damage, then kicking the wheel of the van. Did she recognize any of the other dolls? Yes, these two, Horev and Isaacson—they came over during the argument. The woman with the camera was speaking in another language, and they came over to help her understand the policeman, who was getting mad.

So, Uri summarized, there were four of them on the sidewalk, and Schneiderman over by the van. Any-

154 • William Bayer

body else? Yes, three more men, two of them helping a third who seemed to be hurt. Using the dolls Amit reconstructed exactly what she'd seen: the hurt man placing his arms across the shoulders of the other two, and then the three of them together limping rapidly away.

"All three of them? You're sure, Amit? Up this way, up Berenice Street? And what about the others? Oh, you mean this was *before* the argument? But the other night you said you heard the quarreling and that's when you went over to the window to look out."

Amit had forgotten. When Mrs. Shapira had gone to her bedroom, she had gone over to the window because she wanted to go outside and play. Then she saw the truck coming and saw it hit the van. Then she saw the policeman get out of the driver's door of the van and then she saw the woman who spoke the other language taking pictures of everything. The policeman wasn't nice to the lady, or to the couple who'd been passing by and stopped to help. He made them all show him their identity cards, and then he spoke very angry words and wrote down all their names. . . .

So, three men and a phony cop had been in a dark blue van, and after Schneiderman had hit it the three men, one injured, had fled the scene. The cop, who, of course, had been "Igal Hurwitz," had taken charge, exchanged names with Schneiderman, then demanded that Susan Mills turn over her film. Important evidence, he'd told her, but Susan had refused. Amit Nissim remembered hearing Ruth Isaacson explain to the cop that the American woman didn't like his attitude.

When they left Amit, after thanking her and presenting her with a gift of the policewoman doll, Uri, who'd been so calm and paternal during the interview, began shadowboxing on the stairs. A quick succession of left jabs, then four quick rights, then a hard right cross.

"Horev-Isaacson! Same case! Congratulations, David—
you were right! But you know something? When you
told us that the other day I thought you were full of
shit. . . ."

Horev and Isaacson—all of Israel knew about them.

Aaron Horev: engineer, devoted husband of Rivka,
obstetrician at Hadassah in Ein Karem. Three boys:
Zvi, Yigal, and Ehud. A typical, honest, striving,
middle-class Jerusalem family, with a two-bedroom
apartment in Gillo and a good second-hand Fiat sedan.

Ruth Isaacson: librarian at the Mount Scopus campus of Hebrew University, wife of Asher Isaacson,
professor of geology at Givat Ram. The childless
Isaacsons, close friends of the Horevs, owned a comfortable two-bedroom house on Bezalel. They'd done
their own fix-up, put a sleek modern menorah in their
window, parked their shiny Japanese car out front.

The assignations took place at 49 Alexandrion, in a
second-floor apartment belonging to Ruth's friend, Zena
Raphael. The arrangement, as it was later revealed,
was that for the reasonable sum of fifty thousand
shekels a month, the lovers had the optional use of
Zena's place, including sheets and towels, from noon
to two each weekday afternoon.

How often they actually met there was a matter of
dispute. Zena said possibly once or twice a week; a
neighbor said every afternoon. But there was no dispute about the finale. A little after 6 P.M. on Thursday, April 18th, Zena Raphael returned home by bus
from a long and tiring day. She unlocked her door,
carried her groceries to her kitchen, rinsed her oranges, made tea, then went to her bedroom to lie
down. From the doorway she saw two nude and tan-
gled bodies. The lovers, each shot expertly twice in the
head, lay dead in each other's arms.

Who had done it? Asher Isaacson? Rivka Horev?

Rivka's brother Samuel, who had always despised Aaron? Some said Zena had done it, that she was herself in love with Aaron and madly jealous of Ruth. Rafi's homicide investigators weren't sure. The clean method of the double slaying, four precisely fired shots from a .22 caliber Beretta, suggested the possibility of a professional hit. And since the "injured parties" in the affair had each been at work at the time, Rafi was basing his investigation on the theory that one or the other of them might have contracted the executions out.

All parties claimed innocence. Asher Isaacson hired an attorney. Rivka Horev, persecuted by reporters, took her three sons to Haifa and threatened to leave Israel for good. The religious demagogue, Rabbi Mordecai Katzer, described the double killing as the wages of infidelity, a consequence of "perverted values" and "secular Hellenism" in Israeli life.

"So now you want Horev-Isaacson?" Rafi's sad eyes drooped with skepticism. He sat back in his chair, hands clasped behind his head.

"I've got a witness."

"A six-year-old. David—*please*. . . ."

"I'm telling you, Rafi, she may be six but she's very very good. Look at my tape. See if you believe her. Horev and Isaacson saw the accident—that's why they were killed."

After Rafi looked twice at the tape he agreed that Amit made a convincing witness. "You didn't lead her and she makes good sense," he said. "Too bad there's no corroboration."

"So?"

Rafi paused. "So—okay, you get Horev-Isaacson. I'll have to tell Latsky, but we won't mention this to anybody else. My homicide guys will just have to keep spinning their wheels. Which is about all they've been doing anyway." He leaned back and lit his pipe. "Of course on one level you've solved it. Now we understand the motive. Get rid of witnesses. Conceal two of them in a phony serial case. Sacrifice three other people including an innocent soldier-girl. Knock off a pair of lovers too."

"Ruthless people."

"So what's behind it?"

"A cover-up. The witnesses saw something dangerous," David said.

"What?"

"I've been thinking about that. It couldn't have been obvious, or they would have had to kill all of them right away. The killers didn't do that. They executed them slowly. Spent two months playing out a complicated charade. So the witnesses—Schneiderman, Mills, Horev and Isaacson—saw something that maybe didn't register as important at the time, but that might appear to be very important in retrospect later on. Four guys, one of them dressed like a cop, driving in an illegally registered van. Something about connecting them—that's what it's got to be. Guys who were going to do something so bad they were willing to kill seven innocent people rather than have four of them look back at some future date and remember seeing them together."

David kept his unit up until 4 A.M. talking out the case. Their first decision had to do with Amit. Since everyone else who'd seen the accident had been murdered, she might now be in danger too. She would have to be protected. David assigned Shoshana to guard her, with Uri and Liederman as relief.

Their second decision concerned Susan Mills. She'd refused to turn over her film to the phony Hurwitz. That could account for the fact she'd been tortured before she'd been killed. Had she talked? She was strong-willed, Dov reminded them—he'd always admired the American nun. So it was possible to presume she hadn't talked, which meant the dangerous photos she'd taken might still be around. David gave the order: Go to every photo store and film-processing outlet in the city working in concentric circles from the Holyland Hotel. Show pictures of Susan to the shopkeepers. Had the nun ever come into their stores? Had she bought film, left off rolls to be developed? Had they any uncollected developed pictures in their files?

At dawn David went home to sleep. He rose in the early afternoon, made coffee, ate some yogurt, and fixed himself a salad. He was in the midst of taking a shower, long and hot, thinking of Anna, becoming excited at the thought that she'd be home in just a week, when he heard the sound of the buzzer downstairs. He turned off the water, wrapped himself in a towel, and went out to the intercom to find out who was there.

"Yigal Gati. I tried your office. They told me you were home."

"General Gati?" Even through the intercom he recognized the famous voice.

"Yes. I'd like to come up and talk if it's not inconvenient."

"I'll buzz you in," David said.

He rushed around the apartment straightening up, wondering what he'd done to deserve this visit from a living legend. He was still struggling into his pants when the doorbell rang. He pulled on a sweater before he opened up. When he did, the general stared with faint disgust at the wet bath towel he was still holding in his hand.

"Worked late last night. I just got up."

"Maybe I should have phoned." But, as David noticed, the general continued to stand there, not offering to come back at a more convenient time.

When David offered him a drink General Gati requested a glass of water. "Bottled," he called into the kitchen. When David brought the glasses back into the living room he found Gati standing before the large window looking out.

"Superb view."

David handed him his water. "Never tire of it. We love it here."

The general turned to him slowly. "Of course you do, a lovely home like this in Abu Tor."

Then, it seemed to David, he became the subject of a deep examining gaze, the kind of gaze, he recognized, which he often applied himself. It was as if the general was trying to penetrate his mind, searching out some weakness he might exploit. David tried to return the gaze but found it difficult. All he could see was the public face, so familiar from a thousand photographs: Gati, the retired Air Force commander whose daring tactics had been so decisive in the wars of '67 and '73, his thick short gray hair brushed forward like an ancient Roman senator's, his dazzling dark blue eyes unwavering and cold.

"This is an unofficial visit. I'm an ordinary citizen, just like everybody else these days." A tight little smile, then, that suggested he knew he was a lot more than that. "It's in that capacity, nothing more, nothing less, that I took the liberty of dropping by."

David motioned him to the couch.

"Spent my life in the military. I'm a blunt guy, so instead of jerking you around and mentioning the names of mutual friends, I'll get right to the point. I'm here to plead a case."

David took a long sip of water. "Go ahead," he said. "Plead away."

"This is a request for mercy because from what I

understand there's probably no decent legal defense. You're wondering what I'm talking about." That fake tight little smile again. "A man named Gutman, whom I understand you arrested a few weeks back."

David nodded. "We arrested him."

"He's in a lot of trouble now."

"Not surprising, considering he's a thief."

"Just a thief? Or perhaps a victim too?"

"A lot of Israelis have been victimized, general. Not all of them have turned to crime."

"Ah," Gati smiled tightly again, "a tough guy. I heard you were. I respect that. I am too."

"What's your interest in Gutman?"

"Known him more than forty years. We served together in the Jewish Brigade. After the surrender, I served with him in Germany, British Occupation Zone. Perhaps you're familiar with some of the different things we did."

So this was how father knew Gutman, and how Gutman recognized me the night of his arrest. "You knew my father?" David asked.

"Of course."

"The 'hunting seasons'?"

The general nodded. "We called them that."

"Gutman was a hunter?"

"One of the best. And a fine fighter later on. We killed quite a few Arabs together, Jacob and I. You may not know it, but Jacob Gutman was one of the heroes of Latrum in May of '48."

The thrust to Jerusalem, one of the legendary achievements of the first war fought by the Jewish State. The rusted tanks and broken armor were still in place, reminders to modern travelers driving the highway between Jerusalem and Tel Aviv.

"And now he brokers stolen Torahs."

Gati rose, walked over to the window, stood with his back to David staring out. "Torahs. Sure. Why not? What does he care? He can't survive on his lousy pension so why shouldn't he supplement it by selling Torahs to born-again American Jews? Way this country is today, what the hell should he think? This pretty young virgin we married almost forty years ago. We look at her now. Do you know what we see?" He turned back to the room, stood at parade rest with his legs apart. "A tarted-up old whore. When we can stand to look at her. When looking at her doesn't make us puke."

He turned back to the window. "You were born after Independence, David. Gutman and I were grown men then. We fought for something and we knew what we were fighting for, and one thing we *weren't* fighting for was the soft-bellied society you've got out there today. Oh, sure, it's sweet out there." He gestured toward the city. "Maybe a little decadent, but what the hell? Everyone's got himself a refrigerator, a washer, a drier, and a car, and the people you need to fix your plumbing are extortionists so sometimes, when your toilet leaks, you just leave it that way because you can't afford to get it fixed."

He turned again; now his body was silhouetted against Jerusalem, and David had trouble reading the expression on his face. ". . . except Jacob Gutman doesn't like leaking toilets. Not that he's so fastidious, you understand. Just that in that regard he's like everybody else. So, good Jew that he is, he knows how to survive. He does what a Jew has always done. Opens up a little shop.

"Now there're all kinds of little Jewish shops. Tailor shops. Dry goods shops. Little grocery stores. Places to buy some lace, some shoes, maybe borrow money on a watch. All those kinds of shops have one goal in common: Sell things for more than you pay out. It's called business. And who's to say who's the sharpie and who's the thief and who's the honest Jewish businessman?

"For a guy like Gutman, those kinds of fine distinctions got blurred along the way. He looks around and thinks: 'I was one of those few guys who went around occupied Germany in '45 and '46 cleaning things up, doing a little public-service deNazification with my pals Gati and Doc Bar-Lev. I actually planned a lot of those missions, the way we'd show up at a guy's house, oh-so-polite in our nicely pressed British uniforms, show him our well-forged summons for interrogation, apologize for the intrusion to his wife, then lead him off politely to our borrowed official truck. Then I'd get in the back with him, pull the canvas flaps shut, and break his neck, quick, the way the Brits taught us in their commando school. Then we'd dump him by the side of the road—no burial necessary because you only take that kind of trouble with a human being. Then on to the next guy the authorities didn't care about. You know, the little guy, the average run-of-the-mill little murderer. And I, who'd done all that, who'd taken upon myself the nasty exterminator's job, find that now that I'm old, my wife's gone, and my daughter's dead, I don't have a marketable skill worth shit in this wonderful meretricious New Society of ours. I look around and what do I see? Everyone stealing, extorting, buying luxuries, getting rich. The country I fought for acting like a harlot running to the Americans for hand-outs every time she overspends. So what should I do? Pretend she's still the same? Hell with that! I'll set myself up in a kind of little Jewish shop. I'll pick up old Torahs, not ask too many questions about where they're from, and sell them to Americans who'd rather buy one cheap than pay a scribe to write one new.' "

Gati stepped forward, sat down, looked hard at David, and then, for the first time since he'd come into the apartment, he gave a classic Israeli shrug. As if to say: "Well, that's it, my plea, I rest my case."

Then, while David stared at him amazed, he took up his water glass, and slowly, carefully wet his lips.

When Anna called from Paris after midnight, he sensed the tension in her voice.

"What's the matter?"

"Nothing. I just wanted to talk. I'll be home soon. Just a couple more days. Can't wait. Oh, David—I miss you so much. . . ."

She sounded, he thought, as if she were about to cry.

His door was open but Rebecca Marcus knocked anyway. "Man on the phone, David. Won't give his name. Insists on speaking to you."

Raskov? No, he'd identify himself. "Okay, ask him what he wants—I'll listen in."

Rebecca nodded. David pushed a button and picked up the deadkey on his phone.

". . . say it's one of Peretz's old boys and I know about the 'signature.' "

"Can you describe it?" Rebecca asked.

"Sure. Pairs of cuts across the tits."

Silence for a moment, then Rebecca's voice, controlled: "Just one moment, sir. I'll see if the captain's available now."

When Rebecca reappeared at the door her face looked drawn. David signaled her to start a trace. Then he took the call.

"Bar-Lev here. We don't usually talk to people until they tell us who they are."

"And if they have information?" The voice was rough, the accent North African.

"If you're looking for a reward—"

"I'm not."

"So what do you want?"

"Got a list."

"What kind of list?"

"Guys in Peretz's unit."

"Your name on it too?"

"Fuck you, policeman. Why you giving me all this shit?"

"If you want to help us out and you don't want to identify yourself, kindly drop your list to us in the mail."

"Can't do that."

"Why not?"

"You want the list or no?"

David thought a moment. "Okay, I want the list."

"Come to Anna Freud Garden. Givat Ram. Three this afternoon."

"Wait a minute! I didn't say—"

"Don't stall, Bar-Lev. And come alone. Nobody else. Or you don't get the list." He hung up.

"It's just a patch of bushes in the middle of the campus," said Dov. "Not isolated at all. At three o'clock there'll be a mob."

"So what kind of a secret meeting place is that?" Micha asked.

"Suppose some kid comes up to David with a slip of paper. Go to X. Then go to Y. Treasure-hunt style. It would be tough to keep him covered."

"Anna Freud—maybe he knows about your father," Shoshana said.

"That's pretty sophisticated. This guy didn't sound like that."

"Suppose he's for real?"

"Fine. We could use a list. And if he's faking, part of the conspiracy, we need to know that too." They all looked at him. Dov seemed worried. "What's he going to do?" David asked. "Shoot me in the head?"

"I don't like it. All of a sudden like this. I mean, now we're way past Peretz."

"But we've been working on a list. Word could have gotten around. We know details on the marks have gotten out. Listen—I know if I don't go we'll kick ourselves tomorrow. So I go. Okay? Everyone agrees?"

He waited in the Anna Freud Garden from a quarter of three. The sun was hot and the bullet-proof vest they'd urged him to wear was uncomfortable and made him sweat. Students lay about on blankets sunbathing, talking, several couples kissing, a few actually reading books. By five he'd had it. He got up, shook his head and stalked off. He met Micha and Dov in the parking lot.

"It was a test, David. To see if you'd show up alone."

"Could be. Hundreds of windows around. I could have been easily observed. Or maybe it was just a stunt. So to hell with it! Guy calls back, I don't want to talk to him. Then we'll see how bad he wants me. Next time *he* can sweat."

At ten that evening he was listening to one of Anna's records, an old Pierre Fournier recording, when his telephone rang.

It was the same caller. "You walked out on me."

"Fuck you," David said, and hung up.

When the phone rang again he sat watching it, letting the rings penetrate the music, echo against the apartment walls. Finally, after fifteen rings, he picked it up. "Yeah? What do you want?"

"Sorry. Got held up. No way to get in touch."

"No big deal. Forget it."

"Don't you want the list? I can give it to you tonight."

"Call my office in the morning. Work it out with someone else."

"Wait! I'm serious."

"Funny, I don't think you are."

"Give me another chance."

"Tell me: Why do you care so much?"

"When we meet I'll tell you everything. Then you'll understand." A pause. "I know you're not afraid, Bar-Lev. What have you got to lose?"

"My sleep."

"Oh come on. . . ." There was something coaxing in the man's voice this time, taunting too, that went beyond mere toughness and made him curious.

"How about a café on Ben Yehuda?"

"Uh uh. The Biblical Zoo."

"They lock up at sunset."

"You're a cop. The guard'll let you in."

"What about you?"

"I'll be there."

"So, are you a cop too?"

"Come alone, Bar-Lev. Midnight by the leopard's cage. If I don't show up within ten minutes, go home. Forget me. You'll know I'm just a fake."

Midnight by the leopard's cage—something appealingly melodramatic about that. Stupid, perhaps, to go alone, but even more stupid if anyone tried to harm him. The people who'd done the killings were certain to know that they couldn't stop an investigation by murdering the officer in charge.

Still, he put on the sweaty bullet-proof vest, tucked his Beretta in his belt, and, on his way out, stopped, went back, and picked up an extra clip.

The Biblical Zoo was in Romema, only a twelve-minute drive across the city that time of night. Here were collected all the animals mentioned in the Bible, each cage bearing an appropriate quotation: "He shall come as an eagle against the house of the Lord"; "Can the Ethiopian change his skin, or the leopard his spots?" He knew the place well, had taken Hagith there many times. A good refuge from the noise of the city, a nice quiet place to spend a Sabbath afternoon.

He circled the zoo, noted that in some places its exterior fence would not be difficult to breach. On one side shanties were built right up against it. On another he saw tears and holes.

This, he decided, would be his way in—no reason to use the entrance and alert the guard. He parked, armed his car alarm, walked slowly back to a place where he'd spotted a rip in the lower part of the fence. It was eleven-thirty. He looked both ways, then crouched, spread the fencing, and crawled in on his belly, being careful not to scratch his head or back.

He made his way cautiously into the park. The ground was sandy, the foliage dry. He caught the sharp smell of wild animals, then began to hear strange noises, bleets and howls ("The wolf also shall dwell with the lamb . . ."), squeals and hoots of exotic birds, and an occasional serpent's hiss.

The leopard's cage was between the bears and the storks, beside the pit that contained the lions. A popular place in the zoo. There were wooden benches before it erected under trees. A concrete path wound among the cages. Faint light cast from street lamps across the road filtered through the dusty leaves.

He chose the darkest most shadowed bench, quietly took a seat. As his eyes adjusted to the dark he tried to familiarize himself with the many sounds around. He differentiated among the grunts of the animals, the traffic, and the low-level background noise of late-night Jerusalem. After a while he felt confident he would be able to tell if anyone approached.

Eleven-fifty. There was a disturbance up the hill behind him between the beavers and baboons. The animals up there had suddenly turned silent. David froze, his body tensed. When he first heard the ping against the railing two feet to his right he thought someone had thrown a pebble or a stone. Then, a split-second later, when he heard it again he knew what it was, leapt off the bench, and dove face-first for the ground.

Pffm-pffm! Pffm-pffm! The sound of a Beretta .22, armed with a silencer, fired in rapid double bursts the way they taught trainees at the intelligence schools. As he crawled off the concrete walk into the trees, he knew there was more than one man firing. From the number of double bursts he decided there were two, possibly three, and that they were rapidly closing in.

He drew his own Beretta, fired once, blind, into the shrubbery, then caught a quick glimpse of a figure running, stooped, above him to his left. He was being flanked. He turned the other way, fired again, then rose to a crouch. Then he dashed, head low, to his right past the wild boar, toward a cage where a solitary water buffalo stood gazing out at him with stupid glassy eyes.

Yes, there were three of them, spread out in a line on the high ground, slowly forcing him down into the lower corner of the zoo. He wouldn't be able to crawl out under the fence down there; he wouldn't have the time. But if he could get one of them he might have a chance to break through and lose himself in the woods on the other side. Time now, he decided, to go on the offense, take one out, then try and slip by the other two. He was wondering just how he could do this when he heard a new sound, *burp!-burp!-burp!-burp!*, fire from an Uzi directed from the sector where he'd first entered the park. But this new fire was not aimed at him. Someone, an unseen ally, was there spraying the high ground with bullets, driving his attackers back.

"Hey! Hey, Bar-Lev! They're gone." He recognized the voice and it was not the voice from the phone. He crouched by the buffalo's cage until he saw Peretz, Uzi slung low over his shoulder, striding toward him down the path.

"It's okay. Really. I scared them off. Fuckers too chicken-shit to make a stand. . . ."

David stood up, furious. "This your set-up, Peretz?"

"Relax, Bar-Lev."

" 'Peretz and his boys.' All that phony crap about a 'list.' "

"For a guy who's just been rescued you're a pretty ungrateful son-of-a-bitch."

"You're telling me you were just passing by and just happened to hear the noise? Far as I'm concerned, this was your little show. Consider yourself under arrest."

"For what? Saving your life? Don't make me laugh." But Peretz was laughing anyway.

"You think it's funny?"

"Three guys trying to kill a cop—no, not funny at all. Look, I saw you were in trouble so I decided to intervene. I've been following you the last ten nights. Saw all the stuff you've been doing up on Berenice Street."

"Following me?"

"Bet your ass. I told you: I want this guy. I want to break his head."

"You're crazy!"

"Aren't you glad? If I weren't so crazy, you'd probably be lying dead right now down there by that cage full of baboons."

David shook his head. He believed him. Peretz was a killer, not a man who arranged elaborate practical jokes.

"You and I have to talk."

"Sure. Okay. But let's get the hell out of this zoo. Stinking animals. Another minute here and I'm going to puke."

From Peretz's apartment, David phoned Dov, woke him up, told him to have the zoo sealed off, and then at dawn to send in a team to search for slugs and shells. Then, while Peretz opened a bottle of red Carmel, he went out onto the terrace where he found an odd contraption, a cushioned three-seater swing hanging from a rusting frame.

He walked across the terrace, grasped hold of the railing, and stared out at Jerusalem. Across the Old City he could see the Dome of the Rock, at night a mysterious floating presence, its golden dome glowing softly beneath the three-quarters moon.

His hands were shaking even as he gripped the ironwork. A delayed reaction to the ambush, he knew. He'd been stupid to go to the zoo alone. *Maybe I'm getting soft*, he thought. *Stephanie warned me and I didn't listen. Taking it for granted that no one would go after me—that was really dumb.*

Peretz appeared with the wine and glasses, set them down, sprawled out on the swing and began to push himself back and forth. For a while David continued to stand at the railing. Then, as the creaking of the swing picked up in tempo, he turned and faced Peretz. He didn't bother to conceal his disgust.

"You were following me—*why?*"

"Nothing illegal in that."

"You said you'd be looking up your boys." Peretz nodded. "So, why follow me?"

"I want this guy real bad."

"If I find him, you don't get him, Peretz. Don't you realize that?" No answer. "Mess around with the police, you're going to be in a lot of trouble."

"Okay, Bar-Lev. Let's make a deal. I'm an officer. Put me in your unit. That shouldn't be too hard to arrange. We'll work together. The two of us will be unstoppable. We'll make a terrific team."

When David shook his head, Peretz stuck out his foot and stopped the swing. "Why not? Just tell me— why the fuck not?"

"First, I don't want to work with you. We hate each other's guts—remember? Second, the last thing I'm

PATTERN CRIMES • 171

going to do is give you a license to break somebody's head."

Peretz gazed at him, furious, then shrugged and poured himself a second glass of wine.

"Interesting bunch of guys there in the zoo tonight," he said casually. "First-class ambush tactics. Really had you by the balls. Course they couldn't do much to you, not with those baby pistols. Things are only good for close-up work. If they'd really wanted to nail you they'd have brought in bigger stuff."

"So what are you trying to tell me?"

Peretz hauled his legs up onto the swing, then lay down across the three seats and stared up at the sky. David could imagine the many seductions he must have engineered on this old, rusty, swinging outdoor bed.

"You see, Bar-Lev, I don't think they really wanted you dead. More like they wanted to scare you off. Or, since they probably know you're not the type who scares, wanted to let you know they know you're there and let you know that they're there too. Because those guys weren't amateurs. They were well-trained men. Elite military training. Could be veterans of a crack unit. Or Mossad. Or Shin Bet* guys. Or even active IDF Intelligence Corps. So Big-Shot, ever think of that?"

Sunday at noon he drove down to Ben-Gurion Airport to meet Anna's plane from Brussels. He used his credentials to enter the customs hall, and then, when he saw her, he watched her a while, savoring his joy in her return.

Yosef spotted him first. "David!" Her head snapped up. She saw him and then she smiled, and when she did he knew he was a very lucky man.

---

*Shin Bet: General Security Services, the Israeli equivalent of the FBI.

"We got fabulous reviews," Yosef said, as they started the drive up to Jerusalem. "Anna's gotten very strong. She doesn't play anymore like a talented kid. There's a new confidence. The audiences picked up on it and the better they liked her the better she played."

Yosef was sitting in back with the cello. Anna sat beside David, her fingers resting gently on his arm.

"So is this true?" David asked.

She grinned, then shrugged.

"Now she's ready for America," Yosef said. "Last time she impressed them. This time she'll knock them dead."

Later, when he began the climb into Judea, she and Yosef turned quiet. The hills glittered tan and gold. A lone hawk riding the thermals circled in the distance.

Finally Anna spoke. "Oh how I missed this place!"

"It's home," David said.

She nodded.

"And no one will ever take it away from us," Yosef said. "We won't let them. Ever."

Late that afternoon, after she had hung her clothes, and set up her music stand, and placed her cello in the corner and her pearl necklace on the little table beside the bed, she came to him and they made love. Afterward she slept against him, her head pressed to his shoulder, her body molded to his flank. At eight o'clock, they went out to East Jerusalem to eat.

At the Ummayyah she gazed around, taking in the boisterous atmosphere. As always the place was alive, waiters rushing about with skewers of meat, journalists huddled in booths with Palestinean politicians, Israeli tourist guides exchanging gossip with Roman Catholic archaeologists.

"Welcome back," he said, "to the Middle East."

She asked him about his case. He told her everything, and when he got to the part about the zoo, she reached across the table and grasped his hand.

"No footprints. Or rather too many. The ground there's a mess. We found plenty of shells too—theirs, Peretz's, and mine. A few slugs. They didn't match the ones in the lovers' heads."

"This is too dangerous, David."

He nodded. "Dangerous maybe, but not 'too dangerous'—not yet." He was tempted then to tell her about Stephanie's warning, but decided he had better not. He didn't want to explain why he'd gone to see her, or bring up Stephanie's speculations about Anna's past.

But then Anna surprised him. Without prompting, she told him that just before she'd called him from Paris, Titanov had phoned her at her hotel.

"From where?"

"Moscow. They won't let him travel. Not because they blame him for my defection, but to make an example of him, so that every musician understands he or she is responsible for the person he or she is sleeping with. But he didn't call to complain about that."

"Why did he call you?" David asked.

"To beg me to come back. For the good of the country, he said, but really, he said, because he still thought about me all the time." She shook her head. "I wasn't touched. I didn't believe a word of it. He's a selfish man. Still, he sounded desperate. I think he thinks that if he could persuade me to come back, they'd let him travel again."

"What did you tell him, Anna?"

"That I'm never coming back, that I never cared for him, and that I'm in love now with another man." She smiled. "He took it pretty well, said he knew all that but still he wanted me to come home. You see, he kept giving himself away. 'I *want* you, I *need* you,' never mind what I might want or need myself. He even asked me about you, seemed to know who you were. 'An Israeli cop,' he said, a little contemptuously, and then he asked how could I fall so low. 'You're not even Jewish,' he said. He was speechless when I told him I've been thinking I might convert."

"Is that true?"

"Could be." She gave him her best, most flashing smile. "One thing for sure—I'm going to start studying Hebrew seriously. Tomorrow I'm enrolling in a class."

"Susan Mills used a tourist photo shop, Samuelson's on King George next to that old German bookstore. They remember her well. She bought a hell of a lot of film." Micha spread out photocopies of the receipts on David's desk.

"They did her processing too," said Dov. "But when we add up the number of rolls she bought and the number she had developed, we come up twenty short. We found eight in her luggage and one in her camera. So there're still eleven unaccounted for."

"I doubt she came to Israel without film."

"Right. So *at least* eleven."

"Maybe she took them to another shop?"

"Doubt it. She was a creature of habit. Took the same bus from the Holyland every morning with a list of the places she wanted to see. Then she'd knock them off methodically, then she'd head downtown. She usually hit the photo shop at noon."

David nodded. "Okay—let's see what we've got. They know she has film on the accident, including shots of the guys in the van. They want that film. Their guy 'Hurwitz' has already quarreled with her about it. Now suppose someone new calls her up and apologizes, someone with a very sincere voice who speaks perfect English and claims he's Hurwitz's boss. She agrees—after all, she's a decent Christian lady only too glad to help out police when they're polite. This new guy drops by her hotel, picks her up, and takes her away to be tortured. But why torture her if she gave them what they wanted? No, that isn't how it went. They lured her out, she got suspicious, and when she figured out that they weren't cops, she didn't give them anything at all."

"So where's the film?"

"Maybe still at the shop?"

"It isn't. We checked."

"So maybe she *did* talk," Micha said.

"No. She didn't," Dov insisted.

David glanced at him, wondered if Dov's strong identification with Susan Mills was blinding him to real possibilities. David was all for the investigator immersing himself in the victim's life, so long as the immersion didn't prevent the investigator from facing unpleasant truths.

"Either way it doesn't matter," he finally said. "They took the film from her room, or, if it was still being developed, they found her receipt, took it back to the shop, and claimed the film as their own."

"They knew her at Samuelson's."

"Even when there's a name on the ticket they just look at the number. At least that's how they do it at the place I take my film."

"We'll go back there."

"This time make sure you talk to *all* the clerks. If someone else picked up those rolls, he wouldn't know she usually came by at noon. He'd probably go in late, around closing time when the staff is tired and gearing up for the bus ride home. . . ."

"So then what did Gati say?" Avraham's eyes gleamed as he gnawed on a piece of chicken.

David glanced over at Anna and winked. It had been her idea to invite his father for dinner. She had prepared a feast of chicken Tapaka, using her clothes iron to weigh down the chicken on the griddle.

"He said he thought that if people understood Gutman's background he might never have to go to trial. When I suggested to him that this was maybe a little naïve he didn't seem to understand. 'But don't you see? He's an atheist,' he said. 'Torahs mean nothing to him. Far as he was concerned he was just selling parchment. What's so bad about that?' "

Avraham threw both hands into the air. "This is our Great Military Genius?" David was pleased. The old man was enjoying himself, and, best of all, the two of them were getting along.

"You never told me you knew him, Father." David refilled his glass.

"I've never been one to reminisce." Avraham toasted Anna. "Some of the good old days were better than others."

"What kind of man is he?" Anna asked.

"Not nice. Not nice at all. A warrior. The kind who thrives on war."

"Didn't he go into politics?"

Avraham waved his hand. "He tried, but he didn't have appeal. Gati was a soldier's soldier. Wouldn't kowtow. Didn't know how to play the game." He reached for the platter, took a second piece of chicken. He smiled at Anna. "This is very good, my dear."

"Not kosher, I'm afraid."

"I told you—don't worry about that. You're an excellent cook." He toasted her again, then turned back to his son. "So," his eyes were excited, "what did you say to him next?"

"Told him it wouldn't matter if Gutman had been brokering stolen newspapers. He'd been caught in possession and for that he'd have to go to trial."

"You're right of course. A crime's a crime, a thief's a thief, and," he gave David a significant nod, "a detective, I suppose, is always a detective."

"What will happen to Gutman now?" Anna asked.

"Most likely he'll go to prison. I really can't see them letting him off. Unless, of course, there was something truly extenuating. I told Gati there's a classic method people use. They turn religious—put on a skullcap, grow a beard, and tell the judge about their new-found faith. But I told him that, unfortunately, due to the nature of Gutman's crime, I didn't see how this particular technique could possibly work."

Avraham roared with laughter. Then he wiped his mouth. "You did well, my boy. I only wish I'd been there—just to see Yigal Gati's stricken face."

The remainder of the dinner continued to be fun, Anna was pleased, and when Avraham thanked her and said good night the two of them embraced. In the car, as David started the drive back to Me'a Shearim, Avraham complimented him on having found such a fine companion.

"You should maybe consider marrying her?" he asked tentatively.

David was amused. "She isn't Jewish."

"So what? You can marry in Cyprus. Isn't that what people do?"

They drove the rest of the way in silence. When they arrived at Hevrat Shas and Avraham opened the car door, David saw an old religious man wandering up the street and then he thought he saw his father wince. "Those missing files I mentioned . . ."

"Yes. I meant to ask—"

"Don't bother yourself. Turns out I was wrong. Blumenthal's garage was ransacked but nothing was taken. Whoever broke in was probably looking for valuables. When he didn't find any I think he just got mad and threw around my papers in a fit of spite."

After his father disappeared into his building, David chopped his hand against the steering wheel.

Damn! Why does he lie to me? He pressed his bruised hand against his mouth.

There had been a temporary clerk who had worked at Samuelson's Photo Shop during the height of the April tourist season. A veteran of Lebanon, stoned half the time, according to Mr. Samuelson—nice, but not someone he'd wanted to keep on.

Dov found him working for a rug cleaning firm that serviced the finer homes in Rehavia. He showed him Susan's picture. Yes, the young veteran remembered her, she'd been in the shop, had bought lots of film and brought it back to be developed. But she'd returned to America earlier than expected—he remembered that because her nephew had come in with one of her claim tickets to pick up her final batch of prints.

"Nephew? Her *Israeli* nephew?"

"Yeah, an apologetic kind of kid. Said his aunt was concerned, didn't want to stick the shop, and had made him promise to pick up her film and pay off her account."

Dov ran out to his car for his IdentiKit, spent an hour with the veteran working up a composite of Susan's "nephew." When he brought the composite in David studied it. An ordinary looking young man, clean-cut and nondescript. "Nice Jewish boy," David said.

Yosef Barak had spoken of a new authority in Anna's playing, a new confidence. Yet now, when David watched her practice, he sensed something troubled in the way she played.

"Is anything the matter?" he asked her one morning.

She shook her head. "No. Why do you think there is?"

"You seem . . . I don't know, disturbed somehow. I just wondered if you were having trouble. After such a big success in Europe to come back here could bring you down."

"Oh, David—this isn't a backwater. Jerusalem's my home." She frowned. "You know I set high goals for myself. Sometimes I think Yosef is too quick to praise."

"So there is something?"

"Just concentration. Don't worry, I'll get it back. All I have to do is," she smiled, "you know: 'practice, practice. . . .' " She kissed him on his neck.

Avraham called. "Something I forgot to tell you. We laughed a lot about Gati the other night, but later, when I thought about it, the approach he made to you rang false. He and Gutman always hated each other and from what I've learned there's never been a reconciliation. So the question is: Why is he trying to get Gutman off? I don't know the answer, but it's something you might think about. Employ an old Kabbalistic principle: Look for the hidden cause because the surface is never real."

He went to Rafi, laid out the case, explained why he thought the worst was yet to come:

"Okay, Peretz is a fruitcake. But now I think his crazy forger theory is correct. My symposium idea was good, but not that good—it was a shot in the dark, not an airtight trap. So a certain 'friend,' whom Peretz refuses to name, a guy he trusts who stuck with him when times were tough, tips him off there's a killer using his signature and there's going to be an open discussion at the Rubin Academy about what this killer might be like. Naturally Peretz goes. But we don't notice him. He sits there and listens like a normal member of the audience. Then five days later someone in a dark blue van picks up Yael Safir at the Ben Gurion hitching stop, and just about the time she's being killed and dumped I'm meeting a guy named Ephraim Cohen, who just happens to have been a friend of my brother, and who works for one of the covert services, or so he says. Ephraim wants to pass along a tip about Peretz from an unnamed source whom he claims was helping us in that Mossad-owned video truck. So we go after Peretz, he's a logical suspect, and if he hadn't gone to Egypt we might still be trying to break him down. You see, Rafi—it's much too slick. Peretz is tipped off about the symposium, he goes, and then I'm tipped off that he was there."

"You think this guy, Cohen—?"

"Yeah, I think he's part of it. Wanted me to think he was Mossad, but I checked him out and it turns out he's Shin Bet. Which means his story about passing on a 'tip' from the video technician was bullshit, something he made up to sucker me in."

"What about the ambush at the zoo? How did they find out that you were onto them?"

"Our inquiry about Hurwitz—that must have triggered the alarm. When they heard I was asking about their cop-who-didn't-exist, they realized I was getting close. Which means, far as I'm concerned, that they're wired in here too."

Rafi tensed up. "That's a pretty awful suggestion, David. Hard to go along with it unless you bring me proof."

"Oh, I'll be bringing you proof, you know that. For now it's just a theory."

"Awful. . . ."

"Why resist it? You're always bitching about corruption. Now, faced with the possibility of a really supreme example of official rot, why do you want to turn away?"

"Look, dammit—!" Rafi was angry.

"You look! Everyone knows Shin Bet has murdered prisoners. Everyone knows about Mossad assassination squads. A superpatriot like Peretz recruits violent sociopaths to staff out his counterterror squad. High embassy officials in Washington recruit American Jews to spy on their own government. So how come, when I mention the possibility this thing could reach in here, you suddenly lock up your mind? Why, Rafi? What's so damn sacred about the cops? We're the garbagemen, remember. So maybe we stink a little too."

Rafi sat stiff in his chair. David was glad Sara Dorfman wasn't in the room. "Remember that girl I was going with last fall?"

"The American *shikse*. Yeah. I never liked her."

"She's an agent."

"They all are."

"She gets into the sack with people in the cabinet."

"What's that got to do—?"

"She tried to warn me off. Said she heard I was up to my ass in something big and that if I kept on the way I was going I could end up getting hurt. I'm telling you, Rafi, this thing feels big, feels like it's getting ready to explode. I'm telling you that, now, up front, and that I don't like being set up for a shoot, and I don't like being shot at, and that I'm following this wherever it goes. There've been murders, innocent people killed, and no matter what the reason turns out to be, it's not going to be anywhere good enough. Not for me."

"THE RIGHTEOUS MARTYR"

BIG SUR.
TWO MONTHS BEFORE . . .

They'd just rolled away the scaffolding. The enlargers, a crew of Italians from San Francisco, were busy packing up their gear.

"She's begging now," Rokovsky said.

"So let her beg," Targov replied.

"It's so pathetic. I wish you'd relent. Maybe just this once."

Targov stood, his dogs crouching by his heels, surveying the big sculpture. His second model, the one one-third human scale, was dwarfed now by the full-sized piece.

He glanced at Rokovsky, so stern and gaunt. Pale and skeletal, he looked his part as *homme de confiance*. "I know just what she'll say if I let her in: 'So big, Sasha. I had no idea! But perhaps a little grand, don't you think? Not pretentious. The Great Form-Giver could never be! But maybe just a trifle . . . hmmm. . . . fancy? Grandiose?'"

"Since you know what she's going to say, what difference does it make?"

"It brings me down, Tola. I'm feeling really good just now."

He moved slowly to the large window, trailed by the dogs, then turned back suddenly to confront the work.

"Big impact," he said. "Good shadows, especially

in full light. Very strong, but California light, Pacific light—how much different will the light be there? We don't know. Not yet. No way to calculate. A couple of days smoothing and it'll be ready for the foundry. By the way, I'm driving up to Palo Alto in the morning. Please make sure the car's gassed up. Better arrange for a truck too, and contact our friends at the Israeli Consulate. I want them to see the piece before it's cast."

He gazed again at the enormous overpowering thing he'd wrought. He'd never done anything like it, had had no notion such an image had been harbored in his brain. Part human, part abstract, it would rise, "The Righteous Martyr," a black bronze vision from a black basalt pedestal, his signature against the sky.

At midnight, a pounding on the door. The dogs leapt, then turned to him, their shaggy slobbering faces inquiring whether they should bark. For four months he'd been living in the studio, sleeping on his day bed, eating at his workbench, rarely venturing to the main house. No distractions, just work sixteen hours a day, his only recreation once-a-week fucking sessions with Maureen. Recently she'd taken to dressing up in black silk underwear, then prancing in time to Polish marches while he sat watching from her moldy couch, his cock a cylinder of steel.

It was Irina. He recognized her style: fierce pounding alternated with whimpers. He went to the door. "All right. I hear you. What do you want?"

"Can't sleep, Sasha. Why are you so cruel? I want to see it. Please. . . ."

"When it's finished—I told you."

"Oh, now. Please. Please. . . ."

Christ! She's impossible! He opened the door, she inserted her foot, and then, when he saw her face, he knew he'd been suckered once again.

"Not a word," he warned her. "A quick glance

from here. Then out! Back to the house! I'm exhausted. I need my sleep."

She nodded to assure him she agreed and that she
understood his artist's temperament. He opened the
door all the way and then stepped back. She stared at
the sculpture. He stared at her.

"It's so big, Sasha. And so—"

He brought his finger to his lips. "Shut up!"

She clamped her mouth, then suddenly brought up
her hand to shield her eyes. "Oh no!"

"What's the matter?"

She was frightened. "The face!"

"What about it? *What?*"

"It's him!"

"Who?"

"Sergei, Sasha. Sergei. Just as he was then. But suffering, suffering so, the boot on his neck, his face
ground down into the dust. . . ."

Today Rokovsky was bringing the Israelis—he must
greet, present, explain, persuade. He would pay for
everything, the casting and the pedestal. But in return
he would demand a major site.

Jerusalem. He had never been there but for weeks
he'd poured over photographs and maps. He had a
vision of it: capital city of the world, central city, the
world's heart. City of martyrs, temples, passions, cru-
cifixions, dreams, redemptions, and now an enormous
garden embellished with works of art. He had created
"The Righteous Martyr" especially for this place. His
journey there, accompanying the work, would be his
chance to put the tortured past to rest.

THE
ABATTOIR

While he groped for the phone Anna turned over and faced the other way.

"Yeah?" He glanced at his watch. It was a little past 2 A.M.

"Got him!"

"What?" As he blinked and tried to clear his brain, David realized he was speaking to Peretz. "Been looking for you. Where've you been?"

"Got him. One of my old boys. Questioning him all night. Don't think he's going to last."

David sat up. "What the hell are you talking about?"

"Guy who did the killings. So far he's confessed that much. Funny thing though—says he wasn't trying to pin them on me. Seems it was lack of imagination, old habits die hard. He used our old unit signature because he couldn't think up a new one on his own."

No, that's wrong. . . .

". . . took a lot to get that out of him, and that he was hired, the executioner. Thing is, Bar-Lev, much as he doesn't like the pain, and he doesn't . . ." Peretz must have turned his receiver to the room, because now David could hear some kind of whimpering in the background. ". . . still he'd rather suffer than tell me who's behind this and what it's all about."

"You're crazy!"

Anna turned and buried her face in her pillow.

David cupped his hand over the mouthpiece, got out of bed, and carried the phone into the kitchen.

"Listen carefully, Peretz. You can't do this by yourself. If he dies on you, you'll be a murderer. Stop right now, tell me where you are, and we'll handle this the proper way."

A pause, and then a weary: "You don't understand—he was one of my boys." David shook his head: the old insanity. "I trained him and now he's let me down. I've got the right to waste him if I want."

"Tell me where you are. There's stuff going on here that you don't know about. Who tipped you off about the Rubin seminar?"

"Never mind that shit. Check this out. Mei Naftoah. There's a restaurant there, at the end of the road."

"Yeah, I know it. Eat there all the time." *What a maniac!* "Listen, Peretz, you were set—"

". . . down the slope, below the third house from the end. Smashed-in roof, but there're a couple rooms left intact. He says that's where he killed them. There ought to be some evidence. Says the victims were brought to him there, he cut them, then the people who brought them took their bodies away. Says he worked over the nun when she was still alive but the rest of them he killed right off. Oh, oh . . . he's moaning again." David heard the moans. "Got to get back to work. I'll call you around seven, see how you made out."

"He's lying, Peretz. You *were* set up."

But the line was already dead.

A strange place, Mei Naftoah, especially at night. The west side of Jerusalem suddenly ends, there's a gas station etched in orange neon, then a large dense housing project, five bleak buildings on a ledge, hulking silhouettes against the sky. Below the ledge a steep incline, then a rocky slope crisscrossed with ancient terraces. On this slope there are remnants of an Arab village, a few old stone houses abandoned at the time of Independence. Beyond are the Judean hills.

An occasional olive tree, a cave, discarded broken-up tractor tires, a few burned-out rusting husks of cars. David found the place mesmerizing; he sensed a haunting desolation. The Iraqi-Jewish restaurant where he and Dov had lunched, where he'd first broached his theory of "hidden symmetry," was an oasis at the end of this narrow twisting dusty path.

A light mist filled the valley. From out in the hills the howls of jackals. He smelled wood smoke, perhaps from a Bedouin camp. The air was so still he could hear Liederman strike a match a hundred meters behind where they'd left him to stand guard on the road.

Dov was at his side. Uri had gone ahead to find the house. Shoshana trailed carrying their radio. Micha was on night duty, watching the house of Amit Nissim.

"David, I'm going down," Uri called to them. He'd said he'd heard these old houses were sometimes used by hikers seeking shelter and by narcotics dealers as places to stash supplies of dope. David saw the beam of Uri's flashlight play upon a narrow passage of old stone stairs. Third house from the end, Peretz had said. When he and Dov reached the third house they found both walls were open. They walked through, then followed Uri to the house below, the one with the smashed-in roof.

Charred beams hung above them, black bars cutting across the gray night sky.

"In here," Uri said. "Doesn't smell too good." Dov probed the ruin with his flashlight, fixed it on a doorway.

"He mentioned a couple rooms left intact," David said. Then he moved forward, afraid of what he was going to find, part of him wishing he wouldn't find it, hoping Peretz was wrong.

Immediately he heard the flies, hundreds, thousands,

he thought. The buzzing stunned him, angry, like a roar; he wanted to shut it out, press his hands against his ears. The smell was bad too, sweet putrescence, a rot both lucious and corrupt. Uri and Dov played their flashlights upon the walls, then their beams converged in one of the corners. The flies were there, clustered, picking and licking at splash marks on the stones and an old decaying mattress half torn up and stained.

"David!" It was Shoshana calling from the outer room.

"Don't come in," he warned her.

"See the clothing," Dov whispered. Some soiled garments were piled haphazardly near the corner. Dov swung his flashlight back to the mattress. Something metallic gleamed. "Could be a knife." He moved closer, lifted one edge of the mattress with his foot. The blade of a commando knife was caught in Uri's beam. "He did the cutting here," Dov said.

Uri fled the room. David could hear him retching outside, then being comforted by Shoshana. Sickened by the noise and smell, David struggled to suppress his rage. Susan Mills had died here; these walls had echoed with her screams. She and Schneiderman and Ora Goshen, Halil Ghemaiem and Yael Safir had been forced into this room, pushed down into this corner, slashed, bled, then stripped and laid out on this horrible mattress to be marked. This was the killing room, the scene of suffering, where pain had been endured and flesh had been rent and blood had flowed—blood which, now congealed, was food for flies.

He sent the others home, except for Liederman who asked to stay up on the road to man the barricade. Now he waited outside, sitting silent on a low stone wall while the forensic specialists went about their work. Every so often one of them would come out, pull off his surgical mask, breathe deeply, and stare at the hills. Then after several minutes he would grimace and return to the gruesome task.

Just before dawn the unit chief appeared, a lanky middle-aged American-born immigrant known around the Russian Compound as "Tex." He squatted down and lit a cigarette. David had known this gentle man since he'd joined the police; now for the first time he found him unnerved.

"We found the clothes of four of them. We don't know what the Arab boy wore. Blood's mingled but we'll sort it out. Tissue cells all over the place so, unfortunately, we can't spray and kill the flies. We'll work on the knife at the lab. Probably do that myself. It may take us all day to get this place cleaned up."

Tex stubbed out his cigarette, then shook his head. Moisture filled his eyes. "Worst crime scene I've seen in twenty-five years. You find caring at a murder site sometimes, David—even when a man rips up his wife. But there was no caring here. Nothing here but butchery." He shook his head again and looked away.

Peretz called a little after seven. This time he spoke rapidly.

"I'll make this fast, Bar-Lev. I'm on only for a minute so don't bother to try a trace."

Rebecca had already alerted the police operators; on the old-fashioned Jerusalem telephone system a trace took four minutes at least.

"Okay, it was the place. Victims' clothes were there."

"So he *was* telling the truth. . . ." Something almost lethargic now in Peretz's tone.

"Can I have him?"

"Won't do you any good. He's been terminated. The interrogation was harsh."

Terminated!

". . . signed him, too. Seemed appropriate. He was nothing but an animal. Claimed to the end he didn't

know who hired him. If he knew I think he would
have squawked." A pause. "I'll have to hide him now.
If they find him dead they'll know we've gotten close.
'The closer we come the more dangerous we are to
them and the more vigorously they'll retaliate. You
and I need each other now. . . ."

David's fury suddenly broke loose. "Hell we do! No
alliances! You're the animal, cocksucker. And I'm
going to nail you—"

Click!

"He's off," Rebecca said.

David spun around his chair and faced the wall.

Rafi's large sad eyes sparkled with incredulity. "He
spent the night *torturing* the guy? You don't know
who he is?"

"Don't even know what city they were in. Somewhere on the northern coast."

Rafi leaned back. "David, this is getting out of
hand."

"You're telling me. I've felt helpless for a week."

"Sooner or later Peretz has got to show."

"He doesn't 'got' to do anything, Rafi. He's a law
unto himself. He knows how to live off rough terrain.
He can bury himself in wilderness. Way beyond fruitcake now. He's a sadistic murderer. I told you that
before."

"Yes," Rafi nodded, "so you did." He reached
beneath his glasses and rubbed his eyes. "So, okay,
now that you know where the killing was done, what
are you doing about it?"

"Canvassing for witnesses. Look, Rafi, the time's
come. I want to confront Ephraim Cohen."

Rafi shook his head. "I'm not going into an interservice thing, not until you come up with something
hard. Go in on a bluff and we're certain to lose the
case. Shin Bet takes over and we're out of it for good.

We'll be lucky to read about it ten years from now when some former cabinet minister sneaks it into his memoirs. There'll be a Knesset investigation and a whitewash, so even then we still won't know what it was about. . . ."

At least, he thought, walking out of Rafi's office, Rafi now acknowledged that the case might have roots in some rogue bureau of the government.

At noon, returning home for a shave and a change of clothes, he paused just outside his door. He could hear Anna and Yosef talking inside. Yosef's voice was patient but Anna's sounded petulant.

"I'm very concerned," Yosef said. "And I don't understand. It's not all that difficult."

"It's difficult for me," she said.

"Why don't you try that part again."

She played several bars on her cello, then Yosef stopped her.

"What's the matter now?"

"You're playing notes, not music."

"Damn, damn, damn. . . ."

"Listen, Anna—why don't we quit for the day. This tension isn't doing us any good." He paused. "Perhaps it's not my place, but still I must ask you: Is there some trouble you're having now in your personal life? With David maybe? Or someone else?"

Distressed at the silence that followed, David withdrew down the stairs. It was best to leave them alone to work it out, he thought. He wouldn't shave today.

It was Moshe Liederman who pointed the way to the young vagabond threesome who lived in the broken deserted house across the gorge from the abattoir. No road led down there. It was a mile and a half by twisting path from the gas station on the heights. Like the killing house it was a ruin but most of its rooms were roofed. No outward sign of habitation; illegal to live there anyway. But Liederman was thorough, for the first time in his police career he was working a case with cops who cared, so he checked out every building in Mei Naftoah and at three that afternoon found the bedrolls and water bottles and remnants of a fire.

He radioed this news to David, who brought along the rest of the team. When David sniffed the embers he recognized the fire he'd smelled the night before.

The contents of the bedrolls indicated two males and a female. David called for Shoshana, then sent Micha to replace her as guard and back-up on the road. The five of them split into two teams—David and Shoshana; Liederman, Uri, and Dov—then took refuge in broken outbuildings on either side and waited patiently for the night.

One of the males turned up first, but to David's surprise not from Jerusalem. He appeared suddenly from the west, wrapped in an Arab cloak, an apparition out of the stark and desolate hills.

"An Arab?"

David watched him. "Israeli," he whispered. "Maybe a little stoned."

As this first figure reached the ruin, a second young man and a girl, also cloaked, appeared.

Shoshana blinked. "Someone giving a party out there? Where the hell are they coming from?"

They waited two more hours until the house was silent. The three had built another little fire, and again the smoke hung in the air and the jackals howled. Fortunately no dogs lurked about to give them away as David and Shoshana crawled closer in. David wanted to surprise the three but didn't know whether they stood watches or slept in separate rooms, and, most important, whether, if they were cornered, they would make a stand and fight.

At a quarter past twelve, Uri, Dov, and Liederman were forty meters away, approaching from the other side. David had been through many busts but each time he felt the same tension and fear—tension waiting for the best moment to strike, fear of not striking quickly enough so that the instinct to resist could be vanquished even before it was aroused.

He gave the signal and a moment later the five of them were galloping across the stony fields. David could feel hormones of urgency rushing through his blood.

The young people did not fight and that was fortunate. When David yanked the first boy from his sleeping bag, Dov found a 9 mm. Browning automatic, clip filled and bullet breached, beneath the rolled-up cloak he'd been using as a pillow. The boy glared. His hair was cut short, he wore a Hebrew University T-shirt and gym shorts with a faded stripe. When they yanked his wrists behind his back there was a moment when his pale eyes showed pain. He squeezed them shut as he was cuffed; when he opened them again they showed injured pride.

The naked couple sprawled together on the bedrolls in the second room gazed up at them perplexed. The boy was dark and bearded, the girl beautiful—fine features, fine pert breasts, magnificent flowing golden hair. When the boy reached toward his clothes Uri squatted beside him and leveled his pistol at his head. Their weapons, another Browning and a small Beretta, lay beneath their jeans.

David yelled for Shoshana. She ran in, took the girl away, and a moment later, when David turned on his radio, Micha announced he'd intercepted a second girl carrying groceries walking down the path. From the time the five of them had entered the house until the four were captured only twenty-five seconds had elapsed.

194 • William Bayer

Shoshana came back, pushing the blond. She was still nude. She didn't try to cover up but planted herself arrogantly with her legs apart.

"She won't dress," Shoshana said.

"Not even underwear?"

When David smiled the girl spat at his feet.

"Angry child," David said. "Okay, go naked if you like. We're going to take you in anyway. You'll be smart at least to wear some shoes." He signaled Shoshana to take her away, then turned back to the bearded boy. "You want to go naked too?"

The boy was shaking. "Who betrayed us?"

"Who sold you the pistols?"

The boy turned to the window. His girl friend was dressing angrily. When he saw the second girl, the one who'd been carrying the groceries, his mouth trembled and his eyes turned wet.

"Georgie, wasn't it? She's the traitor. It was her. *Wasn't it?*"

"Better get dressed," David said.

Separate the suspects, put them into tiny harshly lit interrogation rooms, then begin the questioning. Use every little piece you can wrench from one to intimidate the others, make them think their friends have talked. Play on their fears. Tire them out. Suggest betrayal is in the air. Create an atmosphere of insecurity so that their old camaraderie will lapse and they'll begin to think that the only people they can trust are their new friends, the interrogators, who, though they have a job to do, will try and help them beat the rap.

Soon a story emerged. Georgie, the girl with the groceries, was an American. Slave of the other three, she was full of the resentment every slave must feel. She ran errands, brought in food and water, was mad for the boy who slept downstairs. They had never trusted her; now they thought she was their betrayer.

So go ahead, Georgie: What have you got to lose? Betray.

They were drug dealers, she said, intermediaries. They bought from smugglers, who brought the stuff in from Lebanon, then sold it to street dealers they met out in the hills. No, there weren't any narcotics in the house—they stashed everything in caves. Actually she didn't know all that much; she'd only met them a week before.

David ran their names through the police computer. Information was rapidly returned. The lovers were kibbutzniks: Zvi had served with the paratroopers and had studied biology; Hannah was a triage nurse who'd dropped out of medical school the year before. Aaron, the boy Georgie was in love with, the tough one with the crewcut who slept with the loaded gun, was the only son of Brazilian immigrants. He had studied mathematics at Giv'at Ram, had served in a tank recon unit, and had fought and been wounded in Lebanon.

Disillusioned youths, David thought. But he sensed something in Zvi—a connection in his head between women and betrayal. Work on that, he decided. Of the three in the house Zvi was the one who would bargain. Hannah was stubborn, in the midst of some kind of irresolvable rebellion, and Aaron was just too tough.

"That Hannah," he began, "quite a girl. Refusing to dress. Spitting fire." David laughed. "Funny what a couple of hours of stressful interrogation will do. Now she and Shoshana are gabbing away."

Zvi glared at him.

"We're not narcs, you know. Personally I don't give a shit about drugs. A person wants to abuse his body, that's his choice. He wants to be an asshole, let him. He wants to OD—good riddance. Does Israel need more self-destructive creeps? I don't think so. Do you?"

He walked behind the boy, placed his hands on his shoulders. "It's okay, son. Georgie didn't lead us to you. Matter of fact we backed into your little operation by mistake." He circled Zvi again, then sat down, looked hard at him, and shook his head. "We were after something else, but we found you." He shrugged. "Now we can't just let you go. Especially not after Hannah spilled."

Zvi studied him. "You're bluffing. She didn't say anything."

"Have it your way. But you know better. The women always squeal."

Another glare.

"It's true. They get lighter sentences, the courts are more disposed toward them. We point this out. Then, if they're smart, and most of them are, they do what they have to do. When the chips are down people always think about themselves."

"Bastard!"

"Don't be pissed at me, Zvi. I didn't do anything. I wasn't even looking for you. You trusted her, she squawked. Seems to me that's more your fault than mine." David shook his head again. "Georgie folded fast. Why shouldn't she? She knows Aaron doesn't give a damn about her, just uses her as something nice to fuck. Give Hannah credit. She cares for you but in the end she made the intelligent move. Now it's your turn. Are you bright enough to take it? I wonder if you are. I got odds from the other guys that you'll be the final hold-out, that, in the end, you'll be the one who burns. . . ."

A half hour more of this kind of merciless talk and Zvi was trying desperately to hold back his tears.

". . . maybe you *can* help us," David said. "You don't have to betray anyone. There's another abandoned house on the opposite slope. Bad stuff going on in there a couple of months ago. People coming and going, mostly late at night. Did you see anything? If you did, and you tell me about it . . . well, maybe, we can work a deal."

A pause while Zvi calculated. He spoke tentatively at first. "We thought they were cops."

"Really? Why?"

"I don't know. Aaron thought so. He said it was something about the way they moved."

"So?"

"So we laid low a while. We watched them."

"And?"

"We decided they weren't cops."

"So then what did you do?"

"We thought they might be a rival group using the place occasionally to do a trade."

"Did you go over there?"

"Aaron did. Got spooked too. Wanted us to move. But then . . . well, we decided to stick around. And after that they didn't come back."

David watched him. "There's something you're not telling me, Zvi."

"He followed them."

"Who?"

"Aaron."

"How?"

"On his scooter."

"Where?"

"To a private house."

David tried not to let his excitement show. "Which house?"

Zvi shrugged. "You'll have to ask him. He didn't say."

The simplest cleanest deals are always best. When David put it to Aaron, he let him know there'd be no compromise: "So far no one knows we've picked you up. We haven't contacted the Narc Unit and if you work with us we won't. The four of you go free. We never met you, we don't know you and, frankly, we don't ever want to see you again. Naturally we keep the pistols. In return you show us where you followed the people from that ruin across the gorge. That's it. Take it or leave it, tough guy. You got one minute to make up your mind. . . ."

55 Lover of Zion Street. One of the best buildings on perhaps the best street in residential Jerusalem. David knew it well; it was just a block from his father's old house on Disraeli. He'd passed it hundreds of times when he was growing up.

An elegant, subdivided, four-story building with two entrances and an attached garage. An ornate wrought iron wall facing the street with a perfectly trimmed privet hedge behind. A gate for pedestrians and a second bigger one for cars. A small garden built around a mature jacaranda whose spreading branches cut the moonlight that fell upon carefully manicured beds of flowers.

He turned to Aaron. "So what did you see?"

"One guy got out, opened the gate. Then the other drove in the van. The first locked up again."

"How long did you wait?"

"About a minute."

"They didn't see you?"

"My scooter's very quiet."

"That's it? Nothing else?"

Aaron shook his head.

David looked at him, reached out, grasped hold of his hair, pulled him close, and stared into his eyes. "Don't ever pack a pistol again." He pushed him away. Then Dov pulled him out of the car and shoved him from behind.

"Leave Jerusalem," David called after him. "Tell

the others. You're finished here. All of you. We see you again we feed you to the narcs."

He had dropped Dov off at Gillo, was back now in Abu Tor cruising En Rogel Street, searching for a place to park. He found one up the block, locked the car, then walked back slowly toward number sixteen. It was 4 A.M.

He was aware, at last, of his exhaustion. He was filthy from the stake-out, sweaty from half a night spent in humid interrogation rooms. He'd been up twenty-four hours straight, talking with Peretz, crawling around a deserted Arab village, breaking down a gang of drug dealers, and now, finding his thinking scattered and slow, he longed for uninterrupted sleep.

He paused at the front door of his building trying to recall the combination. Three-three-five-something. He hesitated. The dogs . . . he didn't hear the neighborhood dogs which always barked when he came home late.

A squeaking sound, like a car door being opened. He had a bad feeling as he turned back toward the street. The cars all looked familiar, cars of people in his building and of neighbors who lived on either side. Then, when he noticed the boxlike silhouette of the large dark van parked on the other side, saw that its side panel door was open, realized he'd driven past it and then passed it again on foot just seconds before, he cursed and dove for the bushes beside the stoop. A second later there erupted the sounds of war.

Burp!-burp!-burp! Burp!-burp!-burp! Submachine-gun fire ripped across the front of number sixteen biting out little chips of stone. It ripped back again, lower this time, stitching the masonry just above his head. The dogs started to bark, all of them, at once. Chips fell on him as he drew his pistol and started firing back. Something hot touched his cheek. Wild barking.

Another burst of fire. He saw sparks coming from the dark open back compartment of the van, then a figure crashing out headfirst onto the street. The panel door slammed shut. The engine started. The van peeled off toward the corner. It squealed as it turned left at the Ariel Hotel, then roared its way south along Hevron, fading finally until the only sound left was the desperate mad cacophony of the dogs.

Lights came on in the building next door. David heard windows being opened. When he glanced up at his own apartment, he saw the old lady who lived on the floor above leaning over her balcony staring down at him, worry and fascination on her face. It was a familiar expression; he'd seen it many times: fright and curiosity and also something else, that strange twist of the mouth that his father called "the guilty grimace of the survivor."

He pulled himself out of the shrubbery, went to the intercom, buzzed Anna, then touched his burning cheek. He licked his finger and tasted blood. A small piece of stone had cut his face.

"David! What happened?"

"An ambush. Don't worry, Anna. I'm fine. I really am. Please call Rafi for me. Ask him to come over and ask him to send a crew."

He walked slowly back into En Rogel Street toward the place where the van had been parked. He was looking for the figure he thought he'd seen crash out of the back of the van. In the shadow of another car he saw the form of a man lying face down on the pavement. He drew closer, observed large bloody tears in his shirt and that his hands were handcuffed behind his back. He studied him a while, then crouched and touched his neck. Stiff and cold. He turned him over. For a moment he didn't recognize him—features slack, face drained, the edge of anger gone, Peretz looked

like any middle-aged Israeli male, eyes sad and woe-
ful, who'd been dead for several hours.

Precisely at noon, all five permanent members of Pattern Crimes hit 55 Lover of Zion Street hard. Shoshana
and Micha, on instructions from David, went straight
for the garage. There they found a dark blue Chevrolet
van. It was empty but the key was in the ignition.
Shoshana started it, backed it up fast, but before she
could get it out to the street, two men ran toward her,
waving Shin Bet IDs. They blocked the driveway and,
when Micha Benyamani ordered them to move, shoved
him aside, then shut and padlocked the driveway gate.

It was a stand-off in the ground floor apartment too.
When David burst in with Uri and Dov, they found
two men and an attractive young woman in a mini-
mally furnished office. One of the men, stocky and
bearded, was speaking on the phone; the other, young
and musclebound, was flirting with the woman who sat
typing at one of the desks.

When the bearded man saw them he snapped some
kind of alert to his caller, hung up, and faced David
with a sneer.

"Out of bounds here, policeman. This is a Security
Services squad."

"Over against the wall. All three of you—hands
behind your heads. You're under arrest."

Nobody moved. The two men exchanged a look.
The girl peered around nervously.

"We're Shin Bet, asshole," the bearded man said.
"Get your people out of here."

"Who the fuck you calling asshole?" Uri asked.

"He tries anything, Uri, kick him in the balls."

"Your oaf kicks anyone I'm shooting off his foot."
The younger man had drawn a pistol. The beard stepped
forward and planted his feet apart.

"Your illustrious career has just ended, Bar-Lev. Nobody messes with us. Especially no stinking cops."

Uri continued toward him. The beard held his ground.

"We stink, huh?"

"Take pictures," David ordered. Then he picked up the phone.

While he spoke to Rafi, and Dov brought out his camera, Uri turned suddenly on the younger man, flipped him onto his back, disarmed him, and cuffed his wrists. The girl screamed. The beard attacked Dov, trying to rip the camera from his hands. Uri jumped on him from behind. When the beard, too, was subdued and cuffed and the girl had obeyed their order, placing her hands behind her head, Dov took careful mugshots of the three of them, then went outside and took more portraits of the goons blockading the gate.

Ephraim Cohen arrived first. Rafi, who'd used a squad car with a siren, was only seconds behind. Their confrontation took place in the driveway. David, who now had the two Shin Bet men sitting back-to-back, listened from the door.

"She's not taking that van," Ephraim warned.

"She's taking it," Rafi said. "And my forensic guys are going over it."

Shoshana sat smiling in the driver's seat; she'd locked herself inside.

"Listen, Shahar," Cohen said, trying to strike a reasonable tone, "you don't bust in on us. If you think you've got good cause, go to a judge and get a warrant. Until then pull your people out."

"I don't need a warrant, not when my top unit chief is ambushed."

Cohen stared at Rafi with withering scorn. "My guys get ambushed all the time."

"We think it was a couple of your goons."

"You think!"

"What are you afraid of, Cohen?"

"You're on my turf, Shahar. Get off of it."

"You've got no 'turf.' "

"Oh no? We'll see."

They came inside together to use the phone after agreeing that their respective bosses would have to talk.

"Why the handcuffs?" Cohen asked.

Rafi nodded to David, who nodded to Uri, who unlocked the cuffs and set the two men loose. As soon as Uri stepped back the beard lunged for him. Uri kicked him in the shins. He howled. The girl screamed again.

"Control your creeps!" Rafi yelled. Ephraim Cohen herded the three of them out the door. Then, while Rafi phoned District Superintendent Latsky, Ephraim approached David with a smile.

"Last time we met I did you a favor."

"Yeah, you set up Peretz."

"That was a good tip, David."

"So why did you kill him? Is that what you do when one of your crummy operations falls apart?"

Rafi motioned David aside.

"Don't insult him. You shouldn't have done it like this. You should have checked with me."

"I would have, Rafi, but if we'd gone for a warrant they'd have heard about it and buried the van."

"Cohen's calling Levin, a big-shot colonel. We may be in more trouble than you think."

"This is Jerusalem."

"So what? Can we bust IDF Intelligence? Can Shin Bet bust the Russian Compound? This is their territorry, David. Busting in here puts us in the wrong."

"We've got pictures now."

"You're still going to need that van."

"If one of these guys was 'Hurwitz' and Amit Nissim identifies him. . . ."

"They'll tear her apart."

"There's the clerk at the photo store."

"Not enough, David." Rafi shook his head. "With people like this, nowhere near enough."

Superintendent Nathan Latsky huddled with Rafi, while the four Shin Bet men glowered and Ephraim Cohen looked impatiently at his watch. Latsky was an old chain-smoking Pelmach type who'd turned frosty in middle age. Now, near to retirement, he disliked conflict. David knew he barely tolerated Rafi, whose open door policy and undisciplined unit chiefs offended his sense of order.

When Colonel Levin arrived, he and Latsky sauntered into the garden. David couldn't hear what they were saying but it looked very cozy—an elaborate *pas de deux* with lots of friendly smiles, deferential noddings, and polite discussion of interservice protocols, neither man trying to intimidate the other, each positioning himself for the inevitable Israeli compromise.

Latsky came back to talk with Rafi, while Levin conferred with Ephraim Cohen. After a few minutes the superintendent motioned David over.

"Levin says you've blown this headquarters." Latsky lit a cigarette. "He says he's moving his unit out."

"What about the van?"

"What about it? You're sure as hell not going to get it now."

"I need it. There's evidence in there," David said.

"David's been shot at twice," Rafi explained.

Latsky nodded. "You tried to snatch it from them and you failed. Now they're not giving it up. Levin's talking principle."

"So it's an impasse. Now what do we do?"

"In a situation like this I go to the Police Minister and he goes to the Director of Shin Bet."

"Then what?"

Latsky exhaled nervously. "They take it to the Cabinet."

"By that time the van's cleaned up."

The superintendent shrugged. "So what do you want to do? Fight it out with them with guns? You took on these people, Bar-Lev. You should have known better. Now we're in a mess."

"It's a vicious circle," David said. "I couldn't get evidence without moving on them first."

"Sounds to me like you didn't have a legitimate case." The superintendent squinted at him. "Oh yeah. Another thing. No pictures. They want your film back too."

The Police Ministry was in a government building in Sheikh Jarrah, a floor above the larger Ministry of Housing. A decent enough office but nothing grand. The minister, presently attentive to police affairs, hoped shortly to move on to better things.

David only knew him by reputation. He was Algerian-born, a slick, smooth-talking fifty-year-old former trial lawyer with perfectly parted silver-gray hair and beautifully manicured nails. He'd gotten the police as part of a package deal called "Opening to the East," whereby certain presentable younger Sephardic politicians received a limited number of minor ministries in return for joining the coalition of religious and right-wing parties that formed the present government.

The minister sat behind a large wooden desk staring out the window. During David's presentation he had fondled an aluminum ruler, pivoting it occasionally to catch the light. Now, waiting for his decision, David sat nervously in a chair in the center of the room. Rafi Shahar and Superintendent Latsky reclined on a leather couch against the wall. The aromas from Rafi's pipe and Latsky's cigarettes merged and filled the room.

"Anything else?" the minister asked. He rotated his

chair and then he smiled. David shook his head. "You won't mind if I ask some questions?" The minister had won fame for his cross-examinations at a number of spectacular political trials.

"Last night you didn't see anybody in the van?" David nodded. "And you can't positively identify the van as being the one you found in the Lover of Zion Street garage?" David nodded again. "These dope dealers you let go—what made you think they were reliable?"

"Their story made sense."

The minister leaned forward. "But you weren't sure?"

"Of course not. How could I be?" He wondered what the minister was driving at.

"This Major Peretz—how do you know he actually found the so-called executioner?"

"He told me where to find the house and also that Susan Mills had been tortured before she'd been killed. That's something only people in my unit knew."

"He could have discovered those things the same way he found out about the double cuts. You don't have a body so you can't say for certain whether this 'executioner' is dead, or, for that matter, whether there ever existed such a man?"

"There's no certainty about anything in this case," David said. "It's the accumulation of many small details."

The minister snapped down his ruler. "You want me to go to the Cabinet. I'm asking questions I antici-pate will be asked of me. If I can destroy your story, then your adversaries will destroy it. In which case we'll lose. In which case there's hardly any point in taking it to the Cabinet in the first place. Don't you agree?"

David nodded and sat back.

"Okay, did you check with anyone before you re-leased the drug dealers?"

"No."

"Have you the authority to make that kind of deal?"

"Within limits."

The minister turned to Rafi. "Did he exceed his limits?"

"No."

The minister smiled. "That's the first positive link in this extremely peculiar chain of events." He looked at David. "You say this man, Ephraim Cohen, was a friend of your brother. Can you think of any reason why he would want to mislead you about Major Peretz?"

"He was manipulating me. He wanted to throw me off the scent."

"As part of a conspiracy?" David nodded. "But Peretz never told you the name of the 'old friend,' the one he said suggested he attend the Rubin Academy symposium?"

"No."

"So you don't know if he made that up?"

"No."

"You can't be sure anything Peretz told you was true?"

"No."

"And your reconstruction of the accident is based solely on the uncorroborated testimony of a minor child and the hearsay ravings of the discredited, possibly psychotic, and now dead Major Peretz—isn't that correct?"

"Yes."

"So let me ask you, captain: What is this crime that you think is going to be committed? Who are these conspirators? What evidence have you got that Security Services personnel attacked you at the zoo and in front of your house? The answers—correct me if I'm wrong—are: 'I don't know'; 'I don't know'; and 'none.' Right?"

David nodded. "Those would have to be my answers."

The minister sat back and arched his ruler between his hands. "Tell me, honestly, if you were me, would you go to the Cabinet with this kind of speculation?"

David shrugged. "I'm a cop, not a judge. Everything I do is speculative."

The minister bent the end of his ruler, then released it so it sprung at David like a tiny catapult. When their eyes met again David saw a narrow gaze of sympathy; the sharp prosecutorial look was gone.

"Let me make this clear. I understand your actions this morning. On a personal level I'm sympathetic. But if I go into the Cabinet with this I'll end up having to resign. So I'm sorry. . . . By the way, I understand you refused Colonel Levin's request to turn over some rolls of film."

David nodded.

"Okay, you and Shahar wait outside. Latsky—stay. There're a few loose ends to discuss. . . ."

"Oh no! I don't believe it," Anna said. "Oh, David—how awful you must feel."

It was late in the afternoon. They were in the apartment. David, exhausted, was lying on the couch. Anna, perched next to him on her cellist's stool, looked closely into his eyes.

"They were kind about it."

"What did Rafi say?"

"That it was the minister's decision, that it was irrevocable, and he was sorry but there was nothing he could do. I told him I understood. It was my fault. I went in without checking because I knew he'd tell me to wait. My miscalculation. I was sure if I got hold of that van it would lead straight to Cohen and Shin Bet, and I'd have enough to make someone talk. Maybe Cohen counted on that. Maybe the two ambushes were a way to push me into moving too fast so I'd screw up my case."

"Why do you blame yourself?"

"The minister said I was obsessed."

"He's right."

"Sure. And what else should a policeman be? The obsession, Anna, is based on an old Jewish principle: Human life is sacred. You don't allow people to take other people's lives and then not pay for their crimes."

She took his hand. "This is one of the things I love most about you—that you *are* obsessed, that you *don't* give up."

"It's what Judith liked least."

She smiled. "She and I are different. Now what are you going to do?"

"I'm still unit chief. I haven't been demoted. We still have our inventory of pattern crimes."

"And the murders?"

"Rafi'll turn them over to his homicide team, they won't get anywhere, there won't be any more killings, and eventually the case will be allowed to fade. 'Unsolved.' " He closed his eyes. "Rafi wants me to go on vacation. I told him no, that if I go now people will think I've had a breakdown." He paused. "I took a vacation a couple of years ago. Got a passport, went to Paris, then down to Bordeaux, the city my mother left for Palestine. I felt run-down, bad about my divorce, and I thought Bordeaux would be a good place to visit. Mother had described it to me many times, I'd studied maps and photographs and thought I'd recognize buildings, parks, and squares. But it didn't work out. People were haughty and I missed the Mediterranean sun. My second day there I was sitting in a café, sipping a glass of wine, when suddenly I knew I had to leave. I spent a couple of days in Barcelona, then cut my vacation short. When I turned up at the office a week early everyone stared at me like I was mad."

She was gazing at him. "I don't know, David. There's something odd about the way you're taking all of this." She slipped off her stool, settled herself on the floor, pressed her head against his side. "I don't believe you're as resigned as you pretend. Tell me really how you feel?"

"Angry and humiliated. Furious." He paused. "As if I just had my face slapped very hard. But a funny thing, Anna: When Gideon and I were kids our mother sometimes slapped us. But she didn't do it very often, not to me, because she found out that with me it didn't work. Gideon would always respond to it. He could be counted on to behave, adapt himself to the model she set for him. But I was different. Being slapped only made me mad. And when I got mad I told myself: 'Cool down and bide your time.' " He looked at her. "So, you see, this case isn't finished yet." He smiled then as he paraphrased the minister: "There're just a few too many loose ends."

Late that night he called Dov at home.

"We shot three rolls, right?"

"Yeah. Three."

"Hold onto one of them, the one that's got shots of all four guys and the girl. Tomorrow take it in for processing to a commercial photo shop. While you're there, buy a new roll, same type, and stick it in your camera. When you turn in the stuff to Latsky's sergeant, make sure he gives you a receipt so all three rolls are accounted for."

"Sounds good."

David paused. "Guess everyone's pretty depressed."

"Shoshana says she's going to quit. She won't. I had the same idea but I got over it. What gets me is the timing. What happened? The investigation seemed like it was at that point, you know—just ready to take off."

"Oh, a lot of things happened, Dov. I was stupid. I should have ordered Shoshana to run over those goons—anything to hold on to the van. Amit too. I mishandled her. Sticking some photos on some dolls wasn't enough. Should have done it like a line-up with a lot more dolls with pictures on them of people unrelated to the case. Then, if she'd picked out the same dolls, the ones that were related, we'd have had something that might have stuck."

"You think Levin's involved?"

"Doubt it."

"David, what the fuck is going on?"

For a few moments he didn't speak. For the entire evening ideas had been swirling in his brain. "I think originally all they wanted to do was to get hold of Susan Mills's film. But she was a feisty nun, she wouldn't hand it over, so they put pressure on her, and once they did that they had to kill her—if they'd let her go she'd have come straight to us. Once they killed her they were in real trouble. There were other witnesses. So they decided to silence them. One crime led to another. The thing escalated. They killed Yael Safir. We started coming after them. They had to protect themselves. Finally the cover-up became a devouring monster, maybe bigger than whatever it was they were originally trying to protect."

"Yeah, I see, but that still doesn't explain what was so important about the accident. I just can't believe we're really done with this."

"You are."

"But not you."

David did not respond. "For a while now," he said, "like the good cops that we are, we're going to be doing just what we're told."

Mr. Nissim was not pleased to find him at his door.

"You promised us you'd only interview her once."

His wife nodded. "You can't see her now. She's gone to sleep. She's been very nervous since that afternoon."

David apologized. He and Uri had worked gently. They'd done their best to turn the questioning into a game. All he wanted now was to show Amit a few photographs.

"She won't be able to help you," Mrs. Nissim said. But when David lowered his eyes and asked again she reluctantly agreed.

When he came into Amit's bedroom and leaned over her bed to say hello, she reached up and gave him a big wet kiss. Then, when he sat down beside her, she reached for her policewoman doll and rocked it proudly while they talked.

David told her he'd brought along some pictures and all she had to do was look at them and tell him if she recognized any of the men.

He spread the pictures out on her bed. She looked carefully at each photo and was clearly disappointed that she couldn't recognize a face. When he brought out the IdentiKit sketch of the "nephew" who'd picked up Susan Mill's film, she shook her head again.

David thanked her, kissed her good night, and was across the room and at the door when she called out.

"I saw him on TV."

"Who?" He turned.

"Oh, one of the men," she said.

David walked back, crouched down. "The policeman?" She shook her head. "The man who hurt his leg?"

She grinned up at him. "No."

"Oh," he said, "then it must have been one of the two who helped him walk away."

Amit beamed. "Uh huh."

David sat beside her again. "Why didn't you tell me this before?"

"You didn't ask me."

"You're right." He smiled. "So, what did he look like, this man you saw?"

"Oh, he had a beard," she said. Her eyes enlarged. "He looked real scary too."

Mrs. Nissim came into the room. "I thought you'd be finished by now."

"Amit's just telling me about something she saw on TV."

"Tales. Nonsense. Ever since you questioned her she's been pointing at people on the screen. Look! The child's blinking again. It's time for you to go. And I'd appreciate it very much, captain, if this time you'd keep your promise and not bother us again."

There was something overtly irritable in Anna now—a sense he had that she was more than anxious, was truly distraught. Sometimes he would gaze at her and, before she'd notice and recompose her features, would catch a glimpse of pain.

What was bothering her? Whenever he asked she brushed his question aside. One time she told him it was her music—that she had felt she was struggling toward a breakthrough but instead now found herself against a wall.

"Tell me about it," he asked.

She touched her forehead. "It's difficult," she said. And then, after a pause, in a whisper filled with pain: "I want so much to be a major performer, David. Not just a fine cellist but a major one." She looked down then, as if ashamed of sounding grandiose. "Not just major either, David. Even better than major. Maybe . . ." She paused again; she could hardly bring herself to say the word. She whispered: "Maybe even the best."

The next few days were quiet. Members of the unit sat around sluggishly going through old dossiers. There were the unsolved pattern cases of the burglarized grocery stores, the kidnapped pedigreed dogs, and the "gentle rapist" who hadn't attacked in months.

Rebecca Marcus carefully took down all the pictures, maps, and documents relating to the case that were tacked up on the squadroom walls. When she asked David where to store them, he instructed her to pack them up for him in a box.

Moshe Liederman asked to see him. He'd spoken with an officer in personnel and learned that with his accumulated vacation time he could begin his retirement at once. With the murder investigation shut down he saw no reason to wait. He had some papers for David to sign.

"No bother," David said. He signed Liederman's papers and thanked him for his help.

"It's me who should thank you," Liederman said. "I want you to know this—I've been a cop for more than thirty years but until I worked with you I never had any self-respect. I'm not talking about the cruel jokes— 'Why do cops always work in pairs?' 'Because one can read and the other can write.' That kind of stuff never bothered me. What bothered me, I think, was that I never really believed in the concept of a Jewish cop. When I put on the uniform and looked at myself in the mirror I felt I was looking at a clown."

"Maybe you just needed to work in civilian clothes, Moshe. The uniform's not for everyone. You'll be working on your archive now. I'm sorry I haven't had a chance to see it yet."

"Someday you will. Meantime, if you ever need help, unofficially, on the outside, please remember me. I'm not like you, I don't have intuition. And I'm not as smart as Dov or as fast as Shoshana or as ingenious as Micha or as tough as Uri. But after thirty years there're a few things I know how to do. I'm good at following people and I like to look under every stone."

He called in Shoshana. "When you go by Amit's school this afternoon ask her about the man she saw."

"Huh?"

"On TV. The scary looking man with the beard. She'll know who you mean."

Shoshana stared at him.

"You *were* going to stop by and see her, weren't you?"

"Well sure, David. Of course." Shoshana smiled. "I take it, then, we're still. . . ."

He looked at his watch. "Friday afternoon. They probably let the kids out early. . . ."

When he glanced up she was gone.

The Friday morning *Jerusalem Post:* He didn't get to his copy until four o'clock. He read it slowly; he'd been so busy the past week he'd lost track of the stream of news.

A taxi driver's strike looming in Tel Aviv. The plummeting shekel. Gyrations on the Stock Exchange. A suicide car-bomb attack at the Lebanese frontier. Rabbi Katzer, visiting New York, raving against the Diaspora. A settler's demonstration—the Bloc of the Faithful accusing the government of welshing on a deal.

In the magazine supplement there was an article about five self-proclaimed "Messiahs" presently wandering the streets of Old Jerusalem. David moved on to a profile of a Peace Now activist who posed the eternal Israeli Question: "What Is to Be Done?" He was impressed until he reached the second paragraph where the man said he was fed up and moving to England for a year. He crumpled the paper, was about to throw it away, when a caption caught his eye.

A picture of a handsome man with flowing white hair; underneath it a name he remembered from his talk with Stephanie Porter. David spread the paper out and began to read a lengthy interview in which Aleksandr Targov, presently residing at the city's artists' guesthouse, Mishkenot Sha'ananim, spoke of the sculpture he had created especially for Jerusalem and which now he'd come to donate and install.

ANNA

She was nervous—he sensed it the moment he entered the apartment. She was practicing, in a pair of white shorts and a sleeveless white jersey, and when she pulled her bow she looked as though she were trying to saw through the cello's strings.

He moved toward her. Her forehead was dripping. When he raised her hair and felt the back of her neck he found it slick.

She stopped.

"What's the matter?"

"Something Yosef said this afternoon. I got upset."

David sat down. "What did he say?"

"Nothing. He had the right to say it. We criticize each other all the time. It's just that we've been working on the Mendelssohn and he said the way I was doing this passage was 'gypsyish.' " She picked up her cello, played a portion of the D Major Sonata with exaggerated sentimentality. "Later he took it back, said what he meant was I was playing like I was trying too hard to please. I wanted to kill him." She paused. "I think maybe he was right."

He watched as she carefully placed the cello back on the floor, stood up, and walked into the kitchen. When she came back out she was smoking a long black silver-tipped Russian cigarette.

"Smoking again?"

"Just since this afternoon. I got so nervous I walked over to the King David and bought myself a pack." She exhaled. "No wonder Israelis are such smokestacks. Everyone's nervous here. I'd be too if I weren't so damned disciplined."

He studied her. "What's the matter, Anna?"

She started to pace the room. "Every day now you ask me that."

"Someone's turned up, hasn't he?"

She stopped pacing. "David, how did you know?"

"It's Targov, isn't it? There's an interview with him in the *Post*."

She nodded. "But how do you know his name? I'm sure I never mentioned him, unless I talk in my sleep."

"I'm a detective, remember."

The Russian in her accepted that: in the USSR detectives knew everything, so why not in Israel too?

She took another long puff. "Damn him for coming. *Damn!*"

"Sit with me." She came to the couch. "What's the matter? Have you seen him? Did he come here to track you down?"

"No. His secretary phoned. A very strange, very thin man named Anatole Rokovsky. He said Sasha was here and asked me to please come and see him. I told him I'd think about it. I was doing that when you walked in."

Then, suddenly, she began to speak. David was amazed. It was as if she had stored up her feelings for a year, and now, releasing them, was so caught up she couldn't stop.

". . . we were lovers. Did you know that? We had some wonderful moments too. But in the end it was impossible. He flaunted our affair in front of his wife. I was just one in a long string of younger women brought into the house to make her feel like shit."

She was up now, pacing the room again, puffing on

another cigarette, waving her arms as she described the agony of the months she'd spent with the Targovs in Big Sur.

". . . not, you understand, that Irina was some poor abused creature. She engineered a lot of it. He told me once that if it weren't for her contempt, he thought she'd probably die. He's a brilliant man, David. Knows everybody. Quotes great hunks of poetry. Pushkin, Pasternak, Tvardovsky. Huge gnarled hands. 'Sculptor's hands,' he'd say, 'but useless now.' Then he'd start in, his litany: Artistic paralysis. Old injustices. Bureaucrats who'd hated him and detested his style. How they cut him off from state commissions, demanded he sculpt more 'realistically,' and finally how they drove him into exile—or, at least, so he said. Complaints, complaints . . . all the time, too, making sure Irina knew about us. He'd steal pieces of my underwear and hide them in his bed where he knew she'd search them out. Awful scenes at dinner. The two of them screaming at one another standing inches apart. Sasha was good to me, helped me, but he used me too. I was his sounding board. He made me pay a thousand ways."

"How did you meet?"

She shook her head.

"What's the matter?"

"You don't want me to tell you that."

"I love you, Anna. We can't have secrets." He paused. "Listen—I'll tell you one of mine."

She stopped pacing, grinned. "I didn't know you had secrets."

"How do you think I found out about you and Targov?"

"How did you?" She gazed at him.

"An old girl friend of mine. An American. You see—you're not the only one around here with a past."

"She knew?"

"She's some kind of American agent. Jealous, and a liar too. She told me Titanov was seen recently in the West. I checked and of course it wasn't true."

She nestled beside him, hung her head. He stroked the back of her neck.

"I know your defection was legitimate, Anna. But there's something you're holding back. Tell me what it is. You'll feel better if you do."

Tears sprang to her eyes. "I don't think I can."

"Guilt is stupid."

"Do they teach you to say that at detective school?"

He nodded. "They have a name for it. 'The tell-your-story method.' So come on, Anna, tell me your story. A detective who loves you—what better listener could you have?"

She began finally to tell it, starting back even before her defection in Milan. He had heard details of these incidents many times but he didn't interrupt her; he knew she had to work herself up before she got to the part that made her feel so ashamed.

". . . it was a couple of months later, after I got to the States. I was temporarily settled in New York. A cold winter day. The wind was biting. I was hurrying along West Fifty-seventh Street near Carnegie Hall when a man approached. He matched his stride to mine and started speaking to me in Russian. He was friendly, polite, open about who he was and what he wanted me to do. He was with the Soviet Embassy. He proposed a mission, and said that if I didn't perform it my brother would be expelled from Moscow University. He didn't put it to me like a threat. Just stated it sadly as a fact. And when I told him that whatever happened to my brother I wasn't going to be a spy, he said this wasn't like that, that spying was for professionals, that all he wanted me to do was report to him on the thinking of some émigrés. He invited me into a coffee shop to talk. I was a little hesitant. But it

was a public place, he didn't seem dangerous, and I
was worried about my brother's future. There he revealed that he knew I was going out to California to
give a concert the following week. While I was there
he wanted me to telephone the sculptor, Targov, whose
name I recognized but about whom I knew nothing at
all. I was to introduce myself to Targov, arrange a
meeting, then sound him out on his activities and
plans. That was it. Stupidly I agreed. Now I'm so
ashamed. But you see, at the time it seemed like such
a harmless thing. Those people, old émigrés—all they
ever do is talk."

When she met Targov she was surprised. She didn't
discover a militant anti-Soviet activist. Instead she found
a tormented artist, flawed on the scale of a character
from a Russian novel. There was a party that first
weekend in Big Sur—refugees, defectors, other émigrés.
Tables set high with Russian food, meat pies and
cakes, flasks too of spicy vodka endlessly refilled. Targov
was attentive. Within hours she found herself in thrall.
Grizzled, seductive, he swept her up in passionate
talk, flinging out poetry, ideas, raucous jokes. Later,
when the balalaika players sang, they stood and clapped
together and then they danced.

Tears filled her eyes as she told David all of this,
and then of how Irina had invited her to move in. It
somehow fed Irina's fury, she thought, to provide a
young woman for her husband to seduce. Irina's anger, Anna soon realized, was reserved solely for Sasha;
the field of energy in the house was between the
Targovs, not Sasha and herself. Enmeshed in their
domestic melodrama she was only a bit player. And
the longer she stayed the more trapped she felt, feeling she would be devoured if she didn't manage to
escape.

It was then that she begged her agent to find her an
accompanist, and went to San Francisco for a meeting

with her contact from the Russian embassy. She told the man that Targov was harmless, that she was finished and would perform no further missions. Perhaps she was followed that day, perhaps that was how Stephanie Porter had learned of the KGB connection. It didn't matter. She didn't care. All she knew was that if she stayed on in Big Sur her life as a musician would be destroyed.

The last weeks there were especially mean. She sensed Irina was getting ready to reopen some old and dreadful wound. It all culminated on Sasha's sixtieth birthday when, after he jokingly accused her of being a Komsomol girl sent to extract his secrets, he confessed to her that long ago he had betrayed his closest friend. A painful story; he didn't give details and she didn't ask for any. She was too upset by the possibility that he had really found her out.

"That, you see, was the irony," she said. "I brooded on it through that afternoon. He had found the courage to confess his duplicity to me, but I couldn't bring myself to confess mine. Instead we made love, and then I played for him. And late that night Irina stole into my room, woke me up, stood at the foot of my bed, and told me everything in a torrent of triumph, fury and abuse."

Sergei Sokolov was the betrayed man's name, a schoolmate of Targov's, an artist too, not nearly so talented, but sweeter, less bitter, better able to cope with the bureaucrats. He'd been best man at Targov's wedding. For years they'd been inseparable. And after the marriage the three of them were a troika, going everywhere together, dining together nearly every night.

One winter evening there was a tremendous storm. Impossible for Sergei to get home. Irina invited him to sleep over on the couch, and the next morning, over breakfast, suggested he move in. Not long after began the period Irina called 'the sharing.' She was beautiful then, and irresistible; Sokolov could not resist. Thus began her year of ecstasy: swift sweet golden impassioned afternoons making love with Sergei followed by long hard silver nights with Sasha on the marital bed. Two males, two lovers, two men she loved. Her body sang. She gave herself up to pleasure.

But the worm of jealousy was there, waiting to wriggle in and feast upon her perfect joy. Sasha must have suspected. He was paranoid anyway, abused by the blockheads, curtailed and paralyzed in his work. He had a studio on the other side of Moscow, an old garage poorly heated with a wooden stove. He would go there each day and, unable to work, would sit with gloved hands staring at his clay.

One blistering winter day (Irina only learned this later) his self-pity built up to a rage. When he could no longer stand his agony he decided to return home. It was early afternoon.

Irina and Sergei were lying naked on the couch. They didn't hear him enter, didn't turn. He took one long slow look at them, then went out to walk. He would smite them dead, then fling himself upon the frozen Moscow River from the hideous Krimsky Bridge.

Better, Irina said, if he had done so; anything would have been better than what he finally did. For as he brooded through that biting afternoon, he forged a terrible plan. At first stunned and embittered, he now saw Sergei's treason as a tool. If he employed sufficient cunning, he would be able to end Irina's affair, avenge himself, and, best of all, buy freedom in the West.

It seemed there was another old schoolmate, Anna explained, a horrid mediocre KGB official named Zabolinsky. *Yes, there's always a Zabolinsky . . . ,* David thought, as Anna described how, since their school days, this man and Sokolov had been enemies. Now Sasha approached Zabolinsky, presenting him with a way to settle the ancient grudge. All he asked for in return was a pair of passports so that he and Irina could travel abroad for a year of study and "artistic growth."

The plan was simple. Sasha and Sergei often engaged in bitter anti-Soviet talk. Sasha would inform on Sergei, arrange for choice bits of their dangerous conversation to be overheard. Sergei would be arrested, tried, and convicted of agitation. And of course it wouldn't hurt that he happened to be a Jew.

"Irina told me all this," Anna said, "standing rigid at the end of my bed. The relish in her voice was positively evil. It was my last night there and she wanted me to know the truth. Sasha's plan worked. Sergei was convicted and sent to a strict regime labor camp. And then, when the visas came through, Irina, fearful and confused, agreed to take advantage and defect.

"Years later, one drunken night, after they were settled in America and Sasha had gained wealth and fame, he confessed everything, explained what he'd done and why, then wept and begged Irina's pardon on his knees.

"But she would not forgive. No matter her own infidelity, what Sasha had done could never be forgiven. Her husband, she told me again, was a common informer. Moreover, the KGB stories about him were true. 'Oh, sure, he hates them now,' she said. 'Now he can afford to call them snakes. But he's the *real* snake. That's what I want you to understand.'

"For a while she stood there staring down at me with this awful gloating look. 'Listen,' she said, 'I've seen the two of you fucking in the studio like a pair of randy goats. Well now, I want you to know, the circle's turned. By some miracle Sergei's finally out. This morning I told Sasha, his birthday gift. I really fixed him—he's so afraid of being exposed he'll never sculpt again.' And then she laughed."

For a while they sat together in silence, David gently massaging the back of Anna's neck, she sobbing silently by his feet. When she spoke again she did not look at him. "After I met Yosef and we played so well together, I knew it was time to begin my second life. And when we came here to give a concert, and I saw this city, I knew this was the place for me to live."

She kissed his knees, then turned her face to him; he saw the tracks of tears upon her cheeks. "Then I met you. It seemed like such a miracle—the way you looked at me, the way we fell in love. Too good almost. And all this time I've been afraid of what you'd think if you knew the terrible thing I'd done. . . ."

David was moved: Anna's story matched Stephanie's perfectly in certain ways, but in meaning was entirely different. And he understood too how Anna saw her own small moment of weakness grossly mirrored in the Targovs' tale of treachery, deceit, and grief.

Ah, Russians . . . , he thought. "Listen," he said, "you did nothing. Just agreed to contact this sculptor so your brother wouldn't be expelled. You think that's so terrible?"

"David. . . ."

He took her face in his hands. "That's nothing. Believe me. My father taught me about these things. You feel guilty because you equate your original call to Targov with his betrayal of his oldest friend. But you didn't betray him, Anna. You did just the opposite. You told them he was harmless. That's not the same. Not in any way. What you did was nothing— nothing at all."

Later they made love, but not in the wild frisky way they often did. This time their lovemaking was gentle and solemn. Afterward he held her until she fell asleep.

In the middle of the night he sensed her restlessness.

"What's the matter?"

"It's the music," she said. "That sonata—no matter how hard I try I can't seem to get it right." He heard real fear and trouble in her voice, resignation and despair. "For years I've played it. And now, I don't know why . . . I just don't know, David, but now I can't."

He turned so he could look into her eyes. "Anna, how can this be true? You're a musician. You choose a piece, study it and master it. What's so difficult here?"

"It's not so difficult. But it resists. I wander around, get lost, and then I can't find my way out again."

"Play it for me."

"Now?"

"Sure."

"The neighbors. . . ."

"A few days ago we gave them an ambush. Now they'll have a concert."

She got out of bed, pulled on her robe, tuned her cello, then started to play. He listened. He was no expert, but he sensed that though she started out well, and played all the right notes, the music soon lost coherence and that this was what she meant when she said she lost her way.

When she was finished she looked dismayed. "Impossible!"

"No. But difficult. I can think of three solutions. You must choose the one that's best."

"Tell me."

"You can go and see my father, talk it over with him. Perhaps he can help you uncover the cause behind your block." He paused. "Then, of course, you can give it up. Tell Yosef the Mendelssohn's not right for you now and you'd like to work on something else."

"The third?"

"That's the hard one. It's what I've been doing with my case. Work on it. Worry it. Worry all its components day and night. Imagine what it will be like when you finally master it, how magnificently you'll play it, how marvelous it will sound. Labor over every segment until you solve it, then move on to the next. As the segments snap together and your performance builds you'll begin to catch glimpses of the design. It may evade you at first but eventually it will be revealed. And when it is you'll have it. You'll understand it, see it whole and clean. Then it will be yours. The music will belong to you forever."

IF I
FORGET
THEE . . .

As Targov shaved he recalled some lines from "Tourists" by the Israeli poet Yehuda Amichai. Scraping his cheeks he spoke them to the mirror:

They weep over our sweet boys
And lust over our tough girls
And hang up their underwear
To dry quickly
In cool, blue bathrooms. . . .

Half an hour later, trailed by Rokovsky, he mounted the staircase to the lobby of Mishkenot Sha'ananim. The pretty student called to him from the desk.

"Good morning, Mr. Targov. Your taxi's here."

He waved to her, then stepped through the glass doors. A moment later he was showered by blazing light.

The taxi roared out of the drive. The walls of the Old City shimmered.

If I forget thee, O Jerusalem
Let my right hand forget her cunning.

It was early morning. They passed through residential streets, past sad old men sitting on benches and children playing joyously in flowering parks. Then they were on a modern boulevard speeding past buildings faced with lustrous stone. Sculptures were everywhere: works by Arp, Calder, Picasso, Henry Moore. . . . Such company! At the site, the taxi shuddered to a halt.

He liked it. No, he *loved* it. He paced it up and down, and then around in nervous circles. He checked the background (a grove of cedars), the approach (a hedged meandering path). Rokovsky, balanced awkwardly on the pedestal, stood in for "The Righteous Martyr."

Targov squinted. He imagined how the sculpture would look in an afternoon rainstorm or illuminated by a waning moon. Yes, he decided, black bronze was perfect: The metal would fire up beneath this holy molten sun.

"Good," he yelled in Russian, "but where the hell's the lawn?"

"First the plumbers," Rokovsky yelled back. "They must lay water pipes before the gardeners plant the grass."

"Plant!" He moved a little so that Rokovsky eclipsed the sun. "They must be mad. Grass takes weeks."

"They'll lay sod," Rokovsky cried; his voice was growing hoarse and now he looked like a scarecrow silhouette.

Back into the taxi for a round of visits to other public sculptures: Rapoport's "Memorial Wall" at Yad Vashem; Lipchitz's "The Tree of Life" on Mount Scopus; Palombo's "Gates to the Knesset"; Elkan's "Seven-Branched Menorah"; then to the Israel Museum for Agam's "Eighteen Levels" and the Billy Rose Sculpture Garden for Maillol, Marini, and Archipenko amid Noguchi's spectacular system of terraces and walls.

Before Rodin's "Adam," Targov finally stood still. "Now here is *something*," he said.

Rokovsky nodded. He was exhausted, not yet recovered from the long journey from Big Sur.

"Oh, Tola," Targov said, "this is a city built for artists. Such light! Such terrible splendor! I never dreamed. . . ." He turned back to the Rodin, examined it again. Unable to find a single fault, he announced: "But now we have so much to do!"

The grass! The unveiling! The invitations! Relations with the press! Within the hour Rokovsky was dispatched to Haifa to meet the Japanese freighter carrying "The Righteous Martyr" in its hold. Targov, free of his aide's gray grim presence, struck off happily on his own.

He spent the day exploring the Old City, hurrying down angled scorching alleys, shoved and battered by delirious mobs. Moans and mosques, churches and wails. An endless harangue of radio music, florid curses, bargains broken, bargains struck.

Cats prowled, greedy skeletal cats. Bearded men worked iron and boys sawed aromatic wood. Arms thrust out plying him with pastries. Arabs ushered him with sweeping gestures into tiny fetid shops.

In the Church of the Holy Sepulcher he gasped. *Have I lost my mind?* The incense was so powerful it snaked down his nostrils and threatened to burn the linings of his lungs.

Pushing his way past a defecating mule, he paused before a doorway. Twisted metal and discarded rusted machinery parts poured out onto the street. He peered inside. A bare bulb hung from a wire above a decaying table. Nearly lost in the rancid gloom were four old men in soiled undershirts puffing on water pipes and playing cards.

He had a feeling about the Old City, that it was compressed, filled with rancor, held together within an angry fist. A city of secrets, robed figures, hooded haunted faces, stern nuns with bloodied knees and mad messianic eyes. At 2 P.M. on the Via Dolorosa, watching a blind man with a white cane stumble out of the Church of the Flagellation, he thought: *I walk where prophets and martyrs have trod*.

He went to see the Dome of the Rock, waiting in line with the tourists. It was, he knew, the finest building in the city. A superbly tiled octagon supporting a large intricately decorated dome, it not only dominated the Temple Mount, it dominated Jerusalem.

The architecture was superb; he nearly swooned at its beauty. The rotunda was suffused with soft pastel light which entered through the stained glass windows of the clerestory and fell upon the rock. He stood at the railing beneath the cupola looking at this enormous outcropping of stone. To this place Abraham had come to sacrifice Isaac, and from it the Prophet Mohammed had leapt to heaven on his horse.

Anna looked different. In California she was bony and pale but here she glowed with health. Was it the detective? Targov examined him: a stocky, tanned, black-haired almost handsome man with full well-sculpted lips. He had a Roman warrior's brow, projected competence and strength. But there was something sensitive about his eyes; a seeker, Targov decided, a man on a quest. Yes, it's he who's changed her; he makes love to her properly, ignites such a fire that the heat rises even to her cheeks.

". . . so brilliant, you Jews! Relativity. Psychoanalysis. Do I dare mention Marxism?" He glanced at Anna. She shook her head and grinned. "Now you're experts on irrigation, pioneering, archaeology. You raise an army, create new armaments, and against the world's expectations proceed to win all your wars."

He glanced around the restaurant. It was nearly empty. When he turned back he found himself object of the detective's gaze. "Perhaps most amazing to me you have rediscovered the heroic. In an era when we're told the hero cannot exist you have hundreds—soldiers, teachers, wisemen. But for all your virtues you're still fallible." He put down his fork. "This food for instance. It's terrible." They laughed as he pushed away his plate.

"By the way," he asked the detective later, "how do I go about finding someone here?"

"Depends who you're looking for. I use the phone book myself."

"You find criminals that way? Amazing!" He looked at the detective again. "There just may be a few old friends from Russia, new arrivals. Could I find them if I wanted to?"

"Give me their names, birthdates if you know them. I'll be glad to run them down."

"I don't want to trouble you. I thought there might be a bureau."

"The Jewish Agency. Or the Ministry of Immigrants Absorption. But, believe me, it's no trouble. With the police computer—"

"Dear God, computers! I wouldn't dream. . . ."

A quizzical spark, then, in the detective's eyes. "Actually this is a very small country. We all know each other. All you have to do is ask around."

Anna excused herself to make a phone call. Targov paid the bill, then he and the detective walked outside. There was an awkward moment as they waited in the sun staring across the ravine. The light was harsh; it hurt Targov's eyes. Olive trees, powdered with dust, stood stark and gnarled against the iridescent sky.

"Listen," Targov said, "I don't want to sound paternal but you're good for her. I see that. She's blooming here. She needed your kind of strength."

"Thank you for saying that," the detective said. "I appreciate—"

"Ah, but here she comes. She wants to show me things. You're coming with us of course?"

The detective shook his head. "I think you two should speak Russian for a while." He bent to kiss Anna, then offered Targov his hand. Again Targov noticed the quizzical searching look. "Please call if you need anything."

"Yes, I will," Targov said.

Somehow he managed to climb the Mount of Olives. She led him by his hand up a steep path of broken rocks between walls that guarded the ancient graves. He panted. In Big Sur he regularly prowled the forest but here the heat was punishing. When they reached the top he looked back across the valley at Mount Moriah bathed in golden light.

"Why?" she asked him.

He turned to her. Her eyes had caught the sun, now reminded him of the color of the Kremlin's walls.

"I thought I was finished. Then suddenly it came. My best work. Perhaps my last. . . ."

She shook her head. "I know you, Sasha. You didn't travel eight thousand miles just to see a ribbon cut."

He studied her. She did not blink or turn away. "Yes," he said, "the sculpture is only part of it."

"And the rest?"

"There is a settlement to be made."

"What kind of settlement?"

He spread his arms. "What else? My life."

"So it has nothing to do with me?" she asked him later, as they sat in the backroom of a tea shop on sweltering Ben Yehuda. Outside a juggler was entertaining a small crowd. Across the pedestrian mall a seedy violinist was scratching out a rhapsody for tourists.

"Nothing. But I'm very glad to see you."

"Tell me why you've come."

He paused. "Call it redemption. A year ago on my birthday I had a dream. A man shot at me. He missed."

"Well?"

"Perhaps next time he won't. Then there'll be repercussions. Yes, I think there will."

She stared at him. "I must tell you, Sasha, I have no idea what you're talking about."

"Better that way. Listen, I'm here and I have many things to do. To see you was the most pleasant of them. You could have been my daughter. God, how I wish . . ."

Later, nervously pacing his apartment, he received Rokovsky's call. The freighter had been delayed three days. Meantime, bad news: Irina was on her way.

"What?"

"She's flying in day after tomorrow. There was a rambling cable at the hotel. I phoned to try and stop her, but Bianca said she'd left. She's in New York someplace, unreachable."

"Bitch!" *She'll ruin everything.*

"I can't think how you can keep her out."

"All right, she wants to come, be a pest, share in the glory—fine. Meantime, I have a confidential mission and it must be accomplished before she arrives. Find Sokolov. When you locate him, and remember you're searching on your behalf not mine, call me back and give me the address. Under no circumstances, Tola, are you to go near him, or tell Irina anything, you understand? When she comes your job is to keep her away from me. Tie her up in knots."

A short silence while Rokovsky, accustomed to fulfilling unexplained requests, pondered a solution.

"Perhaps she might enjoy a trip to the Galilee," he finally said.

"A MAN WHO HAS BEEN WRONGED"

Everyone in the Russian Compound knew that Pattern Crimes was in disgrace. Cops who'd envied David his status as favorite son of Rafi's CID, greeted him with hypocritical commiseration, while real friends stopped him in the corridors to tell him he'd been handed a rotten deal.

One day in the men's room he overheard himself discussed. A pair of middle-aged narcotics detectives were pounding on the coffee machine just outside the door:

"He's a terrific detective," said the first, "but he's got this complex—he's going to save us all."

"Yeah," said the second, "it's not enough for him to investigate. David has to *understand.*"

He watched his people carefully. Each reacted in his own way. Uri Schuster performed isometric exercises while gazing sullenly into space. Micha made inefficient busywork with the files while Dov braved his gloom by striding aggressively up and down the halls. Only Shoshana seemed unperturbed. She wore the preoccupied look of a detective puzzling out a baffling case. *She's onto something,* David thought. He decided to leave her alone. Whatever it was she would play with it until she dropped it or brought it in.

Sarah Dorfman was kind; she took Rebecca Marcus out to a concert. Then, three days after David's dismissal from the case, Rafi summoned him into his office, dispatched Sarah on an errand, then rose and closed the door.

"You're angry with me. I can tell by your expression. You think I should have fought harder on your behalf." Not true, of course, but David said nothing; his father had taught him to allow guilty-feeling people to express their guilt. ". . . but don't forget: that kind of loyalty has to be reciprocal. If you'd consulted me first, I'd have backed you up no matter what. But you moved in on your own, and went too far. I did the best I could for you. I'm sorry you feel betrayed."

Rafi lit his pipe, then mumbled something about having David and Anna over for dinner. But then, with no date set, the invitation hung between them awkwardly.

The next evening, when David came home, he found a strange assortment of flowers on the windowsill, bizarre epiphytic orchids with oblong ruffled pink-veined leaves.

"From Rafi," Anna explained. "He even sent the vase."

He began to leave the office early to take long walks in the city. His hope was that this exercise would work off his malaise. But these walks made him feel sorrowful. Jerusalem resisted his advances. The city remained elusive, evading his attempts to read her pattern, understand her grand design.

He started to revisit places he remembered from his youth, streets where long ago he and Gideon had walked or ridden bikes. Memories of his brother haunted him; he couldn't understand why. Then one evening he found himself just outside his father's door.

He didn't knock, simply stood outside in the gloom

listening to the commotion within. A quarrel was taking place. The words were indecipherable. A woman whose voice he didn't recognize was carrying on hysterically and his father was responding with angry words. Then there was quiet, then whispers, then weeping again. Fascinated and embarrassed, David hurried down the stairs. In the alley he paused to stare up at the window. Then he rushed back through Me'a Shearim, past storekeepers pulling down their roller blinds, to the bright lights of Jaffa Road.

That night he told Anna about the incident. "Who could it have been? I know this sounds stupid but it never occurred to me that he still has a private life. I always think of him brooding at home alone, and then, when I catch him in an emotional scene, I wonder: Do I really understand him? Do I know anything about him? Oh, Anna, why do I feel so out of touch?"

She said she thought it was his case—that having been deprived of it so suddenly, it was impossible for him not to feel lost.

"Sure," he said, "that's why I started taking walks. But they've only made me feel worse. Things come back, bits and pieces of the past. The more I walk the more morose I get."

"Tell me."

"I've been thinking of Gideon. I suppose it's because of Ephraim Cohen and Peretz. Just this evening I had an idea—that somehow he took upon himself all the problems we should have shared. That he absorbed all the pathology in our family, took on all the abuse. And that now, because he did, I'm walking around alive."

"What pathology?"

"The thing our parents generated. The web they wove around us from which we had to struggle free."

"You think Gideon . . . ?"

"He took it all upon himself, Anna. And by doing that he left me free to become a sane adult."

They went out for a walk late one afternoon along the wall that ran along the western edge of the Old City. They walked silently until they reached the Jaffa Gate. Then Anna turned to him and spoke:

"I love it here, David. I don't know why. I'm not religious but I'm stirred. There's no river, no harbor, but I love it anyway. The city covering the hills like a carpet. The long shadows of people by the walls. Oh, David, it's your place, your city. This magic city-made-of-stones. . . ."

Early Saturday morning he drove to Haifa, arriving at the Raskov house at ten o'clock. It was an extremely large house in Central Carmel, modern, flat-roofed, and sprawling, with a fine view of the harbor below.

A Druse woman opened the door. No sign of Judith or Joe.

"I'm Captain Bar-Lev," David said to her in Arabic.

The woman nodded. "Please wait. Hagith will be right down."

From the stoop David looked around. The lawn was perfectly manicured, and there were two shiny Mercedes-Benz automobiles parked beside the house. The trunk door of one had been left open exposing tennis rackets, an expensive set of golf clubs, a pair of snorkling flippers and a breathing tube.

Hagith's face reminded David of Gideon's, but her gestures were reminiscent of Judith. On the drive up to Tiberias, they talked about her schoolwork, her teachers, her friends, carefully skirting details of her life at home.

"Anna and I want you to stay with us," he said. "For a week, or longer if you like, and your mother approves." Hagith didn't answer. "Don't you miss

Jerusalem? Do you remember it? It's been almost a year since you came up to visit."

"Yes, I remember," she said. And then she started to cry.

"Darling! What's the matter?" He pulled the car over to the side of the road. "Why are you upset? Is it something I said? Please tell me so I can help."

"I *want* to visit," she said. "I miss you and grandfather very much."

"We miss you too. That's nothing to cry about."

"Joe won't let me come," she said.

"What do you mean, he won't *let* you? Why not, darling?"

"He says people will try and kidnap me so they can get his money."

The crude son-of-a-bitch! He fought hard to control his fury. "Listen, Hagith—it doesn't matter what Joe says. Doesn't matter at all. A visit to Jerusalem is between you, me, and your mother—and nobody else."

"I don't like him," she said suddenly. "His breath smells bad." She threw herself sobbing across David's lap. He petted her splayed hair while explaining that no matter where she lived, he, David, would always love her and would always be her daddy. But even as he said all of this he couldn't help but be aware of a surge of joy inside. *She hates Joe Raskov, hates the smell of his breath! She's still my daughter!* Suddenly he felt better than he had in weeks.

I've been thinking about Anna and her problem playing Mendelssohn," his father said.

"Yes?"

"Mendelssohn was a Jewish composer."

"So . . . ?"

"So that could be significant. She's having trouble with a Jew."

"You think she's having trouble with me, father?"

"Maybe. Of course this is only a suggestion, David, but perhaps it would be helpful if you would both examine that."

When he glanced up Shoshana's supple body filled the doorway. She shook her glossy curls and grinned.

"So here you are," he said.

"I know you've been waiting for me."

He motioned her to a chair. She sat and crossed her arms.

"Nine days ago you sent me to catch Amit Nissim. I told you what happened—she couldn't describe the scary bearded man any better than she had for you. So I thought: Okay, I'll keep in touch, she knows something, she's the only one who does, she may be only six years old but right now she's all we've got. Every afternoon I've been dropping by the school just when they let the kids go loose. Amit sees me, runs over, we give each other a hug, then we walk a couple blocks, I buy her an orange, we talk, about police work, this and that, then I pat her on her fanny and send her home.

"I like her. She looks up to me, says she wants to join the force when she grows up. But I'm not spending my time with a six-year-old because I need my ego massaged. I figure she's seen this scary bearded guy once, maybe she'll see him again. Every time we meet I ask her if she has, and she shakes her head and promises she'll tell me if she does.

"Okay, two days ago we go through it again. No, she hasn't seen him, so we go on to something else. Then, out of the blue, she says: 'I saw the other one.' 'Who?' 'The other one,' she says—which just about freaks me out. Turns out, to please me she's been sitting with her parents watching all the grown-up shows. And on one of them, a discussion program a week ago, she recognized another of the three men from the van. Not the scary bearded one, and not the guy who was hurt. But the third man who, with the beard, helped the injured guy limp away. Can she describe him? A little. He had gray hair, sharp eyes, and acted very proud. Since that fits just about every Israeli TV panelist I've ever seen, I asked the broadcast people for a list. It wasn't long. I found pictures of most of the men in old newspapers and magazines. I compiled a little scrapbook and this afternoon I showed it to Amit. She examined every face, then fingered one of them. You know, David, she's been an excellent witness, and so far she's been on the button every time."

Shoshana placed her scrapbook on his desk. He turned the pages: party leaders, former cabinet ministers, public personalities from business and the arts. When he reached an old newspaper photo of General Yigal Gati, Shoshana clicked her teeth.

He glanced up at her. "Him?"

Her eyes were flashing. "Yup."

He leaned back, thrilled. Pieces were finally clicking into place. "You know, Shoshana, you've become one damn fine detective after all."

"Thanks. And now I suppose you'll take this into Rafi since, of course, it's not our case anymore. I hear the new team's discrediting all our work. Dov says they don't even care about the accident. So they'll probably discount this too."

He touched the scar on his cheek. "Fuck them," he said.

"Right! Fuck them!" She laughed. "What are *we* going to do?"

He leaned forward. "I want you to check up on our old friend Gutman, the Torah thief. He's been in the lock-up awhile. Maybe that prosecutor, Netzer, wouldn't mind if you took him out for a little walk."

"Gutman?" She squinted at him.

"Yeah. Don't you think he could use some air?"

"Is there some connection between him and General Gati?"

"Talk to Netzer, Shoshana. We need old Gutman. So when you go in use all your charms."

Late that afternoon she brought Gutman to where he waited beside the Jean Arp sculpture on the western edge of Independence Park. It had been a magical Jerusalem day, the sky deep blue, the dry air fragrant with decaying lilac blossoms. Now Arp's three vertical steel waves stood like profiles of gigantic women, silver silhouettes against the dense summer greenery.

Gutman had aged since the night of his arrest. He'd lost weight, his skin was pale, and he blinked like a man not used to being out in natural light.

"So it's you." When he saw David he lifted his eyebrows. "For this they let me loose?"

"You're not loose," David replied.

"Oh? More Gestapo torture. I get it now." Gutman enlarged his eyes. "Bring the old Jew out of Bergen-Belsen, let him breathe, then send him quick to 'the delousing van.' "

David knew Gutman was a shrewd old crook and that his indignant persecution talk was merely rhetoric. But he found the Nazi references troubling. They were bad enough coming from Arabs, but when a Jew used them they were calculated to injure and infuriate.

"Let's call this a short reprieve."

"Just how damn short is it going to be?"

"Depends on you."

"Do I have to read your mind?"

"Okay, Jacob, let's take a little walk."

He gestured for Shoshana to follow, then guided Gutman up King George toward the offices of the Chief Rabbinate.

"How's your father?" A moderate tone now, as if

Gutman had decided to behave like a normal person for a while.

"You should have told me you knew him."

"And embarrass you?"

"I wouldn't have been embarrassed."

"Oh? So you like to arrest your father's friends?"

The harsh defensive tone again; David ignored it. "You recognized me. Tell me how."

"I knew you when you were a kid. I've seen you a few times since. People point you out: 'Hey, there goes young Bar-Lev, nice boy.' See, David, you're not old enough yet. Later your face will change. Your true cop-type character will assert itself."

They passed Stein's Bookstore. Through the window David saw an old man in a skullcap moving languidly among stacks of moldy second-hand Hebrew and German books. Ahead, grenade screens guarded the entrance to the Jewish Agency. Bands of razor wire caught the sun.

"I haven't seen your father in years. Or many of the others."

"The hunters."

Gutman glanced at him. "What did he tell you?"

"Nothing. It's the one thing about which he's never said a word."

"Didn't he say anything about me?"

"Yes. He said you were a man who had been 'wronged.' "

Gutman smiled. "Still, you knew I'd been a hunter?"

"Yigal Gati told me. He came around one day."

"Hmmm. This is interesting. Tell me more."

"I didn't like him much. Pushy kind of guy."

"He always was. A good commander but no compassion, none at all."

"Yes," said David, "I know what you mean. A real first-class Israeli prick."

Suddenly Gutman stopped. He turned to David.

There was fear in his eyes and wariness too. "What are you telling me?"

"That Gati's not doing you any good. That if you want help with your difficulties, Gati's not your man."

"So who is my man? *You?*"

"Calm down. Let's go into the park. It's nice and cool down there."

He glanced back at Shoshana, then guided Gutman off King George. As they descended by a footpath and entered the trees, the sounds of Jerusalem traffic faded away.

"So what are you going to do for me, sonny-boy? Going to get me off?"

"Can't do that. A reduced charge—maybe. But for that you'll have to trade."

"Trade? You mean bargain? Your camel for my rug—that sort of thing?"

"How about your money for my Torah?" For the first time, David saw Gutman grin.

This, he knew, was the crucial moment, the pivot upon which the interview would turn. Gutman could spill, if indeed he had anything to spill. Or he could tighten up and then it would be useless to try and make him talk.

They passed a young mother in a red blouse pushing a baby carriage, and then a young man with one leg, tall, tanned, athletic, a Lebanon veteran, walking with crutches, his sweetheart by his side.

"I want to explain about the Torahs."

"I'm listening." David gestured toward a bench. Gutman sat down. David sat beside him. Shoshana leaned against a tree.

"I don't want you to misunderstand. I didn't do it for the money. I never cared about that."

"So what did you care about?"

"Religious people. Their stupid *halacha*. The way they've brought this country to its knees. They're de-

testable. The Knesset ought to ban them. Fire the
rabbis. Outlaw the yarmulke. Cut off their damn
earlocks and if they don't like it ship them out." He
shook his head. "One day in 1972 one of them, a
black-suited black-hatted son-of-a-bitch, hit my only
daughter, Miriam, with his car. He was a diamond
merchant, fifty-two years old. She was nineteen, on
leave from the army, a beautiful red-headed kid, eyes
so sweet you'd look into them and want to cry. He ran
her down, squashed her right there on Malkhe Yisrael,
and the bastard didn't even stop. Just drove off with
his precious diamonds, and then, when they caught
him and put him on trial—no doubt of the outcome;
the case was open-and-shut—up pop a dozen of his
friends to say he couldn't have been the driver because
he was with them in their *lernen* group interpreting
Talmud at the time. Then his lawyer starts in on
Miriam like she was some kind of slut, like she practically deserved to be run over for walking in a religious
neighborhood, her head provocatively uncovered and
her bare legs fanning flames of lust. The prosecutor
was a young smart-ass. He didn't prepare himself;
they ate him up alive. Then came the verdict. Reasonable doubt, says the judge. No punishment. No dam-
ages. The fucker walks out of court, a great big smile
on his face. Your father tells you I was 'wronged.'
Yeah, I was wronged. *Oh yeah! I was wronged!*"

Gutman twisted in his seat. There were tears in his
eyes. David glanced at Shoshana; she was staring embarrassed at the ground.

"Give your father credit, he tried to help. Told me I
had to come to terms with what had happened, put it
behind me and get on with my life. I listened and I
tried but I couldn't do it. My wife was dead. I had
nobody left. So that's when I thought up my little
vengeance scheme. Pretty pathetic for a hunter, maybe,
but for me at my age it wasn't bad. . . ."

He shifted position, wiped his eyes, tensed himself as if to show them he was strong. "Trade in Judaica. Export the stuff to the diaspora. The scrolls too. I practically gave them away. Anything to get the damn things out of here faster than the damn scribes could write up more. So maybe it was pathetic. Still it satisfied. Every time I sold off some of that crap I felt a little thrill, a little lighter in my heart." He laughed. "Now they want to lynch me. A Torah thief—they're crying for my blood. Suppose I say: 'Okay, sorry, judge, I'm remorseful, I won't do it again.' Then what? He gives me four years instead of five?" Gutman looked around. "A day like this, you think what prison could be like. I know I'm going there, and I know that's where I'm going to die."

David peered at him. This, he decided, was one very strange human being. Gutman was spilling, so far so good. But there was more, there had to be.

"So tell me, Mister Big-Shot Detective, why do you think Gati's been trying so hard to get me off?"

"You have something on him."

A shrewd smile now. "Pretty smart, sonny-boy. Yes, you're pretty smart."

"Tell me about it?"

"Maybe I will." He paused. "Funny thing, I kind of like the idea of him being so frantic on my account. Hiring that fancy lawyer Abramsohn for me—yeah, that was nice. Then Abramsohn says I should just keep calm and everything will get worked out. By calm he means silent. But now I'm not so sure. I could get killed in jail, poisoned, or maybe one night some-one sneaks in and slits my throat. Anything to silence me, because they don't know what I know. The truth is, I don't know much. Just that there was some kind of accident."

David stared at him. "What kind?"

"An accident. How the hell should I know what

kind it was? I wasn't there. But I do know that's what they're worried about."

"Who's worried?"

"Oh, Gati. Maybe Abramsohn. Maybe some other people too. That's the trouble. I just don't know. I don't know what it means."

"Where did you hear this?"

"I heard it."

"Not enough, Jacob. We already know about the accident. *Who? Where?* You have to say."

"In the first place, sonny-boy, I don't have to tell you anything. But suppose I do? Then what happens? They hear I squawked and decide to kill us both. I don't care about myself, but you're Doc Bar-Lev's boy. I wouldn't feel right my dying moment knowing I'd brought that kind of grief on him."

David peered at him. As much as he wanted to probe he knew it would be a mistake. So they just sat there together in silence until finally Gutman cleared his throat.

"What happened with our hunters group—now that's an interesting tale. First it was just to talk it through, your father's idea after he became a psychoanalyst. We'd all long since gone on to other things, but there was still something lingering in our hearts. Not guilt exactly, but this awful feeling about having killed so coldly and brutally the way we had. So your father got us together. A reunion, he said. A chance to talk things out. Regular meetings. I looked forward to them, the first Thursday of every month.

"But then, after we'd been through it all a hundred times, we began to speak of other things. Israel. Her destiny. What should be done. It was around that time, after the Yom Kippur War, that there occurred what we later called 'the split.'

"I'm not saying up to then we didn't disagree. Gati and I, for instance—we always hated each other's guts.

But this new thing went beyond personalities. It had to do with the way we'd each responded to what we'd done. How to put it? There were two completely different ways. Your father's, the way of most of us, that we'd done what we had to do and that that was over for us now. And the smaller faction, Gati's gang, who felt the opposite. They had this idea we should become an avenging knighthood and go back to doing dirty clean-up work. So that was the division: hunters who wanted to live normal lives, and hunters who wanted to hunt some more.

"After the split we went separate ways. We didn't mix with them and they didn't mix with us. But there were still a few odd contacts, guys who moved back and forth. One of them, Max Rosenfeld, lived in my house on Hananya Street.

"Max died two and a half months ago. Liver cancer. Started feeling bad, went into the hospital, and three weeks later he was gone. I went to visit him four, five days before the end. He sent for me, said he knew something important about Gati and the rest of them, something he wanted to pass on. He was very sick. He didn't give details. Just said there'd been this accident. Gati was worried about it, all of them were worried, and they were trying desperately to cover it up. He also told me they'd robbed your father's papers, files he'd stored in Herman Blumenthal's garage. He said they'd taken stuff to cover their tracks, because they were going to try and set you up."

"Me?" David was astonished. "Me personally?"

"Yeah, you, sonny-boy. Avraham Bar-Lev's Big-Shot Policeman Son. Truthfully, that's all I know. I forgot about it because it didn't mean a thing. But after I got arrested I remembered and sent word to Gati I knew certain stuff, that I needed help, and that if I didn't get it I was going to spill to the police. He was famous. I figured he could pull some strings. Now

I see he can't and neither can that fancy Abramsohn. So now I'm wondering: What's going to happen? Am I going to die in prison? Or, now that I've squawked, is this pretty young police girl here going to trot me off to the delousing van . . .?"

He went directly from the park to see his father. No advance call. The old man's embrace was brittle. The stubble of his beard bruised David's cheek.

"What's the matter? You look unhappy."

"I didn't come for therapy."

"I don't do therapy anymore." A pause. "Why did you come?"

"Which of your papers were stolen?"

"None. I told you that."

David glanced at the photos on the table: Gideon in his Air Force uniform smiling, his mother's sad longing eyes meeting his with reproach.

"Listen, Father, this is difficult to say, but I know you've not been truthful. Dr. Blumenthal never reported the break-in. I checked. And on his deathbed Max Rosenfeld told Gutman that Gati and his faction robbed your files. Which ones? Files on the hunters? I can understand that; Rosenfeld spoke of covering their tracks. But he also said that they were going to try and set me up." Silence. "What files could you have that could possibly help them do a thing like that?"

Avraham stared at him, then turned away. "I'm sorry. . . ."

"Never mind that. What did they take?"

"Remember the concept of the broken vessels. . . ."

"No Kabbalah, Father, please. This one time just the facts."

"You want facts. All right. They did take the hunters files, not that that means anything. Everything we did has been common knowledge for years."

"What else?"

"That doesn't concern you."

"Dammit, Father, don't hold out on me. I must know everything. I may be your son, but I'm also a captain of police."

"Ha! You're going to play the big shot now with *me?*"

"Don't lie to me again. Or withhold or shade the truth."

Just then the window shook: the sonic boom of a fighter crashing across Jerusalem's skies.

"Would you arrest me? Really?" Avraham's voice now was subdued.

David lowered his to match. "If I had to—yes," he said.

The old man winced. The room was steamy. David wiped his brow.

A long pause, and then Avraham spoke: "They also took my file on Gideon."

"Why?"

"I don't know. To hold over me maybe, remind me I'd already lost one son."

"A warning?"

"I think so." Avraham squirmed. "If they read that file they know I blame myself."

"How can you? Gideon was an adult. He made a choice."

"But what compelled him to make it? I don't know. That's the trouble—he was more difficult and perplexing than any patient I ever had. After he died I lost belief. For thirty-five years I gave people answers. Then, when he killed himself, I started wondering: Was my profession just a fraud?"

"You helped many people. You can be certain of that."

"I look around now and I see sickness everywhere."

The light in the little room was dim but David was certain he saw tears in his father's eyes. He wanted to say something, give the old man comfort, then he knew that the best comfort he could give him would be to give up their struggle and allow him to regain his dignity.

"I'm sorry I talked to you the way I did. Sometimes I get carried away." He paused. "It's hard, you know, being the big-shot cop. Sometimes even harder than being Dr. Avraham Bar-Lev's son."

Avraham smiled. "No, you were right. I shouldn't have lied to you. But now I have something more to say." He paused. "This time will you let me tell it my own way?"

"Of course."

"An analogy between the broken vessels and your case. The vessels, remember, were unable to contain the powerful light that poured into them, and thus they shattered into a million shards. I believe that's why your case is so important. The forces you are confronting are very powerful. And if you don't separate them, David, they may blow everything apart."

"You already figured it out, David. You told me before they set you up to go chase after Peretz."

Anna was lying on their bed, hands behind her head. David stood by the window staring out.

"Peretz—yes," he said. "But now I think there may have been something more."

He gazed down upon Jerusalem. In the summer night the lights of the city made a pattern across the valleys and the hills. The Dome of the Rock seemed poised above everything, like a cap holding in the anger boiling out of the maze below.

"Suppose they were planning to create a case," he said, "a pattern case, that would have to be assigned to me. Suppose they deliberately left a trail of killings that they knew would pull me in."

"But why would anyone want to do that? What could they possibly gain?"

"Maybe they thought it would seduce me, and then, on account of some personal flaw, I'd botch it and then they could go ahead with whatever it was they'd planned."

He turned to her. The shadows beneath her arms were pools of darkness. "I wonder . . ."

"Yes?"

"I wonder if they did this so that maybe later on . . ." He shook his head. "I know this is a bizarre idea, Anna, but suppose they did this so that later they could *use* me somehow . . . ?"

He phoned Yehuda Merom at the Ministry of Defense. "Can you get hold of my brother's medical file?"

"No problem. . . ."

But later that afternoon, when Yehuda called him back, his voice had lost its confidence.

"David, I'm sorry, I'm not going to be able to give you what you want."

"The file's missing?"

"Most of it, yes. It'll turn up eventually. Probably it was just misplaced."

"The psychological portions?"

"Yes. But, David, how did you know?"

"It's been almost two years since he crashed. Are the records on a dead pilot kept secure?"

"They're supposed to be."

"But not really, right, Yehuda? You had access to them, so other people did too. Any number of people could have removed them. And no one would have noticed because nobody cares once the officer is deceased."

David was surprised. Israeli generals did not usually

retire into luxury. They tended to favor simple farm-houses or the beloved kibbutzim of their youths. Yigal Gati, however, inhabited a penthouse in the most expensive area of the rebuilt Jewish quarter, the complex designed by Moshe Safdie that overlooked the Western Wall.

The scene below was fascinating as always, but observing it from here David felt detached. So vivid and engaging when seen from out-of-doors, the view seemed dead through Gati's wall of soundproof glass.

He turned back to the room. The general, sipping from a glass of mineral water, observed him from a sleek gray soft glove-leather couch. Except for a pair of expensive contemporary chairs the large living room was underfurnished and austere. Sets of thick glass shelves recessed in the walls contained a collection of archaeological artifacts. David examined them: superb examples of pottery, papyrus, and ancient coins illuminated by invisible lights. There was a large ornate menorah too, the kind one might have found sixty years before in a wealthy synagogue in Prague. And beside it, in a simple frame, hung a fine small glowing oil painting by Chagall.

Gati, offering no explanation as to how he had acquired these priceless objects, watched with curiosity as David took them in. Finally, when David sat down, Gati met his eyes.

"So—nothing can be done. I was afraid of that. Poor Gutman. I had hoped. . . ." He made a gesture to show he understood the inexorable processes of the law.

"Still," David said, "we have loose ends. Gutman's case, it turns out, is not as simple as we thought."

"Oh? I thought you found the Torahs in his apartment."

"Yes. But now it's not the scrolls that interest us."

"What then?"

"Collateral aspects. Certain statements the man has made. He's a strange fellow, clear one moment, barely rational the next. He sees us alternatively as friends and persecutors. In his paranoid phases he sometimes says the most extraordinary things."

"Such as?"

"Well, for one thing, he hints at knowledge of inflammatory facts."

"Is this what you've come to tell me?" Gati was studying him with the same cool evaluating gaze he'd employed on his unexpected visit to Abu Tor. "You have something to say, David, go ahead and say it."

David nodded. "I know now why you came to see me, even though you always hated Gutman's guts."

"Why did I come?"

"You were afraid he'd talk."

Gati didn't wince or blink or exhibit any other symptom of stress. "What could he say, that crazy old man?"

"He had plenty to say about you. Including the fact that you'd been recognized leaving the scene of a certain unreported accident."

Gati laughed. "Ever since his daughter was killed, Gutman's had accidents on the brain." He continued to gaze at David. Then, after a long silence, he shook his head. "You're bluffing. And what's more, you know I know you are." He stood up, went to the huge window, stared out, then turned. "Tell me—what do you really want?"

"Since you ask so bluntly, I'd like to see you without your mask."

"An honest man. You're not like your father. I always found him a little . . . oblique."

"And my brother? Do I remind you of him?"

"No. Not at all. He was a completely different type. Extremely talented, perhaps the most effective pilot I ever had in my command. But he was a coward killing himself the way he did. Not that there's anything wrong with suicide. In appropriate circumstances it can be honorable. The zealots of Massada; that Japanese guy, Mishima; Svidrigailov in *Crime and Punishment.* But your brother . . . look, if he wanted to take his own life, okay. But a single bullet would have done the job. To destroy a perfectly magnificent aircraft in the process—I'm sorry, I lose sympathy. I don't respect grandiose gestures designed to distract attention from—and let's be honest now—unsavory personal flaws."

Gati seemed actually to froth as he said this. Now he stood in a defiant posture as if challenging David to mount a physical assault.

"I notice something about you, general."

"Yes?"

"You like to stand in front of windows when you talk."

Gati grinned. "Not a bad observation. Though I'd have hoped for better from 'the best detective in all of Israel.' " He shrugged. "Anyway, since I'm standing here, let me say a few words about the view." He turned his back, stood at parade rest, and stared out as he had done in front of David's window in Abu Tor.

"We hear a lot of talk these days about territory. It's become our national fetish. West Bank. East Bank. Frontiers. Annexations. Lines drawn and redrawn again and again. Parties are formed. Old friends become bitter enemies. People shout. People scream. But in the end they're squabbling over nothing. Because the real issue isn't territory. It's something else. It's character—who we are and what we want to be."

He faced David again, then pointed through the window toward the Western Wall. "Take the Wall. Sometimes I stand here and stare at it for hours. Such a tired bedraggled place. Such pathetic performances too. A wretched remnant. Old men bobbing up and down. Tourists gushing tears. But look above it. The Mount! Now there's something serious. We took it in '67, paid for it with Jewish blood. And then, like perfect idiots, we gave it back. Can you imagine? The high ground! *Gave it back!*"

He left the window, sat down wearily on the couch. "I ask you: What kind of people are we that we would give up our temple site and settle for a moldy cellar wall? So you see, David, if I give long speeches while standing in front of windows, it's just the reaction of a bitter old patriot to a truly sickening sight."

The man was crazy. It was time to leave. David leaned forward as he spoke.

"I'm going to be very frank with you, general. I didn't come about Gutman. He was my excuse. I came about certain personal papers stolen from my father. You took them, and I want them back."

Then, for the first time since he had entered the apartment, David saw Gati shake. It was only a tremor, it lasted only for a moment; the general regained his composure almost immediately. But in that single instant of trembling all of David's suspicions were confirmed. He knew for certain now that Amit Nissim's identification had been correct, and that Max Rosenfeld, on his deathbed, had told Jacob Gutman the truth.

The Mendelssohn sonata: now Anna worked on it every day. Whenever David came up the stairs to the apartment he could hear her practicing portions through the door.

"It sounds better," he told her. She shook her head. "Well, not hopeless."

"No, not quite hopeless," she agreed.

She had a special way of smiling even when she was sad. That smile touched him. It made him want to take her in his arms.

She was worried about Targov. "He's here for a purpose. He won't tell me what it is, but I think the unveiling is a pretext for something else."

"Sokolov?"

"Yes. But not just to see him—it's not just that. He has a plan. Something complicated. Deep and strange, I think."

"He wouldn't try to hurt Sokolov, would he? To cover up what he did?"

"No, no—he's too torn up with guilt. I'm more worried he'll hurt himself. He liked you, David. Very much. He told me that several times. But he's cryptic. He talks about redemption, making things right, settlements, settling scores. He has something in mind. Perhaps something dangerous. I wonder if Jerusalem is really good for him. He's become obsessed with martyrdom. That's all he sees here, all he thinks about. . . ."

David nodded. The city was filled with repentant madmen—saints and saviors of every stripe. "Messiahs" walked the streets, along with criminals and psychopaths, each harboring his agenda, his plan for redemption, his way of righting ancient wrongs and putting an end to tortured sleepless nights.

THE WIRE
IN THE
BOTTLE

"You hate me. That's only natural," Targov said.

The old man shook his head.

"But that's impossible, Sergei. You have to hate me. You *have* to. You simply must."

Something shriveled about him, Targov thought, as they examined one another now in silence. The room was small and simply furnished—new immigrant's furnishings in a room without character, in a basic housing block without style, in a barren neighborhood southwest of the city. All the flats here were identical; aside from the numbers on the doors the only way to tell them apart was by the laundry hanging from the balconies. Now night was closing in. The room was dark except for the single unshielded low-wattage bulb that burned from a fixture in the wall. Targov pulled his chair forward. He knew he must engage this man. But Sergei sat staring at him refusing to be engaged, huddled in his chair, shriveled, wrinkled, withered, and, Targov hated to admit this, looking almost, yes . . . almost repulsive.

The glossy black hair that had waved up straight up from his forehead was all gone now. His teeth were rotten and his mouth, that mouth Targov had seen one cold afternoon pressed so ardently against Irina's throat, reminded him of a misshapen piece of clay.

But it was Sergei's eyes that frightened Targov most

for they lacked all trace of glimmer. Sergei stared at him with eyes so dead they showed nothing, no pain, not even contempt.

"Listen to me, old friend. We both know what happened. Each of us knows what he did to the other and can see the disproportion. Now I've come to you with a way to even up the score and at the same time stick it to our common enemy. But you say nothing. Don't even bother to refuse. Surely you must feel something about my coming here. Or at least about my plan. . . ."

Silence again, and that implacable deadening stare, the stare that said it didn't matter, nothing did, that life was the same as death.

"I'm recalling now . . ." *At last he was speaking!* ". . . how you always liked it when the irregularities were balanced. In painting, sculpture, architecture most of all. Many times, when we'd walk in Moscow, you'd see it in a building and point it out. 'Look, Sergei Sergeievich! The beauty of it! The subtle symmetry!' I remember . . . so many years ago. And now, well . . ." he smiled, "your taste is still the same."

"You haven't answered me."

"What exactly is your question?"

"Will you do it?"

"I don't despise it," Sergei said. "But it wouldn't mean anything."

"*It would!*"

"To you, perhaps. But not to me." He shrugged. "Now, Sasha, tell me about your work. . . ."

It was only toward the end that Targov saw how cleverly he'd been baited. Those occasional little nods, tight little smiles—small encouragements, perhaps, but large enough to make him boast. Too late he realized he'd sounded like a pompous ass. But why, anyway, was Sergei so interested in his success? He didn't seem like a man who reveled in envy. Why then? What was he after? What did he really want?

Targov found himself beginning to dislike him. He asked himself: Do I really want to put myself into the hands of this withered old man with dead eyes and foul-smelling teeth and a horrible uncentered mouth?

"You needed me as nourishment, to feed yourself. . . ." *What was he talking about?* "If I'd been killed you'd have forgotten me quick enough. But alive, locked up, degraded, my condition incited you to greater triumphs. You had to make up for what you'd done so you became a better artist than you had any right to be. Without me, Sasha, you would have been mediocre. Did you ever think of that?"

No, he hadn't thought of it, but now he saw how the camps had turned Sergei mean. "Is that why you sent the postcard—to tell me this? You've been expecting me, haven't you? You knew one day I'd come."

Sergei shrugged. "I thought you might. But it wouldn't have mattered if you hadn't."

His eyes were very bad, he said; he'd lost seventy percent of his sight. But still he could work, he said, though in a different style and on a much grander scale.

"Do you have a studio?" Targov looked around. He could see no workspace in the little room.

"Don't need one. I lost my touch. I don't work with my hands anymore. I do conceptual pieces now, design them. The bulldozers do all the work."

Conceptual pieces? Bulldozers? Now what the hell was he talking about?

"Only a year here but already I've received a major commission. They've carved it out in the Negev." He stood. "Come, I'll show you." He motioned Targov toward the second room, where, in the gloom, Targov made out a narrow bed and several open suitcases containing neat piles of clothes.

A bare bulb hung from the ceiling. Sergei grabbed hold of it, switched it on, then flung it out by its cord. It swung crazily back and forth casting rapidly moving shadows on drawings and photographs tacked up to the walls.

"What is this?" Targov caught glimpses of an enormous four-sided trench.

"An environmental sculpture. An earthwork."

"Really? Remarkable. But, tell me, what does it mean?"

Sergei turned to him. "Nothing. It means nothing at all."

"So you've become an abstractionist?"

A small smile. "You could put it that way. No more daintily crafted ballerinas or tourist giftshop junk. My sight's too dim for that." He glanced mischievously at Targov. "It does surprise you, doesn't it? And the scale too. Well, it *is* very big." For a moment, Targov thought, Sergei actually seemed to gloat.

"How did you conceive of such a thing?"

"No studios in the Gulag, though some men do nice work with pipe cleaners, discarded chess pieces, assorted odds and ends. I worked differently. I designed sculptures in my mind. And now this one," he said proudly, "has actually been dug. Dug out in the Holy Land."

Targov examined the photographs. He could see trucks, bulldozers, men laboring beside an enormous trench. The shape itself was very simple: a modified rectangle, something like a trapezoid, containing a circle near its center. Simple, geometric, highly abstract, and, according to Sergei, meaningless. It was difficult to believe that this shriveled broken man beside him had been responsible for such an outpouring of human labor.

"It must mean *something*."

Sergei grabbed hold of the cord, stopped the lamp from swinging. "Why must it? *Why?*"

"But it does, doesn't it?"

Then, just before Sergei shut off the light, Targov thought he caught a glimpse of a malignant grin.

"I want you to try and understand. We were victims of the apparatus. The men who ran it were evil. They hurt us both, and now we must hurt them back."

Sergei yawned. "You've already told me this."

"But I promise you, it will work. I'll be punished for the terrible thing I did, and you'll have the pleasure of wielding the punishing instrument. Then we'll both be free, you from all your bitterness, I from all my guilt. A private matter, strictly between the two of us. As for the rest of the world, they will see something else."

"Yes, of course, the famous émigré artist assassinated beside his sculpture in honor of refusenik Soviet Jews. Who else but the KGB would do such a wicked thing? They'll be hated by everyone. Ridiculed. Despised."

"So you *do* understand."

"Oh, I understand all right. And so what? Two days later no one'll give a shit. Aren't you ashamed, Aleksandr Nicholaivich, to come to me with such a deal? To ask me, of all people, to free you from your pain?"

Now he was confused. The meeting was not going well. He was the famous one, the strong one who'd come from halfway around the world with the startling, original, gorgeously conceived and balanced scheme. But things had gotten mixed up, he had misjudged his old friend's feelings, and now Sergei, nearly blind, had somehow gained the upper hand.

"Don't you wonder how it feels?"

"What?"

"To sit here now across from you."

"I—"

"You know only how *you* feel, Sasha. Don't you wonder what it must feel like to be *me?*"

"Yes, of course," Targov said. "Please tell me. I would like to know."

Sergei nodded. "There's an old story by Komroff. A convict is released from prison after many years. As he leaves his guard asks him: 'How does it feel to be free?' The convict goes back into the world but he doesn't fit in. He becomes eccentric, turns his little room into a jail cell, and begins to collect odd little pieces of wire which he imprisons by twisting them, then stuffing them into a bottle. One day, when the bottle is filled, he decides to break it open. But the pieces of wire don't spring back into shape. Rather they remain twisted, a mass in the shape of their old prison, the bottle, from which, in a certain sense, you could say they were 'released.' "

It was difficult to arrange. Rokovsky had to plead. The director of Mishkenot Sha'ananim had received many odd demands from exalted guests, but a private plane, to fly out over the Negev so that Targov could view an "earthwork" that no one on the staff had even heard about, a plane, moreover, that must actually be able to land on the sand beside the site—this one was quite incredible.

Still, Aleksandr Targov was a sculptor of international repute who had every right to view a piece of contemporary Israeli art no matter how obscure. So—okay. The director would do her best. "Here in Israel we have a motto: Nothing is impossible!"

"While I'm away," he told Rokovsky, "take Irina to him. Leave them alone together, wait outside for her in the car. But check your watch—I want to know how much time she spends."

It *had* to mean something. There'd have been no point in creating it if it didn't. Sergei had pointed him toward it, had wanted him to see it. But why? And *what* did it mean?

He had the pilot fly over it several times. The work was huge, its sides a good five hundred meters long. An enormous trapezoid enclosing a circle near its center—it looked exactly as it had in the drawings and photographs, except now there were some craters near the circle.

New embellishments or damage created by the wind? In the latter case, Targov knew, the piece would never last. But perhaps that was the point: It wasn't meant to last, was meant to erode and thereby express the relentless forces of time.

Targov knew about time-dimensional sculpture, but he did not respect it. For him the whole point of a sculpture was that it outlast its maker; art was an act of striving against the certainty of death.

As the pilot made a final pass Targov wondered if the piece might be a kind of signature. Two forms opposed: the sharply angled trapezoid and the smooth-sided circle inside. Sergei's mark, his way of saying: "I lived and one day I was here."

It was hot on the sand. He felt dizzy, nauseous. His eyeballs, shielded by dark glasses, felt as though they were being scorched. The pilot loaned him a hat, handed him a canteen of water, then waited in the plane while he trudged the four outer walls of the enormous thing. It took him nearly thirty minutes to make the march, a tortuous and monotonous inspection that yielded him no new ideas.

Then just as he was about to turn toward the center to inspect the inner circle, he heard a noise, looked up, and saw a lone military jet racing toward him out of the oscillating air. An extraordinary sight because the plane was flying extremely low, perhaps no more than a hundred feet above the sand.

The noise was deafening. He pressed his palms against his ears and flung himself into the deep trench that lined the earthwork's outer wall. He turned onto his back. The plane was a fighter and it was screaming at him. Suddenly it soared up. He watched it, saw it pass directly overhead, plunge down again, then fly off into the haze from which it sent back a terrifying boom.

Ears ringing, Targov rushed back to his own small waiting aircraft.

"To Jerusalem," he yelled at the startled pilot. Then, when they flew over Sergei's earthwork, he looked down upon it a final time. He shook his head, furious with himself that having made such a perilous journey he still could not decipher it.

Irina wanted to fly back to California. That very night if Rokovsky could find her a seat.

"He's *awful,* Sasha. Twisted. A mean little man with nasty empty eyes and terrible stinking breath. To think how all these years I longed to see him. Now I never wish to see him again. Not ennobled either by his tragedy—in fact just the opposite, a deformed old *zek.* So maybe that's the lesson: that in the end we must wear the face of the monster, the one who lives inside."

"You sound more disgusted than heartbroken, Irina."

"I am disgusted. Now I want to go."

"Won't you at least stay for my unveiling?"

She shook her head. "I know you don't want me there. Better to wait for you at home. Our life together could be different now, Sasha. We could change it if we tried. You could give up your girls and I my bitterness. We could forgive each other. If we could do that then maybe some good will have come out of all our pain."

There was *something* about that earthwork, he decided: something tormenting, something not right. It was the one thing about which Sergei had boasted, swinging the bare bulb, then grinning furtively, maliciously, as he'd suddenly switched off the light. He was concealing, or at least pretending to, and, like a damn fool, Targov thought, I was suckered in. I flew out there, thinking I'd discover its meaning at the site, then nearly got mowed down by that hotshot Israeli pilot doing bumpety-bumps in his ear-splitting jet.

But it *did* mean something. Why else would Sergei have designed it? And there was something strange about that too—digging those trenches, creating those walls must have cost a fortune. Who was the sponsor? Who had assigned him such a grand commission? And since when does a trinket carver such as Sergei Sokolov arrive out of the Soviet camps to find Israeli bulldozers ready to execute his "conceptual art"?

It was a task for Rokovsky. Let Tola track the sponsor down. Meantime, now that Irina had left, he would watch Sokolov himself. His old friend, nearly blind, wouldn't even notice that he was there.

GIDEON

"You see, here's where they pried off the lock."

David and Dr. Herman Blumenthal were standing just inside the garage behind Blumenthal's house on Abravanel. David nodded. He could see the chisel marks in the wooden door, could smell a musty odor too, the aroma of old papers, files packed loosely in cartons which, stacked together, filled nearly half the interior space.

"Surely these don't all belong to my father?"

Dr. Blumenthal shook his head. "Some are mine, and some belong to colleagues. Our names are on the cartons. Since I don't own a car and I have this space, it's become a depository for a whole generation of psychoanalysts."

David had always liked Dr. Blumenthal, his father's mentor and oldest friend. With his dancing eyes, kindly features, and wild white curly hair, he looked a little like Albert Einstein without a mustache.

"You weren't here when it happened?"

"Friede and I were visiting our grandchildren in New York. After we came back it was a couple of days before I noticed the hasp had been chiseled loose. The padlock, you see, was still intact. I was in the process of unlocking it when the assembly fell out of the door. Then, when I looked inside—a terrible mess, papers scattered everywhere. I called all concerned.

We spent a weekend sorting things out. None of us could find anything missing so I didn't bother to report it. That's why I was so surprised when you told me what your father said."

"Surely you've noticed how strange he's become?"

"Yes, of course. Everybody has. But the change in his interests may not be as bizarre as people think. Kabbalah, after all, is based on the belief that one can attain great illumination about the nature of God by exploring deeply within. I wonder if the process is so different, really, than exploring the unconscious through free associations and dreams."

"Still . . ."

"I know. In the year and a half since Gideon died. . . . But you say it was Gideon's file that was taken?" Dr. Blumenthal shook his head, perplexed. "I had my own file on him. I wonder. . . ." He moved toward a stack of cartons, removed one, and began prowling through the one beneath.

"You had a file on Gideon?"

The doctor nodded. "For a while he came to me professionally." He glanced up at David. "Nothing strange in that. One never treats one's own child. If one of our children needed help we'd send him to a colleague. A great honor to the person, a gift of trust. I sent my own daughter to Avraham. And he . . . but I'd have thought. . . ."

"No," David said, "I was never sent to anyone."

"Ah, here it is." The doctor extracted an old-fashioned marbled cardboard folder tied together with string. "But now, David, you must tell me what this is all about. Otherwise, even though he's dead, I can't. . . ."

"Yes, I understand."

As they walked back to the house, the old man put his hand on David's arm. "You were upset back there. I noticed. Perhaps for a moment even a little depressed. But you shouldn't have been. If your father didn't send you to one of us for treatment that only means he didn't think you needed it. To feel badly about that would be the same as feeling jealous because your brother got extra attention when he had the misfortune to break his leg."

The interior of the house was dark, furnished with heavy German pieces from the 1930s. After David explained why he was so curious about Gideon—his father's cryptic comments and the strange fact that the psychological portions in Gideon's medical folder were now missing from the central files of the IDF—Dr. Blumenthal agreed to speak freely of what he knew.

"I didn't see him often. Perhaps two dozen times over the years. In no sense was he in treatment; we would just meet occasionally to talk." He untied the dossier, quickly reviewed the papers inside. "Most of these visits were during his adolescence. He had the typical troubles of a boy that age—self-image, sexual identity, some special problems having to do with your mother, and also a rather well-defined self-destructive streak. Later in his twenties he came to see me four times. He feared that he was homosexual. He found himself attracted to other men, but he resisted these feelings and wanted to be cured. We discussed his undergoing regular therapy, but he said this wasn't feasible. If the Air Force found out he'd be finished as a pilot, and he loved flying; he couldn't bear to give it up. I tried hard to reassure him. He was, you see, attracted to women too. But because of his great physical beauty men approached him frequently, and when they did their longing for him had the effect of arousing him as well. That, I think, was his problem. We're all bisexual to a certain degree. But his very attractiveness, which you probably envied as an advantage, became a kind of curse. Every time someone made an advance it only emphasized his ambiguity. Had he been less beautiful he would have been left alone, and thus better able to combat the sexual feelings he despised."

Dr. Blumenthal consulted his dossier again. "The last time he came to me was a few months before he crashed. I remember he was very troubled. In 1981 he had flown an important mission. Perhaps you didn't know this—he was one of the sixteen pilots who flew Operation Babylon."

David was surprised. The brilliantly executed surgical strike against the Iraqi nuclear reactor ranked with the most daring exploits of the Israeli Air Force.

". . . a secret of course. The names of the pilots were never released. They were our best pilots, some even said the finest fighter-bomber pilots in all the world. Gideon had been elated by the mission. He thought of it as the high point of his life. But when he came to me he was depressed. He had finally become involved with another man. He was terribly frightened he'd be found out, frightened of disgrace, perhaps frightened most of all of the possible reaction of your mother. And yet he felt helpless to break it off. I had the feeling then . . . well, I could have been wrong."

"What?"

"That he feared he might be blackmailed by this man. Not for money. I don't think that. And I'm certain it had nothing to do with espionage."

"What then?"

"I don't think he knew himself. Just that he felt trapped, that he was being led along somewhere, and that sooner or later he might be forced to do something against his will."

"I don't understand. What did he say?"

"I didn't make a transcript, David. My notes are only impressions of what I think I hear between the lines."

David nodded.

"But there's something else here. Another kind of note." Dr. Blumenthal shook his head. Suddenly, David thought, his face was flooded with grief. The doctor handed him a page out of the dossier. "Look there at the bottom."

David squinted. Blumenthal's handwriting was spidery and difficult to read. But finally he was able to decipher the bottom line: "Treatment? Problem of exposure. *Unorthodox Solution?*"

"What does this mean?"

"At the time I didn't know, which accounts for the question mark. But just now. . . ." He shook his head again. "It could explain. . . ."

"What?"

"The fact, David, that your father even had such a file. I didn't mention this to you before, but when you came to me this morning I thought this whole business about Gideon's file and the break-in was extremely odd. Of course Avraham kept papers pertaining to his sons. Every parent does. But why would they be mixed in with his patient files? Then you told me he referred to Gideon's being more perplexing than any patient he ever treated. That, I think, is a clue to the 'unorthodox treatment' Gideon was talking about. Suppose your brother, feeling he had nowhere else to turn, took his problems to your father. And suppose your father tried to treat him—an impossible task, a thing that simply cannot be done. The treatment failed, as it had to. Gideon killed himself. Your mother fell ill and died. Your father, blaming himself, became consumed by guilt. He renounced everything, sold his beautiful house, gave up his profession, went to live in a wretched neighborhood and immerse himself in Jewish mysticism. If you look at everything he's done this past year from that point of view, then his behavior starts making sense."

David nodded. "And so does the stealing of all

these papers. Whoever removed my brother's military records would also want my father's file." He paused. "But only someone very close to Gideon would have known he'd been my father's patient. You didn't know."

"No."

"So it had to be Gideon's lover, this man you say he feared might push him to do something against his will. . . ."

Later, when Dr. Blumenthal walked him to the street, David asked why Gideon hadn't come to him for treatment. "Surely he knew you'd be discreet. You wouldn't tell the Air Force."

"He knew that, yes, but still he was afraid even to be seen making regular visits here. Afraid too that your mother would find out."

"What was going on between them?"

"Mother and son? Ah!" Dr. Blumenthal smiled. "The answer to that would have been the quest of the therapy—another reason your father could never succeed with it."

"He was a soldier," he told Anna, "and my mother loved him for it. The sharp uniform, the perfect haircut, the beautiful clean-shaven chin. He was the favorite warrior-son with the strong tanned arms and legs. He was also—and it hurts me to say this—a bit of a fascist too. He was particularly vicious in hand-to-hand combat training, and he gloried in the Israeli war machine. The helmet visors, the zippered flight suits, the cult of manliness. Muscled flesh, polished paratrooper boots, smart salutes—the whole esprit of the pilot corps. You wonder why he didn't run away. Where could he go? Cyprus? England? The United States? Without his aircraft, without the cult, he was nothing and he knew it. Fact is, he had no place to go except into the sky . . . so that was where he flew."

Rafi called David in. He looked embarrassed. Superintendent Latsky had assigned a case to CID with the strong suggestion it be assigned to Pattern Crimes.

"What kind of case?" David asked.

"Actually a species of street scam." Rafi glanced up, met his eyes, then focused on Sarah Dorfman at her smaller desk across the room. "Small gangs. Three or four kids. One of them, eating a sausage sandwich or ice cream, picks out a well-dressed tourist, approaches him, then stumbles against him smearing mustard or syrup on his clothes. Profuse apologies. 'Oh! Dear sir! Dear madame! I'm so sorry!' Enthusiastic efforts, then, to clean off the disgusting mess. Other kids come forward. 'Let us help. We have a rag.' Soon three or four of them are working the poor guy over, dabbing at his garments, thoroughly grinding in the mustard or syrup. Meantime, of course, expertly removing his wallet, passport, and watch. The tourist is so upset by the horrible mess they've made of him that it's only later that he realizes he's been picked completely clean."

David stared at Rafi. "You can't be serious?"

"It is a pattern crime, David. Though not, I admit, our usual kind."

"Rafi, this isn't new. Arab kids have been doing it for years. It's petty street crime."

"Yeah. Of course. But the point is, Latsky wants it stopped. The mayor's office has been complaining and the Ministry of Tourism says it costs us friends."

"But why use detectives? All you need are a couple of cops." He felt a welling up of bitterness.

"I have the impression Latsky's got it in for you, David. You caused him trouble with the minister. So now. . . ." Rafi shrugged.

"Do you have it in for me too?"

"Of course not!" Rafi spread his arms. "When Latsky

proposed this I told him it wasn't for us, but he wouldn't budge. He's a pissed-off old man without the guts to call you in and chew your ass. His is the old bureaucrat's way: Humble the subordinate, assign him a degrading task."

"Listen, Father—I don't want to embarrass you, or pry into your business, or reproach you about something that happened in the past. Just two questions. No explanations required. None needed. No apologies either. All right?"

Avraham nodded. "That sounds reasonable."

"Who was Gideon's lover?" David blurted the question out.

"Oh, David. . . ." His father's voice was filled with pain.

"Do you know his name?" Torment now disfigured Avraham's features. He turned away. "For years, Father, we left all this unspoken. Maybe it's time now to talk it out."

When Avraham turned back to him the mixture of fear and relief on his face reminded David of Gutman on the night of his arrest.

"It was his old schoolmate Ephraim Cohen."

Cohen! "You're sure?"

"Gideon told me." Avraham shook his head. "What's question number two?"

Now David was almost afraid to broach it. But, having pushed so far, he knew he could not retreat.

"What was the pressure Gideon feared? What was he afraid he'd be compelled to do?"

Avraham grimaced with disgust. "The pressure, I assume, was that the affair would be revealed. As for what Ephraim wanted him to do—I haven't the faintest idea."

"But he didn't do it, did he?"

"No, he didn't. Which is why I think he killed himself."

"So as not to have to bear disgrace? I think he could have handled that. I think he was strong—"

Avraham cut him off. "Disgrace he could have handled. But not betrayal. You see, David, I think he was so wounded by Ephraim's threat, he couldn't bear to live."

"You never pursued this?"

"No. How could I?"

"You could have discussed it with Ephraim."

Avraham shook his head. "Gideon was gone. What would have been the purpose?"

A long pause then before David spoke: "Thank you, Father. I know how painful this has been. I'll try not to bother you with this again."

David assigned Shoshana to be the decoy in his scheme to entrap the mustard-and-syrup pickpocket gang. Now she had to assemble a suitable wardrobe.

"How far can I go?" she asked.

"Far as you like so long as you end up looking rich. You know: nice rich Jewish-American girl on her first UJA leadership tour."

"She'd stay at the King David."

"Naturally."

"So what about a handbag from that gorgeous leather shop in the Cardo?"

"Sounds good."

"Expenses?"

"See Rebecca. She'll get you an advance from The Claw."

"Afterward, David—do I get to keep the stuff?"

But before he could tell her "no" she had disappeared.

He put Micha on Ephraim Cohen.

"We know he's Shin Bet, but not much else."

"What do we want to know?"

"Everything. Military background. Reserve unit. Marital status. His private life too. Any weak spots you can find. Particularly any rumors about outside love affairs."

"This'll be hard, David. A Shin Bet guy. How can I sniff around without his finding out?"

"Just do the best you can. Go for what you can get out of the files. But use your own contacts on this one, Micha. Whatever you do, don't cut in Police Intelligence. They're in bed with Shin Bet. They share with each other all the time. There's more loyalty between them than between PI and us."

"It's shit, David. The whole compound knows about it. David's Dogs doing patrolman's work."

Dov's face expressed his fury and disgust, also his feelings of betrayal. Uri wore a similar expression, but less intense because he was less outraged. He was older, had more years in and thus more experience with the ups and downs of being a cop.

Dressed in various combinations of T-shirts and track pants they were lounging against a wall just inside the Jaffa gate. For four days they'd been staking out Shoshana, who, in her high fashion garments, was strolling now around Omar Ibn El Khatab square inspecting trinkets in the windows of the tourist shops.

"Thing that gets me," Dov said, "is that even after you bust your ass to make detective, they can break you back down this way."

"Take it easy," Uri said. "Remember we were riding high a while back. Couple of weeks ago we were David's Dogs. Now we're being punished so we're the Rabies Squad."

"Rabies Squad—that's not bad," David said. "Maybe we can do something with that."

"Foam at our mouths and drool?"

"Or maybe turn it into something," David said.

Dov looked at him. "What do you mean?"

"Suppose we call ourselves the Rabies Squad and take on every stinking job Latsky's got. Suppose we start acting like we've got a case of rabies—guys you don't fuck around with, guys who bite."

He could see they liked that; he liked it too. More than anything he wanted to show Latsky that he wasn't going to be humbled or beaten down.

"See that kid. Looks like he's cruising. He's munching something too." Uri nodded toward an alley that converged upon the square. An Arab boy, spooning ice cream from a cup, was moving toward them at a leisurely pace.

"Remember, if he spills on her, wait till his buddies cluster around."

Uri smiled. "Then kick ass, right?"

David nodded. "Okay, let's spread out."

Actually, they all agreed afterward, it was Shoshana who kicked ass the best. Even before they reached her, she had unleashed a series of ferocious chops and kicks. The Arab kids were devastated; no rich tourist woman had ever come at them like this. She badly bloodied two of them, and smashed her foot into the crotch of the third. He fell to the pavement, curled up, held himself, and whimpered. Fascinated passersby pressed forward while frightened tourists fled the scene.

When it was over Shoshana's fine silk blouse, which she'd bought at an expensive boutique in Yemen Moshe, was split straight down the back. But she didn't care. She loved to fight. Studying her afterward David thought: *Today a decoy has been born.*

When they delivered their prisoners to the booking room at the Russian Compound, Dov introduced the beaten-up Arab youngsters as the harvest of a brilliant trap.

"We're the Rabies Squad," he announced to the astonished guards. "We skim scum off the streets."

He remembered an incident between Gideon and his mother. Gideon was still in high school; David was on leave from the army. He'd spent two years as an intelligence officer compiling psychological profiles of the Egyptian General Staff.

In those days he was courting Judith Weitz; the incident occurred one night after they'd gone out. David had returned late to the house on Disraeli Street, was mounting the stairs to his old bedroom on the third floor, when he heard voices coming from the closed upstairs sitting room, and paused on the steps to listen.

His mother was speaking. There was something fierce and unfamiliar in her tone. She was berating Gideon, mercilessly, David thought, all the while punctuating her speech with what seemed to him to be inappropriate endearments.

"Darling, darling . . . absolutely not acceptable. You must never do such a thing! . . . vile and cowardly . . . selfish . . . horrid. No, sweetheart! No son of mine . . . !"

What were they talking about? David retreated two steps, to bring himself closer to the sitting room. Just then the door opened and Gideon appeared, wearing a pair of jeans and nothing else, his upper torso bare, gleaming with perspiration.

" . . . disgusting . . . vile. . . . Don't you *dare* walk out on me!" Their mother's voice continued to cut through the house as Gideon raised his head, saw David, and they locked eyes. Gideon's, David saw, were streaming tears.

". . . come back in here, darling! I insist! *Immediately!*"

But Gideon just stood there, eyes still locked with David's, his chest heaving as he wept. Finally unable to bear this vision of anguish and vulnerability, David broke contact and continued up the stairs.

"Okay," said Micha, reading from his notes, "we got ourselves a pretty fancy boy. Ephraim Cohen: thirty-two years old, born on Kibbutz Giv'at Haim. Graduate of Balliol College, Oxford. Did two years' graduate work in Arab studies at Harvard. Distinguished military record: fighter pilot, later detached to General Yigal Gati as a special aide. Served in Air Force intelligence. Six years ago he transferred to General Security Services. Married to Dr. Shira Aloni, another kibbutznik, now associate professor of botany, Hebrew University. The Cohens have two children, a boy and a girl. They live in a handsome flat on Arlosoroff just across from the Van Leer Foundation. Cohen is known as an Anglophile; he favors fine English tailoring and speaks the language like an upper class Brit. He's also fluent in Arabic. Far as his politics go, I couldn't pick up much. He's not religious, nor, so far as I can tell, associated with any particular faction within Shin Bet. Basically, David, what you've got here is a typical young, elite, secular Israeli, well-off, probably Labor Party liberal, ambitious, hardworking, superbly educated, and very well connected. If there's a blot I can't find it. In a funny way he seems . . ."

"What?"

Micha squinted. "A little too perfect, know what I mean? Maybe just too good to be true."

"So, Rafi," David asked, "has Latsky found us another dirty little job?"

Rafi laughed. "Latsky's shitting in his pants."

The last time Rafi had described Latsky's anxiety, he'd told David the superintendent was pissing blood.

"Why? All we did—"

"No, not that. A male body turned up, hidden pretty well in a gully near Kafr Aqab. It could have lain there for years if some Bedouin hadn't stumbled by. The vultures made a pretty good meal of the guy, but the forensic team managed to get some prints. He checks out as a bully-sadist from the Haifa waterfront. Military records show he was sentenced to five years in prison for assault on an officer. Then suddenly he was released."

"One of Peretz's boys. The 'Executioner.' How was he killed?"

"Hard and slow."

"He was marked, of course." David didn't bother to conceal his sense of vindication.

"Since Peretz's story to you finally checks out, the minister's changed his mind. Congratulations, David." Rafi grinned. "As of now you're back on the case."

Anna described *"toska"* to him—a melancholy longing that struck her sometimes when she played, a sad and anguished yearning for her motherland.

She smiled when she told him that *toska* was a feeling no expatriate Russian could avoid.

"Targov feels it very strongly," she said. "I think he could die of it if he allowed himself." Then, after a pause: "Sometimes, David, I think that's why he came."

"To die?"

She nodded. "To die here in Jerusalem."

On a golden Sabbath they went together to The Shrine of the Book to see the Dead Sea Scrolls. "They are like title deeds to us," David explained. "Proof of our ownership of this land."

Later, facing the black wall outside, the wall that

symbolized the forces of darkness that prevailed before the revelations of the Book, he said: "The case involves my entire life. I keep looking for an elegant solution. There're all these different paths leading off in different directions, and I don't know which one to follow to get me through the maze."

She placed her hand against his cheek, then arched up on her toes and kissed him between his eyes. "The same problem with my sonata," she said softly. "A thicket of ideas. Lots of different ways to play different sections. But no clean clear line leading to the finish."

Sometimes, after they made love, early in the morning or late in the afternoon before the sky turned dark, he would turn to her, look directly into her eyes, and then would see all the colors of the sun spreading out from her pupils in a wheel of fire.

A fine private house in the German Colony. An old lady in a green housedress, her white hair arranged in chaotic wisps, greeted David at the door.

"Moshe Liederman? Yes, he's here, young man. Up three flights, then follow the corridor."

Old wood steps creaked beneath his feet. He smelled dead flowers, and then, on the third floor, the dark aroma of rooms closed up and rarely aired. Down the corridor past old black-framed schoolroom etchings of classical Roman scenes. At the end an open door revealed a narrow attic room.

Liederman, wearing a worn gray sweater, sat crouched over a wooden desk. He was reading clippings, a cigarette in his hand. When he heard David's steps he looked up, surprised.

"Captain Bar-Lev!" He started to rise.

"Stay still, Moshe." David peered about. The room was lined with shelves packed with folders containing old newspapers and books. "So this is your archive. Okay if I sit down?"

Liederman cleared a pile of papers off a chair. His thumb and forefinger were stained with nicotine.

"I'm honored. But you should have warned me. I'd have straightened things up and bought some beer."

David inspected the room again. "Tell me what you've got here? And what you're trying to find out?"

Liederman was cautious at first, perhaps afraid David would find him Holocaust-obsessed. But soon he revealed the dimensions of his archive: a vast collection of Polish newspapers from the years 1938 to 1944, in Polish and Yiddish, as well as mimeographed underground newsletters and other circulated tracts produced after the Yiddish papers were closed down. It was an archive that documented the destruction of Polish Jewry, the core collection inherited from his father, then supplemented by years of methodical attendance at estate sales, and purchases made at flea markets and in secondhand stores.

"So what are you seeking in all this?"

"I read through it looking for an answer."

"An answer to what?"

"To how it could have happened, how this culture, so bittersweet, so vibrant and alive, was so suddenly and utterly destroyed. But of course I know how that happened. The historians have explained it very well." Liederman paused. "Perhaps I read through it just to feel the loss. Perhaps," he added, "just to feel."

"Listen, Moshe—there's something I'd like you to do. I can't promise it'll be useful, but it's possible it could prevent another tragedy. You told me you're good at following and that you like to look under every stone."

Liederman smiled. "I like that more than anything."

"In that case," David said, "you may enjoy this

very much. I want you to follow a certain Shin Bet officer. His name is Ephraim Cohen. . . ."

"Shoshana, remember that little scrapbook you put together for Amit, the one with all the men who'd been on TV panel shows? I want you to make up another one for her, this time of 'scary-looking' guys with beards."

Uri lived North of Jerusalem on Le'a Goldberg Street in the suburb of Neve Ya'acov. David drove out there on Saturday afternoon, spent twenty minutes searching out the address, and then, when he finally found the Schuster's first-floor apartment, came face to face for the first time with Uri's wife.

"You must be Captain Bar-Lev," she said. She was a stout broadly built woman with gleeful twinkling eyes. "Uri's down there." She pointed to the basement stairs.

He made his way to the cellar, then followed a corridor that led past storage and utility rooms. He passed a laundryroom, smelled the dry hot air of the driers, the aroma of detergent, and the sweat of people waiting for their wash. He was about to return to Mrs. Schuster for more detailed directions, when he heard sounds of panting and then a harrowing groan.

"Uri?"

He moved toward the sounds, found himself in the doorway of a windowless low-ceilinged room. The bare concrete walls were dank. Uri, wearing a sleeveless singlet, was working out with a set of ancient barbells. There were beads of sweat on his hairy shoulders, and, when he recognized David, a sudden expression of distress, as if he were embarrassed at being caught doing something so stupid as lifting weights.

As they talked Uri mopped himself with a towel.

"I want you to find the van."

"That's impossible. They got rid of it."

"Cleaned it up, painted it, altered the registration, hid it away. But junked it? No. That's too rich even for them."

"How am I going to . . . ?"

"Auto paint shops. Repair shops. Gas stations. They have to maintain the vehicle. And this isn't New York—there aren't that many fancy American vans around. I brought the pictures Dov took of the four goons and the girl." He handed them to Uri.

"Well, with these it's different, David. Yeah. Maybe. . . ."

"When you find it don't move in, just let me know."

"No criticism intended, David," Rafi said. "But aren't you putting an awful lot of your case into the hands of a six-year-old child?"

"She's almost seven."

"Be serious."

"Okay, Rafi, if it weren't for Amit we wouldn't know about Gati or be able to place four of our victims at the accident scene. If I really thought she was going to be our star witness at a trial, then, sure, I admit she couldn't possibly support the case. But I don't think of her that way. For me she's a source, very reliable up to now, who just might lead me to another one of the three guys who were in that van. When I finally find out who they are, then I'll know what this case is all about. And then, maybe, I'll be able to figure out a way to break it open and bring in the bastards who think it's okay to kill some 'wild cards' so they can make suckers out of stupid cops."

"Was Gideon really so vulnerable?" Anna asked. "From the way you've described him I've gotten an impression of a kind of icy prince."

"Sure, he was that, but underneath he was troubled.

When I listened to Dr. Blumenthal I felt sick at heart. I wished we'd been closer. I wished he'd trusted me. But the way things are here I can understand why he didn't think he could."

"Yosef's gay."

"Yosef's an artist. When he does his reserve duty he gives concerts at military bases. Pilots are different. And Israel is different too. We're just starting to acknowledge life-styles that are taken for granted in the States. To live openly as a homosexual here is to accept the fact that generally one is going to be reviled."

"Would you have helped him, David?"

"I like to think so." Sorrowfully David shook his head. "On his own terms he was in a terrible kind of bind."

"So he committed suicide."

"At that time, in his particular state of torment, he must have felt that was his only way. Ephraim wanted him to do something and threatened that if he didn't he'd be exposed—grounded and disgraced."

"But wasn't that a bluff? Ephraim was involved too. Worse, he was married. Seems to me he would have been even more disgraced."

"That's logical, Anna. But this wasn't a poker game in which Gideon was coolly sizing Ephraim up. The issue wasn't whether Ephraim would follow through on his threat. My father put his finger on it: It was the betrayal implicit in the threat itself. The thing you have to remember about these Shin Bet creeps is that almost all their operations are based on manipulation. They're trained to find a person's weakness and then exploit it. Ephraim, who'd known Gideon since boyhood, must have thought he knew all his weaknesses: his fear of exposure, and of being shamed before our mother, and his self-hatred on account of being attracted to men. The one weakness that perhaps he didn't know about was Gideon's extreme sensitivity to the slightest hint of personal betrayal. So here he was threatened with betrayal by one of his closest, oldest friends, a man moreover with whom he may have been in love and with whom he was physically involved. What could he do? Yield to Ephraim's blackmail and perform the illegal mission? Or kill himself because he couldn't perform it, and couldn't face the threatened consequences? In an extreme emotional crisis situation like that, the question of whether Ephraim was bluffing would have been almost irrelevent."

"But, David, what was the illegal mission?"

"That," he said, "is what I'm going to find out."

THE
UNVEILING

Here was Sergei, living free and retired in this gorgeous sun-struck city, behaving like a bored old pensioner in Minsk. He rarely ventured out, and, on the few occasions that he did, it was to buy a Russian language newspaper and take it to a drab suburban park. There he'd read it, leave it on his bench, then walk back to his hideous housing block. He did not look around, gaze at buildings, absorb the beauty, breath deeply of the air.

Targov spent three days following him. When it became too tedious he turned the job over to Rokovsky.

"Listen," Targov told him, "this is a little man who lives a little life. Not one who dreams up vast schemes to be carved out in the desert sand."

"The work is his. I've verified that."

"Who paid for it?"

"I told you. An American group, some kind of fine arts foundation."

"Why choose him?"

"Perhaps out of pity."

"Perhaps this, perhaps that. There's something wrong here, Tola. I want facts. You must find out for me: Why Sokolov? *Why?*"

At night Targov visited the warehouse where "The Righteous Martyr" was stored. Rokovsky had arranged for the sculpture, covered with a plastic sheet, to be placed upon timbers so that it was suspended a foot above the floor.

Targov, wearing work clothes, wriggled beneath it, dragging along a flashlight, a hammer, and a pot of clay.

If it should fall now and squash me, he thought, *it would probably serve me right.*

Once beneath the hollow bottom, he sat up straight so that his torso was literally inside the statue. Using the hammer, he carefully broke the seal he had painted to match the bronze, then reached up, unclasped the hidden tube, pulled it out, and set to work patching up the hiding place with clay.

When he was finished he shined his flashlight around. Finding his repairs seamless, he lowered himself and wriggled out. When he stood up, triumphant, grasping the tube, he moved too fast and strained his back.

In three days the unveiling would take place. The plumbers had installed the pipes, the sod had been laid, and now masons were busy positioning the paving stones so that viewers could circle "The Righteous Martyr" without treading on the grass.

"There seems to have been some sort of military fund," Rokovsky said. He and Targov were on the first of their three daily inspections of the site.

Targov grimaced. "You told me a foundation."

"A joint venture. Each put up a certain amount. The foundation funded the design; the military paid for the actual work. The work, by the way, is entitled 'Circle in the Square.' "

"How much?"

"Ten thousand for Sokolov. Impossible to estimate how much to move the sand."

"Ten thousand dollars! Impossible!"

"That much, Sasha, is a fact."

"But something's not a fact—is that what you're telling me?"

Rokovsky nodded. "There is something queer about the deal."

"What?"

"Difficult to say. Maybe it's just my feeling. The designs were drawn in a most exacting manner, like architect's plans, precise to the centimeter, as if the measurements were crucial, and the exact angles to the compass points as well."

"Tola, for God's sake! What does all that mean?"

Rokovsky shrugged. "Maybe Sokolov didn't make the drawings."

"He could have come up with the idea, then hired a draftsman. . . ." *But why the hell am I arguing the other side?*

"I spoke to the engineer in charge of the project. He was quite certain about this, absolutely firm: Sokolov never, ever, not one single time, contacted him or visited the site."

Targov strode away. He couldn't understand it. The whole business was just too maddening.

"Okay, rent a car," he yelled across the freshly watered lawn. "No more planes. This time we drive. We'll leave right after lunch."

Down rocky roads, across sinuous sands, through a stony wasteland of sweltering emptiness. When they finally arrived, exhausted, eyes tired, throats parched, Targov shook his head.

"You see, Tola, in the middle of nowhere it serves no purpose, none at all. Oh, I know the theories—I've read them in the art magazines: how the difficulty in reaching the site is inextricable from the work; how the inaccessibility is the point, blah-blah-blah. . . . But Sokolov the trinket carver! Such grand concepts never entered his brain. I'm telling you: *Israelis don't waste money*. There's a fraud being perpetrated here."

"Good. Now what are we going to do about it?"

"To begin with, get out the Polaroid and photograph the damn thing from every side. I'm telling you, this shape means something. 'Circle in the Square' —that's not even what it is. It's a circle in a trapezoid. I've seen it before, too, but, in my pathetic dotage, I just can't remember where. . . ."

On Sokolov's face an expression of bemused contempt. "So it's you," he said, blocking the door.

"Pardon me, Sergei, but were you expecting someone else? Irina's gone home. She didn't say good-bye? Oh dear!"

Sergei, glancing meaningfully at the tube in Targov's hand, stepped back into his room. "Is that the punishing instrument?" He asked. "I meant it, Sasha. I decline to participate in your self-serving little farce."

"I brought it anyway, in case you changed your mind."

"I won't."

"Don't be so sure. I may give you a new reason to want to knock me off."

"Don't you understand: the sweetest vengeance I can have is to wake up every morning thinking of you waking up remembering what you did."

"I'm not here to discuss vengeance, Sergei. My unveiling is tomorrow. I'm inviting you to come. I'd like you to be my honored guest."

"So if I won't lie in the shrubbery with your ridiculous rifle, I'm to sit at your right hand cheering with the notables."

"You're in trouble, Sergei Sergeievich!"

"Not me, Aleksandr Nicholaivich! I bear no guilt."

"Twice I've been out to see your earthwork. You didn't design it. You acted as a proxy. For whom?

And why? You'd better tell. Because I promise you this, Sergei: The fraud won't stand."

Now, at last, a stricken look. The crafty old *zek* was scared. He said nothing, just gulped and turned away. "I don't know what you're talking about."

"Well, here's food for thought," Targov said, rising, pulling out an envelope, laying it carefully on his chair. "Since I know you've never been out there, you couldn't possibly know what's been going on. Here are my photographs. When you recover from your little terror, examine them closely and compare them to your own. I think you'll find some interesting changes. There have been—how shall I put it?—erosions. Yes, certain erosions which most certainly do not coincide with the pristine vision you conjured up during all those painful years on strict regime."

Out on the street, Targov walked briskly to Rokovsky, waiting in the rented car.

"He's scared now. Maybe unnerved enough to move. Wait here and follow. I'll get myself back to Mishkenot."

They were alone in the luxury restaurant behind the artist's residence. Anna, looking unhappy, said that she and her cello had unaccountably become estranged.

"Renew the friendship," Targov suggested.

"Easier said than done."

"The detective—maybe he's the problem."

She shook her head. "David wants desperately to help."

Targov thought for a moment. "There's a drawing by Balthus. 'The Guitar Player.' It's very sexual."

"Naturally." She smiled.

"A man sits on a stool plucking at the genitals of a woman who lies across his lap like a guitar. He makes her sing. You could do that with your cello. Indulge yourself. Make love to your instrument. Think of it as, well . . . a little outside affair." She giggled. "Seriously, I wonder if it was a mistake for you to settle here. Everyone's so tormented. Loudmouths too. The pressures. The paranoia. All that's bound to take a toll."

"Oh, Sasha," she said, "you don't understand. I wouldn't dream of living anyplace else. No outside affairs either—if that's what you're hinting at."

He grinned, shrugged, then turned serious. "I've seen Sokolov several times but our encounters have not been satisfactory. He refuses to despise me—he won't forgive, and he won't retaliate. But I don't bring him up to burden you with that. For years I've lived with guilt; I'll manage to live with it some more."

"Then why do you bring him up, Sasha?"

"Because there's something very peculiar going on. He's involved with something here, something that's not quite right. He claims to have designed some simple-minded pattern they've carved out in the Negev, some sort of enormous environmental sculpture. But I'm absolutely positive he had nothing to do with it even though he's listed officially as the artist."

Anna shook her head. "I don't understand why you're telling me this."

"It's a fraud. Your boyfriend, the detective—I thought he might be interested."

"David's working on a murder case, Sasha. He barely has time now to sleep."

"Yes, of course. I'm sorry. Will he at least come to my unveiling?"

"Both of us will come, of course."

"I promise to astound you, Anna. . . ." Tears filled his eyes.

Rokovsky, usually so glacial and ironic, was excited,

nearly feverish. He paced about Targov's apartment at Mishkenot, puffing vigorously on a cigarette.

"Oh, he moved all right! In a way I'd never seen before. Agitated. Extremely agitated. Like a tightly wound spring just starting to uncoil."

Targov smiled. "So the twisted wire no longer holds the bottle's shape."

Rokovsky stared at him. "Pardon me?"

"Nothing, Tola. Just a passing thought. Where did he go so fast?"

"He boarded a bus, got off at Zion Square, plunged into the mob. He headed up Ben Yehuda like a demon, then, at the intersection near that big department store, he looked around as if afraid he was being followed."

"He didn't see you?"

"He doesn't know me. Anyway, he can barely see. But he was scared and angry. I'm telling you, Sasha, whatever it was he saw in those Polaroids, it gave him one big boot in the ass."

"So where . . . ?"

"The foundation, the one that funded the design. He stormed up the stairs, then walked straight in without bothering to knock. I stood outside and listened to the argument. He was furious. The other man tried to calm him down."

"What did he say?"

Rokovsky stopped pacing, spread his arms. "You know I don't speak a word of Hebrew. But Sokolov doesn't speak it so well himself. Occasionally he'd slip into Russian. I understood enough. He was demanding extra money."

"More than the ten thousand? Incredible!"

"Maybe not so incredible if he was threatening to talk."

"I see what you mean. The fraud. . . ."

"It's fishy as hell. Sokolov signed the drawings and

was paid. But now things are different and he thinks he's entitled to more."

"Did he get it?"

Rokovsky shrugged. "I don't know. Finally he quieted down. When he left he looked exhausted. I followed him back on the bus, saw that he was going home. Then, when I started to look for a cab, I was stopped by another man who turned out to be a cop."

"What?"

"I'm telling you, Sasha—this thing is serious. The cop started yapping at me. Wanted to know who I was following and why. When he saw my American passport he changed his tune. Said he'd picked us up when we left the office building. He wanted to know which office Sokolov had been visiting. I told him, of course. He let me go and it was only later that I realized he'd been following the other guy—the guy Sokolov had gone there to meet."

Targov, astonished now and totally confused, slapped himself on the top of the head.

The unveiling took place at noon. The sun beat mercilessly, but the Israelis, out of respect for the occasion, had placed umbrellas behind the dais.

The Mayor of Jerusalem was there; he made a gracious speech. Several ministers attended, the Director of the Israel Museum, and leaders of the Russian émigré community, each of whom embraced Targov in a slobbering Russian hug.

Targov was tense. Would Sergei change his mind? The plan, fashioned so coolly back in California, now struck him as insane. *Fact is,* he thought, *I'm a terrible coward. I'm nearly sixty-one and still afraid to die. Irina was right: I want to be like Trotsky. But even Trotsky would have flinched if he'd known the hour of his death.*

There was another thing—"The Righteous Martyr"

didn't look all that splendid or even righteous anymore. It was one thing to view it inside a studio; here, beneath the sky, it seemed smaller, somehow diminished. Jerusalem was a great city packed with great works of public art. The Martyr was good, but no masterpiece, and it most certainly did not dominate its site.

So, another illusion melted away, along with the image of the saintly Sergei and his sense of himself as a man who could face bullets with a smile. Now all he wanted was to get through the unveiling—get through it alive.

". . . and so we give our fondest thanks to Aleksandr Targov, who has donated this fine bronze work to commemorate the martyrdom of the suffering refusenik Soviet Jews. Let this site henceforth be the rallying point from which we demonstrate. Let it be the place from which we shout: 'Let My People Go. . . .' "

Targov modestly accepted the mayor's thanks, then the mayor's wife pulled the cord. The veil fell. "The Righteous Martyr" stood revealed in all its mediocre competence. Polite applause. Targov stiffened. *If he's going to shoot he'll do it now.* But there was no shot, the applause faded, and then the audience started to disperse.

Anna kissed him on both his cheeks. The detective warmly shook his hand. Rokovsky led him to the car that would carry them to the reception at the mayor's home.

As they drove off from the site Targov slowly shook his head: He had survived, and, perhaps best of all, Sergei Sokolov had proved himself a coward too.

Early the next morning frantic knocking at his door. It was the director of Mishkenot, her face contorted with distress.

"An outrage, Mr. Targov. A desecration. No words

to describe our shame. That such a thing could happen here—it is not, I assure you, the Jewish way. But," she added sternly, "the damage will be repaired. And the culprit, we vow it, will be punished as he deserves."

"What culprit? What the hell are you talking about?"

"I just don't understand it," the woman said. "Sometime in the night a maniac fired bullets at your sculpture. He hit it, too, and, I regret to say, shot off the martyred figure's nose."

Targov stood stunned for a moment. Then he began to laugh. "Have you read Gogol, madame? If so you'll understand. The nose, you see, is an organ with which all of us Russians are constantly obsessed."

ROOM 304

When Shoshana told David that Amit Nissim had identified rabbi Mordecai Katzer as the "scary-looking man with the beard," he could see the pattern beginning to come clear.

The morning after Amit's revelation he called the PC Unit together. Stationing Rebecca Marcus at the door to be sure no one walked in, he picked up a piece of chalk and approached the blackboard which Dov had mounted on the squadroom wall.

At the top he drew a rectangle with three large circles inside. Below he drew a smaller box, and then another larger box at the bottom.

He pointed to the rectangle. "The van," he explained. He pointed to the three circles. "The three men who fled." He pointed to the smaller box. "The Chief of Operations." He pointed to the large box at the bottom. "The operations group—the guys we've been calling 'the goons.' "

Dov and Shoshana grinned. Micha and Uri moved uneasily in their chairs. David approached the board again.

"Okay, here's what we know." In the circle on the left he wrote "Gati" and in the circle on the right he wrote "Katzer." He stared at the circles for a moment, placed a question mark inside the one in the middle, wrote the name "Cohen" in the Chief of Operations box, and, in the goon box, wrote the names of the four men they'd confronted and photographed when they'd raided the house on Lover of Zion Street.

He pointed to Gati:

"Retired Air Force general. Doesn't like the direction the country's going. Sickened by it. Thinks we're 'soft.' Cold, secular, elitist. A failed politician with grandiose fantasies of being a 'hunter' again, maybe leading an avenging knighthood and taking on some dirty clean-up jobs."

He pointed to Ephraim Cohen:

"Former Air Force intelligence officer, once Gati's aide-de-camp, now an official in Shin Bet where he commands the Lover of Zion Street baboons. Tried to steer us wrong on Peretz. Up to his ears in the cover-up. Intermediary between Gati and the operations group which recruited the executioner, operated the van, and transported the victims to the Mei Naftoah slaughterhouse."

He returned to the rectangle, pointed to Katzer:

"Racist religious demagogue. Strong connections with Jewish terrorist groups. Has called for annexation of the West Bank, an end to 'Hellenic culture,' creation of a fundamentalist theocratic state, expulsion of Arabs, and a 'Holy War of extermination' if we're ever attacked again. Much too crude for Gati. A man of an entirely different style. They don't belong together but there they were. At a certain point in time, our cool elegant retired general and our sweaty rabble-rousing rabbi were seen, at the corner of Yehuda Ha-Nasi and Berenice streets, getting out of Cohen's van."

"A third man too." He rapped his knuckles hard against the question mark. "All we know about him now is that he was injured and limped away. He's the link. Find him and we'll have a shot at figuring out what they were doing. Do that and maybe we can stop them in their tracks. Based on what we know so far I'd say it's a safe guess these guys were hatching some kind of right-wing plot. At the very least I want to charge them with conspiracy. The preferred charge will be premeditated murder."

He told Anna: "I didn't tell them about Gideon. I didn't think they needed to know. The way I'm going to handle this is send each of them out to work on separate pieces, then put the pieces together myself. But now I wonder: not saying anything—maybe that was a mistake. It isn't that I'm ashamed, you see, or that I want to cover up for Gideon, or that I think there's anything wrong that he had those feelings for other men. But somehow dragging that in. . . ." He shook his head. "It didn't seem appropriate."

She looked at him. "You weren't trying to cover up for Gideon, David. You were protecting your father. But I think there's going to come a point in all of this when you're going to have to think about protecting yourself."

Uri was driving. They were in an unmarked police Subaru. They had just passed the large red Calder sculpture at Holland Square and now were heading west toward the small suburban village of Ein Kerem. It had taken Uri only four days to find the van. David couldn't believe it. "How?" he asked.

"Took your advice," Uri said. "Started with gas stations. Went to the one nearest Lover of Zion Street, then tried the one just after the turn-off to the slaughterhouse. First guy I talked to there knew the car. Seems they had an account and gassed up there regularly. When I showed around Dov's pictures, a couple of the guys recognized them right away. The manager said that Yoni, the short musclebound one who drew the gun on Dov, came by every week to pay off the account. But no one's been by lately, not since the day of our bust. So I thought: Okay, they must have stashed that damn vehicle just the way you said.

"I started calling on garages. Anyone remember housing a big dark blue Chevrolet van? About number thirty-six down the list I hit this greasy place in Romema. They remember keeping it a couple of days, but it's not there anymore. I showed around the pictures. The boss picked out Yoni again. He even knew him by name." Uri glanced at David. "He knew him as Igal Hurwitz."

"The phony cop who took down all the names."

Uri nodded. "That's the one. Too bad little Amit doesn't remember him, but that's okay—now I know I'm onto something good. I call the boss aside, swear him to secrecy, tell him I'm with a special undercover unit investigating corruption in the Jerusalem police. Now he's interested—everybody hates the cops. So I tell him Hurwitz is suspected of taking bribes, which he's invested in this big fancy American van, and now I'm looking for the van because it could be crucial evidence when Hurwitz goes to trial. By this time the guy's frothing—he thinks he may know where that van is stashed. Hurwitz was looking for a place to store it cheap, and the garage owner sent him to a friend who owns an old ruined Arab farmhouse down in Ein Kerem."

They had entered the village, birthplace of John the Baptist. They passed a ceramics studio, a leather shop, a good art gallery, a nonkosher Hungarian restaurant, and finally an inn, a gathering place for the crafts-and-culture set, famous for its macrobiotic Sabbath lunch.

It was late afternoon. The town was almost empty. Uri swung the Subaru up a narrow road that ran back toward the Jerusalem Forest. They passed several farmhouses that had been gutted and turned into villas, then followed a dirt track which led to another farmhouse, this one still in ruins.

"The guy who owns it hasn't raised the money yet to fix it up," Uri said. "I checked him out. He's probably on the level. Didn't contact him though. Didn't want to alert our friends."

Uri parked behind a gnarled old olive tree. There were stones scattered everywhere, pieces of the house torn loose from its walls. David got out and followed Uri around to the back. Here there was a second stone structure in better shape than the first, built into the side of a slope, with a large set of padlocked wooden doors.

"Farmers used it for storage," Uri explained. "Over on the right there's a little gap in the slats." He pulled a flashlight from his pocket and gestured David forward. "Shine this in and take a look."

David found the gap and peered inside. The chromed front grill of the van was just inches from his face.

"We have to get in here."

Uri nodded. "I brought along some tools."

While he went back to the Subaru, David looked around. The stone barn could not be observed from the road, but there was a direct sightline, across the gully to the rear, to the Franciscan Church of St. John situated on the hill just behind Ein Kerem. A man, posted up there with binoculars, would be able to keep a watch.

Uri returned with an automobile jack and a pair of plumber's pliers. He set the jack under the right-hand door, then, attaching the pliers to the lower hinge-pin, carefully worked it loose. He removed the upper pin the same way, then knelt to pump the jack. The door, creaking, rose a fraction of an inch. Uri lowered the jack and pumped it up again, gently working the door up and down. When he was satisfied it would swing out, he stepped back, looked around, fetched a large flat stone, placed it a foot from the edge of the portal, then knelt again and carefully grasped hold of the bottom of the door.

"Here's where the old weight-training comes in."

He squeezed his eyes, screwed up his face, and sucked in his breath. Then, exhaling, he pulled the door off its hinges and, with an enormous groan, set it down upon the stone.

There was a ten-inch entry gap into the barn.

"Can you squeeze in there? I sure as hell can't," Uri said.

Shoulder first, David wedged himself inside. When he was clear of the portal, Uri handed him the flashlight. He switched it on and began to inspect the van.

There was barely enough room to turn around; the sides of the vehicle were just inches from the walls. He managed to get into the driver's seat, then crawled over its back into the compartment behind.

He shined his flashlight around, looked under the seats and then inside the ashtrays. Nothing. He had expected that—he knew Cohen wouldn't allow the van to be stashed until it had been thoroughly cleaned out.

Of course there was a chance the clean-up had not been perfect, something that could only be determined by a police forensic team. He could call one in now and gamble they'd pick up traces of powder or even Peretz's blood. But the odds of that were low, Cohen and his people would be tipped off, there'd be another interservice dispute, and in the end, David knew, forensic evidence wouldn't be enough. In fact, if there was any evidence, it would only point to the goons. David didn't particularly care about them. He wanted Gati, Katzer, the third man who'd been injured in the accident, and, most of all, he wanted Ephraim Cohen.

Now he sat in the rear seat of the van trying to imagine what the accident had been like. Two of the three were probably sitting where he was seated now, the third on the bench opposite. The driver, using the alias of Hurwitz, had been driving them in random circles around Jerusalem. A moving safe-house. Ex-

treme precautions. Everything arranged so that three
men would not be seen. But then the unexpected:
Schneiderman's truck smashed into the side of their
secret mobile conference room. Suddenly, in front of
witnesses, the three men had been exposed.

He slid open the side panel door, squeezed out,
closed it, bent down and ran his fingers lightly over its
entire surface. The paint looked fresh, unscratched,
and he could find no trace of damage. Which meant,
he concluded, that Ephraim's men had replaced the
entire panel door.

Later, when he was outside, Uri pointed out the
sightline to the church.

"I saw that," David said, "but you could sit up
there for a month and still miss out. When they take
the van out, if they do, they'll be smart enough to
move it out at night."

"So now what? Is this a dead end?"

David shook his head. "There's still the damaged
door, Uri. Probably still lying around wherever it was
they had it replaced."

The next morning he invited Micha out for coffee to a
police hangout on narrow Rivlin Street. When they
had ordered and were seated in a quiet booth in back,
David asked him if he'd be willing to take on a small
piece of unofficial work.

"Sure. You know me, David. What do you want me
to do?"

"For a guy like you the padlock on that farm building would probably be a cinch."

Micha's hand, holding his cup of coffee, was trembling
just a little bit. "What do I do once I open it?"

"Wire the ignition of the van. Nothing big, you
understand. We wouldn't want to blow off anybody's
legs. Just a small charge, enough to send a message.
The kind of message they sent to me when they used
me for target practice at the zoo."

Micha's hand was suddenly still. "Yeah, I think I'd like to do that."

"How about tonight?"

"Tonight would be good."

David stood up. "Get together whatever you need and we'll drive out there after work."

"Micha says he's just too perfect, that there's got to be some dirt."

"If there is, it's hard to find, captain. No sign he fools around with boys."

"What about girls?"

Liederman shrugged. "If he does he's pretty careful. But maybe he's got no need to fool around. His wife's the kind we used to call a 'dish.' "

They were standing at the overlook on the top of the Mount of Olives. It was a blazing summer day. Air-conditioned tourist buses were parked in the circular drive, tourists were milling about, taking pictures, exclaiming at the view. Several waited in line to mount a bedraggled camel which stood, its snout dripping foam, in a small dry pile of camel excrement.

"He drives a BMW. Works at that Shin Bet sub-headquarters beside the Brandeis School. Couldn't hang around there. Security's too tight. But I caught him a couple times driving home at six o'clock. In the evenings he and the wife go out, usually pretty well dressed. Cocktail parties, restaurants, one night to see the Danish ballet. One evening he took off by himself. I broke contact when I saw he was heading down to Tel Aviv."

"Maybe he's got a boy down there."

"That's possible. There were fifteen of us the night we tracked Peretz. By myself in Tel Aviv. . . ."

"Yes," David said. "I understand."

Liederman cupped his hands to light a cigarette. The gold hemisphere of the Dome of the Rock glittered far below.

"One interesting move he made. He was walking around downtown, aimlessly I thought. Then suddenly he started acting furtive. I turned away. Next thing I knew he wasn't there. I figured he'd slipped into this office building, 28 Histadrut. There's an American-style hamburger joint out front. I took a seat. Sure enough, about twenty minutes later he came out of there walking fast.

"I still had this feeling his antennae were up so I didn't take off after him. But when he was gone I went into the building and had a look. Lots of offices, small businesses, gem wholesalers, import-export firms. Then on the stairs I bumped into this old man stumbling around like he was in a daze. Minute later I saw this other guy, tall and very thin, lingering in the hall. So on the off-chance there was some connection I decided to hang around. And guess what? The thin guy was tracking the old man, which was not very difficult because the old man was almost blind. I followed them a couple of blocks—"

"Moshe, please—is there a point to all of this?"

"Well, you know me, captain. I'm not intuitive."

"So you always say."

"But still, you see, I felt it was all connected. Don't ask me how. I just had this feeling the two of them, the old man and Cohen, had come there separately to meet. Never had a hunch like that before. Never had any kind of hunch. So I thought: 'Okay, Moshe, now you finally got yourself a hunch, start acting like a detective, see where the hell it leads.' "

David nodded. He was interested.

". . . by this time it was dark. They got on a bus for Talpiot. I got on too. Then, when they got off near an apartment project, I did the same. Okay, the old half-blind guy was stumbling his way toward one of those new immigrant housing blocks. Suddenly the thin guy broke off and, couple of seconds later, he and

I were face to face. I stopped him, flashed my ID, demanded to see his, discovered he was an American, and then, in my rotten English, asked what the hell he was doing following around an Israeli citizen in the dark. I tell you, captain, the guy was scared. He started fumbling around. Something about his name, Rokovsky, gave me an idea, so I started talking to him in Polish, and from that point he started to relax."

"Rokovsky? *Anatole Rokovsky?*"

"Yeah, something like that. Do you know him, captain?"

"Not exactly," David said. "Go on. What happened then?"

"Long and short of it, he finally admitted he was following the older guy. And when I asked him why, he started telling me this story about some missing money and a loan. So where had he followed him from? I asked. In the end he told me what I wanted to know: the office at 28 Histadrut where the old man had met Ephraim Cohen. It's some kind of arts foundation. Room 304. . . ."

HER
DREAM

David was speaking to her. Anna looked up.

"Now we have a very peculiar situation," David was saying. "The man Liederman is following meets the man Rokovsky is following. Ephraim Cohen meets Sergei Sokolov. What's the connection? *Why?*"

He had broken in on her mid-afternoon when she'd been practicing. Now, trying to concentrate on what he was saying, the tortured sonata still whirling through her brain, she was aware only of a feeling that she was needed. *Yes, now finally he needs me,* she thought.

". . . but how can this be?" David continued. "Of course I remembered what you told me—Sasha saying he'd uncovered some kind of fraud. But still. . . ."

"David, I'll find out for you." At the moment she had realized that he needed her, she had felt a surge of joy.

"I thought of that. But I'm not sure I want you involved. What if Sasha's implicated? This is a nasty case. If only there were some other way. . . ."

She stood up. "There is no other way."

He smiled. "Well, since you're so insistent, I'll drive you over there. We'll talk about it. You'll have to be careful, guarded about what you say."

"Oh, I'll be guarded." She was already at the door.

"Anna! Wait! Where are you going?"

"I'll walk," she said, gripping the knob. *"You* be

308

careful, David. Don't step on my bow." And at that she slipped out quietly, then fled down the stairs.

As she crashed out the front door of the apartment house the hot dry August air hit her in the face. Hurrying up En Rogel, past the old Arab houses and the path to the Abu Tor observation point, she brought up her hand to push aside her hair, smelled the rosin on her fingertips, and felt an urgency she hadn't felt in weeks.

At the corner, where the five streets met, she waited impatiently for the traffic light. *If I can help him now,* she thought, *then maybe I can help myself.*

Yes, she thought, if she could help David break through the wall of his case, then maybe she could break through the wall that blocked her too. She had no idea why this would be so, but was absolutely certain that it was.

Crossing and then starting down the hill, her nose caught the aroma of pines; the scent wafted to her from the trees that grew on the slopes of Mount Zion. That was the way she liked to walk, the regular march she'd been making these broiling summer afternoons: from the apartment on En Rogel up Mount Zion to the top; then into the strange room called the Coenaculum where The Last Supper had taken place; then down to the cellar which was called King David's Tomb; then out past the Diaspora Yeshiva and around the side of the Church of the Dormition; and then along a whitewashed wall that glowed in the fading light. And whenever she went that way she thought of David, but not of David the ancient King. She thought of David Bar-Lev, the strong, intense young man with whom she lived; the obsessed, tormented, endlessly probing Israeli detective with his despair at disorder and his love of patterns; her handsome, tender, dark-haired Jewish lover; this David whom she loved, *her* David . . . *hers.*

There was new construction on Derekh Hevron; the sidewalks had been torn up. On her descent she had to pick her way through clay and sand and chunks of Jerusalem stone. She paused at the corner where the street swerved down toward the Cinemateque and Bloomfield Park began. Thirty feet from where she stood sat the rusting Dumpster of David's case, where, on the second night of Passover, he had gone to see the marred and naked body of Yael Safir.

There it was—that awful hollow metal coffin to which David had rushed that evening through the storm. When he'd returned, shoes muddy, clothing soaked, he'd spoken of Ephraim Cohen. He hadn't been furious the way he was now; now he hated Ephraim more than any man on earth. But he was angry even then, when he still thought Peretz was the killer, and she had sensed his anger and because of it had made no overtures, although all that afternoon she'd been looking forward to making love. Instead she had touched him gently and cooked him an omelet and then watched as he had faced the window, staring out bitterly as the lightning cracked the sky. And she had known even then that he would not be whole again, not until his case was solved.

She entered Bloomfield Park, then walked along the paths which crisscrossed the manicured lawn. Approaching Mishkenot she compared the two men in her life: David, on whose behalf she was now on an important mission, and Sasha, her former lover, whom she was now on her way to meet.

David first, of course; his body seemed to have been made for hers. When they made love they fit together perfectly. There was lightness in their play and never repetition. They were like two musicians who played intwined variations, joining perfectly in the obbligato, and always arriving with perfect timing at the coda.

Sasha had felt heavy upon her, a good fatherlike

heaviness. His old skin was leathery, his hands power-ful from smoothing clay, and he was always eager, ready, huge, and always, endlessly, erect. Something a little perverse about him—Sasha's tastes were some-times odd. He liked to nibble on her toes, have her pose in strange positions. He'd ask her to play her cello half nude, then stalk behind her and plant kisses on her shoulder blades. In bed he'd make her giggle. "Now *I'll* be the cellist," he'd whisper, "and *you'll* be the instrument." And so she would let him play her until he made her moan, and afterward she would grin and he would laugh and pat her head and compliment her on her tone. She knew he didn't love her; he enjoyed her as he'd enjoyed all the many women he'd possessed. She knew that all of them, herself included, were but surrogates for the Irina of his youth.

The Jerusalem Music Center was situated just above the entrance to Mishkenot. Coming upon it, thinking suddenly of Igor, she froze on the narrow stone stairs.

It was her first thought of him in weeks, since she discussed him with David on her return from Europe, and now she remembered his voice when he'd called from Moscow and awakened her in Paris. The pleading in it, the cries, the sobs—so pathetic and so different from the Igor Titanov she had known.

The musicians had all called him "Wild Man," on account of his grandiose, swooning, arm-thrashing style. It was a manner he had copied from Leonard Bern-stein, even to the flashy tossings of his mane, and into which he'd integrated several gestures of Stokowski, trying sometimes to actually model the music, using his hands to carve the air and sculpt it out.

But when he took her to bed the gestures were not refined. He hurt her, hammered her, turned sex into a game of conqueror and slave. If she and David always climaxed together, following separate threads that al-ways knotted in the end, and if she had found release with Sasha because he had played upon her with a certain tender wit, still it was only Igor who had had the power to make her howl. He was her conductor and she was his orchestra and the music he made her play was a long symphony of ecstasy and pain.

How she'd loathed him! How she'd longed for him! During the year that they'd been lovers a single lustful glance from him was enough to make her wet. She'd both hated and craved the sharp tang of his sweat as he pumped roughly up and down upon her, the hard slap of his hard body, and the obscenities he whispered as he bit her ear. "Resist!" he'd commanded. "Resist! Enjoy!" And so she had resisted, allowed him to beat upon her as if she were a drum, listening to him vow that this time he would break her to his will.

Sometimes she wondered if she had not defected in Milan just to escape his rule of her. Sometimes she wondered if she had really defected to escape her shame in her pleasure at being ruled.

A productive hour spent at Mishkenot with Sasha and Rokovsky, and now she was back at the apartment to give David her report. He was on the phone, but had looked up at her and squinted when she came in.

"Why do you always look at me like that?" she asked, when he had finished his call.

"Like what?"

"Like you're relieved to see my hair still in place, my clothing untorn." He smiled. "It's Sasha, isn't it? You think I go to see him to tear one off."

"Never, Anna! Never have I had such a thought! But don't be too clever. It's an old trick—trying to throw off the investigator by mocking his accusations in advance."

She growled at him, formed her hands into claws, pulled off her blouse, and pounced. She ripped the upper buttons off his shirt, then they rolled upon the floor. They grabbed and clawed and pretended they were cats. He took her finally, laughing, facing the window, over the back of the couch.

"This is the way you like it, isn't it? *Isn't it?*" she hissed. "The way you did it all those times with Stephanie. Wrestling with her. That bitch! That Lynx!"

He was sitting now smoothing out his clothing, while she sat in a chair opposite and formally presented her report.

"Sasha says Sergei received a grant from an American foundation. It was to design some kind of abstract environmental sculpture in the Negev. The thing's actually been built—Sasha's gone out there twice to look at it. He says it's a phony: Sergei didn't design it, and Sasha doesn't even think it's a work of art. He wouldn't care except that Sergei made such a big point of telling him he'd created it and boasted to him about how big it was. So after following Sergei around for several days, he decided to put on some pressure. It seemed to work. Sergei took off, and Rokovsky followed him to the offices of that foundation where he overheard him demanding extra money."

"From Ephraim Cohen?"

"Rokovsky doesn't know. He never saw the other man. And since he doesn't speak Hebrew he could barely make out what they were saying."

"But he's certain Sergei asked for money?"

"Yes, and that he was very angry too. The other man tried to mollify him. Rokovsky, by the way, was very frightened when Liederman stopped him in the dark."

For a few moments David gazed at her. His silent intensity always fascinated her—she could sense the wheels turning in his brain. Finally he spoke: "How did Sasha pressure him?"

"Apparently by handing him a stack of Polaroids,

ones he'd taken at the site. And then by taunting him and telling him straight out he knew the sculpture was a fraud."

"That's it?"

"Pretty much. I didn't tell him about your case. Just that you'd been interested in what he'd told me and asked me to find out more. He'd like to talk to you about it directly, David. He's obsessed with it." She smiled. "That's what struck me most of all."

"What?"

"The way you both feel—so strongly. This obsessive intensity about you both. You're different men, completely different in most every way. But in that you're nearly the same."

She had a secret: that when she played she could *become* the cello. She could enter into it until she merged with it, and then she could find the music, and then the music could flow out. That was the way she felt when she was playing well—that she *was* the cello, that there was no distinction between it and her, and that the music was not to be found on the sheets of the score, but deep inside, in the dark interior cavity of the instrument. The music, all the cello music ever written, was there, waiting for her to hear it, waiting to be released. Playing, then, became releasing—she was all that stood between the hearing of it and the silence; when she became the cello all she had to do was open up.

But now, for some reason, she could not become the cello. She was merely a cellist, as she had been when she was a student, before the secret had been revealed. *I have no trouble opening up,* she thought; *I do that all the time with David. My trouble now is that I cannot become the cello. I must find my way back into it, squeeze myself back inside.*

She decided that night that she would dream her

way inside her instrument, and that when she did she would listen carefully to the music so that she would know how it must be played.

But it was very difficult to will herself a dream, and that night this dream she longed for did not come. Instead she dreamed of something else: two men, David and Sasha, moving on separate vectors toward a particular meeting point in space and time. But hard as she tried, she could not see the place of their convergence, though she could see very clearly that they were moving toward it at increasing speed.

DAVID'S DOGS

It was past midnight. Shoshana was posted on watch in the lobby at 28 Histadrut. Uri had the janitor and night watchman ensconced in a first floor office, while David, Micha and Dov set to work opening up room 304. The words "Holyland Arts Foundation" were stenciled in black on the frosted glass door. The lock was serious; Micha said he wouldn't be able to open it without leaving marks. But there was a transom, also made of frosted glass, which Dov felt certain he could breach, then fish through to catch and throw the bolt inside.

As Dov unscrewed the transom fixtures, Micha, who'd done preliminary research, filled David in.

"Very low-key type of operation. They buy up paintings and sculptures by Israeli artists, arrange shipment to the States, and then exhibit the works over there. They also make contributions to Israeli art schools, encourage exchange of art teachers, fund promising young Israeli artists, and occasionally commission a major work to be placed in a public location—a development town, say, or on an army base."

"So who's behind it?" David asked.

"Americans, some kind of Christian evangelist group. Been operating here close to three years. They pay their rent on time, never bother anybody and, according to their neighbors, seldom get visitors. The old mama-type who works in the front room is sweet and kind of dumb. She sits out there, smiles, and sorts the mail. Actually, since she's only here part-time, the place is mostly closed."

Once they were inside, however, David was disappointed: no hidden safe, no concealed tape recorders, no windows made of one-way glass. Just two small offices, both shabbily furnished—a waiting room with hard wooden chairs, a desk, a phone, and an answering machine, and an inner office with another desk, a metal filing cabinet, and on the walls photographs of various works of contemporary Israeli art.

He opened a drawer of the filing cabinet and started rifling through file folders. Most contained copies of letters between the Foundation's home office, in Dallas, and various Israeli galleries. He found one marked "Negev Earthwork: 'Circle in the Square.' " It was the only folder that was empty.

"Of course it's empty," Dov said. "It's the one we're interested in."

"Is this some kind of Shin Bet safe-house?" Micha asked.

"A good safe-house is a residence. Here, there's only access during business hours."

"Still it could be a front," Dov said. "Money gets sent in, art gets shipped out. It's looks like any one of a hundred little foreign religious charities. No one pays attention, because what they do is so ineffectual and nice."

"Maybe just a little too ineffectual," David said. "Question is: Is this a legitimate Shin Bet operation, or is it related somehow to our case? How's your English, Dov?"

"Damn good—you know that."

"Ever been to Dallas?"

Dov shook his head. Then suddenly he grinned.

"Hey! You're kidding, David. You are, aren't you? Oh wow! Just turn me loose!"

Latsky bit into his lower lip. "Suppose it *is* a valid Shin Bet operation?"

"So what's the harm?" David asked. "All we want to do is check it out."

"Come on. What's bugging you? Is it the money?"

"I have a discretionary fund. . . ."

"So what's the problem?"

"Too much of a longshot." Latsky squinted, then lit a cigarette. "You got some hearsay Cohen went in there. So what does that prove? Nothing." He squinted again, then exhaled. "You're floundering. Because you can't make head or tail out of this you want to dispatch twenty percent of your force to the goddam U.S.A."

"Give me five days. If Dov doesn't come up with anything I'll haul him back. He can hitch free on El Al far as New York, and from there—"

"Fine! Send him! Do whatever the hell you want. Since they found that 'executioner's' body you've been the minister's fair-haired boy." Latsky stubbed out his cigarette. "Just don't ask me for any written orders. As far as I'm concerned this meeting never happened. I never authorized anything. You're operating on your own."

David drove Dov Meltzer down to Ben-Gurion Airport, waited while he cleared customs, then escorted him onto the plane.

Dov looked nervous. "I've got reserve duty coming up, so maybe I won't come back. Maybe I'll join the traitors driving taxis around New York."

David leaned over the seat. "Find me something, Dov. Investigate the hell out of this. Because Latsky's right, I *am* floundering. I'm not sure what I'm doing anymore."

He and Micha drove out to the Negev to look at the earthwork. After half an hour of trudging around it, Micha gave his verdict: "I see why they call it 'Circle in the Square.' But you know something, David—it's a crock of shit."

"So why's everyone so concerned about it? What's Cohen's involvement? Why is Sokolov acting panicked? If Targov's right and Sokolov didn't design it why pay him good money to sign the plans?"

Micha looked at him. "There's something going on."

"That's right, but what? I want to know. Use your contacts, Micha. Find out who authorized this thing. No one lives around here. There's no decent road in, and when you get here there's nothing to see. So if it's really just a crock of shit, then what the hell's the point?"

Liederman wanted to go down to Tel Aviv: "To try and find that Arab kid," he explained. "You know, the one Peretz picked up off the beach. If I could find him I could bring him up here and then try to sick him onto Cohen. Dangle him, you know. Maybe Cohen would bite."

"Forget it," David said. "He's too smart to bite an Arab."

But later he realized Moshe Liederman had begun to think like a detective. He was getting hunches, following them up, and he'd grasped the basic method of entrapment—finding the suspect's weak spot and then exploiting it by dangling bait.

He told Anna: "I'd like to have some photographs of Cohen together with a man. Then I'd haul him in, and, if he refused to cooperate, I'd threaten to show them to his wife."

"David! You wouldn't do that!"

"No, of course not," he said. "But I sure as hell wouldn't hesitate to make the threat."

Uri found the panel door through a garage in Netanya that specialized in Chevrolets. The foreman of the bodyshop remembered replacing the door, and directed Uri to a junkyard further down the coast. Here Uri made his way between carcasses of demolished Fords and torn-up Fiats, broken axles, shattered windshields, smashed-in radiators, and assorted burned-out truck engines crusted with grease and dirt. It took him two days but he finally found the panel door, and when David sent it over to the forensic lab at National Police H.Q., they were able to match paint marks in the dents with scrapings of paint taken from Schneiderman's truck.

"All of which proves," Rafi said, "that Schneiderman hit a van. But doesn't prove it was the van in Ein Kerem."

"Maybe not," David said, "but I never counted on establishing a solid chain of evidence."

"Then why did you go to so much trouble, David?"

"Confirmation. You see, Rafi—now I *know* I'm right."

Dov's first call came through in seventy-two hours:

"Think it's hot in Jerusalem. You should see the way we're sweating here."

"What have you got?"

"First, and this wasn't hard, Holyland Arts is owned by a Texas corporation called Militants for Christ, Inc. It's a spin-off of an Oklahoma oil company. The sole owner is a certain Harrison Stone, a big-deal oil and gas multimillionaire. He's also a part-time TV preacher— cool, soft-spoken, and very very slick. Around here they call him 'The Wizard of Ooze.' Some kind of local joke—I don't get it, but what the hell. Anyway, though Stone's certainly a fundamentalist, he's not a fire-and-damnation type. Makes his TV sermons in a cool reasonable tone of voice from behind a corporate desk. Something interesting: There's no church—no staff, no building, no parishioners. It's a private philanthropy and strictly a one-man show. And according to people in the Jewish community, Stone's a very big fan of Israel."

"Has he been here?"

"Plenty of times. Trouble is I can't find out exactly when. But get this, David—he's also a close pal of Rabbi Katzer. Katzer was here last year soliciting funds, and not, I hear, just from local Jews. Stone supposedly arranged several very private meetings between Katzer and wealthy Texan Christian fundamentalists. Pledges of serious money are rumored to have been made in exchange for unspecified promises. It's all kind of vague, no one knows exactly what went on, but from the little I've been able to uncover I'd have to say your conspiracy theory is looking good."

David felt a rush of excitement; a little more of the concealed pattern had been revealed. "How did you dig all this up so fast?"

"I had help from a local lady reporter name of Gael Rubin. She wrote a series of articles on Stone, something very difficult to do because it's almost impossible to get near the guy. He's a take-over specialist who operates with a lot of secrecy."

"What do you think?"

"Don't know yet. But the operation here doesn't fit with those crummy offices we saw."

"You got pictures?"

"I shot some off the TV."

"Have the consulate wire them to me. So—what does your pretty reporter girl say?"

"Did I say she was pretty, David?"

"She is, isn't she?"

"Yeah, she is." Dov laughed. "And she says Stone is pretty sinister. Says that except for the religious stuff he plays it quiet, stays in the background, always works through proxies. Then, when he's ready to gobble something up, he strikes out of nowhere like a shark."

He told her: "Here I am working on a murder case that in some tangential way involves my brother, my father, and myself. And now it seems to involve you too. Your old lover has somehow stumbled into some strange back room of it. At least I think he has. So many intersections. . . ." He shook his head. "I think this could only happen here. Only here, Anna, in Jerusalem. . . ."

Micha confirmed that Holyland Arts had funded the design of "Circle in the Square" and that Israeli military engineers had done the actual work, paid for out of an IDF cultural and recreational fund.

"Far as I can tell, no specific individual authorized it. The way it works with this fund is that once properly prepared papers are filed in the appropriate manner they get shuffled through the bureaucracy from desk to desk. Each officer adds his initials and several months later the project comes out the other end approved."

"If that's how it works then I pity Israel," David said. But still he wasn't satisfied. "Bring in Sokolov," he instructed Micha. "Time now to put him on the grill."

There was something about the old man that filled David with ambivalence. His face bore the stamp of vulnerability one saw often in the older generation of European-born Israelis. The look of internal disturbance, of having been deeply and indelibly wounded in the past, totally opposed to the famous "Sabra look"—the strong, set, committed features and direct unblinking gaze. A disturbed face but David knew he must distrust his sympathy. Often those who looked most disturbed had been deformed in sinister ways.

Was Sergei evil? Targov had told Anna that he was, but examining him now, across the small table in the tiny basement interrogation room, David could not be sure. There was pathos in the taut forehead, the terrible teeth, the bushes of white hair that sprang Ben-Gurion style from the sides of his shriveled head. His eyes, greatly magnified by his extra-thick spectacles, were frightened. No wonder—he had received an official summons; the man had spent fifteen years in Soviet camps.

Still, there was a hint of craftiness that belied the injured stare. David recognized the face of a man who could channel his hurt into a mercenary rage. He knew the type—the cheater, the stealer, the professional litigant, the man who behaves as if money can salve his wounds.

"Before I start asking questions, let me make several matters clear. We're investigating a case in which you may or may not be involved. As of now you're not a suspect, and we have no plan to bring any charges. However, if you lie to us you'll be charged with perjury, and, I warn you, the penalties for that can be severe. I say this because I want you to understand that there's nothing to be gained by concealing the truth."

Sergei nodded, his face alert and tense.

David flicked his finger at the pile of drawings which Micha had removed from the walls of Sokolov's bedroom and which now lay between them on the table. "We know you didn't make these. We know you were paid to sign them and claim authorship of 'Circle in the Square.' For us that's no crime. What we want to know is how you came to sign these drawings. Who approached you? What did they offer you? What deal did you strike? And, most important, *why*—why did *they* need *you?*"

Sergei hesitated. His hugely magnified eyes blinked and darted and finally came to rest. They were aimed at the place where David's forefinger touched his signature on the top drawing of the pile.

"This is your signature."

Sergei nodded.

"But you didn't make these drawings?"

Sergei shook his head.

"Who asked you to sign them?"

"I received a letter from the foundation."

"The Holyland Arts Foundation?"

"Yes."

"What did the letter say?"

Sergei coughed, then looked nervously away. "That my situation, as a new citizen and a sculptor, had come to their attention. That I was invited to come in and discuss the possibility of receiving a commission to create a public work."

"So you went to the foundation offices. Whom did you meet?"

"Mr. Hurwitz."

"Igal Hurwitz?" Sergei nodded. "So what did this Mr. Hurwitz have to say?"

"He was sympathetic when I told him about my loss of sight. He convinced me this would be no problem— that it would be possible for me to conceive a work and then leave its execution to someone else."

"Had you ever been involved in conceptual art?"

"I was a carver. My specialty was carved ballerinas."

"Did you tell this to Hurwitz?"

"He said it didn't make any difference."

"Did he then suggest a particular 'conception' to you?" Sergei hesitated. "Well?"

"Yes."

David tapped the pile of drawings. "And this is what he suggested?"

"Yes."

David sat back. "You're being truthful. I appreciate that you're not trying to mislead me or shade the truth. Let's go a little deeper now. Who brought up the matter of money?"

"Hurwitz did."

"What did he say?"

"He told me there would be a fee."

"Did he say how much?"

"Depending upon the size of the final work, it would range between five and ten thousand dollars."

"That's quite a lot of money just to sign some drawings."

"Apparently it was worth it to them." Sergei smiled. It was that smile that caused David to decide that he disliked him, but he kept his dislike to himself.

"Yes, I see that," he said. "Of course they wanted your signature. But didn't you think it a little strange to be offered foreign currency?"

"The foundation is American."

"But Hurwitz was Israeli."

"He was a foundation employee. He made that clear."

"And you didn't ask him any questions about why you'd been chosen, or why the fee would be so large, or what the 'Circle in the Square' was supposed to represent?" Sergei shook his head. David sat back again. "Yes," he said, "I understand. There you were being presented with a once-in-a-lifetime opportunity. Here was this foundation representative offering you a substantial sum of money, and not only that—also legitimacy as an environmental sculptor. Who were you to question what was behind this fortuitous stroke of fortune?"

326 · William Bayer

"Exactly!" Sergei smiled; his interrogator understood him. There was no danger for him here, no need to conceal the truth.

"So you signed the drawings?"

"I signed them, of course."

"All of them?"

"Yes."

"Without asking any questions?"

Sergei smiled again. "I don't believe I said a single word."

"Of course not. Why should you speak? To ask questions then could have blown the deal. In fact the drawings were already prepared, weren't they? They were right there waiting for you in the office when you arrived. And the money was there too, wasn't it? A pile of it. Cash." David gazed at him. "The drawings were there, and the pile of cash right there beside them. That's how it was, wasn't it? *Wasn't it?*"

Sergei nodded eagerly. His interrogator was such an intelligent man. He seemed already to know the answers to everything he asked.

"And you never asked any questions, and you have no idea why you were chosen, and that's all you do know."

"Yes!" Sergei exclaimed. "Yes!"

David leaned forward. "So why is it that you went back and demanded additional money?"

Sergei shook his head. "I never did!"

"Several days ago you were seen returning to the foundation offices."

"I went back—yes! I saw Hurwitz—yes! But I never demanded anything."

"So why did you go back?"

"I needed a loan."

"You'd already spent the full ten thousand!"

"Life is expensive here, difficult for an immigrant. You must know that."

"Yes, I know," David said. "The foundation had helped you. Now you hoped that they might help you again."

"That's it!"

"Did Hurwitz agree to make the loan?"

"He said he'd have to consult the Dallas office."

"And now you're waiting to hear?"

"Yes, I'm waiting. I'm waiting. . . ." Sergei's eyes glazed over as his voice drifted off.

Seeing that he was finally exhausted, David stood up and extended his hand. "Congratulations, Mr. Sokolov. You are now a legitimate Israeli artist. We appreciate your coming in. Sergeant Benyamani will return you to your home."

Later, with Micha, he examined the videotape of the interview.

"He's slick. He could be lying, but I don't think he was," Micha said. "The setting was too intimidating."

"He lied about the loan."

Micha agreed. "But he's shrewd, shrewd enough not to ask questions when he sees a pile of cash."

"They were shrewd to pick him," David said. "He was perfect. He made a perfect schnook."

"The one thing I don't get is Hurwitz. We know he dealt with Ephraim Cohen. But we know Cohen wasn't the phony cop who took the names at the scene of the accident."

"Suppose 'Hurwitz' was a floating false identity. Shin Bet guys like tricks like that. Suppose everyone involved in this thing carried Hurwitz papers. Whenever one of them needed a false name, he simply called himself Igal Hurwitz. And if anyone asked any questions, he'd just reach into his pocket and pull out his Hurwitz ID."

"That's good, David. Sure. That makes sense." Micha hesitated. "Now what do we do?"

"You go down to Tel Aviv and check with Immigration. See if there's any record of a Harrison Stone entering Israel this past spring."

The following night he was staring out at the city while Anna struggled with her music. For a moment he thought he heard something promising, as if she were breaking through at last.

The telephone rang. He went into the kitchen to answer it.

"It's me." He recognized Stephanie's voice. "I can hear her practicing. Works late, doesn't she?"

"She works," David said, "until she gets it right."

"Yeah—well, that's really great." Another pause. "Listen, about our last encounter, I know you're not too happy about some of the things I said."

"Forget it, Stephanie," David snapped. "Just say what's on your mind?"

"Strictly business. Okay. I called because for a while now I've been hearing various odds and ends. You may remember that we discussed your murder case."

"Way I remember it, you tried to warn me off."

"I was worried for you, David. Then I heard you *were* off of it. I forgot about it until this afternoon when I happened to pick up something new."

"What?"

"The ninth."

"The ninth what?"

"I don't know. But there was something emphatic about the way this source of mine—"

"Who?"

"Can't tell you that."

"What can you tell me?"

"Come on, David, give me a break. This man, whom I'm not at liberty to name, moves in what we call extremist circles. He keeps his ears open, and, for as long as I'e known him, he's been a highly reliable source. Today, at our regular get-together, he mentioned he's heard that something big is due to happen soon. Then he muttered something about the ninth. Since today's August fifteenth, I figured he meant a month from now. But there was this sense of urgency, you know—of imminence. And since it was in the context of the killings, which he once told me meant a lot more than met the eye, I thought I should, though I have no idea what any of this is about, call you up and pass the information on."

"Tell me more."

"Can't. Can't jeopardize this relationship over an internal Israeli matter."

"How do you know it's just internal?" She was silent. "Have you any idea, Stephanie, how many times I've been deliberately misled on this? I hope you're not trying to do that now, because—"

"You're fucking impossible! I try to help you and you practically accuse me—oh! never mind! You know, David, I think that sometimes, really, you do expect too much. Anyway I'm running late. So, anyway," she paused, a little mournfully, he thought. "I hope we run into each other one of these days. . . ." And, when he didn't respond to that: "Well, that's it, I guess. Good-bye."

When Dov's photographs came in, he showed them to Shoshana.

"Piss-poor pictures, David."

"Show them to her anyway."

She glanced at her watch. "I'd better hurry then. School lets out in twenty minutes."

Yeah, David, he was here all right." Micha was telephoning from Immigration Central Records. "Harrison Stone, U.S. citizen. I'm looking at his form."

330 • William Bayer

"Date of entry?"

"One day before the accident."

"Departure?"

"The day after. Not too bad."

Another rush of excitement. "What else is on the form?"

"He gives tourism as the purpose of his trip and the Tel Aviv Hilton as his address. I just checked with them. He had reservations there, but then he canceled out."

"So where did he stay?"

"Hey, David, I only just got this a couple minutes ago."

"You're down there now, so you work Tel Aviv. Check everywhere. I'll have Uri call around up here."

"David—"

"I want to know where the hell he stayed. So stay on it till you find out. Good-bye."

Shoshana was pouting. "Amit doesn't remember him. For a second there I wanted—but then I remembered what you said about not trying to lead her on."

"Forget it, Shoshana. She's just a kid. And now we're getting close. I want you to work now with Uri. Help him find out where Stone spent his nights."

Dov called again: "Big roaches here. Between them and the heat you nearly die. Okay, with Gael Rubin's help, I finally got in to see Peter Crownshield. He's Stone's public relations representative, whose job, according to Gael, is to deflect all queries and protect Stone from the press. This Crownshield's a real smoothie. He wanted to be sure to set me straight. Mr. Stone's a firm supporter of Israel, rumors notwithstanding that his support is based on Biblical prophecy. 'What prophecy's that?' I asked, playing the not-too-bright Israeli journalist. 'That the Second Coming of Jesus Christ,' he said, 'cannot occur until Israel is destroyed.' He's talking about the prophecy of a war of Armageddon. And he wanted it clear that Stone doesn't think that way. 'Mr. Stone,' he said, 'sees no reason why Christ can't return to earth tomorrow. His support for Israel is unequivocal. Far as the foundation's concerned, Mr. Stone set it up to nurture art and beauty in the Holy Land.' "

"So that's it?"

"Pretty much."

"How's Miss Rubin?"

"She'd like to come over for a visit soon."

"American girls are nice."

"I know you're an expert, David—that's why you're living with a Russian. Seriously, I don't think there's much more for me to do over here. I've got reserve duty. . . ."

"Come home, Dov. You've done a terrific job."

David had never been inside Mishkenot Sha'ananim, although he knew the "Peaceful Dwelling" well. One of the first buildings constructed outside the walls of the Old City, this nineteenth-century landmark had been converted, after the Six Day War, into a guesthouse for visiting writers, artists, and musicians.

He and Anna walked to it from Abu Tor. Anatole Rokovsky met them in the lobby. He embraced Anna, gravely shook David's hand, then escorted them down a flight of stairs to a corridor off which there were numbered doors, and a series of small perfectly kept internal sky-lit gardens.

This was the first time David had seen Rokovsky; he studied the Russian as he led them along the long stone corridor. Thin, stooped, his thick gray hair cut almost to his scalp, Rokovsky loped along gently on the balls of his feet. The way he moved reminded

David of the surreptitious gait of a jailer who sneaks around the halls of a penitentiary trying to catch the prisoners breaking rules.

Targov's greeting was effusive, his handshake powerful. "Come in! Come in! We have tea prepared. And also we have vodka. I'm *so* glad to see you again. And Anna, too. I always love to see her." He grasped Anna in his arms.

When David mentioned he'd never been inside Mishkenot, Targov took him on a brief tour of the apartment. There was a master bedroom and bath, a kitchenette, a study, and, on the second floor, a second bedroom suite. When they returned to the living room, Anna was reclining on the sofa sipping tea from a tall glass and speaking Russian with Rokovsky.

"They treat us well here. No disturbances so we can work. And if we want to meet somebody—anybody, including the president . . ." Targov clicked his fingers. " . . . like that! It is instantly arranged!"

David sat beside Anna. "In the matter of Sokolov—"

"Yes, yes!" Targov leaned forward eagerly. "I'm dying to know: What did you think of him?"

"Not too much really. A complicated man. A man who knows not to ask questions when there's money on the table. A man who doesn't care about anything, except, of course, survival. No more ideologies, no more loyalties or principles for him. In short, a man who in a situation like this, offers himself as the perfect shnook."

Targov glanced quizzically at Anna.

"A Yiddish word, Sasha. David means he thought Sergei was more than willing to play the patsy."

"Yes, that seems right. He's a hard old *zek*. But don't forget—convicts become experts at concealment."

"Concealing or not, he claimed he didn't know anything. He'd been paid to sign the drawings and that was good enough for him."

"And the extra pay? What did he say about that?"

"He denies he asked for or received any extra pay."

"He's a liar! Rokovsky heard him."

"I know. That's why I'm here. I want to know why he lied about that. It must have had something to do with the photographs you gave him. If you still have some from the same series, I'd like to see them."

Targov snapped his fingers. Rokovsky jumped up and headed for the study. "When I handed them to him," Targov said, "I pointed out that there'd already been erosion. I wanted to be sure he saw how quickly his masterpiece was deteriorating, and that it couldn't possibly last."

Rokovsky returned with a sheaf of Polaroids.

While David examined them, Targov fumed on. " 'Circle in the Square.' It's ludicrous. If that's what passes for sculpture these days, then maybe it's time for me to think about retirement."

"We thought it could be some sort of ideogram," Rokovsky said. "A symbol. Or writing. Ancient Hebrew perhaps."

David looked closely at the photographs. "It's no kind of writing I've ever seen."

"So—what is it?"

"Perhaps not a symbol. Not abstract at all. Perhaps something very concrete."

"Such as what?" Targov asked.

"Who knows?" David shrugged. "Perhaps some kind of replica. Perhaps even," he paused, "something that points to something . . . some kind of chart or map."

Uri found the hotel: Stone had spent two nights at the King Solomon Sheraton in Jerusalem. The suite had been reserved a month in advance through a Dallas travel agent.

David spoke to the manager and informally requisitioned a copy of Stone's bill. No log, of course, of his

incoming calls, but Stone had phoned out four times.
The first call was to Dallas. David dispatched Shoshana
to the telephone company to track the other three.
Then he recalled Micha from Tel Aviv, suggesting he
meet Dov's plane and bring him up as well.

Half an hour later Shoshana was back with names
and addresses. The first local call, to TWA's Jerusalem office, was made to confirm Stone's departure the
following night. The second was to the Histadrut Street
office of the Holyland Arts Foundation, and the third,
made at precisely 11 A.M. the day of the accident, was
to a public phone booth in front of the Alba pharmacy
on Jaffa Road.

"That was the contact point," David said. "The
meeting was prearranged."

"So that's it," Uri said.

"Not quite. It's still a theory."

"Come on! He makes two sets of hotel reservations,
then puts the one he cancels on his immigration form."

"Pretty suspicious," Shoshana said.

"Forget suspicious. We need something solid."

Uri and Shoshana looked at one another. David
wondered: Was Stone going to be another dead end
like the van?

"Somehow they got him back to the Sheraton,"
Shoshana said. "Found a taxi or took a bus. Trouble
is, no one would remember now."

"But suppose they didn't get him back so quick.
Remember: He was injured. Suppose they took him to
a hospital first?" He could feel their excitement. "Well,"
he said, "what are you waiting for?"

They called hospitals, spoke to registrars, checked
the records of emergency treatment rooms for the day
of the accident. Then, when nothing came of that,
they started calling every private physician in Jerusalem. When Micha turned up with Dov, who was jet-

lagged and blinking and longed for sleep, David put them on the phones too. At four o'clock Uri stood up.

"Okay, I got him nailed."

Dr. Shmuel Mendler, interviewed in his Balfour Street consulting room, remembered his American visitor well.

"Oh yes," said the middle-aged orthopedist when David showed him the TV-set photographs, "this is the gentleman, Mr. Gerald Morris. No doubt of that. He came to me that day on an emergency basis, referred here by a friend. He'd been in a little automobile accident, he said, and he was in a good deal of pain."

Dr. Mendler reviewed the patient's chart. "It was his knee that was injured. I X-rayed it. Nothing shattered, nothing serious. I gave him a shot of Demerol and taped him up. He was flying out to the States that night. I advised him to see his own physician immediately on his return."

And who was this friend who had referred Mr. Morris?

"A neighbor of mine actually. We live in the same building around the corner."

"On Arlosoroff?" David asked.

"Yes, that's right."

"A man named Ephraim Cohen?"

"How extraordinary," Dr. Mendler said. "How absolutely extraordinary that you should know."

David entered Stone's name in the middle circle on the blackboard, then stood back and shook his head. "Gati. Stone. Katzer."

"So what does it add up to? You told us the middle guy would be the link."

"They don't belong together, that's for sure," Uri said.

"Why not?"

"Two Jews and a Christian. That's some weird kind of match."

"Yeah, but what kind of Jews are we talking about? And what kind of a Christian? Two Israelis, one a fundamentalist rabbi. And the Christian's a fundamentalist preacher too."

"So what's Gati doing there?"

David thought about it. "Maybe we've been looking at this wrong. Maybe Gati's the real link." Silence. ". . . Three very different guys and all three claim great devotion to Israel. We've got right-wing Jewish politics and fundamentalist foreign money and in between we've got a military mind. Enough there, seems to me, for one hell of a conversation. And then we've got a half-blind old Russian paid off by Ephraim Cohen, fronting for Stone's Holyland Arts Foundation. He signs drawings of an environmental sculpture that no one authorized, no one cares about, and that's practically impossible to find. Whatever the hell's been going on, we ought to have enough now to put it together. So let's sleep on it, meet here tomorrow at seven, lock the doors, and brainstorm until we figure it out."

That night he told Anna: "I keep coming back to this: Ephraim Cohen was a flight commander in Gideon's squadron, and later he was detached to Gati's headquarters as a special aide. You see how it links up. This is just a guess, but suppose Ephraim wanted Gideon to perform some sort of unofficial military mission, the order coming down from the general. When Gideon killed himself, his flight group was out on a practice exercise, each plane fully armed. Then, when Gideon peeled off, no one chased after him or tried to call him back. Gideon was an expert in precision bombing. He'd been one of the sixteen pilots on the Iraqi reactor raid. Gati himself told me Gideon was one of the most talented pilots he'd ever had in his command. Suppose Ephraim told him to fly somewhere and use all those deadly armaments. Suppose that was the mission Gideon refused to perform—to fly someplace and drop his bombs."

After she fell asleep, David thought about Gideon flying the reactor mission. Enough had been published about Operation Babylon for him to replay the mission in his mind. The planes had taken off mid-afternoon from the Etzion base, descended to less than a hundred feet off the desert floor, then had crossed the Saudi Arabian frontier, and flown for two monotonous hours barely skimming the sand. As they'd crossed into Iraqi territory and approached the reactor, the pilots had suddenly turned up into the sky. Focusing on the great dome of the Tammuz reactor, they dove for it, one plane at a time, each attacking from a different angle and direction. They unloaded their bombs, and screaming up again, flew very high in pairs until they reached Israel and home.

The dome, the great dome of the reactor—it was so thick, so strongly reinforced, that it required direct hits from every plane. . . .

At five o'clock that morning he woke up in a sweat. At last the design was clear: *The craters!*

There had been no craters in the original drawings, or in the photographs taken just after "Circle in the Square" had been completed. But craters were clearly visible in Rokovsky's Polaroids. They were what had excited Sokolov and sent him rushing to the foundation to try and extort extra money.

Craters meant bombs. Bombs meant a bombing target. The pilots who'd flown against the Iraqi reactor had practiced for months against a target carved out in the sand.

"Circle in the Square" was a practice target for bombers. And this time too the target was a dome.

He shook Anna awake.

"Now I know," he said. "I know what they're going to do." *The Ninth!* He reached for the phone.

"Rafi?"

He shook his head. "Today's the Ninth of Av, anniversary of the destruction of our ancient temple. No time now to go through channels. I have to go directly to the minister."

TO DIE IN
JERUSALEM

After Targov woke up he lay in bed, eyes closed, breathing in the sweet aromas. These scents, released from the terraced gardens surrounding Mishkenot, seeped into his room each morning through the barred windows he left open to the breeze. Sometimes there was another smell too, dry and ancient, that came to him from the Old City across the ravine. And occasionally a stray Jerusalem cat would jump through the window, and he would chase it around the apartment, finally corner it in the tiny kitchen, then the two of them, old sculptor and slinky cat, would bare their teeth at one another, then Targov would grin, yield, and turn away.

But this Friday morning as he lay in bed his mind struggled with the puzzle of the earthwork. He had been astonished by what David Bar-Lev had suggested: that it was not an ideogram, not abstract, that it could be some kind of replica or map.

But a replica of what? An image of the thing, which he now wanted to recapture, had come to him in his sleep. He had seen it from the air, just as he had on his first visit; there was a terrible roar and then Sergei's markings had grown larger as he'd approached. Yes, he'd been flying toward the earthwork, soaring down upon it like a hawk. What was it then? The idea was within his grasp. Recalling a line from Macbeth, he opened his eyes: "O! full of scorpions is my mind."

Sergei had not designed it and it had nothing to do with art. But it did have a purpose, which he might have guessed if he had paid proper attention to that roaring Air Force jet. Its rush at him from off the sand, its surge and plunge could have explained the markings. But he had refused to acknowledge their significance, preferring instead the torment of a mystery.

His mind racing, he played with the shape, turning it, revolving it, looking at it from every side. He'd seen it before. Many times. Here. In Jerusalem. His was a sculptor's mind accustomed to manipulating forms. He fixed the shape in his brain, then strode across the room, opened the top drawer of his bureau, rumaged inside until he found his pocket city map, took one glance at it, and knew that he was right.

"Faster!" Targov cried. Rokovsky was racing around the Old City walls. "Faster! Faster!" Targov felt an urge to punch groggy unshaven Tola in the arm.

The road curved and swerved as they passed the Dung Gate, plunged down into the Kidron Valley, then rejoined the Jericho Road. As they turned to climb Mount Scopus a truck carrying vegetables almost ran them down. But Rokovsky drove skillfully. Eleven minutes after he'd picked up Targov at the door of Mishkenot, he deposited him, with a screeching of brakes, at the overlook on the crest of the Mount of Olives.

It was 7 A.M. The sun, which had risen an hour and a half before, hung behind them in the east. Below the city sparkled; in another hour it would begin to steam. The crenelated walls that surrounded the Temple Mount were a blinding pale beige, the trees upon the Mount were dusty green, and its two great structures, the silver dome of El Aqsa and the larger golden Dome of the Rock, shot back the sun like mirrors.

"Tola, look down there at the city."

"I'm looking," Rokovsky stared. "What am I looking for?"

"The shape out in the desert. The thing we saw. The map."

Rokovsky squinted. "I know Bar-Lev said it might be a map, but I don't see—"

"We've seen it at least a hundred times."

"Please, Sasha, help me out."

"Look at the shape of the Temple Mount—it's the same, a trapezoid. And the circle in the center." Targov pointed at the golden dome. "That circle is the Dome of the Rock. Now do you see?"

Rokovsky nodded slowly. "The shorter end faces south and . . ."

"Yes. It's a full-sized replica, oriented the same way too. And those craters we saw near the center. . . . Think, Tola, think of what we saw out there: a map of the Temple Mount, signed by my old friend Sergei, constructed far out in the desert. So, think about it—for whom? and why?"

"They want to start a war," David said. He twisted around to watch the minister. He had awakened him and now the older man, expression still opaque, paced the living room of his villa in leather slippers and a silk floral-patterned dressing gown.

"Yes—a war. I like the shape of that," the minister said. His perfectly parted silver hair caught the early morning light. "As a man with such an extraordinary mind, I think you may be wasted in the Jerusalem Command. I could use you on my personal staff."

"I didn't come—"

"I know why you came. You have a very pretty theory. Your only problem is that you can't prove it."

"I'll do my best," David said. "Meantime, by the Jewish calendar—"

"The holiday—yes, I understand. But what does that have to do—?"

"What better day, minister, than the anniversary of the Romans' destruction of our temple? The pilot, whoever he is, flies in, drops his bomb, and blows up the Dome of the Rock now situated on our sacred ground. Then Jewish fanatics rush the place and cheer— Jewish sovereignty has been restored; the temple will be rebuilt, the Messianic Age has come. Meantime, of course, every Arab in Jerusalem becomes a homicidal maniac. A sacred shrine of Islam has been destroyed. The rampaging Jews must be fought off and killed. So, to defend ourselves, we shoot the rioting Arabs, blood flows in the streets, and suddenly we're up to our ass in a holy war. Considering that since sunset we've been facing that kind of threat, do you really want me out scrounging around for proof?"

The minister had stopped pacing and was examining him now with curiosity. "No need to patronize me, captain. Either you've got a case, or you've come here with a fantasy."

He was right; David knew that sarcasm was not going to help his cause. "I apologize," he said. "I understand that what I've told you must strike you as farfetched."

"Farfetched? It's outrageous! We know fanatics want to do these things. But people of such stature, whether we like them or not—it's almost too much to believe. . . ."

"I agree, which is why it took me so long to see it." David paused. He knew now that he had the minister's attention, recognized that same narrow, somewhat skeptical, yet sympathetic gaze he'd observed in his eyes the day he'd removed him from the case. "Let me try and explain it again as simply as I can. Each of the men in that van had reason to enter into this conspiracy. Katzer because he *wants* a bloodbath—it will justify his plan to expel the Arabs. Stone because he believes in biblical prophecy. And Gati because the Mount's the 'high ground' and the fact that we 'gave it back' in '67 proves to him we're soft. So bomb the Dome, retake the high ground, and, while you're at it, redraw the map. But this time don't stop at the Jordan River—take the East Bank too!" David paused. "They make a perfect threesome: an ideologue, a moneybags, and a military genius. A year and a half ago they tried to blackmail my brother. He didn't like their scheme so he jettisoned his bombs and crashed his plane. My guess is that this year they're simply paying the pilot off. Which is why now I want to move very fast, and stop this thing before it gets off the ground."

"That's quite a little speech. What exactly do you want me to do?"

"Authorize arrests."

"Without warrants?"

"Here we have an imminent danger to human life."

The minister winced. "I'm a defense lawyer. General Gati's a national hero. Katzer, horrible as he is, is an important politician. If they were my clients I know exactly what I'd do. Threaten. Sue. Make sure the police never heard the end of it. And while I was at it I'd go straight to a judge and have them out within the hour."

"You're saying they're untouchable. I don't think so, but I'm not a lawyer—I'm a cop. Anyway it doesn't matter. The point is to expose the plot. Once it's exposed they'll have to cancel it. Exposure is what they fear the most, which is why they had the accident witnesses killed."

"And if you're wrong?"

"I'm not."

"What if you are?"

"You'll kick me off the force."

The minister stared at him, appraising. "I could do that now if I wanted to."

David met his gaze straight-on; this, he knew, was not the time to blink.

"You'll really stake your career on this?"

"I wouldn't have come here otherwise."

David sat quietly; the minister was making up his mind. He hesitated, squinted, then gave a short swift nod.

"Okay. Make your arrests." He moved toward his desk. "But you'd better make them fast. I'll phone the prime minister, recommend the grounding of military aircraft for just one hour." He turned to David. "You understand what that means? You'd better be right, captain, because if you're not, and something happens, and Israeli airspace is undefended, then you and I are going to be the biggest assholes this country's ever seen."

Targov wandered the Old City for hours. The heat was punishing. The dry dust of Jerusalem clung to his clothes. There were so many mysteries here, interstices, hidden corners, tunnels that led to bolted doors. But above the labyrinth, dominating everything, was that great and stunning golden dome.

To want to destroy beauty like this—what could be Sergei's purpose? But the moment Targov posed the question, he knew what the answer had to be. It was the classic rage of the unsuccessful artist against anything that mocked his mediocrity. If you can't create great art, then feel free to destroy it. Sergei was no better than that miserable little Dutch painter who, despairing at his own failure, had slashed out at Rembrandt's "Nightwatch" with his knife.

He phoned Rokovsky from an Arab money changer's shop just outside Herod's Gate.

"Fetch him!"

"Where are you?"

"The Old City. Bring him to David's Tower."

"When?"

"When you find him."

"And what if I can't?"

"Find the bastard!" Targov hung up, then plunged back into the labyrinth.

"You bypassed me and Latsky!" Rafi was furious.

"I did what I thought I had to do."

"Send an oaf like Uri Schuster to handcuff Rabbi Katzer! Send twenty-two-year-old Shoshana Nahon to arrest General Gati!"

"They're my people, Rafi. Who else was I going to send?"

"I understand you personally hauled Ephraim Cohen out of bed in front of his wife and kids."

"So what?"

"*So what!* Cohen's a hard-ass. You don't make an enemy of a man like that. You must be out of your mind."

"If I am I'll pay for it, won't I?"

"Oh, you'll pay for it all right. Latsky's neck's gone purple. His blood vessels are about to burst." Rafi shook his head, tried to calm himself. "You're over-involved, David. Twisted around and riddled with guilt. This whole business about Gideon and Ephraim Cohen. . . ."

"What about it?"

"It's taken its toll on your good sense." He picked up a pipe, knocked it against his palm. "As for Miss Stephanie Porter and her unsourced rumors about 'the ninth'—the bitch is jerking you off. She's got her own agenda and she's got you pussywhipped, and you don't even see how you're being used."

David felt the heat rise to his cheeks and sweat

break out on his brow. He felt like punching Rafi in the face.

"Oh, Rafi—what a stupid lousy thing to say. . . ."

When she put down the phone after Rokovsky called, Anna knew this was the day that David's and Sasha's vectors were destined to converge. Each of them had been following a separate trail with obsessive intensity, and now they were both running around madly in the city, and she felt that the meeting of their trails, of which she'd dreamed the night she'd tried to dream herself inside her cello, could end in some kind of tragedy, and that she must not let them meet alone.

When David finished telling them of Rafi's doubts, all except Dov stared at the floor.

"He's wrong, David. You solved it and he's jealous." Dov smiled. "It's as simple as that."

"Screw Rafi anyway," Shoshana said. "Who wants to be in an outfit where the fucking commander doesn't know what the fuck is going on?"

Rebecca Marcus, offended by Shoshana's language, sat ramrod-straight in her typing chair.

"It felt great to arrest Katzer," Uri said. "His breath stank. He must have eaten sausage before he went to bed."

"He's already out," Micha said.

"He keeps a lawyer on tap. His thugs called the guy and he turned up all bristly with a writ."

"Gati wanted to strangle me," Shoshana said. "He gagged when I told him the charge." She made her voice severe: "Obstruction of justice and conspiracy." Then she broke down and giggled.

"Ephraim played it cool," David told them. " 'So what did I do? Called a doctor for an injured American, a good friend to Israel.' He laughed in my face.

But he was faking it. One side of him thinks he's immune; the other side knows he's in very deep shit."

"We did right, David," Dov's voice was steady. "Those guys play rough. They don't worry about the rules."

"Anyway, we're the Rabies Squad." Shoshana's black eyes flashed.

David loved them: They were his people, they'd done something extraordinary, and now, like a small commando unit reassembled after a dangerous operation, they were reliving the drama of it, laughing, exchanging stories, astounded by their own audacity.

Even Rebecca Marcus, normally distanced from their camaraderie, seemed excited by their tales. When the telephone rang she snapped it up.

"For you, David. It's Anna. She says it's urgent."

At 2 P.M. every Friday, tourists throng the sides of narrow Via Dolorosa while pilgrims gather near the First Station of the Cross waiting to be led along the route by priests. Church groups from Mexico, the Philippines, rural France, men, women, and children, many obsessed with martyrdom and stigmata, some even bearing huge oversized crosses on their shoulders, assemble to make the march and relive their Savior's Passion.

It was amid this throng that Targov now found himself. The procession was already in progress. He could barely push his way past the stream of pilgrims. *But oh!*, he thought, *the faces!*

Targov studied them: Haunted faces with jutting chins, and stern determined glowering eyes. Fanatical faces, otherworldly and smug. Superior scowls that said: "We Know. We are the elect. We have seen the Light. And now we own the Truth."

Suddenly Targov hated that burning look, and hated the passions, generated within this city, which powered it. He too had longed to wear it, to die intoxicated by righteousness. But now, seeing it on others, he understood the arrogant pride in which he'd spun his plan. In that same instant of awareness, he was flooded with self-contempt, for he finally understood the idiocy of the notion that a man can achieve redemption by acting out another's pain.

David entered the Old City by Jaffa Gate, then followed narrow David Street, unmarked dividing line between the Christian and Armenian Quarters, jammed that Friday afternoon with pilgrims, shoppers, tourists, and miscellaneous Jerusalemites. Pushing past people and mules, through the aromas of sewage and roasting meat, David fought his way into the tunnel that connected up with the old Roman Cardo. Recently excavated and restored, it had been turned into an underground street of fashionable Israeli shops.

Anna was waiting for him in front of Steimatsky's newsstand. He ran up to her, planted a kiss on her brow.

"What's going on?"

"It's Sasha. Rokovsky called. He said the old man's acting crazy, wandering around in here, babbling something about Sokolov being party to a plot to bomb the Dome of the Rock. Sasha demanded a confrontation at David's Tower, and Rokovsky gave Sergei the message. Now he's scared. He thinks they're both crazy and there's a real danger one or both of them will be hurt."

The Citadel, called David's Tower, was attached to the Jaffa Gate. Here Targov stood on the highest parapet awaiting Sergei Sokolov. There was no breeze this torrid August afternoon. The tower was deserted and the Old City baked. His ears took in its sounds. Shrieks, moans, and wails of Arabs, Christians, and Jews thronging below in the labyrinth, each scheming to increase his fraction of the precious space.

"I am summoned!"

Targov stared down. Sokolov was standing legs apart in the center of the courtyard while a nervous looking Rokovsky waited several meters behind.

"The Great Sculptor wants to see me. He *demands* my presence." Sokolov made an exaggerated bow, then began to scamper up the first flight of narrow steps. Watching him approach, Targov saw something new in his face. The deadness, the emptiness were gone, replaced now by mockery and spite.

"It's about *the nose,* isn't it?" Sergei's tone was bitter. Charging up the second flight, his entire face was animated by rage.

"Fuck your goddamned nose!" Targov yelled when Sergei was just one flight from the top.

Stunned, Sergei paused on the landing. "What do you mean—*my* goddamned nose?"

"Yours, idiot! You were the model for The Martyr, but too stupid to recognize it." Targov laughed. "You shot off your own nose, don't you see? Shot it off to spite your face!"

Sokolov reddened. His body began to shake. A perfect portrait of a vandal, Targov thought, at the moment he realizes he has inadvertently defaced himself.

"You stole my face!"

"Stop whining. I know what you've done. It would be pathetic if a masterpiece weren't at stake."

"A masterpiece! Ha! That's what you think of that big black ugly thing of yours?"

"I'm talking about the map, you fool—the map you got ten thousand dollars to sign. You hate that dome, don't you, Sergei? It's just too perfect, isn't it? Nothing you could ever make, could ever dream, could ever be compared to it. Mediocrity! Trinket carver! Impotent little man!"

Grasping hold of Anna's hand, David plunged into the mass of pilgrims, shoving, pushing, elbowing his way through. At last ahead of the procession he looked back upon it, the leading priests chanting, costumed like actors, the pilgrims following them, a delusioned mob.

As they fought their way through the Christian Quarter, he briefly explained to her the history behind the conspiracy: how the site of the original Jewish Temple was now occupied by a sacred Islamic shrine, and how several times Jewish extremist groups had tried to blow it up in order to hasten the fulfillment of the prophecy that the Messiah would appear only when the temple was rebuilt.

"They've tried with dynamite," he said, "but they've never managed to get close enough. We guard the Dome of the Rock and the El Aqsa Mosque as fiercely as the Arabs. We know the kind of tragedy that will occur if Jews ever manage to destroy it. But if a plane attacked, piloted by a skilled professional who'd practiced his run again and again on a full-scale model like the one Sergei Sokolov pretended he'd designed, then there'd be no defense—he could take it out in a single pass. When Gideon flew the Iraqi reactor mission, he and his squadron practiced for weeks against such a target. That's how I figured it out. I was thinking about Gideon, and then it came to me in a flash."

They'd reached Omar Ibn El Khatab Square. David pointed up at the Citadel. "Look!"

"Sasha!" Anna yelled. But Targov and Sokolov couldn't hear. David could see them high up on the parapet, two distant figures about to come to blows.

Anna turned to him. "This is the place," she said.

"What place?"

"Where the trails you have been following will meet. I dreamed about this, David. But I couldn't see it in my dream."

"Come!" He grasped her hand. "There's a way in around the other side." He guided her toward Jaffa Gate.

Even in his anger Targov wanted a confession. Whatever he'd done to Sergei, it was as nothing compared to this. "Admit you knew," he shouted at him. "Admit you wanted to destroy it! Confess, dammit! Confess, and redeem your wasted life!"

Sokolov rushed at him then, fueled by some newfound fount of demonic energy. The old man, supposedly broken in the Gulag, now charged up the last six steps like a savage, stood before Targov, thrust both his hands at his chest and gave him an enormous shove.

Targov stumbled back, nearly lost his balance.

"Sergei! Be careful!"

But Sokolov charged again. This time he threw his entire weight against him, driving Targov so hard against the railing that he reeled and nearly fell.

It was madness, David thought, the way the two of them were wrestling up there while he and Anna rushed to the center of the courtyard and reed-thin Rokovsky yelled: "Look out! Look out!"

Two old men, locked in combat perilously above them, one husky with a wild white mane of hair, the other bald and cadaverous. Their movements were jagged as they grasped hold of each other's shirts. Spittle shot from their mouths as they screamed obscenities and fought. They swayed together wildly, first toward the railing, then away from it, then toward it once again. Two old men out of control, like robots whose mechanisms had gone berserk. Their wild struggle was etched out against the crenelated tower and the hot Jerusalem midday sky.

Each was battling, brawling, scrambling to kill the other while struggling to maintain his balance and stay alive. *Madness! Madness!* David thought, as he saw the railing start to give. He stared up at them, helpless, and then turned to Anna, standing beside him, who had just let out a scream.

"*Sasha*. . . ."

They were falling now, twirling together through space, and even as they did they continued to fight like animals. Targov knew that in a second they would both hit the courtyard and die. He saw Rokovsky, the detective, and Anna looking horrified. His last thought, before he hit the stones, was: *I will die here in Jerusalem.*

THE NINTH
OF AV

When the story broke in the press the references were discreetly veiled:

Sources within the Ministry of Justice allege. . . .

Sources have revealed that persons as yet unnamed. . . .

Knowledgeable sources suggest that murders were committed to cover up a conspiracy that reached into the highest levels of the government. . . .

But then, when the Ministry of Justice spokesman refused to comment, shrewd editors, smelling something big, sent out their best reporters to dig around.

On the following morning the dispatches were sharply focused. Over breakfast David translated a story for Anna entitled "The Ninth of Av Conspiracy." He had given a long background only interview to its author and was now pleased to find himself described as "a confidential source within the Jerusalem police":

Wild rumors are circulating at the Etzion Airbase that a Lieutenant Ya'akov Ben-Eleizer, a pilot, has been placed under arrest. Lt. Ben-Eleizer, it is rumored, had been paid to bomb Jerusalem's Dome of the Rock at noon on the recent holiday, the Ninth of Av.

354 • William Bayer

There are rumors too that soon after the arrest a large number of army bulldozers were sent into the Negev to destroy a surreptitiously constructed bombing target there. Unnamed IDF sources confirm that the money used to construct this target was diverted from funds appropriated for the cultural improvement of military personnel.

These same sources state that the designs for the target were prepared under the auspices of an obscure American charitable arts foundation with offices in Jerusalem. Attempts to obtain confirmation have met with official rebuffs.

But a confidential source within the Jerusalem police, who spoke only on condition that he would not be named, has confirmed that the bombing plot is connected to a string of unsolved killings, including the double murders of Aaron Horev and Ruth Isaacson, which rocked the capital this past spring.

This same police source, who is very close to the investigation, points to a power struggle now taking place between the Police Minister and the Director of the General Security Services. According to this source this struggle revolves around the roles played in these killings by certain unnamed Security Services personnel.

Arrests, this source says, are imminent. Meantime, there are rumors that a well-known religious figure and politician may also be involved. Rabbi Mordecai Katzer has publicly called many times for the destruction of the Dome of the Rock. And a retired Air Force general, whose name is a household word, is reported to have left the country hurriedly. . . .

When the phone rang, David and Anna were still sipping coffee discussing the article. It was Latsky's Moroccan secretary, The Claw.

"The superintendent's shitting green," said The Claw. "He wants to know what the hell you think you're doing."

"Right now, dear, I'm reading the papers. Sorry he's having trouble with his bowels."

"Cut the crap, David," she said. "People around here think you're the leak."

"So what can I do about it? People can think what they like."

"People can also wonder why you're looking for a lot of trouble."

"I'm looking to close out my case. If Latsky would listen I'd explain to him why he ought to divide it in two. Let the national headquarters big shots investigate the bombing conspiracy. Just let me wrap up the homicides."

"Hmmm. Interesting idea."

"Why don't you see that it gets around."

"I just might do that," said The Claw. "Of course, this isn't official."

"Of course not," David said. He grinned at Anna. "So tell me: How long, really, are your nails?"

"The Dome's one thing," he explained to Anna, "a political-religious conspiracy. That's solved for now, though I haven't the slightest doubt that sooner or later fanatics will try to blow it up again. The killings, however, are something else."

"You feel that way because of Gideon."

"Sure, I admit the case got personal with me, but there's another reason too. Latsky says: 'Don't rock the boat. You saved the Dome. Isn't that enough?' Not nearly enough! To leave it at that is to tell the Security Services: 'You can get away with murder.' So what message does that send to people who work in all the other special bureaus? 'You're immune from Justice. You can do anything in the name of National Security. You can kill and go unpunished.' That's intolerable. When people start believing that, then Israel is finished."

Later he said to her: "Sure, maybe someday they'll bomb the Dome, but if they do I think they'll be surprised. They'll have their riot all right, they'll have their war, but their Messiah won't appear."

Even as he said that he was startled by his tone: He knew he'd sounded just like his father.

Just after lunch, Rafi called him in.

"Okay, you've got the go-ahead. Cohen and his four goons will meet you in front of the compound tomorrow at seven A.M. Colonel Levin's ordered them to submit to arrest. You can hold and interrogate them for a week. Only condition: So long as they're in custody here they're to be kept separate from everybody else."

"Private cells? Must be afraid we'll bunk them with informers. What about the girl?"

"She was just a secretary."

"They've cooked something up, haven't they, Rafi?"

Rafi tapped out his pipe. "If I were them I sure as hell would," he said.

Two hours into the preliminary questioning David understood their strategy: Deny any connection to the homicides; produce unimpeachable alibis from impeccable Israeli citizens; stick to a claim that they constituted a special unit assigned to infiltrate right-wing Jewish terrorist groups.

Ephraim Cohen had brought along a file of his orders, each one properly dated and signed. He tried not to smirk as David read them, but couldn't disguise his confidence that very soon he'd have to be released.

At eight that evening, David called his people together.

"We're going to have to scam these guys."

"They're tough motherfuckers," Uri said.

"Right, so first we've got to wear them down. They think we're finished with them for the night, so in half an hour we'll start in on them again. Hard tough questioning. Make them go over everything ten, fifteen times. Start chipping at those phony alibis. 'What color shirt were you wearing?' 'What color shoes?' 'What did you eat for dinner that night?' Make them think their stories maybe aren't meshing all that well. Every so often ask if they're sure they don't want a lawyer. Confer in whispers. Smile knowingly. I don't care how tough they are. Cohen chose them because they're goons. If we play them right, we can make that choice backfire in his face."

Because his prisoners had put together a phony story, he reasoned that sooner or later it would have to fall apart. He didn't spend much time with them; he'd drop in every so often, but mostly he listened and watched from the observation rooms. He was looking for stress points, the little things that made them hesitate. Their reactions to each other too, the particular way their eyes would move at the mention of their colleagues' names.

When he did enter one of the tiny basement interrogation rooms he went out of his way to sound reasonable: "Need anything? A sandwich? A glass of water? A lawyer? You're not being mistreated, are you? No one here's going to be abused or hurt."

He stayed completely clear of Ephraim Cohen. He knew Ephraim would wonder about that, prepare himself to be on guard when and if he did appear. Maybe he'd wonder if David had been taken off the case, or if he'd disqualified himself because of Gideon.

At the end of the second day, he had them sorted out. Two sets, he decided, the first smarter and more efficient than the second. The two European-types who'd been in the office, Gabi and Yoni, were the senior men. The two North Africans who'd stood before the gate, Ari and Shlomo, were the thugs. The senior guys had done the planning; the thugs had done the bad stuff. They'd picked up the victims, dumped the bodies, fired on him from the van, killed and dumped Peretz.

By the third morning David's people had narrowed the weak spot down to two: Ari, the Tunisian who'd set him up at the zoo, and Yoni, the short muscular one who'd pulled the gun in the Lover of Zion Street office and had stored the van out in Ein Kerem.

Uri and Micha liked Ari, because, they said, he seemed the angriest of the lot. Dov and Shoshana preferred Yoni, because, they felt, he had the most to lose.

"Why should Yoni do heavy prison time for Cohen?" Dov asked. "He followed orders, and he never actually killed anyone."

"Yeah, but Ari's bitter," Micha said. "He knows he's got no future here. And just because he was a triggerman doesn't mean he wants to spend the rest of his life in prison, especially when he thinks of Ephraim Cohen strutting around free in his hand-tailored British suits."

They turned to David for a decision. He said he liked Yoni best.

"They don't know we found the van. Yoni stored it out there, so on that he's vulnerable. If we play him right, he'll think he was betrayed. If he asks for a lawyer, we'll know he's ready to deal."

"Shouldn't I go out there and unwire that ignition?" Micha asked.

"No, we're going to be using that. Leave it just the way it is."

They drove out to Ein Kerem after lunch in a three-car

caravan, Yoni with Micha and Uri in the lead, Dov
and Shoshana with the videotape equipment just behind. David, with Ephraim Cohen and two pairs of
high-powered binoculars, trailed the two lead cars by
several hundred meters.

"Where are we going?"

David glanced at Ephraim. "Out for a drive," he
said. Ephraim smiled. He looked, David thought, particularly handsome today, an idealized Israeli male
with fair hair, clear eyes, and tanned and sculpted
cheeks.

"I know you're pissed at me," Ephraim said. "And
not just because of Peretz. On account of Gideon."
Then, before David could respond: "I wish you could
believe this—I considered him my closest friend."

"Almost like a brother?" And then, when Ephraim
nodded: "Little bit like a lover too?"

Ephraim turned away. When he answered his voice
was subdued. "Yes, that too for a while."

"So tell me something, Ephraim—since you cared
for him so much, why did you betray him the way you
did?"

"Oh, David, really—I didn't."

"He thought you did. Doesn't that maybe make you
feel just a little bad?"

"He was unstable. You know that."

"You exploited his instability."

"It wasn't like that. I didn't deliberately—"

"Oh, I get it," David said. "Your blackmail was
unintentional." He showed Ephraim his most sarcastic
grin. "Yeah. I understand."

They drove on in silence after that. Then Ephraim
turned to him again. "Because of you, David, the
Dome plot came apart. In some circles you're a hero
now."

"So?"

"Why not rest on your laurels?"

"Still a few little things that bother me." David looked at him. "Such as seven homicides."

"You're not going to get anywhere with that. Quit now and save yourself the trouble."

"Just give up, is that what you're saying? Withdraw honorably from the field?" When Ephraim nodded, David said: "I'm a cop. We don't fold our tents."

After that they didn't speak until they reached Ein Kerem. Ephraim glanced at him, confused when the other two cars turned off toward the farmhouse and David continued to drive straight on. Then, when David parked at the foot of the drive that led up to the Franciscan church, Ephraim shook his head.

"What are we doing here? Is this some kind of outing?"

"Sort of. Let's take a walk." David motioned toward the top of the hill. "Help yourself to a pair of binoculars, Ephraim. You'll want to take full advantage of the view."

He got out of the car. Ephraim scowled but took the binoculars, then the two of them started walking up the drive. It was a fine day for a walk in the country, David thought, the air fresh and clear, butterflies fluttering and bees humming and songbirds flitting from tree to tree.

David paused outside the gates of St. John's. Here, from a stone wall, there was a direct sightline to the ruined farmhouse below. David set his field radio on the wall, leaned against it, and began to sight in his binoculars. Ephraim stood beside him and did the same.

"I see them," Ephraim said. "They're down there in a field of rubble."

"Your man Yoni—he's looking kind of nervous."

"He's going to show you the van. What's that going to prove?"

David continued to observe the scene. He spoke

casually. "You've got it wrong, Ephraim. Yoni hasn't said a word. Not yet. But I think he will. Just keep a watch on his face. It'll be interesting to see his expression turn when he realizes he's been betrayed."

Uri and Dov had gone around behind the stone barn. Now they were returning with the broken panel door.

"See that door? Yoni's wondering how we found it. He stashed the van, and, since he didn't tell us about that, he knew, when we drove him out here, that one of his pals had blabbed. But that door's something else, an added complication, because it was damaged in the original accident. That was long before there were any pickups or killings of whores and hustlers and soldier girls. In a way you could say that door is what those killings were about. So now Yoni's maybe wondering if the person who blabbed was you."

Ephraim laughed. "Very clever, David, but, believe me, it's not going to work. Not with Yoni anyway. His balls are made of brass."

"We'll see. Personally I think he'll spill. Don't forget: He knows how far you'll go to cover something up."

"What's that supposed to mean?"

"That under the right kind of pressure he'll wonder if you'd kill him too. To save yourself. It's only logical. After all, if you'd order the killing of a soldier girl to fancy up a phony murder series, why would you hesitate to kill the very guy to whom you gave that order, a guy who could really roast you if it came down to a forced choice between him and you."

"Bullshit, David. You'll never force that kind of choice."

"Let's just see what happens, shall we?"

As he peered down again through his binoculars, he sensed that Ephraim was becoming unstrung. David's posture throughout had been directed at convincing him that, on account of his bitterness over Gideon, he was prepared to go a lot further than a cop might ordinarily go.

The view through the binoculars was extraordinarily clear; the light fell just right upon the group below. David could see the strained expression on Yoni's face as Dov gestured toward the barn. The doors were open now. He could see the gleaming front end of the van, and the ruined panel door lying on the ground. Yoni seemed to hesitate. But then he shrugged and began to move.

He walked straight into the barn. After David lost sight of him he imagined him squeezing himself inside the van, then rolling down the window to air the vehicle out. Dov would call to him: "Drive it out," and Yoni would fumble around searching for the key. He'd remember finally where he'd hidden it, on top of the visor on the passenger side. He'd reach for it, bring it down, then insert it into the ignition switch. And then he'd hesitate again.

"What are you waiting for? Get that crate out of there," Dov would shout.

Yoni would sense that something was wrong, but he wouldn't know exactly what. Ephraim had told him to wipe everything clean and now he was leaving prints on the steering wheel and the key. But what difference would prints make if someone had actually squawked? So, okay, he'd drive the damn van out and pray there weren't any old prints or bloodstains in the back.

David imagined him reaching down, turning the key, pumping on the gas. And then how the whole front end of the van would seem to explode right in his face.

Smoke poured out of the barn.

Ephraim turned to him. "What the hell!"

But David didn't turn, just planted his elbows on the wall to steady his binoculars, and continued to observe.

They all ran forward at once to pull Yoni from the driver's seat. They brought him out, badly shaken, then laid him carefully on the ground. Shoshana, playing Good Nurse, knelt beside him and began to mop his brow.

"What happened?" Ephraim demanded.

"Someone wired up your van."

"*You!*"

David shrugged. "Question now is, what does Yoni think? My guess is he thinks it was *you.*"

"Your people wouldn't be trying now to put that crazy notion in his head?"

"I have to admit that in this particular case, Ephraim, my people most definitely are."

"That's coercion. Coerced testimony can't be used in court."

"Up to Yoni to say whether or not he felt coerced. I'm betting he'll say he wasn't. But let's not argue about it. Let's see how it goes. His ears are ringing and he's scared and he's not all that bright anyway. My people are telling him what they think must have happened, and, believe me, he's getting the idea. You blabbed on the van so we'd bring him out here, but you'd had it wired so it would kill him when he started it up. Something went wrong. The charge wasn't big enough. So he escaped, he's shaken up, and now he's starting to grasp the implications. And here comes the clincher, Ephraim. Watch this carefully. This is the part where you actually get to see him turn."

Yoni was sitting up now. Dov and Shoshana were talking to him, showing him the kind of sympathy a man betrayed and nearly killed deserved. Shoshana handed him a pair of binoculars, while Dov pointed up at the church. Yoni put the binoculars to his eyes, peered through them, and saw David and Ephraim spying down on him. "See, Yoni," Dov was saying, "he's up there watching. He set you up." And then

Yoni grasped it—like a lightning bolt it suddenly struck him in the brain: Ephraim wanted him dead, and the only way he was going to survive was to tell these people every single thing he knew.

David turned on his field radio.

"Micha, how's it going?"

"He says he wants to talk, and that he doesn't need a lawyer. We're setting up now to videotape."

David shut the radio off and turned to Ephraim. "Well, guess that kind of settles it," he said.

"You can't do it like that."

"We can't? Why not?"

"*Because it's not legal, dammit!*" Ephraim kicked the wall.

David turned to him then, and examined him with great curiosity. "Tell me something, Ephraim: Just what kind of game is it that you think we're playing here, where there's one set of rules for you and another set for us?"

Yoni talked for three days straight; it took him that long to tell them everything. They followed him around frantically with camera and videotape recorder as he led them to the killing house in Mei Naftoah, the place on the Tel Aviv beach where Shlomo had picked up Halil Ghemaiem, the hitching stop at Ben-Gurion Airport, the Damascus Gate, and the place Yaakov Schneiderman had parked his truck the night that Ari had hidden in the back. Then on to all the different places where the bodies had been dumped: the ditch beside the road to Mevasseret; the Old City wall near the Dung Gate; the construction site behind the Augusta Victoria Hospital; the road up the Hill of Evil Counsel; and the Dumpster in Bloomfield Park.

He talked so fast, so furiously, and with such conviction, that no one who would later see the tapes could doubt for a moment that his confession was freely given. He offered so many details that, when the others were confronted with them, they too quickly crumbled and confessed. And then there ensued a kind of contest in which each of the four tried to outdo the other in quality of testimony and remembrance of detail. In the end David had four sets of videotapes containing four interlocking confessions. And whenever he asked the questions: "Who gave these orders?" "Who told you to do this?" "Who ordered this to be done?," the answer came back, "Ephraim Cohen," "Major Cohen," always the same, again and again.

The night after he turned everything over to the prosecutors, David said to Anna: "Now it's done. It involved everything, you know—my father, my brother, my sense of myself. It consumed my life and now that it's all over I feel empty just a little bit. But you know something? The more I think about Gideon, the more I admire what he did. He was a real patriot; he preferred to kill himself rather than start a war. Gati had contempt for him for destroying his aircraft, but if he'd gone quietly, his death wouldn't have haunted me as it did. In a strange and unforeseeable way he sent me a message. If I hadn't been so disturbed by the way he'd died, I don't think I'd have broken the case."

The next morning he drove down to Haifa, met Hagith, and took her out for the day. Judith was in the front hall when he arrived.

"Congratulations, David," Judith said. Hagith ran toward him, then threw herself into his arms.

Later, when he returned Hagith to the house, Joe Raskow opened the door. He didn't say anything and he didn't meet David's eyes. Judith did not appear.

He had solved his case but still something bothered him: Hurwitz, the phony cop.

Yoni and the others had admitted that "Hurwitz" was a floating false identity. They had all carried fake Hurwitz ID, to be used whenever they felt it necessary. Yet not one of them would admit he had been in the van at the time of the accident, a relatively trivial matter in the context of the seven homicides.

Amit Nissim, confronted with them in a lineup, could not identify any of them as the difficult cop she'd seen. So who was this Hurwitz, this mean non-English-speaking cop who had driven the three conspirators around Jerusalem?

The question nagged at David; he could not get rid of it and he knew that it had to be answered. Because the man who had driven the van that day was the only witness to the conversation between Gati, Katzer, and Stone, and thus the only link between the killings and the Ninth of Av conspiracy.

Although Amit had not picked out Ephraim Cohen, David still thought he might be Hurwitz. He asked Micha to check out his alibi. Two days later Micha reported back.

"It wasn't him, David. I know most of his alibis are phony, but on the day of the accident Ephraim Cohen was definitely not in Israel."

"Where was he?"

"London. Seems he and his wife travel there every spring. Probably to order a couple of new suits, the fancy kind he likes. His passport confirms that he was there, so do the customs and immigration records, and so do the airline passenger lists."

"Could he have faked all that?"

"He could have, but he didn't. Look, I know you're wondering how, if he was that far away, he was able to call Dr. Mendler on behalf of Harrison Stone. I don't know how, David, but somehow someone got in touch with him. Because in the billing files of the Hotel Dorset in London there's a record that he called Mendler, and that's something even he couldn't fake."

He went to see Jacob Gutman. It was late afternoon, the floors of the jail were shiny, the corridors reeked of disinfectant, cigarette smoke, and prisoners' sweat.

Gutman grinned when the guard showed David in.

"So it's you, sonny-boy? They're all talking about you now. You did some pretty fancy stuff, I hear."

David handed him a carton of cigarettes. "From my father. He sends his best."

"Thank him for me."

David nodded. "Netzer told me you won't have to go to trial. Said you're going to plead guilty and then he'll move for a suspended sentence."

"So what do you think of that? You didn't put in the good word by any chance?"

"I'll testify at your sentence hearing, Jacob. Unless the judge is a creep, you won't serve any time."

"Thanks, sonny-boy. Anything I can do for you?"

"Yeah. I want to know more about something we discussed that day we met in the park."

"We discussed a lot of things."

"This is about what Max Rosenfeld said. As I remember it he told you that people had stolen my fathers files to cover their tracks, and, this is the important part, that they were going to 'set me up.' "

Gutman nodded.

"Is that really what he said?"

"Yeah. Something like that."

"You remember his exact words?"

Gutman shook his head. "Max said they had you all set up."

"But that isn't what you told me," David said. "You told me he said they were *going* to set me up."

"Did I? Wait a minute. I'm getting confused. No! I remember how he said it: 'They're even playing games with Bar-Lev's boy, the cop,' Max said. 'They got him all set up.' "

"You're sure?"

"Yeah, I'm sure. What's the big deal anyhow?"

David didn't reply. He simply patted Gutman on the arm, left the cell, then took a long walk through the deserted night streets of M'ea Shearim.

As he stood beside the schoolyard fence waiting for Amit, he felt a welling up of melancholy. For all his pleasure in seeing Hagith he missed her daily presence in his life.

A bell rang inside, and then, a moment later, he heard the high-pitched voices of children charging down tiled halls. The kids emerged from the building in a mob, then flooded the playground, laughing, skipping, jumping, running, their packs of books and luncheon boxes bouncing on their little backs.

It was a while before he saw Amit; she spotted him at the same time. She took leave of her friends, walked slowly up to him, and shyly said hello.

"Hi," he replied.

"You want to show me pictures?" David nodded. "Where's Shoshana today?"

"She's busy. Anyway, this is confidential. Do you know what 'confidential' means?"

She looked up at him. "That means it's a secret."

"That's right," he said. "A secret just between the two of us."

They walked a block up from the school to a bus stop where there was an empty bench.

"Let's sit here," he suggested. And then, after they

sat: "I've got six pictures of six different men. I've never shown them to you before."

"You want me to tell you if I recognize them." She smiled. "You know, I'm not a baby anymore."

He dealt the photographs onto the bench as if they were playing cards. While she studied them he watched her face.

"This one," she said immediately, picking up a picture. "This was the policeman who tried to take the lady's camera away."

David didn't look at the photo. Instead he peered into Amit's oversized eyes. "You're sure?"

"I'm sure." She stared straight back. "Now can I go home?"

He waited until she had disappeared, then glanced down at the photograph. Then sadly he shook his head. It was the one he'd been afraid that she would choose.

It was nearly dusk when David approached the old house on Shela Street which Rafi had inherited from his father and then subdivided, reserving the ground floor apartment for himself. While he waited at the door he marveled at the superb condition of Rafi's garden. Even now, in August, with Jerusalem so dusty and hot, the lawn and shrubbery here were dense and green. There was a sweet aroma too of hibiscus and of the exotic air orchids which Rafi bred.

Ruth Shahar answered the door. "David!" She embraced him. She was a small wiry woman with gray bangs and nervous eyes. "How's Anna? Rafi keeps saying the four of us are going to get together. But you two guys are always busy." She stood back from him, smiled. "Don't stand out here. Rafi's in the greenhouse. Wander around back. Surprise him. He'll be delighted. I know he will. . . ."

David retraced his steps, then followed the narrow

stone walk that led around the side of the house to the garden in the back. He stood there a while watching Rafi moving inside the greenhouse, an unlit pipe clenched between his teeth. The long fluorescent tubes of the greenhouse were lit, bouncing purple light off the top of Rafi's head. He carried a plastic bottle and every so often dipped into it with a dropper which he then squeezed above the hanging plants.

Rafi must have sensed the presence of a stranger; he froze and peered out toward the lawn. Then, when he recognized David, he smiled and beckoned him in.

"This must be important. I've barely been home an hour. Be with you in a minute, soon as I finish giving dinner to my beauties here."

He gestured David to a wicker chair, then began to move again among the orchids. They were strange tormented-looking things clinging to bunches of bark and masses of moss that hung from the greenhouse ceiling. Sometimes, after Rafi had finished his hybridization experiments, he would release a group from his control, setting them outside in the branches of shrubs and trees where a few, although not all, survived.

"I can't tell you how relaxing it is to garden after a day of crime and punishment. Do you have a hobby, David?"

"Nothing quite like this."

"I know you love music."

"I like to listen to it, but I never learned to play."

Rafi put down his bottle and dropper and slipped into the other chair. "I'm glad to see you. I know we've been tense with each other. I'm sorry that we have."

"Why do you think there's been so much tension, Rafi?"

"Strain of the job, I guess. Stress of the case."

"Do you remember that symposium back in May, the first one we held in Latsky's conference room?"

"With Sanders and your father? Sure."

"You told them I was the best detective in Israel. Do you remember saying that?" Rafi smiled. "But you didn't mean it, did you?"

Rafi squinted at him. "Why do you say such a thing?"

"You didn't think I'd see through your bullshit then."

Rafi's face turned stern. "What's on your mind, David?"

"You were 'Hurwitz.' I know that now. You were the driver of the van. You overheard everything, and you took down all the names so that later the witnesses could be killed. You played me for a fool, Rafi, with your 'our first Israeli serial murder case' and 'consistently marred flesh' and 'you're my best man so I'm giving this to you' and 'it's a pattern crime so you solve it because you're in charge of pattern crimes.' "

Rafi stared at him. "So that's why you came. You've come here to arrest me."

"Is that all you have to say?"

"You sound bitter."

"I trusted you. How should I sound?"

"I suppose I ought to say I'm sorry."

"Don't apologize to *me*, Rafi. Just tell me why did you do it? *Why?*"

"You've heard me complain often enough. You know how I feel about things these days."

"I thought you hated the intolerance, the polarization. I thought you hated the way the fanatics have been gaining power."

"Yes, I hate all that. But you didn't listen carefully. If you had, you'd understand why I think Gati's right, that our only long-term hope is to become bigger and more powerful."

"And if—"

"Yes, if that means making alliances with pigs like Katzer or screwballs like Stone, that's okay too. When you need allies you take what you can get. Which is why Israel's allied now with South Africa."

"*A war,* Rafi?"

"A war might be the best solution."

"*Might be!*" David shook his head. "But, you see, I don't give a damn about your politics. I only want to know how you could bring yourself to set those people up?"

"Will you believe me, David, when I tell you that that wasn't what I was trying to do, that the thought that they might be killed never entered my head? When the accident happened and Stone got hurt, my first priority was to salvage our cause. It had taken months to set up that meeting. It was the crucial meeting where the final deal would be struck. So I started shouting and pretending I didn't speak English to draw attention to myself and give the three of them time to get away. Then that damn nun started snapping pictures. I tried to grab her camera, but she wouldn't give it up. Then other people crowded around. So to distract them I took down their names. It was only later, after Cohen's assholes killed the nun, that he decided to get rid of all the witnesses and bury the killings in a case I could control. None of it was directed at you personally. I never doubted you were a fine detective, maybe even the best in Israel. But best or not you're plenty good enough, otherwise I wouldn't have you on my staff."

They sat facing one another, two men who'd once been friends. Finally David spoke.

"I can forgive you for using me, but not for being party to the murders." He stood up. "I'll arrest you in the morning. That way you have tonight to explain things to Ruth and organize your affairs."

"I did what I did for love of Israel. You must believe that, David, if nothing else."

David looked at him and shook his head. "Oh, yes, Rafi—for love. For *love*. . . ." He turned away.

The next morning when Rafi did not appear, David was not surprised. He called the house. Ruth told him that Rafi had been up the whole night working in his study, and then, just before dawn, had driven off without saying good-bye.

That afternoon, when an envelope addressed to David was hand-delivered to the guardhouse of the Russian Compound, he had an idea what had happened. Inside the envelope was a complete sworn and signed confession of Rafi's role as conspirator in the Ninth of Av affair.

Two days later an army patrol found Rafi's body in the Judean Hills. His police Beretta was still in his hand. There was a single bullet in his brain.

MUSIC

At the end of September, just three days before the Jewish New Year, the weather in Jerusalem changed. The sun, which for months had been baking the streets, suddenly became more temperate. The harsh white sky turned a deep fathomless blue, and the dry cutting winds gave way to a gentle breeze. Jerusalemites, welcoming these changes, congratulated themselves on their good fortune. It was such a privilege to live in a city imbued with so much radiance!

The following afternoon David left work early, then walked from the Russian Compound over to his father's room on Hevrat Shas. The ostensible purpose of this visit was to invite Avraham for Rosh Hashanah dinner. But David had other matters on his mind.

"Irina Targov is back," he told his father. "Remember how she insisted her husband and Sokolov had to be buried side by side? Now she wants a new inscription cut into the base of Targov's sculpture: 'Dedicated by Aleksandr Targov to His Oldest Friend Sergei Sokolov in Honor of His Lifelong Struggle on Behalf of Imprisoned Soviet Jews.' "

Avraham shook his head. "On some level she knows she ruined their lives. Now she wants to force them to forgive each other."

"But they never would have done that."

"No, of course not. But still I think Irina did a healthy thing. Now she should feel less guilt."

Hearing his father say that David couldn't help but wonder: *Does he now feel less guilt himself?*

They talked for a while then about a conference Avraham was going to attend on Kabbalah and psychology.

"I think you're still interested in psychoanalysis, Father."

"On a theoretical level I am."

"But you won't go back to taking patients?"

Avraham shook his head. There was silence then between them, a silence David did not wish to break. He could feel there was something the old man wanted to say. He would wait until his father said it—the "tell-your-story method."

"You were right, you know?"

"About what?" David asked.

"Something you said to me last spring."

"What was that?"

"You said you felt that we were very much alike—that we both wanted to get to the bottom of things and neutralize the demons." Avraham paused. "I mocked you for saying it. Mocked you many times for the work you chose to do."

"I remember. . . ." *Was the old man really going to apologize?*

"Now I know that you were right. Not only about our being alike, although I believe your observation there is most acute. I also think you were right for making the choice you did. Your work is immensely valuable, David. You *do* render the demons harmless."

David was speechless. His father could have given him no greater gift than this: acknowledgment that he, the surviving son, had been passed the torch, and now was carrying it well.

His eyes strayed to the photographs of his mother and Gideon. Avraham must have noticed because he suddenly began to speak of them.

"She and I destroyed him," he said. "Instead c loving each other, as we did when you were young, w focused all our love on him. We struggled over him and, in the end, I think we tore him apart."

"Maybe it's time, father, for you to forgive yourself All this tortured thinking—it can't do you any good.'

Avraham did not answer, but David thought he saw a subtle nod.

To divert him David told him the latest news on the case: Ephraim Cohen's attempt, through his attorney to have the videotaped confessions ruled inadmissible

"He wants a political trial so he can claim the role of victim. He'll depict me as his persecutor."

"What will happen?"

"He doesn't have a chance. Rafi's confession nails him and even Levin's disowned him now. There's a big shake-up going on inside Shin Bet. Lots of fancy talk about abuses of trust and power."

"The others?"

"Stone can't come back. He's *persona non grata*. No way to touch him—basically all he did was write a check. Gati's still away in France. I think it'll be a long time before we see him again. And Katzer is still raving and holding rallies. He predicts he'll be prime minister in six or seven years."

"Unfortunately, a lot of people would like to see that happen. Katzer is our collective sickness, the dark side of everything we built. When people like him and Gati talk about Israel, they always end up discussing territory. They don't understand what Israel is. The territory here." Avraham pointed to his head.

"There was a public brawl in Tel Aviv the other night. Katzer zealots battling Peace Now sympathizers. They smashed up a café on Dizengoff, toppled tables and broke a lot of mirrors."

Avraham thought about that for a while, and then finally he nodded. "Perhaps instead of breaking the mirrors," he said, "they should look more closely at their faces."

Later, outside on narrow Hevrat Shas, David found himself surrounded by youngsters. They were pouring out of the yeshivas, young men and boys garbed in black, and they pressed against him as they passed. But strangely he found he was not annoyed. For the first time in memory he did not recoil, nor wish to break loose from contact with these people, nor did he see, as he looked into their faces, suspicion or contempt, nor feel, on his own part, any of his usual distaste.

A man his age, a rabbi, with milky skin and heavy spectacles and a thick black beard, nodded as he approached. David nodded back. Their eyes met, they smiled, and then David felt something pass between them, some fine, rare form of acknowledgment.

He thought about it as he walked away, asked himself what it was. Recognition, he decided, recognition that although each had chosen a different path, an opposite way to live, still they were connected. And that although this meeting of their eyes would be broken off in a moment, still they were both men and Jews and thus tolerance and even love were possible.

As he stood on the edge of Me'a Shearim, looking across the rubble-strewn lot that separated the ultra-orthodox quarter from the Christian churches and hospices and nunneries to the east, he was struck suddenly by an extraordinary change in the quality of the light. The western sky had luminesced, was now a soft dark violet. The sun, covered a few moments before by thick ribbons of clouds, had slipped and found a window; now a thin band of it, a bar of fire, burned out of the darker sky like a spotlight.

Perhaps two or three times in his life David had seen light like this, slanting in from the west, flowing down upon Jerusalem. It was a hard strong focused light that hit the stones, then seemed to penetrate them, then etched long velvet shadows on the ground.

The effect was magical. As David walked toward the Old City he stopped several times and stared. He saw other pedestrians doing the same, and drivers stopping their cars, then getting out so that they too might feel the radiance. Jerusalem was being transformed. Its beauty was being multiplied. And as each moment passed, and the sun slipped a little lower and its color deepened, all the stones of the city seemed to come alive. The shadows lengthened, and the lines and angles of buildings grew sharper and the curves of domes softer, and towers seemed to stand straighter and walls to enclose more warmly and steps to invite and arches to protect and doorways to beckon, and he thought: *This is special. I must not forget this; I must remember this afternoon for the rest of my life.*

He decided to walk home. He entered the Old City by the Damascus Gate. There were mobs of people in the little square but very little noise. He was surprised. Where were the dissonance, cruel clash of languages, wails, usual sounds of torment and abuse? Instead a oneness of sound, almost mellifluous. He recognized it as harmony.

Through the Moslem Quarter, across the Via Dolorosa, down El Wad, then through the long vaulted tunnel that led to the Western Wall. The palpable anger he usually sensed when he crossed these unmarked frontiers between the Quarters was not apparent to him tonight.

The sky was darker now, deep purple like wine, but the sun, nearly red, still burned through hard and strong. The floodlights had not yet been turned on, but the glowing Wall beckoned to him. He gazed at it, then drawn by some instinct he did not understand, approached, picked up a cardboard yarmulke at the barrier, set it on his head, and strode closer, paused, then moved directly to the stones.

Religious men stood around him; the air vibrated with their prayers. And the rough surface of the rocks vibrated too, dancing before the dying sun. The crevices, crowded with petitions, crushed one upon the other, seemed to devour the light. Just in front of him was darkness; he reached forward, touched the place, placed his palm against it. It was his own shadow he was touching and the stone that held it felt warm. Another connection, he thought. It was as if, finally, he had touched the city's heart.

Later he stood in the center of the plaza and gazed at the buildings all around. The golden dome of the Dome of the Rock caught the dying fire, held it a while, and glowed. Beside the shelter on the top tier above the rabbinical tunnel he made out soldiers, and, on a ledge within the Mount, several men, garbed in cloaks, staring down. He turned, looked up at the apartments just behind, found Gati's great window, and saw that it was black. It was from here the general would have viewed his spectacle of destruction: the bomb floating down to meet the Dome, the explosion, the fire, and then the beginning of the Holy War. Except that Gati hadn't cared about Armageddon, or the rebuilding of the Temple, or even recapture of the "high ground," the Temple Mount. What he had wanted was a provocation that would ignite a War of Wars. His dream was of a final decisive war of conquest, in which all Arabs would finally be driven from the land, and the borders of the Jewish State would become those of the biblical "Greater Israel."

A mad scheme. It would never have worked, and it would have cost hundreds of thousands of lives. Three fanatics, each with his own horrible agenda, conspiring together in a van. . . .

He left the plaza, ascended into the Jewish Quarter. Here, on this cool autumn night, the narrow pedestrian streets were still. He passed a soldier in battle dress, submachine gun hanging from his shoulder, kissing his girl in a quiet corner.

Lights burned in apartments. He peered in and saw families, people talking, children playing, women preparing meals. These domestic scenes filled him with a great longing to be home.

He rushed through the maze of alleys, then out through the Zion Gate. Descending Mount Zion, there came a point when he caught sight of his own apartment across the valley of Hinnom. His window was lit, which meant that Anna was home. He strode faster, and, on the descent, began to run. The air, scented with an intermingling of pine and rosemary, parted easily before him. He was barely winded when, a quarter hour later, he arrived in Abu Tor.

En Rogel: a special street of old Arab houses and new apartment buildings and gentle dogs that communicated with savage barks. Hinnom was all blackness now. The Arab town of Shiloah sparkled in the east. The Jerusalem of Gold Folklore Club was empty, and the street lamps projected shadows upon the cars parked along the curb.

The moment he entered number sixteen he heard the music. Faintly at first, as he passed the doors of apartments where people were listening to radios and TV news, then more clearly on the second floor. He thought: *It's the sonata. She's finally gotten herself a record.* But as he climbed to the third floor he realized this wasn't true. There was no piano part, which meant that the music was live. But played by whom? Could another cellist be working with Anna now?

Whoever this cellist was, he was playing the sonata well, David thought. Playing it very well. He paused outside the door and listened. Then he thought: *Is it possible? Could it be?*

He opened the door quietly. Anna was perched on her stool facing the window. Her back was to him, her body was swaying; the music swelled up and filled the room.

She was playing, and when she sensed his presence she turned to him. He saw the triumph on her face. And then he realized that even as he had entered the building he had known that the music could not have been played by anybody else.

He walked to the couch, sat down, and listened. Her eyes glistened with pleasure and a glow of conquest reddened her cheeks. She bowed and swayed and her expression said everything. She had it now—every phrase, every nuance. She'd mastered it. Now the music was hers.

Later he thought: *Perhaps now too this city belongs to me.*

It was past midnight. Anna was asleep. The sound of her breathing filled the room. David sat before the large window staring out at Jerusalem. The buildings were the same—the hills, the lights, the shadows and silhouettes. On a thousand clear nights like this he had gazed upon them. But now, on this particular night, at last he was seeing them whole.

It was the pattern of Jerusalem finally revealed, the pattern he had been seeking and which until now he had not permitted himself to see. He recalled the events of the afternoon: the way the light had struck and made perfect all the domes and minarets, the look of sad pride in his father's eyes, the nod of shared acknowledgment with the rabbi, and the satisfaction on Anna's face when he had come upon her at the moment of her conquest. He knew that each of these events was a part of some inexpressible whole, and that his embracing of this whole meant that at last his fractured world had cohered.

Staring out at the moonlit city he trembled at the lucid power of this vision. It was as if, until this moment, there had been no design. But now, like iron filings suddenly organized in the presence of a magnet, everything, every person and place he knew, came together in a pattern demarcated by the city spread below.

It was a beautiful pattern, moral too: Everything was connected, every life touched every life, and he himself was part of all of it.

As he gazed out marveling, he knew that this vision was one he would not forget. And he knew too that if one day he confronted chaos again, worked a case again that would perplex, obsess, and taunt, he would be able to look back upon this night, recall that he had seen the pattern, and then his world would become orderly again.

ABOUT THE AUTHOR

WILLIAM BAYER is the author of *Switch* (available in a Signet edition), the award-winning *Peregrine*, and other novels. He and his wife, food writer Paula Wolfert, divide their time between New York City and Martha's Vineyard.

AN AWFUL SECRET.
AN UNSPEAKABLE OBSESSION.
TWO HIDEOUSLY PERFECT MURDERS . . .
"HAS STUNNING INTENSITY!"
—Mary Higgins Clark

a novel by
William Bayer

It was a grisly work of art, a crime as perfect as it was
pointless. And it was Detective Frank Janek's job to get inside
the mind of the lethal genius who had decapitated two women
and *switched* their heads. He would need to be as cold, as
creative, as insanely *brilliant* as his killer prey . . . "Superior
characterization, movement, tension."

—John D. MacDonald